ALSO BY LISA GRUNWALD

Whatever Makes You Happy
New Year's Eve
The Theory of Everything
Summer

WITH STEPHEN J. ADLER

Women's Letters
Letters of the Century

The Irresistible Henry House

THE

Irresistible
Henry House

‖ A NOVEL ‖

Lisa Grunwald

RANDOM HOUSE

NEW YORK

Published in the United States by Random House, an imprint of The Random House Publishing Group, a division of Random House, Inc., New York.

RANDOM HOUSE and colophon are registered trademarks of Random House, Inc.

The photograph on page 409 of this edition is used courtesy of the Division of Rare and Manuscript Collections, Cornell University Library.

Owing to limitations of space, copyright credits can be found on page 413.

Library of Congress Cataloging-in-Publication Data
Grunwald, Lisa.
The irresistible Henry House: a novel / Lisa Grunwald.
p. cm.
ISBN 978-1-4000-6300-0
1. Women teachers—Fiction. 2. Attachment behavior—Fiction. 3. Orphans—Fiction. 4. Home economics—Fiction. I. Title.
PS3557.R837T78 2010
813'.54—dc22   2009019720

Printed in the United States of America on acid-free paper

www.atrandom.com

2 4 6 8 9 7 5 3 1

FIRST EDITION

For my son, Jonathan Grunwald Adler,

with love and wonder

With the lips and eyes of a valentine
And a smile from the Sunday comics,
He was the Practice Baby in a College of Home Economics.
"Oh what a lucky baby I am!"
He often used to cry,
"To have a hundred Mammas
To make me hush-a-by!"

—Morris Bishop and J. H. Mason, "The Practice Baby,"
   The Saturday Evening Post, May 1928

PART ONE

The Practice Baby

1

Welcome Home, Henry

By the time Henry House was four months old, a copy of his picture was being carried in the pocketbooks of seven different women, each of whom called him her son.

The photograph showed Henry on the day he arrived at Wilton College in 1946. He was lying naked in his crib, his backside bare and sassy, his hair already shiny and dark, and his grin already firmly in place as he pulled up on his chubby hands and turned back toward the sound of his name.

Henry House was a practice baby, an orphan supplied by the local home for the purpose of teaching college women how to be proper mothers. For more than two decades, since the early 1920s, colleges across the country had offered home economics programs featuring practice kitchens, practice houses, and, sometimes, practice babies. Henry was the tenth such baby to come to the Wilton practice house. Like the other so-called House babies before him, he was expected to stay for two years and be tended to in week-long shifts by a half dozen practice mothers. In earnest, attentive rotations, they would live and sleep beside him as they learned the science of child rearing—feeding and diapering, soothing and playing—until it was time to pass him on to the next devoted trainee.

Raised, as a consequence, not with a pack of orphans by a single matron but as a single orphan by a pack of mothers, Henry House started life in a fragrant, dust-free, fractured world, where love and disappointment were both excessive and intertwined.

IN 1946, THE CAMPUS OF WILTON COLLEGE sat like a misplaced postage stamp in the upper-left-hand corner of the mostly flat, still mostly rural Pennsylvania rectangle. Established in 1880, the college was one of the oldest in the country created solely for the education of women, and it drew, in nearly equal numbers, girls from the nearby farms and girls from the distant towns and girls from the glittering, ambitious East. If some arrived with the thought that home economics would offer an easy path, they had only to enter the practice house to be disabused of this notion.

Martha Gaines ran the program with an iron fist and a hidden heart, living full-time in the practice house while the undergraduates came and went. Martha considered the building hers, the students hers, the program hers. In 1926, she had been reassigned from her original post as a textiles instructor to design and run the practice baby program, and she had been in charge since the arrival of the very first House infant. Martha had overseen all the House babies since then, the single exception being during the previous year, when she had been urged (the gossip, she knew, said *forced*) to take a leave of absence. On this sharp, brisk autumn morning, with a new school year, a new group of mothers, and a new baby before her, Martha had never felt a deeper need to be in command.

Henry was in her arms. He was wearing bright red cotton pajamas and was wrapped, budlike, in a pale green cotton blanket. The date of his birth—June 12, 1946—had been written on a piece of orphanage stationery and fixed to his blanket with a large diaper pin. The orphans always arrived with numbers and, thanks to Martha's one streak of whimsy, stayed on with cutely alliterative names: Helen House, then Harold House, then Hannah, Hope, Heloise, Harvey, Holly, Hugh, and Harriet. Only when they were adopted—which they invariably were, quite eagerly, as the prized products of modern child-rearing techniques—would they finally be given real names.

At the door of the practice house, Martha now exhaled a home-coming sigh, then expertly shifted the baby onto her left arm to open the door with her right.

"Welcome home, Henry," she whispered, stepping into the en-tranceway and turning on the light.

Then she kissed one of the baby's tiny, still-clenched hands—not his face, of course, for she rarely deviated from the rules she imposed on her student mothers, and one of those rules was not to indulge in undue physical affection. ("MOTHER MUST NOT BEGIN WITH S" was the admonition that Martha had stitched as a sampler years before.)

Now she tucked Henry's fist back under the blanket and stepped into the nursery. It was ten-thirty on a Monday morning, and the girls weren't scheduled to come until eleven, and that would give Martha barely enough time.

Henry looked at her, his eyes just mature enough to focus on hers. Martha shrugged off her tweed jacket, keeping the baby snugly against her chest and inhaling the talcum-y smell of his neck.

There had been times, in her previous year of exile, when Martha had not been sure she'd ever get to hold a House baby again. Relief and the lingering loneliness of her time away now galvanized her. With Henry up on her shoulder, she all but spun around the room, reach-ing for her tools: a fresh journal, a sharp pencil, a measuring tape, a di-aper. As she gathered the things, she hummed the song that Bing Crosby had been crooning since the end of the war:

Kiss me once, then kiss me twice
Then kiss me once again
It's been a long, long time.

THE NURSERY HAD REMAINED LARGELY UNCHANGED in the year of Martha's absence. The walls were still the palest shade of green, with crisp white wainscoting that hemmed them in and kept them from seeming completely institutional. The changing table and a small dresser flanked the left-hand wall. A rocking chair and an oak side table sat beside the far window. A faded Oriental covered most of the dark wooden floor.

In general, the room was—like Martha herself—not altogether cold but not particularly inviting. *Functional* described them both. At forty-eight, Martha was no longer confident, slim, or remotely happy enough to be what most people would consider attractive. In recent years, her face had become doughy and less defined, as if the lines of her features were starting to smudge. Her body, often plump, had become heavyset, and she had taken to wearing, along with her tailored suits, a series of eccentrically colorful silk scarves that were meant to distract attention from the rest of her.

Today Martha's scarf was bright turquoise and orange, and as she laid Henry on the changing table, he seemed transfixed by its pattern. Staring, he didn't protest as she unwrapped his green blanket and, ribbon by ribbon, undid his red pajamas. Only then—from the cold and the shock of not being swaddled—did he begin to yell and squirm. Resolutely, Martha ignored his cries and unfastened his diaper pin. "You're a strong one," she said to him, unfolding her tape measure.

She measured the circumference of Henry's head, then his height, his hands, and his feet. She noted the color of his skin, his eyes, his hair. She noticed and recorded a small extra flap of skin on his right ear, like the ear tags that came on those German teddy bears that had been so popular before the war.

"What's that doing there?" she asked Henry, while he kept on bellowing.

He was only fourteen weeks old, and Martha usually preferred the practice babies to be five or six months when she got them. Irena Stahl at the orphanage, however, had been unusually firm in insisting that Henry was the healthiest candidate, and Martha—anxious to resume her duties—had been in no mood to argue, and certainly not to wait.

She turned Henry over on his belly and scrutinized his skin, running one large hand across the tiny span of his shoulder blades, no wider than an octave. She studied the small of his back, his buttocks, checking for imperfections, marveling at their absence.

She knew that the girls would be coming soon, and that she should dress the baby, and prepare him, and prepare herself as well, but for this one moment, he was hers, entirely hers, and all of his magnificent future, and his already insignificant past, fit grandly within the span of her hand. She scooped him up, and, despite herself, she kissed him firmly on the cheek.

For a moment, their eyes met again, and Martha felt a surge of longing. Furtively, she looked around the empty room. "Now you know," she whispered to Henry. "I think I'm going to love you," she said. "Don't tell a soul."

MARTHA HAD PUT HENRY IN THE CRIB for his nap and had only just finished filling the diaper pail with cold water and borax when she heard the bustle of girls approaching the front door. She struggled not to envy them—their youth, their freedom, their endless choices. All of them would be freshmen this year, and though the freshmen were always more energetic than the sophomores, they also required more guidance.

Three of them stood in the doorway now, and Martha guessed they'd not come together. Two were conspicuously beautiful blondes and the third an agitated brunette in an ill-fitting boiled-wool jacket. "Beatrice. I'm Beatrice Marshall," she said as if reciting a line she'd spent time rehearsing. "Did they tell you I was to join your class?"

"I have your name right here," Martha said.

Beatrice attempted a relieved smile but revealed instead yellow teeth and anxious eyes. She removed her hat hastily, and her hair, which was fine and the color of brown sugar, flared up with static in a nervous halo. Inside, she took off her jacket, uncovering a dress that was clearly a hand-me-down special, or at least the veteran of one too many a harvest ball. By contrast, Grace Winslow, the taller of the two blondes, was perfectly done up in a camel-hair skirt, a white blouse, and a tidy French twist. The third girl, Constance Cummings, held a smart red purse in one hand and, in the other, the new bestselling paperback that Martha had already come to loathe, though she hadn't yet managed to read it: *The Common Sense Book of Baby and Child Care*, by Dr. Benjamin Spock. Swinging her long, straight hair over her shoulder, Connie settled into an armchair and sat—grave and expectant—with her bag at her side and her book in her lap, as if she was waiting for a sermon to start.

The fourth student to arrive was Ruby Allen, from West Virginia. Another farm girl, she was wearing a polka-dot dress and enormous Minnie Mouse shoes, and she greeted the others with an exuberant "Hi, y'all." She was followed quickly by Ethel Neuholzer, who walked in with an Argus camera around her neck and a Clark Bar in her hand. She was a slightly chubby brunette with a Veronica Lake swoop to her hair and a blue bow that completely extinguished the intended smoldering effect. Within the next five minutes, she had reached into her voluminous purse to offer her new classmates Lucky Strikes, Life Savers, and Doublemint gum.

"Where's the kid?" she asked.

By noon, the only one absent was Betty Lodge, but Martha already knew her. Betty Lodge—née Gardner—was the daughter of Dr. Nelson Gardner, the Wilton College president. Betty was a long-ago graduate of the Wilton Nursery School, which was still located just next door. Martha had known her since the day she turned two, because the staff and faculty had always been encouraged to attend her birthday parties.

At the moment, Betty had again become a much-clucked-over presence on campus, this time because her young husband, Fred, had been included in the War Department's final list of dead and missing. With every month that passed, the chance of his being found alive became more and more negligible. Yet Betty, or so the chatter went, clung to reports of captured pilots and amnesiac prisoners. The year before, a bomber pilot who had been listed as dead had been found alive in a Rangoon hospital, and most people saw Betty's enrollment in the home economics program as a testament to her faith that Fred had, like that pilot, survived the war.

She walked in nearly forty-five minutes late, a short, frail-boned eighteen-year-old with thatched blond hair and an almost storybook face. A sweetheart face, people called it. Slightly boyish, even more elfin, she would have made a perfect Peter Pan. She had pale skin, long, thin wrists, and oddly stubby hands. The lightness of her skin and the unusual brightness in her eyes made it look as if she might have just been beamed in from a neighboring star.

"Where's the baby?" she asked before the front door had even closed behind her. Maybe it was something about the expectancy in her voice; maybe it was the little pearl buttons on her pale blue sweater set; maybe it was simply that Martha had known her for so long. Whatever the reason, Betty looked no older than twelve as she asked the question, and Martha felt a stab of sympathy for her.

"Sleeping," Martha told her.

Betty turned immediately in the direction of the nursery and walked in without hesitation, a sense of entitlement trailing her like a scent. Martha's sympathy ebbed. So this was what it would be like to have the president's daughter here, she thought.

In a few moments, the rest of the girls had left the embrace of the living room chairs to form a clucking, perfumed bracket around the sides of Henry's crib. It was a configuration they would resume any number of times in the many months that followed. And Henry, awake or asleep, in glee or discomfort, health or illness, would always be the exact focus of their six pairs of searching eyes. He would rarely disappoint the needs and hopes those eyes conveyed.

"He will wake up at one o'clock," Martha began, with the certainty of a fortune-teller. "When he wakes up, he will need to be changed. He will then have his lunch. Eight ounces of formula, at room temperature. I will show you in a moment how to sterilize the bottles."

"Do we get to play with him?" Ethel asked, fingering the strap on her camera.

Martha scowled. "When it's your week to live in the practice house, you will of course prepare for and give all his feedings, including the ones in the middle of the night. You will take him outdoors for walks, maintain his crib and carriage bedding, bathe him, shampoo him, weigh and measure him, soak and wash his diapers—"

"Wash his diapers!" Grace said in horror.

"Wash. His. Diapers," Martha repeated. She looked at the six women one by one, trying to make sure they were listening. "Taking care of a baby," she said, "is the only important job that most of you will ever have."

ONLY BEATRICE HAD BROUGHT A NOTEBOOK, and while the girls resumed their places on the armchairs and sofa, she clutched it as if it was a kickboard and she was just learning to swim. A few years back, Martha mused, she had taught another kid like this. Dumb as a spoon. Nervous as a fish. "Do we need to take notes?" Beatrice asked now, dropping her pen.

"Who didn't bring a notebook?" Martha asked. Hands sprang up in unison, as if the girls were here not for a class but for a swearing-in.

NOT EVERYONE WHO STUDIED HOME ECONOMICS at the practice house was completely incompetent, in Martha's view. But even some of the most basic skills—like sterilizing a pacifier, say, without cloaking the place in the smell of burning rubber—seemed at times to tax the students' capabilities. Martha had grown up the child of an Army captain, and inefficiency bothered her almost as much as carelessness did. She understood that her growing inability to hide her impatience was the main reason that Dean Swift, the head of the Department of Home Economics, and President Gardner had insisted she take her sabbatical. And that Carla Peabody, the insipid young college nurse, had gotten to run the practice house in her absence. And that Martha had spent most of the previous few weeks trying to eradicate the last traces of her.

Other than the previous year, that had been the only time when the leaders of the college had intruded into Martha's life. She was determined that they would not do so again, and yet the shameful reality—so completely at odds with her character and the impression she usually gave—was that she was as perfectly vulnerable to their wishes as a baby like Henry was to hers.

AT 12:45, WHILE MARTHA was still demonstrating bottle sterilization and formula preparation, Henry woke up, yelling. Martha had to suppress a smile as she watched the looks of fear pinch and pull at the girls' faces. Within seconds, both Connie and Betty were on their feet, and Beatrice had dropped her pen again.

"He's crying!" Ethel said.

"Yes," Martha replied languidly.

"Shouldn't we—" Connie began.

"Shouldn't you what?" Martha said.

"Shouldn't we go pick him up?" Connie asked, brandishing her paperback Spock. "Spock says—" she began.

Martha squared her shoulders and fingered the gold honor society pin she always wore on a chain beneath her scarf: Omicron Nu, the home economics sisterhood that was the only group to which Martha had ever belonged.

"There is no textbook for this course," Martha said. "If there were a textbook for this course, it would not be Spock."

Connie looked contrite, then concerned. "What's wrong with Spock?" she asked.

"Now. What time did I say his nap would end?" Martha replied.

Henry's cries were rising in primal rhythms now, and there were gasps between his calls, a forlorn, slightly desperate sound that even Martha, if she were honest, would have to admit she would rather not hear.

"You told us one o'clock," Beatrice said.

"It's nearly one!" Connie added.

"If you don't train him now, you can't train him later," Martha replied, and so, for the next thirteen minutes, until precisely one o'clock, seven women stood in the kitchen, listening to Henry House cry, watching the minute hands on their watches crawl toward the refuge of the hour.

"NOW?" CONNIE ASKED at one.

"Now," Martha said, and, despite herself, she led the way a little too eagerly back into the nursery.

Henry had managed to come unswaddled, and his face was nearly as red as his cotton pajamas. He did not stop crying when Martha picked him up, or when she changed his diaper, or even when she carried him, up on her shoulder, to the rocking chair. Only when she had guided the bottle firmly into his mouth did Henry stop. There was a kind of collective loosening in the room then, like the relief that follows a storm after the lights have been restored.

IT WAS AFTER HIS MEAL—eight ounces of formula exactly, drained to the last drop—and after the lesson in burping—over the shoulder, then over the knee—that Henry House was briefly returned to his crib, his backside naked, and that Ethel took the photograph they would all carry in their wallets. For although these women were present, on this September morning, to begin their education in the science of child rearing and the science of home economics, there was nothing in the least bit scientific about the feelings already engendered in them by this winsome, brown-haired, dark-eyed, sweet-cheeked baby boy.

2

Six Different Lullabies

Like the other academic disciplines at Wilton College, the Department of Home Economics required a four-year commitment from its students, and a course load as heavy as that of any department on campus. Despite the assumptions it inevitably provoked, home ec had for decades been a quietly subversive portal to a traditionally male world. In the name of home maintenance, menu planning, and stain removal, students took mandatory courses in physics, chemistry, statistics, bacteriology, biology, nutritional analysis, and electrical circuitry. At the end of one course, called Household Equipment, every girl was required to dismantle and reassemble an entire refrigerator by herself. This was no sorority tea.

Yet in the buzz of postwar enthusiasm, as the Baby Boom began in the reclaimed bedrooms of three million couples, the cooking, cleaning, and household maintenance seemed to take a backseat to the child-care course. It was the practice house, with its tiny, living embodiment of a great American future, that seemed to draw from the students the most somber sense of purpose. When Connie came for the first day of her first week as practice mother, her shiny red shoes were the only suggestion that she would ever bring anything light or fun—anything but grave ambition and patriotic intensity—to the tasks involved in helping to raise a fine young American.

Martha did nothing to perk up the mood. In her nineteen years as head of the practice house, she had trained more than fifty student mothers. But she had yet to find one who didn't need sober reminding that the joys of tending a child should never be separated from the risks.

With Connie, Martha did what she had always done for a novice on day one. She commented on the weather, took the girl's jacket, gave her an encouraging smile, thrust the baby into her arms, and said she had something to attend to upstairs.

It was a necessary initiation. The deep end of the pool, the rudder of the sailboat, the wheel of the car. All those situations that ultimately had to be handled by one person alone. There could never be any true preparation. Just defeat or survival.

Of course in this case it was Henry's survival that was the initial concern. Henry, who had tightened his tiny fist around Martha's index finger this morning and brought it directly into his mouth, as if it were his own thumb. Maybe it was his size—so much smaller than the usual practice babies—that made him seem more vulnerable. But in all the years she been running the practice house, Martha had lost only one baby, and that one had been her own: a tiny, awful, unbeautiful thing, born dead and bloody and premature, a hundred seasons ago, on a winter night when she'd still been loved.

Martha saw herself in the mirror at the top of the stairs and readjusted her scarf, forcing the memory out of her mind. Once a day. She allowed herself to think about that only once a day.

Like the first floor, the second floor of the practice house featured one small and one large bedroom, as well as an ample parlor. The rooms upstairs were as personal and crowded as the main floor's were generic and pristine. Martha had not yet found places for the souvenirs of her semesters away: pale pink shells and bleached white coral from Bermuda, a woven blanket and a clay bowl from Mexico, the inevitable Statue of Liberty from New York. She surveyed them now with mixed feelings. It was true that she had seen many wondrous sights she would never have seen unless Dean Swift and Dr. Gardner had insisted she go. It was also true that those sights had made her miss the practice house more deeply, made her feel the peculiar imbalance of having a home in which one lived only at the pleasure of an institution.

The many photographs framed on the walls upstairs were not of family, exactly, but rather of families formed and dissolved every few years: classes of women with House babies, babies long since returned to the orphanage, long since adopted, long since renamed. On the rare occasions when their adoptive families brought them back to visit, they never remembered Martha anyway.

"Mrs. Gaines?" Martha heard Connie call. "I think he may be—"

May be what, Martha thought, already fighting the same impatience that had led to her recent exile. There were really only a few options with a four-month-old baby. He could be hungry. Tired. Dirty. Hot. Cold. Sick. In pain. And that was all.

Martha checked her watch. It had been only ten minutes. She would give Connie five minutes more.

"I'm sure he's fine, dear," Martha called, and then she sat at her desk and waited, ready to move only at the sound of a life-threatening disaster.

MARTHA GAINES IN HER TWENTIES had never once looked into a mirror with apprehension or dismay. She hadn't been striking, but she'd been pretty, her features a warm invitation: hazel eyes, ascendant cheekbones, upturned nose—all broad and Irish. It hadn't yet crossed her mind that she wouldn't find love, a husband, children, and, someday, a house of her own.

She had been twenty-five on the Christmas Eve when Tom Gaines, the baritone who'd been promised all week by the choir director, had loped into the church, late. Tom had been stocky and rugged-looking, with an unexpectedly tidy and debonair side part in his hair. His place among the baritones had been opposite Martha's among the altos. Their eyes had met three or four times that night, looking up on a hallelujah.

He was a maintenance man for the Pennsylvania Railroad, painting the bodies of locomotives in their signature dark green, maroon, and gold. Martha would have married him no matter what his job had been. He smelled of sweat and shaving cream, and he sang or hummed love songs, sometimes without even knowing it.

She had been so in love with him, and when they married she had taken such joy in practicing all the large and little skills of home economics. She had tried to please him in the other ways too, but unlike cooking or canning or sewing, there had been no lessons in sex. She hadn't loved it, but she'd loved him, and when she'd gotten pregnant, she'd been proud of herself in a quiet, conventional way. The night the baby was born dead, Martha woke from the ether to see Tom at the foot of her bed.

"Please," Martha said. "Where's the baby? Please. Let me hold the baby."

"Hush, sweetheart," Tom told her. He climbed into the bed beside her, allowing her to lean against his green checked shirt, allowing her to weep into the taut, clean, smooth, just-shaven crook of his neck.

Only later, after the tales and confessions of his many dalliances had surfaced, would it strike Martha as incriminating that he had been so fragrant and clean-shaven at eight o'clock in the evening.

BACK DOWNSTAIRS NOW in the practice house, Martha found Connie waiting at the foot of the stairs. Henry squirmed in Connie's arms and made the little bleats that came from behind babies' motionless mouths, the way that purrs came from cats.

"What does he want?" Connie asked Martha.

"You're supposed to be the mother," Martha said, struggling with the impulse to take the baby, lift him high, and make him laugh, as she had this morning.

Martha showed Connie how to fold and pin a diaper, how to clean and powder a bottom. She had Connie put Henry on his back, and he flapped his arms up and down, as if he was making snow angels. He kicked his chubby legs, still curved like parentheses, so that it looked as if he was trying to clap with his feet. His slightly open mouth formed a smiling pyramid, the top lip rising into a little peak. Connie laughed, and, for a moment, Martha felt the old pleasure of watching a student warm to her task. But the third time Connie called the baby Harry, Martha picked him up herself. "It's not Harry," Martha said protectively. "The baby's name is Henry."

Eventually Martha would learn that Connie had a brother named Harry who had died in the Ardennes Forest. For now, Martha didn't realize that what she assumed in Connie was carelessness was only lingering numbness. And that like Betty—even like Martha herself, if she'd let herself think about it—Connie had shown up to care for Henry with a willing smile but a missing part.

IN FUTURE DAYS, Henry's afternoon walk would be an independent activity for Connie, but on the first day for each practice mother, Martha went along. She had found over the years that if she didn't set the initial course, the mothers would always come back after only ten breathless minutes.

It had seemed, a week before, as if autumn would be a long Indian summer. But for the last three or four days there had been a chill, and many of the leaves, which had seemed so thick and fixed in their bushy green embraces, were now skittering around Martha's sensible shoes and Connie's shiny red pumps. The leaves got stuck to the white sides of Henry's carriage tires, which picked them up and spun them over like passengers on a Ferris wheel.

The campus buzzed with the freshness of fall, and the thrill—still so unaccustomed—of a world no longer reeling from war. Young women in blunt pageboy haircuts and bright-colored lipsticks traversed the grounds, carrying books and satchels, swinging skirts cut full for the first time since before the war. Their laughter and gossip preceded and followed them, but several times rose and then fell to silence when they saw Martha approaching. The leaves went around on the carriage wheels. The brick buildings held the sun.

Passing one threesome, Martha could just catch the words *Gaines* and *baby* coming over them, like the backwash of a tide.

"What have you heard about me?" Martha asked Connie.

"Well, I only just got here a few days ago," Connie said.

"And—?"

"And, well. They say you took time off."

"Do they say why?"

"Not really," Connie said.

Of course, Martha thought. *Not really* meant *yes*. She shouldn't have asked the question; it betrayed self-doubt. She didn't need reassurance anyway, she told herself. What she needed was for everything to be back in its tidy place, with the girls and the school relying on her to set and enforce the standards.

A chill swirled the leaves at Martha's feet.

From his carriage, Henry let out another cawing sound, then flapped his arms emphatically and tried to get his hand to his mouth. Instead, he hit his own nose, then looked surprised.

Connie laughed. "Poor little fellow," she said, just as Henry burst into startled tears. Connie stopped the carriage and bent over the baby.

"What are you doing?" Martha asked.

"I thought I'd pick him up," Connie said.

"Not necessary," Martha said. "He'll be all right."

"But—"

"You can't fuss over every little thing."

IN THAT REGARD, the nights were always the hardest. No matter how many times Martha explained to the girls that babies needed to learn how to get to sleep by themselves, it was always a struggle to enforce the hands-off policy.

On Connie's first night, Martha lay in bed upstairs, sleeplessly hearing the all-too-familiar sounds of a new practice mother on the job. The restless pacing in the small downstairs bedroom while, in the nursery beside it, the baby cried. The premature trip to the kitchen to warm up the 2:00 A.M. bottle. The murmured endearments as he drank. The creak of the rocking chair. The lullaby: in Connie's case, as far as Martha could make out, it was "Don't Sit Under the Apple

Tree." The crying as Henry was put back in his crib. And then the pacing again.

Did it matter that, over the course of the next six weeks, six different women would sing Henry House six different lullabies? Or hold him in six different favorite positions? Or nuzzle him close in the pillowy haven of six different perfumes?

A WEEK LATER, during the nighttime feeding, Martha heard Grace sing "It Had to Be You." Ethel, who it turned out had the best sense of humor, sang "Is You Is or Is You Ain't My Baby." A week after that, Ruby sang "Mairzy Doats." When it was her turn, Beatrice offered up a surprisingly sweet "All the Pretty Little Horses." And finally, in the last week of October, on her own first night in the practice house, Betty fed Henry and rocked him, and sang:

They say that falling in love is wonderful

Martha had actually seen the great Ethel Merman sing this song in *Annie Get Your Gun* just this past summer in New York City. She had laughed at Merman's antics, the way she'd hammed it up through "Anything You Can Do," but when she sang "They Say It's Wonderful," Martha had found herself standing in the darkness, weeping, her arms resting on the smoky-smelling plush red divider at the back of the theater.

To hold a man in your arms
is wonderful . . .

Downstairs, now, there was a woman crooning this very song about another man who had left. More than a year after V-J Day, the only word from the Army was that Betty's husband, Fred, had almost certainly died in battle. Of course, unlike Tom Gaines—who had been killed in a train station accident, a paintbrush in his hand and a woman's phone number in his pocket—Fred was being universally mourned, and Betty universally comforted. There was nothing new to Martha about this injustice, the inequity of competing solitudes. Yet somehow, at two o'clock in the morning, with the first winter air sneaking in like a suspicion through the cracks around the windows, Martha suddenly couldn't lie still.

Breaking one of her myriad rules, she pulled on her old chenille bathrobe and tiptoed down the stairs.

As she suspected, Henry had long since finished his bottle, and Betty was rocking him unnecessarily, rocking him back to sleep, exactly as she wasn't supposed to do. There was one small lamp on the oak side table, and by its light, Martha could just recognize the look on Betty's face as one of depthless longing. The girl nearly leapt when she saw Martha, as if she'd been caught petting with some boy from a nearby school.

Jostled, Henry blinked and started to bleat, then closed his eyes again in sleep.

"What's wrong?" Betty asked Martha.

"Why are you still rocking him?"

"He was—"

"I've told you he shouldn't be rocked back to sleep. All babies wake up for all sorts of little disturbances. This one's no different, and you can't interrupt *your* sleep every time."

"I don't mind," Betty said.

"You should mind," Martha said.

Betty took this in for a moment, still apparently confused and surprised by Martha's presence in the nursery.

"I'm sorry," she finally said, but for some reason she seemed to hold Henry a bit closer.

Martha put out her hands for him, reinforcing the sense that she was interrupting some illicit schoolgirl behavior, now confiscating an offending item.

"The other girls told me you never come downstairs during the night," Betty said, still holding Henry.

"Well, clearly the other girls were misinformed," Martha said, though in truth she could not remember a single time when the need to check on a baby had overwhelmed her in quite this way. "Give me the baby," she said curtly.

Deposited back in his crib, Henry woke again and this time wailed. Betty was at the side of his crib in one long, urgent step.

"Don't pick him up," Martha said as Betty's fingers curled around the wooden railing of the crib.

Betty stood beside Martha and stared down into the shadows, as if she were standing at the edge of a canyon.

"I thought I was supposed to be the mother," Betty said.

3

A Dangerous Instrument

At five months, Henry House could sit in a high chair, reach for a block, and laugh at a good funny face.

Martha found him to be unusually smart. He had already begun saying his *B*s—almost always the first consonant, but quite early in this case. *Ba,* he would say. *Ba ba ba ba,* and even when he was sleepy or hungry, he seemed to follow the action around him with shiny, apparently mirthful eyes.

Now, in November, as first Connie, then Grace, Ethel, and Ruby completed their second rotations as practice mother, the sounds that came from the living room and nursery were louder and bolder than they'd been two months before. The tall, wooden, cathedral-style radio provided constant background noise; Henry seemed to love music and usually waved or kicked to the beat. The kitchen had become a chemistry lab for the mixing of his favorite meals, and debates raged during the long, darkening Sunday afternoons about when Henry had first crawled or clapped.

As always, getting the girls to pay attention to the baby was never as hard as getting them to let go.

"HAND HIM OVER," Ruby said.

It was Monday morning at nine o'clock, the official beginning of the practice house week. At this hour, the current practice mother was supposed to hand off the baby in time for his first bottle, then sit with his baby journal for a half hour or so, updating the information while remaining on hand in case the new mother had any questions.

They had all heard Henry cry before. Even on the very first day, they had heard that wrecking combination of scream and gasp. By now they had all learned to tell the hot, hungry cry from the fitful, sleepy cry; the warning cry from the whinny of being startled. This was different.

Henry, on the blanket, had been laughing with Ethel and had tumbled over, falling mirthfully in his red pajamas into a soft blue silk throw pillow. When he finally crept forward on his elbows and managed to raise his head back up, he found Ethel gone and Ruby in her place. For a moment, he stared the way grown people do at a magic act, right before they applaud. Then he started screaming.

He made pained, puncturing sounds, the kind that animals make, the kind that scream emergency, outrage, catastrophe. Ruby, reaching down for him; and Ethel, on her way to his baby journal; even Martha, who knew better than to be alarmed—all stopped as if ordered to do so. Then they converged on Henry.

"What did you do?" Martha asked Ruby.

Ruby looked just as startled, and nearly as tearful, as Henry. "I don't know!" she cried. "I don't think I did anything!"

"You must have done something," Ethel said.

"I just bent down to pick him up."

Henry's screams had risen beyond the beastly and transformed themselves into something almost mechanical—a siren, an alarm, constant and unstoppable.

Martha regained her composure, mortified by the thought that she'd been shaken, however briefly, by this outburst from a baby. Every child-care expert she respected believed that it was wrong to indulge such behavior. Every House baby she'd cared for had had to be broken at some point. And, far from damaging them in any way, the process seemed to calm the babies down, at least eventually.

"Oh, Mrs. Gaines," Ruby began, making a move toward Henry.

"Don't even think," Martha said, "of picking up that child."

Ruby looked to Ethel, as if for a reprieve. Ethel, for her part, looked to Martha, who turned with military precision and walked toward the living room. The baby screamed. The girls sagged and stared.

A MOMENT LATER, Martha was sitting in the living room, serene and expectant, her legs crossed at the ankles, a book already open to the page she wanted.

"Have a seat," she told Ethel and Ruby, above Henry's cries and the girls' bewilderment.

"Mrs. Gaines," Ruby began again.

"You've all just been handling him too much," Martha said, and then she read from her favorite child-care book, the one by John B. Watson:

" 'The mother picks the infant up, kisses and hugs it, rocks it, pets it and calls it "mother's little lamb," until the child is unhappy and miserable whenever away from actual physical contact with the mother.

" 'When you are tempted to pet your child,' " Martha read, " 'remember that mother love is a dangerous instrument. An instrument which may inflict a never-healing wound.' "

In the nursery, Henry was asleep, a patch of spit-up milk darkening the front of his red pajamas, his face slick, drained of all color, and, in slumber, seemingly without life.

IN THE FIRST WEEK OF DECEMBER, during her second tour as practice mother, Beatrice let Henry nap with the windows wide open, then took him out for his afternoon walk without a sweater or hat. The cold he caught was a lulu, and though caring for a sick baby was an inevitable part of the lesson plan, Beatrice proved no more adept in her nursing than she had been in her regular ministrations. She slept through one of Henry's doses of eardrops, and she was so awkward with the nasal syringe that Martha had to take pity on the baby and do the job herself.

She was, as it happened, sitting with Henry in the bathroom, hoping the steam from the shower would unclog his chest and nose, when Beatrice pounded on the door.

"There's a visitor," she called.

"A visitor," Martha said to Henry, mimicking Beatrice's awed tone of voice.

Beatrice pounded again, and Martha turned off the shower, just as Henry began to cry.

"Just a moment," Martha called.

Beatrice opened the door. The steam instantly engulfed her, and she looked terrified.

Martha took a tissue and wiped the streams of mucus from Henry's nose and mouth. She stepped past Beatrice and then saw President Gardner standing at the end of the hallway, framed like a guard in a tower.

He was a stout man with bushy eyebrows and a beaked nose and, in Martha's experience, an always slightly irritated air, as if he had spent his whole life waiting to hear something just a little more brilliant than whatever anyone said. As far as Martha could remember, he had never set foot in the practice house.

"Mrs. Gaines," he intoned above Henry's whimpers. His voice was a low and elegant hum.

"Dr. Gardner," she said. "This is— How nice to see you."

Beatrice, her hair even more electric than usual because of the steam, started off toward the kitchen.

"Beatrice," Martha said sternly. She handed Henry to her, despite his wailing, his filthy face, his fever, her love.

"What was wrong with the little fellow?" Dr. Gardner asked, after Beatrice had wafted away down the hall.

"A terrible cold," Martha said. "I'm afraid he needed a little extra attention from me."

"A cold?" Dr. Gardner said. "Isn't he rather young for a cold?"

It was a stupid question, but that didn't startle Martha. The few men she'd known had always asked stupid questions about babies.

"Babies are always susceptible to colds if they're not being breast-fed," she said matter-of-factly, and watched, with some vague satisfaction, as a flush of embarrassment crossed Dr. Gardner's face.

SHE OFFERED HIM TEA, which he declined. Instead, he lit a cigar and settled by the fireplace in one of the living room chairs. He chatted about the Nuremberg trials, and about the board of trustees, which had just announced its plans to endow a chair in the Department of Psychology. The whole time, Martha's mind raced with possible scenarios. He had come to tell her she was being fired. She was being tenured. He had come to ask her to give a presentation to the trustees. To alter her curriculum. Her methods. Her décor.

When, after fifteen minutes, he stood up and walked down the hall toward the nursery, Martha was reminded of Betty on her first day in the practice house: those exact same strides, that same odor of entitlement.

"Dr. Gardner, can I help you with something else?" Martha asked, following him.

"No, I just want to see where the baby sleeps."

"Where he sleeps?"

"Sleeps. Plays. Crawls. What have you."

"You want a tour?" Martha asked, still surprised.

"Perhaps the student I just met will do the honors," he said, and it was not a request but a command.

IT WOULD REMAIN UNCLEAR TO MARTHA for weeks what Dr. Gardner had been looking for, but something told her that it would be unwise to question Beatrice too closely about what, if anything, he had asked her. If the president's real purpose had been to confirm either new or old accusations about Martha, then she didn't want her questioning to be construed as insecurity.

Even two hours after the president left, the smell of his cigar hung thickly in the air.

———

HENRY DIDN'T RECOVER FULLY from his cold until nearly a week later, and it was only then, with an attentive Betty on hand for her second stint in the practice house, that Martha decided it was safe to go into town to do her Christmas errands.

It was a Tuesday morning, still just the second week in December, but Martha hated to fall behind on tasks that could be done in advance.

Wearing rubber boots in case of snow, she walked the red-brick streets from the campus into town. The market had the new Green Stamps catalogue, just in time for the holiday season, and Martha picked one up at the counter, then moved on to the Spring Street church, where the annual manger scene filled the front lawn. Martha paused before it, wondering if the sheep and goats had been re-painted, or if they just looked more vibrant because of the bright sun. The gold on the wings of the angel caught the light, and even the Baby Jesus seemed to have a pinker pair of lips. Jesus was nearly as big as Henry, his arms and legs chubby and outstretched, and his eyes wide open and smiling. Martha didn't think any newborn would look like that, but she realized, not for the first time, that she had never seen a newborn. Not any practice house baby. Not even her own.

Around the corner at the post office, Martha bought a page of Christmas Seals. At Hamilton's Hardware, two blocks down, she read-justed her scarf when Arthur Hamilton told her he liked its colors, and she ogled the signs for the latest household wonder: a new Hoover that was said to vacuum up twice the dust in less than half the time. At the toy store, Martha stood by the window, admiring the new train display; it had grown less elaborate with each Christmas of the war, but now, with peace blooming, it was exuberant with fresh cotton snowdrifts, a well-frosted church, and new fir trees. For a moment, Martha tried to imagine what Henry would be like when he was old enough to play with trains like these, and then she thought again of her stillborn child, and then of her lost marriage, and then, banishing the thoughts from her mind, she needlessly pushed at the vertices be-tween the leather-gloved fingers of first one and then the other hand.

———

"HE'S GOING TO BE AN ARTIST, I just know it," Betty said as Martha stepped into the kitchen that afternoon.

Henry, his hands covered with applesauce, had smeared large circles onto the tray top of the wooden high chair, and he was now busily smacking the centers of them, as if they were rain puddles.

"An artist!" Martha said, putting her bags on the counter.

"Picasso! Rembrandt! Look at how he uses his hands!"

Martha wanted to pick Henry up. She wanted to nuzzle him, to rock him, to feel the perfect fit, the weird completion, in the moment when Henry's hands found their way to the nape of her neck. Martha wanted to carry him in a perpetual embrace, to have those tiny arms seek and choose her shoulders, her cheeks, her nose. Momentarily frozen by the desire, she stared at Henry, unmoving, until Betty finally looked up and said, "Don't worry. I'll clean him up." Martha nodded. She gathered up her roll of Green Stamps, her new catalogue, and her Christmas Seals. "All six-month-olds use their hands," she said to Betty. "That's the main thing six-month-olds do."

"Ga!" Henry shouted, and Martha forced herself to go upstairs.

IN THE EVENING, she sat at her desk, listened to her tabletop Philco, wrote notes on her Christmas cards, and neatly affixed the Christmas Seals. This year, the seals had a bright blue backdrop framing the image of a lamplighter. They were the perfect match for Perry Como's hit about the old lamplighter who leaves the lamps dark for all the courting couples:

> *For he recalls when dreams were new,*
> *He loved someone who loved him, too . . .*

Martha's Christmas card list was not terribly long. Other than two cousins in Santa Anita whom she'd only met once, she had no family.

Her father had died a decade before, and her mother a decade before that. There were no siblings, no surviving aunts or uncles. The list was mostly made up of Martha's fellow faculty members—her colleagues in the home economics program, her neighbors at the Wilton Nursery School, Irena Stahl at the orphanage, and of course Dean Swift and President Gardner. There were a few former students with whom she'd stayed in touch, but if two years passed without them sending cards in return, she would automatically remove their names from her list. Her father had impressed on her years before the sin of wasted effort.

. If Dean Swift and President Gardner had not welcomed her back, Martha thought, how many Christmas cards would she be sending out now? And from what tiny, barren rented room would she be addressing the envelopes? She tried to calm herself by remembering that at forty-eight, she was still not too old to seek a new job. Wilton College, however, was the only place where she'd ever worked.

The house was so quiet tonight that she could hear Betty turning the pages of her book in the bedroom below. And once, she heard Henry let out a sound, like a laugh, in his sleep. Still at her desk, Martha moved on to the trading stamps, using a sponge to wet them and then pasting them tidily into a book. "Would you throw money away?" she had often asked her students when they grumbled about having to paste in the stamps. She would point proudly to the practice house toaster, the new electric coffeepot, and the brass-tipped fireplace tools by way of showing them what a little time spent pasting could buy.

Martha paused to look around her room. The wood floor, with its wide, warm boards the color of a cello; the tall windows that framed the campus's tall trees; the wainscoting on the walls; and the photos, and the mementos—these last, it was true, would come with her if she was ever forced to go. But how—and where—would she ever find any new ones?

Sometimes—in the rare moments when she had Henry all to herself—she would let him put his arms around her neck, and she would whisper to him, "Hold tight." Now, sensing change like a scent in the air, she heard the words in her own mind, just as clearly and firmly as if she were talking to him. *Hold tight.*

CHRISTMAS FELL ON a Wednesday. All the girls would be going home for the holiday. So on the Saturday before they took off, they gathered at the practice house for their own practice Christmas.

Martha gave Henry a red fire truck, her standard gift for practice house boys. Beatrice had knitted him a stocking with an *H* that sagged dramatically across the top. Ruby had crocheted him a bright red sweater using yarn that had been sheared and dyed on her parents' farm. The rest of the girls gave presents that suggested their own expectations of Henry, or perhaps their own views of themselves. Betty gave him a set of finger paints and a box of crayons. Connie gave him books. Ethel gave him a silly pull-toy dog on a little string leash. And Grace, who had the most money, gave him a miniature white piano that even Mozart would have been years away from being able to play.

When they had all opened their gifts for him, Henry sat on the rug next to the Christmas tree and, ignoring each of the actual presents, chewed merrily on the plastic lid of a box that had held Christmas cookie sprinkles. After a while, Grace sat beside him on the rug and plinked out "White Christmas" on the little piano, and Henry grinned, allowing a mouthful of saliva to drop onto the rug.

Surrounded by his seven mothers, only one of whom had tried to conceal the wish that her gift—and her arms—would be chosen above all others, Henry sat in his red sweater, plump and passionate, like a tiny Santa Claus himself, and looked from one to another of them, as if trying to figure out what he should give to whom.

4

Give Me the Baby, Dear

Two weeks later, Martha heard the news from Ruby—that Betty had finally received a letter. From the somber tone in Ruby's voice, Martha could only assume that this would have to be *the* letter.

"When did it come?" Martha asked Ruby.

Henry was in the nursery, taking his nap, and Ruby was helping Martha take down the Christmas tree ornaments.

"I think it was just this morning," Ruby said.

"Did you see Betty yourself?"

"No. I saw Beatrice in town on our walk," Ruby said.

Martha knew it was unkind, but she couldn't help feeling angry that her whole routine and the house's routine—and the whole routine of the college, for that matter—would be thrown off by the inevitable bustle and sadness over Betty's husband's death. There would be a memorial service, of course. And compulsory condolence visits to Dr. Gardner's house. Maybe even a plaque or portrait at some point. And there would be Betty herself, whose needs would now come before anyone else's.

Martha had seen Betty's husband only once—about two years before—the week he had come back on leave, when he and Betty had stopped to see her father briefly just before he shipped out again. To Martha, he had looked odd then, like an undernourished Popeye, with a goofy, slightly uneven face. He was still young enough to be wearing—like tiny badges—bits of tissue on the places where he'd cut himself shaving.

Martha sighed as she took a wrapped ornament from Ruby and tucked it into a corner of the hatbox in which she kept the most delicate of the Christmas decorations. She wondered why it was that her own husband couldn't have died valiantly, guaranteeing not only his martyrdom but hers as well. "Poor Martha," people would have said, the way they had already spent the year saying "Poor Betty." And everything she did, or tried, would have been construed as courageous. Yes, Betty had lost her young husband. But at least she would have good wishes, sad smiles, and all of her future before her. And she would have her father's help and protection. That couldn't hurt much, either.

The real courage, Martha was starting to believe, was going on when no one cared if you went on or not.

"Mrs. Gaines?" Ruby was asking from her perch at the top of the stepladder. She was trying to liberate a string of cranberries from the highest branches of the Christmas tree, and the challenge was clearly unnerving her. "Can you give me a hand, Mrs. Gaines?" Ruby asked.

"We throw the cranberries out with the tree," Martha said abruptly, her anger surprising them both. "You've been studying home economics for more than three months now, Ruby. Surely you would have learned that if you keep berries in a hatbox for a year you can expect them to rot."

Stung by Martha's tone, Ruby let go of the strand and looked down from her tangled heights. "I'm sorry, Mrs. Gaines. I was just trying to—"

"Yes," Martha said, and, distracted, walked into the kitchen, still carrying a striped crystal bell.

In the kitchen, she stood by the stove, looked down at the green and white checked linoleum tiles, and tried to govern her feelings. Then, unexpectedly, Betty was at the back door, her face slick with tears and hurt, which made her look even younger than usual.

"Is he still asleep?" she asked as she barged into the kitchen and jostled Martha. The bell in Martha's hand dropped and broke, melodically, on the pristine floor.

With barely a glance at the ground, Betty was already heading down the corridor to Henry's room, the soles of her brown and white saddle shoes squeaking on the warped wooden floor.

"Betty!" Martha shouted after her.

"What was that?" Ruby called.

"Betty!" Martha repeated, stepping over the broken glass.

In the nursery, Betty had already picked Henry up and lifted him onto her shoulder, so that his face fit neatly against the pale curve of her neck. She was crying, but soundlessly, and her eyes were shut, as if she was praying.

"I'm sorry," Betty said.

"What?"

"I'm sorry I made you drop that. What was it?"

"Only an ornament. Let me take the baby, dear," Martha said.

Betty shook her head as fiercely as having a sleeping baby crooked into her neck would allow.

"I know you must be devastated," Martha said. "Believe me. You have all my sympathy. But really, you know. The baby shouldn't be held so much."

Betty shook her head again and seemed to hold Henry even tighter.

"Would you like me to call your father?" Martha asked, as gently as possible.

"No."

"I think you should give me the baby now," Martha said. She had the illusion that she was talking to a jumper who had already decided that nothing made more sense than jumping. But it was not exactly worry for the baby that was making Martha nervous. It was not worry for Betty, either. It was actually the premonition that something was going to be physically ripped away from her.

"Come," Martha said one last time, and then she took a step closer to Betty.

"Let us alone," Betty said, her neck and head bent over Henry's head, like a third, protective arm.

"Dear, I'm so sorry about your husband," Martha said. "Here. Give me the baby, dear. Let me get you a tissue."

Martha grabbed three tissues from the box she always kept on the dresser, beside Henry's little blue plastic brush and comb. She fought the impulse to wipe Betty's face the same way she cleaned Henry's. Instead she thrust the tissues into Betty's hands, essentially forcing a trade, and finally Betty handed the baby to Martha and started to wipe her eyes.

"Do you know how Fred died?" Martha asked gently.

Betty shook her head again, and then began to sob. Every gasp showed the girl's tiny ribs and perfect waist. It was hard to believe that a vessel this small could hold such enormous pain.

Finally, with what seemed a mythic effort of will, Betty stopped crying and put her hands at right angles to her body, as if trying to push down her feelings, or at least the air around her.

"With any luck it was quick, and he didn't have to suffer," Martha said.

"No," Betty said, gesturing again to hold down the air. "It's not like that. Fred isn't dead. He's alive." And she burst into tears again.

AFTER MARTHA HAD SENT RUBY OUT with Henry for his walk, Betty unfolded the letter for Martha to see. Though it had only come that morning, it already had the look of something nervously overhandled, as if with each opening there had been the hope of finding a different message. Stamps with oval faces bordered the top of the gray-blue envelope like guards, and the words BY AIR MAIL were printed across the cover in bold blue capital letters. The message inside was equally forceful, written in capitals too, as if intended as a telegram for which the characters had to be counted. Martha read:

NEVER WENT BACK. AWOL ITALY, THEN HID AUSTRALIA. THEN
ASHAMED TO EXPLAIN. BUT REALIZE CAN'T LIVE WITHOUT YOU.
COME MEET ME. MELBOURNE P.O. KNOWS ADDRESS. LAST NAME
NOW WHAT YOU USED TO CALL ME FOR FUN. SOONEST.
DEAREST. NEW LIFE AHEAD.

For several minutes, Martha read and reread the note, trying to figure out what to say. Gingerly, as if she were tucking Henry into bed, Martha put the letter sheet inside the envelope and handed it back to Betty. As she did so, she noticed the tiny, pale blood vessels fanned out across Betty's exhausted eyelids. The teakettle whistled, another cry.

"I know this must be a shock to you," Martha finally ventured, taking down a bag of Lipton to dunk in each of two china cups. "And that you must be a bit confused about the idea of your husband—"

Betty shook her head again.

"What did Dr. Gardner— What did your father say?" Martha asked.

"My father doesn't know yet," Betty said.

"Why not?" Martha asked, nonplussed. But it would be another week before Betty would tell that part of the story. For now, she merely stared at Martha, as if from a roiling ocean.

"But, dear, Fred *is* alive," Martha finally said. "I would think that would be more important to you than anything else."

Betty poured what must have been five seconds' worth of sugar into her teacup, then stirred it with needless vigor. "Where's Ruby?" she finally asked. "It looks like rain. She should bring him back," she said.

"Betty. It's Ruby's week."

"She doesn't know how to handle him."

"She's learning all the time," Martha said. "You all have your strengths and weaknesses."

"He's mine," Betty said.

"We all feel that way sometimes," Martha said.

"No," Betty said, with surprising strength. "I mean he's mine. I had him this summer. He isn't Fred's. Fred doesn't know," she said. "Henry's my son."

5

A Puppy in the Sun

The facts were fairly simple, though it took Betty time to admit them all, and she changed them several times before she stuck with one story. The most important fact was that the baby wasn't her husband's.

Henry, it turned out, was the child of a man whose first name was Jerry and whose last name Betty would never know. She had met him in a movie line in Pittsburgh three months after Fred shipped out. She had let Jerry bring her back to the apartment where she and Fred had been living. Unglued by fear, wine, and loneliness, she had let him spend the night. Not even the whole night, actually. Barely the length of the movie they'd seen. Then he had disappeared.

Betty had been eighteen. For nearly three months, telling no one, she'd simply hoped that the baby would go away. She was working at a hat shop, and on her break one afternoon she read an ad in the back of the *Pittsburgh Sun* about how to get the problem fixed. For two weeks, she drank a daily concoction of rosemary, bay leaves, pumice, pepper, vinegar, and Coke. When that didn't work, she began to exercise constantly, exhaustingly. She did a hundred sit-ups each night and another hundred each morning. Finally, she summoned the courage to ask a pharmacist if there was someone she could see. The druggist gave her an address. She lost her nerve at the last moment, though, when she overheard some coffee-shop talk about a girl "botched" in a back-alley job.

When, in Betty's sixth month, an old woman gave up a bus seat for her, Betty broke down, called her father from Pittsburgh, told him what had happened, and asked if she could come home.

"And what did he say?" Martha asked Betty over the cup of tea that had become, by the following week, their daily ritual.

"He cursed at me first," Betty admitted, wrapping her hands around her teacup as if clasping them in prayer. "He actually used a swearword. Then he said thank God my mother was dead, or this would kill her. Then he asked me where the father was, and when I told him I didn't know, he said thank God I didn't know, or he would kill *him*."

"And then?" Martha asked.

"Then he asked if there was any chance Fred would believe the baby was his, and I said no. And then he sent me to the Home."

Martha sighed. Of course. That was what girls did if they were pregnant and unmarried or in disgrace. They went to stay in maternity homes—in one door secretly, pregnantly; then out the other, welcomed back to resume their lives as if nothing but time had been lost. It was from exactly these homes that orphanages like Irena's—and in turn programs like Martha's—were able to get their babies, and to pass them on, if all went well, to real families who would want them.

ON THE FIRST MONDAY after Betty's revelation, President Gardner made another unannounced visit to the practice house. This time, Martha felt quite sure that she knew why he had come.

"You've come to see your grandson again?" she asked him softly after Beatrice had taken Henry down the hall.

"We will never call him that," Dr. Gardner snapped.

The president strode into the living room and took his seat by the fireplace.

"I apologize," Martha said quickly. "I didn't realize."

"I obviously cannot change the fact that Bettina chose to tell you her entire wretched story," he began without preface. "But I will say that if you repeat to a single soul even a word of this very personal business, you will be out of a job on the very same day that I hear about it. I will not have the name of this college being dragged through the mud," he said. "Do you understand?"

"Of course," Martha said. "I would never say anything."

The president looked around, presumably for somewhere to put his frustration.

"Don't you ever light a fire in here?" he finally asked.

"Well, we do worry a bit with the baby so close to walking," Martha said, getting to her feet.

"When Bettina was a baby and we still lived in Vermont, we had a potbellied stove, and all our neighbors with children kept their stoves surrounded by wrought-iron gates. Every day, Bettina's mother warned her not to go near ours, and one day she did, and she burned her hand, and she never went near it again."

Martha paused for a moment, considering how to respond to this pearl of wisdom.

"I don't think I'd get a lot of babies from the orphanage if I sent them back with burnt hands," she finally said.

"You will go on getting babies from the orphanage as long as I tell the orphanage that we need babies," Dr. Gardner said.

Martha, expertly wielding the fireplace tongs as if the logs were lumps of sugar, allowed this to sink in. "Irena Stahl knows about Henry, then?" she asked as she arranged pieces of kindling into a perfectly balanced tower.

"Absolutely not," Dr. Gardner said.

"Then how did he come to be here?" Martha asked. It was Irena, after all, who had insisted that Martha take Henry, despite his having been only three months old. It couldn't have been a coincidence.

"It's perfectly obvious," the president said. "I told Irena I had heard about a baby who needed to be placed. Until we knew what had happened to Fred, Bettina simply refused to give the baby up. Do you see?"

"Yes," Martha said.

"I know I should have insisted, right from the start, that he be sent far away. I've already regretted that. But Bettina seemed so fragile."

"Yes," Martha said again.

Then Dr. Gardner brushed a crumb from the lapel of his jacket, as if he were shaking off the moment. "Imagine," he said. "Thousands upon thousands of girls give these babies up *all* the time, and get on with their lives. Not Bettina. She even wanted to keep him with us at my residence. Can you imagine?"

"No," Martha said, but she could.

The president let out a kind of laugh. "I told her if we did that, it wouldn't be my residence for long."

That was true, of course. A college was a place where people expected—and, Martha felt, deserved—to find propriety. Martha took two logs and carefully laid them across the andirons.

"And now? Will Betty keep him?" Martha asked, as gently as possible.

"Keep him! A bastard?" Dr. Gardner intoned. "A *bastard*?" His eyes flashed at Martha. "Bettina's place is with her husband. She *will* be going to Australia, and I can promise you she will not be showing up there with some other man's child." From the nursery, the sound of Henry's laughter emerged, like an unexpected song. Somewhat more gently, the president added: "And in time, she and Fred can have children of their own."

BUT BETTY DIDN'T LEAVE right away. Over the months that followed, she twirled the practice house into a constantly moving, ever-more-powerful, Betty-centered vortex. She was nearly always the subject of conversation, even though she had told no one but Martha that she was Henry's mother. Instead, all the girls—and most of the campus—knew only that Fred had deserted the Army. They believed the reason Betty was always in tears had to do with the shame of being married to a deserter, and the sadness of having to leave her home and her family in order to be with him.

The girls—Connie and Grace particularly, who were closest in upbringing if not experience—complained about Betty's frequent pop-in
visits, which they attributed to her position not only as daughter of
the president but also as resident diva.

"Why doesn't she just go, already?" Connie asked.

"I suppose she's not sure she wants to live in Australia as the wife
of some guy who could be court-martialed any minute," Grace answered.

"So she'd rather leave her husband when he needs her most," Connie said.

"And stay with Daddy? Why not?"

And Martha, though tempted, offered no answer to that question.

OVER TIME, HOWEVER, it became abundantly clear to Martha that, despite the agonized (and frequently confided) vacillations of Betty's
heart, there was no way that she would or could stay at Wilton. Staying would mean ending her marriage, outraging her father, bringing
scandal to the college, and, apparently, raising a child without any financial support. In 1947, what was unusual about Betty's situation
was not that she would give up the baby but that she had managed to
stay in his proximity for so long.

By March, Betty began to make plans to join Fred in Australia, and
by May, she had begun showing up less and less often at the practice
house.

SHE LEFT FOR AUSTRALIA three days after Henry's first birthday. She
was thin and pale and sick and cried-out. Henry, too, seemed not himself that day—or perhaps that was simply Martha's imagination, or a
new phase of his development. It was typical, Martha felt, for one-year-
olds to be withdrawn. At least that had been her experience. Certainly
Henry could have no sense of what he was losing. No one around him
did.

What Martha would remember most about the day was what
Henry did when Betty walked out the door. Though he had just

started standing up, he crawled onto the living room rug and into a trapezoid of sunlight, toppled over onto his side, and—despite the bandage that was supposed to deter him—put his thumb in his mouth. For a long while, Henry stayed there, like a puppy in the sun, the trapezoid perfectly framing him, as if he were trapped in a weird, warped viewfinder.

Then Ruby ran back inside and told Martha that Betty needed to tell her one more thing, and Martha walked out to the front yard. Amid the lushness of the new green summer, Betty looked down at the ground, where two bees chased each other past a fallen rose. She whispered, "Take care of him for me."

Martha nodded firmly, deciding at that moment not to ask Betty *for how long*. If she didn't ask, she could always believe that Betty had meant forever.

6

You Know More
Than You Think You Do

With Betty gone, the practice mother rotation would need to be shifted, at least until September, when there would be new students hoping to join the program for the second year. The night Betty left, Martha sat at her desk and weighed the pros and cons of substituting herself for Betty in the coming weeks. On the one hand, it would be setting a new and possibly unwieldy precedent; on the other, it would relieve the girls, who had already scheduled their summer trips home and would otherwise have to revise their plans. Martha imagined strolling with Henry in the summer evenings, or letting him splash in the kiddie pool when the days got long and sultry.

But just a few days after Betty's departure, an official envelope appeared in the practice house mailbox, a letter from Dean Swift suggesting that Martha attend the Matson College Conference on Child Care in July.

There was no mistaking the underlying message in this suggestion, which was that Martha, despite a basically peaceful, patient year, was still being doubted, still somehow in need of further training. Throughout the afternoon's errands, Martha tried to find a way around what she knew was tantamount to an order. Buying the week's groceries. Taking her old tan pumps to be resoled. At Hamilton's, she stopped to look again at the new Hoover. "For every woman who is proud of her home," the poster beside it said, and Martha *was* proud of her home, as half hers and half real as it might be. She had gone to these sorts of conferences before and had enjoyed rubbing shoulders with her counterparts from other programs. But this was not the right moment to leave the practice house. Perhaps, she thought, she could explain to Dean Swift the effect that Betty's departure was bound to have on the schedule. Perhaps, she thought with even less hope, she could appeal directly to Dr. Gardner.

Martha walked through the pale, warm afternoon, besieged by the sounds of summer: music coming from open doorways; the jangly car horns, which seemed louder than usual; the shouts of liberated children; and the gentle metallic grating of their roller skates on the pavement. It suddenly seemed to Martha, in fact, that children were everywhere: their Mercurochromed knees and unkempt hair and untied hair bows and their bicycles with the limp red, white, and blue streamers dangling from the grimy beige handgrips.

How could she leave Henry now, so soon after Betty's departure?

How could she ever leave Henry?

EVEN BEFORE MARTHA CALLED MATSON to register for the conference, she knew the main topic was bound to be Dr. Spock, whose book-length ode to permissiveness had become only more ubiquitous since Connie had first brought her copy into the practice house. Late that night, Martha forced herself to read, for the first time, what everyone had been talking about. Spock's first section was titled "Trust Yourself," and his first sentence was just as ridiculous: "You know more than you think you do." In Martha's experience, most people in most endeavors invariably knew considerably less than they thought they did. And what was true in most endeavors was doubly true in the raising of children.

She could hear Henry fussing downstairs now, as he often did when he was with Connie, who remained the most indulgent and least effective of his mothers. It was heartbreaking to overhear them sometimes, especially his crying, which was the simple result of Connie's having given in to his crying before. If a child knew that crying would get him attention, the child cried. If a child knew that crying didn't work, the child stopped crying. She supposed Dr. Spock would say the crying *meant* he should be picked up. But Martha's teaching depended on believing that a child was something to manage, not to be managed by. She read:

> Every time you pick your baby up, even if you do it a little awkwardly at first, every time you change him, bathe him, feed him, smile at him, he's getting a feeling that he belongs to you and that you belong to him.

Belonging, Martha thought. Since when did *belonging* matter?

THE MEETING ROOM AT MATSON was warm and wood-paneled, glittery with old silver and good crystal. Everything was perfect, the tea cakes laid out symmetrically, the doilies fresh, the tablecloths not overly starched. It was exactly what one would expect at a convocation of domestic experts, and the undergraduates who were serving were eager and polite. The mood was festive. Like other areas of American life, academia had found new energy since the end of the war, and in her welcoming speech, the president of the National Association of Child Experts virtually exulted at the convention's unprecedented number of participants.

Over the next two days, Martha took part in seminars on toys, influenza, and finger painting. She attended lectures on speech development, toilet training, and genetics. Sitting in a darkened lecture hall, enveloped by the slightly burnt smell of the Kodaslide projector and the wheezes and clicks of the dropped slides, she looked on, utterly engrossed. She felt, at once and all over again, that these subjects and systems mattered. The use of schedules. The maintenance of charts. The parsing of children's needs and impulses. She glanced down the row of rapt women, whose gold Omicron Nu pins gleamed identically from their necklaces and lapels. The home economics society had never meant more to her, and amid the comfort of note taking, she had to admit to herself that she had allowed Henry to blur her focus. What was the practice house, after all, if it wasn't a testament to the belief that women could replace the mysteries of child rearing with mastery?

For a moment, Henry became not the child she had always wanted, or even the one she was trying so hard not to love, but rather the tenth of ten children whom she had started on their way. She conjured a mental picture of the baby journals on her shelves, and the children they represented, raised according to time-tested methods. Methods that women had trusted, long before they'd been set loose by Benjamin Spock to trust themselves.

RUMORS AND UPDATES of Dr. Spock's whereabouts preceded his movements around the Matson campus. Wilton had had its share of famous visitors too, but Martha could not remember any who'd been received with such giddy enthusiasm. She did not get to see Spock's face until late the last afternoon, when, along with the approximately forty heads of child-care programs, she attended the most selective seminar of the weekend.

Sitting at an enormous conference table just a half dozen seats from the famous doctor, she found it hard to look at him. There was an intense kind of solicitousness about him, as if he was so used to listening to people's symptoms that he viewed all statements made to him as clues to something else. Martha didn't want to be analyzed. She didn't want to be diagnosed.

"Has that been your experience?" he kept asking when people made their opinions known. There was nothing even slightly nasty in the way he asked the question, but somehow it still seemed to be an accusation.

Spock was disarmingly modest. He appeared to be almost shyly surprised by the success of his book, whose very "Trust Yourself" message seemed so self-effacing. He was the anti-expert: Some Midwest common sense, some reasonable rules, some sensible behavior, and children would be just fine.

"So what do you say to Holt and Watson about baby's schedule of feedings and eliminations?" one woman asked.

"Well, different things may work for different types of children," the doctor answered congenially. "In my experience, it causes more harm than good to try to keep children to strict schedules."

"Is there anything, then, that you disapprove of in an infant?" another woman asked.

Spock smiled benignly. "Well, let me ask you this," he said. "What infant behaviors do *you* find objectionable?"

"Thumb sucking," Martha said. She hadn't realized she was going to speak until the words were out of her mouth. The women at the table all turned in her direction, like the members of a choir looking for their cue.

"It's a dreadful habit," Martha continued, "and apart from the fact that it's unsightly and unsanitary, it can do permanent damage to the teeth and the jawline."

"Is it safe to assume, then, that you subscribe to traditional methods to deter this?" Dr. Spock asked.

"Yes," Martha said.

"And may I ask which of them you have found to be most effective?"

"Well, it varies from child to child," Martha said, aware that several of the women were now looking at her exactly as they would if she had just stepped onto a train track at the commuter hour. Her hand moved nervously to adjust her scarf and necklace, but she overcame the impulse. "Sometimes," she continued, "I've found it effective to be vigilant about offering a toy as a distraction. Sometimes I'll combine that with bandaging the thumb, or putting on a scratchy mitten. In the most extreme cases, I've employed a celluloid cuff."

She watched some of the participants look down, as if in pity.

"And please don't all of you pretend you haven't done the same," Martha said. "This has been the accepted practice among educated child-care providers for the last forty years. Surely you'll acknowledge that, Dr. Spock," Martha said.

"Of course," he answered quickly, with a twinkly, avuncular smile that made Martha cringe. "But in my experience, restraining a baby physically only frustrates him."

"Of course it frustrates him," Martha said sharply. "How can any habit be broken without it causing some frustration?"

Spock nodded his agreement and then, as if offering a perfectly made, neatly trimmed tea sandwich, laid out his belief: that thumb sucking, like so much else in infant behavior, was the reflection not of habit or will but rather of simple need.

"A baby sucks because it needs to suck," Dr. Spock said.

"I wasn't suggesting, Dr. Spock," Martha said archly, "that a baby sucks because it is one of Satan's minions."

That brought a much-needed laugh from around the table.

"I don't have much patience for people who soften at the slightest sign of resistance," Martha continued. "Of course it's disturbing to upset an infant, but I always tell my students that if they think about the long-term benefits, they'll be able to withstand the feelings of the moment."

"And do you have children of your own?" Dr. Spock asked.

"That's not the point," Martha answered, perhaps a bit too sharply.

"I wasn't trying to make a point," the doctor said. "I was just curious."

"I have helped raise ten babies over twenty years in the home economics program at Wilton College," Martha said, finally adjusting the scarf around her neck, fingering the Omicron Nu pin beneath it.

"I just wondered whether you yourself had ever experienced these kinds of emotions," Spock said.

"What emotions are those?"

"The emotions of being a mother."

"Have you?" Martha said. And apart from whatever facts and figures they took away from the conference, the impertinence of this moment was what most of the participants would long remember, and what Martha, in her fervor, would think about with pride.

But the liberation inherent in Spock's message, which in essence was love over law, was for Martha as inescapable as it was secretly welcome.

7

The Center of the World

All the way back from Matson on the bus, Martha savored her moment. Martha Gaines and Benjamin Spock. She had told him what she thought. She had stood up for the program she was going back to reclaim. The summer world slipped by, alive with flowering bushes and flowered hats, children playing on swing sets and running through the rainbow spray of sprinklers. There was something cool and comforting in the act of passing these lives by: not at all unlike the role she had played for all those practice house children. They existed, in her memories, as if on a series of front lawns, waving at Martha as she rode by. There had been many. There would be more.

But the clear, impartial, professional path became instantly muddied, and nearly obscured, as soon as Martha walked back into the practice house that afternoon. Ethel was lying, fully prone, on the living room rug, a camera in her hands as usual. Henry, wearing only a diaper, was standing against the couch: beautiful, hopeful, and irresistible. He was looking at Ethel, wobbling a bit, and seemingly unsure about what to do.

"Come on, Hanky-Panky," Ethel was saying, oblivious to Martha's presence. "Come on, Hanky-Panky. You can do it. Walk to Mama Ethel's camera. Walk the way you just did."

"Eh-oh!" Henry shouted, which was as close as he could get to *Ethel.*

"Yes, Hanky-Panky. Eh-oh."

"Eh-oh!"

"You can do it, Hanky-Panky. I know you can. Let Eh-oh take your picture." She lifted her head from the viewfinder and smiled at him. "Then we'll show all the others." At this, Henry grinned extravagantly.

"Ethel!" Martha shouted.

They both turned, startled, toward Martha. Then Henry plopped to his backside, hard.

"Boom!" Ethel said—no doubt intending to keep the wailing from Henry to a minimum. Intending to suggest that every boo-boo could be a source of joy.

"Really!" Martha said, and Henry, somehow, decided not to cry and got up onto his hands and knees and started to crawl toward Martha.

"Why isn't he dressed?" Martha asked Ethel, putting her suitcase down so that she could stop Henry from crawling past her.

"He was," Ethel began. "That is, I was just getting ready to dress him, and then, son of a gun, Mrs. Gaines, he took a step."

"He's taken steps before," Martha said drily, picking Henry up.

"Without holding on to a darned thing," Ethel added.

In Martha's arms now, Henry put his hands on either side of her face and bent his head forward so that his forehead was touching hers.

"Mah!" he said, which was as close as he could get to *Martha.* In the tiny tent of intimacy created by their touching foreheads, Henry looked into Martha's eyes and Martha looked into Henry's. His eyes were completely enthralling to her—green, with flecks of orange, now—promising love and magic. For a moment, she felt the moist sting of tears coming, and she had to force herself to walk forward, into the living room, and to hand Henry to Ethel.

"Put some clothes on him," she said huskily. "I'm going to go unpack."

UPSTAIRS, HOWEVER, Martha did not unpack. She did not even bring her suitcase into the bedroom but left it, unopened, on the landing and sank into her parlor chair, beset by the ache and helplessness of being in love.

Had he really taken his first step without her?

It was an hour before Martha walked back out onto the landing to retrieve her suitcase. In the mirror at the top of the stairs, the mirror in which she had greeted and calmed herself so often, she now saw the folds of her neck, as copious as the creases in the proscenium curtain she had seen last summer on Broadway.

They say that falling in love is wonderful.

She thought of Betty, crooning that song to Henry in the first weeks of his stay. To hell with her, Martha thought. If Henry were Martha's, she thought, she would never have left him—she could never have left him—no matter what her husband needed, no matter what her father said. If Henry were Martha's, she thought, his needs would be the only ones that mattered. Perhaps they already were.

WEEKS PASSED, and the late summer bloomed and smoldered. Henry, for his part, betoddled the world. He understood himself to be an extraordinary being, unlike anyone else. He was the only one of his size, the only one people bent down to greet. He was the only one who seemed to be the center of the world.

By autumn, after more than a year of coming and going, he knew how to get the most from each mother. With Beatrice, he did his crawling, his walking, his dancing, his jumping; everything giddily physical and bold made her squeal with excitement. Ruby seemed to inspire the longest contemplative times, times spent reading or doing puzzles, side by side, with Henry standing and Ruby kneeling at the coffee table. Sometimes she would loop her arm around his waist, and he would make himself lean against her in a kind of swoon, and when he got a particularly difficult piece in place, he would let her give him a little squeeze and he would say "Wooby!" which reliably made her giggle. Or he would say "Deed it!" with a huge, proud grin.

With Ethel, at mealtimes, he would look up with his orange-green eyes, full of glee and eager anticipation, and she would swoop a spoonful of applesauce by him, like a tiny plastic B-25, and he would sit up in his high chair and swat a hand at the spoon, like King Kong. Then Ethel would laugh and laugh and give him as much more as he wanted.

His baby journal was nearly three-quarters full now, and on weekends, the women smoked their cigarettes, sipped Dole pineapple drinks, turned the pages, and argued about who had taken which photograph when, who had been with Henry to crystallize this moment of his milestone-rich life, or that one. The journal was a pointillist painting. A stained-glass window. A fly's eye. But in any case, an undeniably, terribly fractured thing.

Goodbye, baby boy. I will never, ever, forget you.

Betty had scrawled that across the bottom of her last page.

Henry would forget her, though, Martha thought, and a plan began to form in the least reliable corner of her divided mind.

8

He Wants a Cookie

Irena called from the orphanage on a mild day in early November, her soft, cool, annoying voice coming over the phone like the air from a fan.

"Are you having a good autumn?" she asked.

"Very nice, thank you," Martha said.

That was it for the small talk. Irena got straight to the point: She had a family, she said, for Henry.

"A family," Martha repeated. It was the moment she had been dreading, and it had come too soon.

"They live in Wilkes-Barre, and she has simply been unable, poor thing, and they very much want a little boy, and your June baby would be just perfect for them."

"June baby," Martha repeated, dully.

"I'm sorry. What is it you call this one?"

"Henry," Martha said, and she found that just saying the baby's name at that moment was like playing a rich chord, a chord with nearly infinite aspects: images, phrases, feelings, all of which echoed and altered and then resolved.

"Well, Henry, then," Irena said, a bit impatiently.

"It's too soon," Martha said. "He's only seventeen months. I keep the babies until they're at least two. You know that."

"Yes, but you have had this one a bit longer than usual, because we gave him to you at three months," Irena said.

Martha instantly saw—as if the image had been projected like one of the slides at the Matson lecture—the photo of Henry in his crib that Ethel had taken of him on that first day.

"Why does it need to be so soon?" Martha asked. "You know, the students are just about to take their midterm exams. Then it'll be the holidays—"

"But that's just the point," Irena said, and Martha could hear her exhaling her cigarette smoke and could imagine her sitting at her desk, shuffling her file cards and papers, arranging lives. "This couple, more than anything, wants to have their baby in time for Christmas."

Irena said she had not one but two other babies who would be five and six months old, respectively, come January. Either, she said, would make a suitable replacement for Henry.

"I know how hard it always is for you to juggle the girls' schedules at Christmastime," she said, as if what she was saying would be making things easier for Martha. "And this would allow you to have a few days to yourself, for once."

Martha imagined the practice house at Christmas, with no baby beneath the tree, no girls circled around it. What would be the point, then, of having a tree?

"Just think what a lovely Christmas the baby will have, being with his new parents," Irena said.

THAT NIGHT, MARTHA STOOD at the bookshelf, where two decades of practice babies' journals were lined up chronologically, starting with little Helen House in 1928. The books, despite their generations of different bindings, evoked the orderliness and rationality of an encyclopedic world, but instead of alphabet letters, they were labeled by the babies' names: Helen, Harold, Hannah, Hope, Heloise, Harvey, Holly . . .

Martha took down the first book. The photographs, slightly brown and blurry with time, were framed by now-old-fashioned white scalloped borders and had been given captions by an exuberant if haphazard first group of practice mothers.

What am I doing here?
Are all these presents really for me?
Don't I look nice and clean?
Mildred Fairfax made me this hat!
I'm a big girl today!

Time unfolded behind her, and Martha remembered the excitement with which those first early months had progressed: the frequent talks with Dean Swift, the introduction to President Gardner, the decision to make child rearing a permanent part of the curriculum. She remembered the first trips she had made to the orphanage—run then by a different woman, whose name now escaped her. She remembered offering Helen House, just after her second birthday, back to the orphanage, in exchange for a younger baby—and the thrill of knowing that Helen would be raised by a married couple who would prize an infant launched with all the latest and best methods. Tom Gaines had been courting her then, wooing her, attending her, and the whole world had seemed bright with certainty and safety: a home, a job, a mission, a man.

Martha realized that Helen House was now twenty years old. That tiny, woebegone infant, around whom an entire academic institution had been started, and a career launched, was now old enough to be a student here herself. Which made Martha—what?—ancient, irrelevant, done.

IT TOOK A FULL TWO WEEKS to get an appointment set up with Dr. Gardner, but the meeting was finally scheduled for the Tuesday after Thanksgiving, and until then, Martha avoided Irena's calls as assiduously as the president had seemed to be avoiding hers.

For the holiday weekend itself, as she almost always had, Martha sent all the practice mothers home and cared for the baby herself.

The night before Thanksgiving, Martha put Henry to bed and then sat downstairs, listening to Burns and Allen, then to Jack Benny, then the news. A Communist rally in Connecticut had been broken up when a group of veterans started stamping their feet and singing

"God Bless America." And Harry Truman, apparently, had come up with the idea of pardoning a turkey that would otherwise have been served the next day at the White House.

Martha darned a pair of socks as she listened. The house was quiet in the absence of a practice mother, but this was nothing like the silence that overcame the place when days or weeks went by between House babies. That was a silence of barrenness, of loss, a silence so deep that it made Martha want to move around to fill up empty spaces. This silence—with Henry sleeping just yards away—felt something more like peace.

Martha sat in the chair till nearly midnight, rehearsing in her mind the conversation she would have with President Gardner after the weekend was over. What she would ask him for. What he would say. How she could keep from ever having to face that other silence.

WHEN THE PHONE RANG on Thanksgiving afternoon, Martha at first thought she would ignore it. She reasoned that it could only be a wrong number, or someone trying to urge her to participate in some local food drive, or—worst case of all—Irena, with her menacing holiday spirit. On the sixth ring, however, Henry said, "T-t-t-t. T-t-t-t. Tellie. Pickee up." And Martha, following his instruction, was nearly astonished to hear President Gardner saying hello.

"I was thinking," he said, "that we might have our chat today."

"Today?" Martha repeated. "On Thanksgiving?" she asked.

"I'm sorry," he said. "Did you have other plans?"

"No, it's just that—well, I'm alone with the baby today. The girls are all home for the holiday."

"Why don't you bring the little fellow along?"

IT DIDN'T OCCUR TO MARTHA until she was seated on the couch in the president's house an hour later that, like her, he would be alone today. There were no warm oven and gravy smells wafting from his kitchen, which, in fact, was completely dark. The dining room table—also visible from the living room—had clearly not been the scene of any festive celebrations. But unlike Martha, President Gardner no doubt had been served a Thanksgiving dinner at the home of some faculty member who was trying to curry favor with him.

"Did you have a nice Thanksgiving?" Martha asked him.

"Very nice, yes, thank you. The Haywoods had me over this year. Very kind of them."

"Yes," Martha said. "Well, Henry and I had a lovely time, too." Together their eyes fell on the little boy, who was sitting on the floor, zooming his red fire truck over the clean beige carpet, then using his hand to sweep away the parallel tracks left by the wheels. Martha sensed that President Gardner would try as hard as he could to ignore him, but also that Henry was present to be looked over somehow.

"So," the president said. "I gather you wanted to see me."

"Yes," Martha began. "I wanted to ask you—I *want* to ask you—"

"Yes?"

"Well, first, have you heard anything from Betty?"

He paused a moment, as if trying to place the name. "Anything like what?" he asked finally.

"Anything like if she's coming back."

"Coming back," Dr. Gardner repeated coldly. "Why would she be coming back?"

Martha looked over at Henry. He had left his truck by the fireplace now and was using his hands to sweep new patterns into the plush of the carpet.

"Look!" Henry said to Martha, and then he dove forward onto his hands, as if he was plunging into a snowdrift, and giggled with the sheer joy of falling forward.

"What is he doing?" Dr. Gardner asked Martha drily.

"You can ask him," Martha said, but it was immediately evident that Dr. Gardner had no interest in asking him.

"Tell Dr. Gardner what you're doing, Henry," Martha said.

"Tell a joke!" Henry said proudly.

"What does he mean?" Dr. Gardner asked, and Martha felt a momentary pang for Betty, having grown up with such a father.

"He means he thinks it's funny to do what he's doing," Martha explained.

"Ah," Dr. Gardner said.

"Have you been in touch with her?" Martha asked. "Do you have an address for her? May I write to her?"

"Have her address? Why?" he asked, and Martha regretted that she had asked him three questions at once.

"Because I'd like to get in touch with her," Martha said. "There's something I need to ask her."

"She's not coming back," President Gardner said. "She's not coming back, and I know you've heard from Irena Stahl that there is a family waiting for this boy."

"This boy" is your grandson, Martha thought but didn't quite have the nerve to say.

Henry, having temporarily tired of his carpet games, toddled over to the desk and picked up an empty ashtray. Carrying it in both hands, as if it held frankincense or myrrh, he zigzagged toward Martha, more than a little off balance, and handed it to her.

"And what's this?" she asked him, suddenly conscious of wanting to show off how adorable he was.

"Sa plate," he said.

"And what's on the plate?"

"Sa cookie!"

"A cookie? Mmm," Martha said, pretending to take something from the plate. "Chocolate chip! My favorite! Why don't you see if Dr. Gardner would care for one?"

Henry turned toward the president and took three shipboard steps forward. "He wants a cookie?" he asked a bit uncertainly.

"No, it's 'Do *you* want a cookie?' " Martha said, correcting him.

"Do *you* want a cookie?" Henry asked in a perfect imitation.

The president laughed, no doubt despite himself, and squinted down at Henry, not unkindly.

"Why, thank you, young man," he said, and, with a touching kind of purposefulness, he pretended to take a cookie and to pantomime eating it.

"Cookies!" Henry squealed with delight and went back over to the president's desk to load up his imaginary plate with more imaginary food.

"There's something Betty left with me," Martha said pointedly. "She told me to take care of it. And I need to know what to do with it now."

Dr. Gardner followed both her glance and her meaning.

"There shouldn't be any confusion about that," Dr. Gardner said.

Martha looked toward the desk, where Henry had readied another plate of pretend cookies and was beginning his next gleeful transverse of the carpet.

"Sir," Martha finally said. "Did it occur to you that Henry might— that I might—"

Never had Martha felt so betrayed by her emotions. Voice quavering, nose reddening, and, she knew, face flushing. Exactly the opposite of the stable, nonerratic, trustworthy person she needed, right now, to be.

She began again.

"If I kept Henry," she said, "you'd still be able to see him, and no one would ever have to know he was your grandson."

Dr. Gardner, truly taken aback, sat upright and moved away startled, as if from a sudden shock or flame.

"You?" he said.

"No one," Martha said, her voice gruff with too much emotion. "No one could be a better mother to this little boy. I know it."

Dr. Gardner lit a cigar, keeping his silver lighter at the tip and puffing emphatically. Then he snapped the lighter shut and waved away the little bit of smoke he had made. He pulled an ashtray near and then tapped the cigar against it needlessly.

Powerless, Martha waited, the balance of her life encompassed somewhere in this man's mind, the child both hers and a Wilkes-Barre family's, his future both known to her and forever lost.

"I don't see how that's possible," Dr. Gardner finally said.

"Why not?"

"Well, for one thing, because I think it's patently unfair to the young lad. How could you want him raised in a practice house—however expertly by you—when he could have his very own family, and two parents, two young, healthy, well-educated parents?"

"And for another?" Martha asked, her heart in a kind of cramp.

"Well, for another, Mrs. Gaines, *Qui procul ab oculis, procul a limite cordis.*"

"I'm sorry, Dr. Gardner. I don't know Latin."

"Out of sight, out of mind," he said.

Henry, a yard or so away from Dr. Gardner, stumbled a bit and fell against his knees, where he scrunched down, whether in glee or embarrassment, it was hard to tell. Then he looked up, nearly triumphant, into the president's face.

"Tell a joke," he said and then collapsed into peals of laughter.

TWO DAYS LATER, Martha walked down the aisles of the orphanage nursery, looking through the prison-bar slats of the cribs, which, at this time of the afternoon, were throwing harsh striped shadows onto the backs and sides of the sleeping babies.

Staring at a multicolored glass mobile that hung in the window, Martha mused that, if the colors of her life before Henry had been all pastels and beiges, they were now bright blues, greens, and reds. Reds especially, Martha thought. She saw Henry's cheeks, his fire truck, his fire hat, his rubber ball, his favorite crayon, his lips, his Christmas sweater. The ketchup he called *chup* and the strawberries he called *stawba*, and the toy stop sign that he somehow preferred to the toy cars.

She knew, as she had never known anything in her life, that she would never be able to let him go.

HIS FAVORITE GAME WAS Where's Henry? There were several ways to play it. You could hide yourself under a napkin, or behind your hands, or you could put a napkin over Henry's head and pretend he had disappeared.

Henry didn't seem to have a preference. He loved the game, no matter how it was played, and no matter who was playing it.

"Where's Henry?"

Giggles, squeals.

"There he is! Peekaboo!"

Giggles, squeals.

"Again!"

"Where's Henry?"

Giggles, squeals.

And on it could go, for a very long time.

What was in those beautiful green eyes, Martha believed, was not only need, but hope. She told herself for the first time that to disappoint either one of those might break someone's spirit, and to disappoint both might break his heart.

The day that Martha decided to take Henry was the day that he began crying when Grace hid under the napkin too long, and then walked out of the room. She was intending it, no doubt, as a joke—just an extended peekaboo for maximum effect. But she stayed out of the room too long, and Henry started screaming, just as he had that fall day when he had looked up to find Ruby instead of Ethel.

"Gray! Gray! Gray! Gray!"

Martha was simply past the point where her feelings about Henry could be disciplined by science—or perhaps by anything. It no longer mattered why Henry was crying. Henry was crying.

Upstairs, the way a tide gradually takes a part of the shore away, Martha's heart began to erode her reason, and she pulled a suitcase down from her closet and quietly began to pack.

SHE DIDN'T KNOW WHERE they would go. There were no people to pull her toward one destination or another. No safe harbors or family reunions. Only New York, for some reason, beckoned. Everything Martha had feared about the place now seemed alluring: the crowds, the numbers, the confusion. Maybe in that chaos, she thought, she would find some peace and some order.

And so she went to work. First she stacked clothes on her bed by item—the long-sleeved blouses; the short-sleeved blouses; the scarves, all folded neatly in squares, with their tags lined up in the lower-left-hand corners; the suit jackets; the skirts; the stockings; the girdles. All her clothes rising in tidy piles, a sensible city made from tweed and silk.

Until the previous year, Martha had owned only one small overnight bag. For her leave, she had traded eighteen of her Green Stamps books for two large Hartmann suitcases that were midnight blue with cream trim and dark blue satin linings. She could pack several weeks' worth of clothing in these and put Henry's things in the overnight bag. But of course she would have to get trunks for the rest. And cartons or crates for her books, pictures, and knickknacks: her life. She thought about Arthur at the hardware store and felt sure that he would sell, if not give her, the trunks—and that he might even store them for her until she could find a new home.

SHE WOULD NEVER KNOW what changed the president's mind.

Maybe, when she was downtown at Arthur's, Ruby had come upstairs and seen the suitcases and the stacks of clothing, and maybe she had told Dean Swift she thought Martha was leaving, and maybe Dean Swift had told President Gardner, and maybe they had decided that Martha was too valuable to lose.

Or maybe, and coincidentally, there had been some secret message from Betty.

Or perhaps President Gardner had simply understood, in the late afternoon of Thanksgiving Day, that he had his own Christmas emptiness to fill.

Whatever the case, when Martha returned to the practice house, she found Ruby waiting for her with an eager, slightly gossipy look—and a message that said Martha should go at once to the president's house.

Back in his living room, Martha braced herself for dismissal, threats of bad references, anything. Feverishly, her mind plunged into a hallucination of order, and, even as she waited for Dr. Gardner to speak, she began to re-sort her clothing mentally, and then to choose which toys of Henry's to take. Why would it matter to Dr. Gardner if she raised the boy—as long as she disappeared from his view? Surely he wouldn't come after her.

"I'm glad that you came, Mrs. Gaines," Dr. Gardner said.

"Of course," she answered.

"And I'm sure you'd like to know why I've asked you here."

He never really told her.

Henry House ended up staying in the practice house, not because President Gardner would admit that he didn't want to lose his grandson; not because President Gardner said straight out that Martha could adopt the boy; not because President Gardner was in any way explicit about how long this arrangement might last, or under what set of circumstances it might change. Henry stayed only because President Gardner said to Martha that evening: "You know, I've been thinking it over, and I think perhaps you *should* keep the boy for now."

‖ PART TWO ‖

We Come and Go

1

Emem

One day late in the summer of 1948, the women Henry House had loved so much and who'd seemed so much to love him showed up together at the practice house carrying gift-wrapped presents and fancy food. They drank pink lemonade, ate chocolate cake, gave Martha and Henry notes and gifts, and snapped endless rounds of photographs. Then they took turns holding Henry, looking sad, and saying good-bye.

Soon after that, a new group of women—with different names and faces, colors and smells—came to take their place, but Henry himself moved upstairs to live with Martha, who now told him to call her Emem (for the two Ms in Mama Martha). Upstairs, in the extra room that was directly above the nursery, Henry now had his own bed, dresser, and shelves; his own sheets and lampshades, which were covered in cowboy fabric; and even his own closet, where he sometimes tried, in vain, to hide.

During the days, it was always Martha who took care of him now. Between and sometimes during her own tasks and duties, Martha went for pretend drives with him in every kind of vehicle, showed him picture books, let him draw and finger paint, or chased him around the furniture, saying, "Emem's going to get you!" Downstairs, the baby named Herbert occupied all Henry's favorite places, and drew the attention from the other mothers the way the moon draws the tides.

Henry asked frequently where Connie, Grace, and Ethel were, and Martha always answered by saying how lucky Henry was to have her all to himself now. Whenever he could, though—whenever Martha let him go downstairs with her—he would toddle up to the week's practice mother with his hopeful, slightly anxious eyes and say, "Can do eet. Want tea?" Then he would reach out a little hand, and before Martha could say anything, he would be pulling the other mother upstairs, in a cloud of hope and charm.

In later years, expounders of attachment theory would suggest that permanent damage could be done to any infant who was denied the chance to form one reliable connection, even in just the first year of life. Eventually, they would examine the approach to children in programs just like Wilton's and conclude that to be treated like a human baton, continually handed off in the grueling relay of the first hundred weeks of life, was a situation that would have left any child's heart untrusting and splintered, if not snapped. But three months into Henry's third year on earth, it certainly hadn't struck Martha that there was anything odd in the way he was behaving. In fact, never having concerned herself with any children older than the age of two, she had no working model against which she could compare him.

An experienced mother of an older child might have thought it bizarre, for example, that Henry at two showed absolutely no signs of the usual separation anxieties. Far from clinging to Martha when other people were around, he would race down the stairs on Sundays to be with the whole lot of practice house mothers. With Martha all but forgotten, he could spend hours handing out pretend cookies and telling them pretend jokes and, perhaps most strikingly, asking them questions: "How are you today?" "You like singing?" "Which do you want?" No trip to the park with Martha, no special breakfast, no promise of toys or favors could compete with the lineup of multiple visitors below.

"Henry tella joke," he would say to one practice mother or another.

"What's the joke, Henry?" she would answer.

"Lion, ROAR!" he would say, and he would follow it with the peals of laughter that inevitably pulled the women's smiles away from the baby and back toward him.

An experienced mother of an older child might also have found it odd that Henry never looked for Martha when he was in the other women's company—or rather, that he looked for her no differently than he looked for anyone else. The women would have seemed, to an outside observer, equal and interchangeable parts in the engine that kept Henry going. The spark was his considerable charm. The women held and humored him. They trained their cameras on him. They passed news of his cutest expressions and precocious questions around like rare fruit.

"Drinkee milkee." "Brushee teeth." "Are you happy now?" "Do you feel bad?"

Jealously, Martha frowned on and tried to shorten these encounters, claiming to be worried that the new baby, Herbert, wasn't getting the attention he deserved. Privately, she blamed the practice house mothers for luring Henry, not Henry for luring the mothers. Martha was besotted enough to be nearly overwhelmed by the novelty and the magnitude of what might come next in his life, and by the hope—growing tentatively into faith—that she would have the chance to see it. It was as if, all her life, she had been served the same first course of the same meal, and now she was finally being given a chance to sample the rest. She had no intention of sharing, even as she had no ability to discern what it was that she wanted to devour.

"wanna go down," Henry said to Martha one afternoon in September, as she tied the shoelace on his left Buster Brown for the third or fourth time that day. The autumn sun was just finding its way through the upstairs windows and varnishing the floor.

"No, not now, Henry," Martha said. "Baby's trying to take his nap."

On the radio, the Andrews Sisters were singing their latest hit:

You call everybody Darlin',
And everybody calls you Darlin' too

"Wanna go down," Henry said again.

"No, Henry, Emem said no," Martha said.

"Wanna see Sally," Henry said.

"It's not even Sally's week downstairs today," Martha said, though Henry was sure he had heard Sally's voice just before.

If you call everybody Darlin',
Then love won't come a-knockin' at your door . . .

"Wanna see Sally," Henry said again, with a sad, strained look on his small face, and, after stepping on and once more untying his shoelace, he slowly began to move toward the door.

"Henry," Martha said in a warning voice. "Stay here."

"Can do eet," he said. "Wanna see Sally."

And as the years go by,
You'll sit and wonder why
Nobody calls you Darlin' anymore.

"Henry," Martha said again, following him quickly out to the landing.

"Can do eet," he said one more time, and then he fell down the stairs.

He fell with his limbs splayed in all directions, as if he was an armload of firewood tossed down from the landing.

HE WAS STILL FOR ONLY a moment or two—just long enough for Sally to come running from the nursery and for Martha to fly down the stairs. It seemed unlikely for a two-year-old not to have been killed by such a fall. And yet, with the exception of the mushroom cap–shaped bump that rose immediately on his forehead, he seemed to be unharmed.

"Want Sally!" he cried, and he refused to look at Martha, even when she picked him up like a baby and cradled him in her arms.

He strained toward Sally—a nineteen-year-old farm girl who was as embarrassed by Henry's preference for her as Martha was wounded by it.

Trying her hardest to seem impassive, Martha handed Henry to Sally and began her examination: feeling his ankles, wrists, elbows, knees—and then, once she was satisfied that his bones had not been broken, staring deeply into his eyes.

"What are you looking for?" Sally asked her.

"Signs of concussion," Martha said.

"And what are they?" Sally asked ruefully, trying to give back the upper hand.

"Several," Martha said distractedly, but she seemed to be searching Henry's eyes for something less clinical.

From the nursery, they could all hear the sounds of the baby, Herbert, crying as he woke from his nap.

Sally started to hand Henry back to Martha.

"Sally! Sally!" he cried, and so, with barely convincing nonchalance, Martha said, "Well, dear, I think you should go on holding Henry for now. I'll just go see to Herbert myself."

2

Nursery School

Two years later—almost two years to the day—a four-year-old Henry ran down the stairs as soon as Martha answered the ringing telephone at her desk. His still-chubby fingers barely touched the banister, and he jumped over the last step. Then he slipped into the nursery, and, for the first of many times to come, he climbed up into the crib where the newest House baby was sleeping. Her name was Hazel, and Henry called her Hazy.

Both Elsa, that week's practice mother, and Martha appeared in the doorway just seconds after Henry landed beside Hazy.

"Henry! No!" Martha shouted, and before he could even touch the baby, Martha had snatched Henry out of the crib.

It was September of 1950, the end of a peak polio summer, a time in American life when every child, no matter his or her age or background, was seen—in equal shades of terror—as being both a potential victim and a potential threat. No one had yet discovered the cause of polio, let alone its cure, so children were kept apart from each other whenever possible, in case proximity increased the risk.

All summer, Martha had seen the photographs everywhere—in magazines, on newsreels, and even as part of the new health curriculum—of children with the disease who had been consigned to those enormous, coffinlike breathing machines that were known as iron lungs. The terror of Henry ending up in one of those contraptions— or worse, the terror of him dying—was one of the reasons that Martha leapt to take him away from Hazel. Though Irena at the orphanage had assured Martha that there had not been a whisper of polio there, Hazel had been in residence for only two days, and Martha did not want to take any chances.

The other reason, which Martha was less inclined to admit to the practice mothers, was that she thought she saw in Henry growing evidence of jealousy.

"Why is she crying?" he had asked Martha about Hazel the night after her arrival.

"Why do you think she's crying?"

Darkly, it seemed, he had answered: "She wants to go back where she came from."

During Hazel's bath the next evening, Henry appeared just in time to thrust a washcloth onto her face. He was uncharacteristically boisterous around her, especially when she was sleeping. And twice, Henry said he wanted to sleep in the crib with Hazel, a bit of solicitousness that seemed suspiciously enthusiastic.

Realizing she was in an entirely new area of child rearing, Martha furtively consulted the copy of Spock that she had never quite gotten around to discarding after the conference a few years back. She looked in the section called "Jealousy and Rivalry," and she saw an ink drawing of an apron-clad mother kneeling on the floor, a pot holder beside her, where, presumably, she had dropped it on her way to attend the crisis. In her arms was a fidgety toddler in a striped shirt and saddle shoes; beside him, a crying baby with spidery hair and tears flying like arrows off his face. Spock wrote that a mother might say to a jealous child: "I know how you feel sometimes, Johnny. You wish there weren't any baby around here for Mother to take care of. But don't you worry, Mother loves you just the same."

That night, when she tucked Henry into bed, Martha took a breath and said: "I know how you feel sometimes, Henry. You wish there weren't any baby around here for Emem to take care of. But don't you worry, Emem loves you just the same."

Henry looked at Martha, confused. "I just want Hazy to love me too," he said.

IN FACT, FAR FROM SEEING HAZEL as a threat, Henry saw her—or per-haps simply sensed her—as another potential alternative to the formi-dable singularity of Martha.

His attentions to Hazel were dramatic enough, however, for Martha to conclude that it would be prudent for Henry to start at-tending the Wilton Nursery School next door. So, as the Indian sum-mer cooled into fall, Martha prepared Henry—and tried to prepare herself—for the first days of his life beyond the practice house.

A STATE OF MILD BUT MUTUAL condescension existed—and always had—between the nursery school and the practice house. Martha saw the nursery school as a college service, a necessary institution within an institution, like the infirmary, or Buildings and Grounds. The nursery school was at but not of the Department of Home Econom-ics, and though its teachers—a succession of Wilton professors' wives, whose children had usually been among their "students"—were per-fectly well-intentioned, there was nothing remotely pedagogical about the approach they took to the children's days. They were, in Martha's view, merely glorified babysitters for the faculty and neighborhood brats.

Not surprisingly, in light of this, the women who ran the nursery school had always tended to look on Martha and her students as un-bearably snooty, and it was with no love lost that Edith Donovan greeted Martha on that first September morning.

There were six other children in the Wilton Nursery School in the fall of 1950. Four were toddlers, still taking naps, wearing diapers, and doing things that to Henry were of little or no interest. But the other two were the same age as Henry, and he had watched them across the backyard with increasing curiosity for the last many months. Martha had never let him talk to them for more than a minute or two. "Germs," she had said, as if referring to the children themselves, and not to the threat they supposedly carried.

This morning, however, on the first day of nursery school, there was no large shadow on the ground beside Henry, no heavy hand on his shoulder hurrying him back to the practice house. Instead, after Martha had introduced him to Mrs. Donovan at the back door, and one of the toddlers had arrived at the front, Martha reluctantly followed Mrs. Donovan inside, leaving Henry in the backyard with the two older children.

"My name is Henry," Henry said to the girl.

"I know that. You live next door," she said. "In that house," she added, and she pointed at it, accusingly.

"Where do you live?" Henry asked her.

"In a real house," she said, although she didn't say it meanly.

Her name was Mary Jane Harmon, and she was the history chairman's daughter. She was six months older than Henry and the exact same height. Like Henry, she had pale skin, as if the protection of growing up on a college campus had meant protection from the elements as well. Her hair was wavy and somewhat sparse, but white as vanilla pudding. But her shoes were brand-new, bright red Keds, and her eyes, as Henry saw them, were the same shade of blue as the game piece in the board game Sorry. He loved her immediately.

"I live in a real house, too," another voice added, and Henry looked from the blueness of Mary Jane's gaze into the tiny, dark, stuffed-animal eyes of Leo Friedlander. For no apparent reason, Leo jumped down from the back steps, grabbed a fistful of leaves, and threw them at Henry's face.

Henry bent down to pick up his own bunch of leaves, then thought better of throwing them and tried to make it look as if he had picked them up not to throw but to study. "When do we go inside?" he asked, just as Martha and Mrs. Donovan appeared again at the back door.

"Oh. Dirty," Mrs. Donovan said to Henry about the leaves in his hand, and Leo smiled.

"Leo did it first," Mary Jane said quickly, and Leo shoved her, accidentally-on-purpose, as they walked up the stairs.

It didn't seem to faze her. She looked back over her shoulder at

Henry, as if he was the gift she had always wanted, and Henry, following Mary Jane up the stairs, ignored Martha's long, yearning gaze and merely waved a slightly dusty hand goodbye.

THERE WAS A THIRD SET OF WOMEN in the practice house now, and Henry saw them every day when he came home from nursery school. A woman named Celia gave him grape juice and called him Henny-Penny and liked it when he hugged her. A woman named Mildred saved him the red Life Savers and called him Heinzy. Marilyn always kissed both his cheeks and shouted "Thank you, thank you!" when he kissed both of hers. Vera called him Sweetmeat and gave him cookies. Kitty liked it when he handed her the diaper pin for Hazy and asked if she wanted him to help. Bev didn't call him anything special, or seem particularly interested, until the day that he asked her how *her* day had been, and after that she hugged him, hard, and called him her special soldier, which he didn't understand but liked.

Except on Sundays, the women never got the chance to see Henry with one another, and by now he had developed a new habit for the Sunday crowds, which was to avoid lingering too long when everyone was together. Martha hoped this meant he was growing more attached to her, but in truth, without actually knowing it, he was trying to protect what he had with each of the others. He made sure that when more than one of the mothers was around, he never answered questions like what his favorite nickname was, or his favorite color, or his favorite book or card game or food. Stating his favorites, he understood instinctively, could mean making one mother happier with him than the others. It was safer not to admit he liked purple more than orange, or chocolate more than vanilla. Sometimes he wasn't sure what the real answer would be anyway.

LIKE THE PRACTICE HOUSE, the nursery school was a modest two-story home that had been purchased in 1924, during the college's first big expansion. Despite Mrs. Donovan's opening-day admonition, it was neither exceptionally clean nor particularly tidy, and this was one of the reasons that Henry—with wet sneakers, free-roaming juice glasses, and even the occasional indoor game of catch—liked being there.

The days at the nursery school lasted from eight in the morning till three in the afternoon. At the start of each day, the three older children usually played inside, building houses from blocks, or drawing, or stringing beads. Henry liked to draw most of all, and often he would give Mary Jane his drawings, somehow never minding when she asked him "What's it of?"

When Mrs. Donovan wasn't too busy with the toddlers, she would sit at the upright piano in the living room and play exuberantly while they all sang and danced. Mrs. Donovan was tall and angular, and when she played, she bent over the keys and rolled her shoulders forward, looking like a question mark.

Lunch, usually around noon, was a daily delight, featuring foods that never took long to make and that Henry had never sampled before. There were Van Camp's pork and beans from a can, or Ritz crackers with Velveeta cheese. There were sandwiches with the crusts left on, and bread-and-butter pickles, and potato chips. On warm days, there was Kool-Aid to drink, and on cold days, there was Ovaltine. For dessert, there was almost always canned fruit cocktail, served in small Pyrex dishes with different-colored spoons.

After lunch, there was Rest Time, and Mrs. Donovan would open up little cots made of scratchy blue fabric, and the big children would have to lie there and listen to her read. Mrs. Donovan's reading voice was the exact opposite of her singing voice—hesitant and soft—and she seemed to lose her place a lot and read the same page twice. Still, no one ever came close to sleeping, even if they were bored.

In the afternoons, Mrs. Donovan would usually hold what she called Science Class. Once, she helped the children plant Dixie cups with grass seeds, sand, and soil, and they watched over several days to see them produce their tiny green circles of turf. Another time, she let all of them—including the toddlers—pretend they were planets and act out the solar system, and she chose Henry—wearing a yellow towel, yellow rain boots, and yellow dish gloves—to play the part of the sun. It was Mary Jane who gave him her own yellow rain hat to complete the costume.

Toward the end of the day, the older children played out back, almost always led by Mary Jane. She had the kind of confidence that could start a conversation, invent a game, or demand a secret.

"Let's pretend you're a dog and I'm a cat."

"Let's pretend you're the babies and I'm the mother."

It wasn't exactly bossiness, not as simple as having to have things her way; it was something more like leadership: the belief that her way would be best for all—that she knew what would be the most fun, or funny. Usually it worked out that way.

"Raise your hand if you like *Amos 'n' Andy*."

"Raise your hand if you hate broccoli."

In answer to these directives, Henry almost always raised his hand, and Leo almost never did. "You're not the boss of me," Leo would say to Mary Jane, or "You can't tell me not to!"

Like Mary Jane, Leo had been at the nursery school for several years. He was the son of one of the physical education teachers, and he was tall, strong, and nasty, and, on top of that, a nose picker who used his thumb and forefinger to roll his various extractions into tiny, dry balls, which he would then flick indiscriminately into the middle distance.

Apart from avoiding these small projectiles, Mary Jane and Henry had to cope with the fact that about once every half an hour, Leo would yell "Tag, you're it!" and chase the two of them through the backyard. If the toddlers were outside, Mrs. Donovan would kneel beside them, closing one skinny, protective arm around them, just like the arm of a padlock.

Sometimes it bothered Henry that Leo spent so much time talking to Mary Jane, even though he mainly insulted her. Leo said she looked like Howdy Doody, an assertion that neither Mary Jane nor Henry could refute, since neither yet owned a TV set.

Henry had no insults for Mary Jane. He thought she was beautiful, especially when she was laughing, or when she was hiding with him from Leo—lips closed tight, eyes wide open—in the space behind the couch. Mary Jane was the first person Henry had ever liked who didn't make a fuss about what he said or did. Mary Jane didn't call him cute or darling, or repeat what he said, or write it down. But she made him feel good, and, other than his drawings, he never had to explain anything to her.

On Mary Jane's birthday, her mother brought homemade cupcakes to the nursery school house and special balloons that had other balloons inside them, shaped like Mickey Mouse's head. Mary Jane's was pink; Leo's was green; Henry's was blue. The balloons were filled with helium, and they bumped and sprang along the ceiling, nudging each other like puppies as their owners guided them by their strings. Then Leo grabbed a pencil and popped the outer skin of his balloon, leaving the green Mickey inside it to shrink, rather gruesomely. Then he went after Mary Jane's. She squealed a little, grabbed her string, and raced back through the house. The chase went on for quite a while, several times past Mrs. Donovan and Mary Jane's mother sipping coffee; past the toddlers at their feet; past Henry, who knew better than to think it was all in fun.

When Mary Jane ran outside to escape Leo, her balloon left her hand and flew upward, into a sky nearly the color of her eyes.

The maple tree in the backyard, the one with the swing, provided a moment of shelter, arching like a parent over the lost balloon. Henry, holding his own balloon, stood beside Mary Jane, the two of them looking up helplessly.

It took only a few moments. It seemed much longer. Eventually, the pink mouse bounced free from the black branches and shot upward. Mary Jane took her loss stoically. She wept but did not cry out loud.

"Wait," Henry said, but he didn't give his balloon to her. Instead, he opened his hand, like a magician revealing a missing coin, and let his balloon fly up, too. They rose, nearly side by side, the blue chasing the pink against a cloudless sky, and for years to come, from that moment on, Mary Jane would try and fail to love other people the way she loved Henry.

THEY DID THINGS TOGETHER every day. Sometimes they sorted the autumn leaves into colored piles. Sometimes they made faces. In the make-believe game that they frequently played, she was called Miss Fancy, which she said with an elegant, drawn-out *a*. He was called Mickey Mouse. From time to time, they married.

In Henry's imagination, they were also sometimes Dick and Jane. Though he could not make out the words in the New Basic Readers yet, he could see that Dick, pushing Jane in her wagon, wore a red and white striped shirt and a pair of khaki shorts just like his own. Dick's hair was also the exact same color as Henry's, Jane's hair was the exact same color as Mary Jane's, and their wagon was the exact same kind as the one that stood in the backyard of the nursery school. The characters in the book also had a little sister named Sally, a dog named Spot, a cat named Puff, and a normal mother and father, but these were details that Henry forced into irrelevance. As he knelt in the small space behind the couch in the nursery school, turning the pages of *We Come and Go,* he allowed himself to imagine that he belonged in a place like Dick and Jane's, where when people left they came back, and they pretty much stayed the same.

Dick pulled wagons. Dick looked out for Jane. Dick played ball. His mother gave him jobs to do, cooked him dinner, never asked for a kiss, never held him too tight, never wept in her room at night. Dick never needed comforting, and he never needed to comfort. His mother never looked into his eyes, long and pleading, the way Martha did, as if there was something that he alone knew and was supposed to tell her.

DAILY, MARTHA SAID she loved Henry. She called him Henrykins, Henny-Penny, Hanky-Panky, and, most often, My Boy. As in "How is My Boy feeling today?" "What does My Boy want for lunch?" From this it was clear to Henry that Martha thought he belonged to her. But she remained vague about his origins.

Once, after Dr. Gardner had come over and sat for a long time in the living room with Martha, smoking his cigar and talking low and secret, Henry asked her if that man was his father. Other than Mr. Hamilton at the hardware store, Henry had never actually seen a man talking to Martha at any length. So it seemed not so silly a question. Henry wasn't sure he understood about either mothers or fathers, but he knew, from the other kids and of course from reading *Dick and Jane*, that there was usually one of each kind of person somewhere in a boy's life.

"Is Dr. Gardner my father?" Henry asked Martha, and he watched the tops of her cheeks turn the color of tulips.

"Your father?" she asked. He had noticed that Martha sometimes repeated what he said, though he wasn't sure if she did it when she was angry or only when she hadn't heard him in the first place.

"My daddy?" Henry said, just in case Martha hadn't understood the question.

"Don't be foolish," Martha said. "Dr. Gardner is the president of the college."

Henry wasn't sure he understood what one thing had to do with the other.

"They can't be a daddy?" he asked.

"Of course they can be a daddy," Martha said. "Where's your fire truck? Shall we play firehouse?"

"*Is* he a daddy?" Henry asked, ignoring, for the moment, the lure of the pretend flames.

"Yes," Martha said. "He's a daddy. Go get your truck. We might have to put out a fire tonight. But he's not *your* daddy."

"Are you my mommy?"

"Do you want me to be?"

"Are you?"

"You're my boy."

It would take another five years before Henry would feel that Martha's answer, while not exactly a lie, was an unforgivable evasion.

3

Alone at Last

Though most people feared polio more in spring and summer than in fall or winter, Martha had read that there had been a deadly outbreak of the disease in the Canadian Arctic just two years before, as well as some local cases even in the colder, supposedly less contagious months. So when, in December, Henry came down with what seemed an unusually bad cold, Martha kept him home from nursery school, barely concealing her panic. All she told him was that she didn't want the other children at the school to catch his cold, but he sensed, from the way she whispered to Mrs. Donovan and to the practice mothers, that there was something more serious going on.

Upstairs, he inhabited the pillowy landscape of Martha's bed, and she brought him chicken noodle soup on a pale green plastic tray with a doily and one of the white dinner napkins. She brought him juice with a straw that folded down on a little hinge. There were two pillows, not one, and the bed was almost as wide as it was long. Several times a day, Martha would sit on the side of the bed and cross her thick, stockinged legs at the ankles and play cards with him. Game after game of War, Rummy, Go Fish, and Old Maid. After each game, she would refill his juice glass and fill one for herself. Then she would make them clink glasses, just like grown-ups. "Here's to your health," she would say.

When his fever rose, she gave him orange-flavored chewable aspirin, which made his whole mouth pucker and his teeth feel like chalk.

Frequently she said things like "Alone at last," and "It's just the two of us, isn't this nice?" Henry wasn't sure if it was nice or not.

Sometimes he would fall asleep and wake to see her shadow on the wall and then turn to see her at her desk, writing out checks with her face scrunched up, or pasting trading stamps into books. Several times a day, she would reach for a small blue jar with a turquoise top and label. She would open the jar and dip two fingers in and then slather Vicks VapoRub onto his chest, rubbing and rubbing beneath his pajama shirt, looking into his eyes while the smell of the menthol mingled with her intensity. Henry, not for the first or last time, experienced the sensation that to breathe, he might first have to be engulfed.

CHRISTMAS CAME ON a Monday, but it snowed the whole weekend before, and all but one of the practice mothers were stranded at school for the holidays. Though Martha had been looking forward to having a break from the girls, she found herself relieved that there were extra hands to care for Hazel while she ministered to Henry. And then there was Christmas Day itself—for once not a practice Christmas for the students but the real thing. Henry heard the bustle of the mothers downstairs, but Martha told him he wasn't well enough to leave the bedroom.

"You don't want to get the baby sick, do you?" Martha asked.

"I wouldn't."

"I know you wouldn't on purpose," she said. "But sometimes you can get people sick without meaning to."

Henry ran his fingertips along the loose crisscross stitches on the shiny border of the blanket.

"Anyway," Martha added mysteriously, "I have a surprise for you later, and I think you're going to like it."

All morning long, Henry slept and woke, hearing the sounds of the mothers downstairs as they fussed over the baby and opened their presents for her, then giggled and said their goodbyes. Finally, he heard whispering on the stairs and wanted to go and look, but he knew that Martha would be angry with him for getting out of bed. He dozed again. When he woke, Martha was standing at the foot of his bed, shielding a large object with her body.

"What is it?" he asked her groggily. "Is it my Christmas present?"

"Ta-da!" she said, and stepped aside to reveal a brand-new TV set.

IT WAS THEIR BEST TIME TOGETHER, and years later—even after he couldn't forgive her for so much else—Henry would be grateful to Martha for this. All afternoon, they sat side by side on her bed, and every few minutes, she would pop up to change the channels, as magically as if she were changing the view outside the window. They saw a cooking show called *Stop, Look and Cook,* and part of an opera called *Hansel and Gretel,* and at three they saw something called *Uncle Miltie's Christmas Party,* with a strange, exuberant man named Milton Berle, who at one point wore a dress. Then, at four o'clock, they stopped changing channels, because they found a show called *One Hour in Wonderland.*

Henry didn't understand the significance of it then, but the Wonderland show was actually Walt Disney's first television program, a prototype of the series that would captivate American audiences throughout the decade—and that Henry would watch, almost without fail, every week for his whole early life.

This afternoon—Christmas afternoon, 1950—was the afternoon he met Walt Disney, a man with the twinkliest eyes Henry had ever seen, a kind voice, a trim mustache, and hair that formed a peak above his eyes, making his forehead look just like Mickey Mouse's. During this show, Mr. Disney was hosting a party for the stars of his movies, and one of the guests was the puppet Charlie McCarthy, who was even funnier on TV than he was on the radio. At one point, Mr. Disney said the words "Bibbidi-Bobbidi-Boo," and magic happened inside a special mirror, and a man with a slightly scary face appeared and granted Mr. Disney's wish to see special things.

Henry had heard about cartoons from Leo, and of course he had seen drawings and pictures of some of the characters. At the nursery school, Mrs. Donovan even served Donald Duck orange juice. But to see these characters do what they could do was amazing: how when they ran, their legs sometimes spun around like wheels; how when they reached for things, their arms sometimes grew longer. For an hour, Henry giggled and Martha fingered the gold pin at her neck and said, "Oh, my, that's funny, isn't it?" But as much as he loved the creations—Mickey and Pluto and Donald and Alice and the Seven Dwarfs with their silly song—it was Mr. Disney, the creator, with his sparkly eyes and the kind way he seemed to listen to everyone, who stayed with Henry longest. Forever, in fact.

THREE DAYS LATER, when Henry had not had a fever for a whole day and was barely coughing anymore, he woke from a nap in the early afternoon and called for Martha but got no response. Henry hesitated, then pulled back the covers and climbed from the cozy confines of her bed.

"Emem?" he called, first from the top of the stairs, then from midway down, then again at the base of the stairs. There was no answer. "Vera?" he called next, because Martha had told him to call for Vera if he needed anything.

There was silence from downstairs, except for what sounded like the baby, babbling.

The wood floor on the stairs was cold under Henry's bare feet, and he knew Martha would want him to wear his slippers, but he didn't like the silence.

When he walked into the nursery, he saw Vera leaning over the crib, wrapping a blanket around Hazy, who kept kicking it off.

"Come, now, Hazel," Henry heard Vera saying. "Why won't you take your nap?"

"Why isn't Hazy sleeping?" Henry asked from the doorway.

Startled, Vera turned and looked scared. "What are you doing here?" she asked.

"Want to play Go Fish with me?" Henry said.

"You can't be here," she said.

"Why not?"

"Because you might get the baby sick. You wouldn't want that, would you?"

"I woke up," Henry said. "Will you take me back upstairs?"

"I have to put the baby to bed."

"She's in bed," Henry said, then watched Vera smile at his logic. He looked at the floor, then back at her. "Vera," he said sweetly. "I'm scared to go upstairs by myself."

She turned completely around from the crib then, letting the blanket drop onto the baby's hands.

"You know, sometimes," Henry said, "a kid needs a little help."

HENRY WAS SETTLING BACK INTO BED, and Vera had just dealt them each seven cards for Go Fish, when she noticed the flush on his cheeks. First there was just a little pinkness, across the tops, where his freckles were. Then, after what seemed like only seconds, the color moved down his face, like the deepening of a sunset, and he shivered, noticeably.

The cards they were playing with were shaped like fish and had colors, instead of numbers, on them.

"Any reds?" Henry asked, and Vera realized that it was the second time he had said it.

"Do you feel all right?" she asked him.

He said: "I feel okay. Do you have any reds?"

Vera shook her head. "Go fish," she said.

Henry reached down to the pile of fish fanned out on his bedspread, but when he did so, Vera could see that his hand was shaking.

She put her hand on his forehead, which was smooth and hot as a rock in the sun.

Vera put her cards down and stood up, and at the exact same moment, Hazel started to cry downstairs.

"Damn," Vera said.

"Damn," Henry said.

"You didn't hear me say that," she told Henry.

"Say 'Damn'?"

"Right."

"Damn."

"I don't suppose you know where your thermometer is?"

Henry shrugged. "Do you have any reds?" he asked.

He coughed then—one deep, long, alarming bronchial bray. When he was finished, his eyes had filled with tears. Meanwhile, Hazel's protests from downstairs had turned into a full-throated yell.

"I have to go see to her," Vera said. "Are you going to be okay?" she asked.

He nodded and was about to speak, but then he started to cough again.

"No. You'd better come back downstairs with me," Vera said.

"I can make Hazy laugh," Henry said, on the stairs, when he'd stopped coughing.

"No, you can't be with Hazy," Vera said, and she was startled to find Henry's warm, dry hand reaching out for hers. "But I bet you can make most people laugh," she said.

"Yes," Henry said. "It's not so hard."

THE AFTERNOON LENGTHENED, along with its shadows. Winter blew in under the doors and windows, cold as the bare trees that bowed outside.

Just beyond the door of the nursery, Henry sat in the rocking chair, uncomfortable with the spindles of the chair back behind his head. In one hand, he still held the Go Fish cards he had been dealt upstairs, and his fingers closed tightly around the narrow parts of the fish tails while he watched Vera bouncing Hazel around the room.

"Where in heaven and earth is Mrs. Gaines?" Vera asked.

"Probably earth," Henry said, curling his feet up beneath him and scrunching over so that the side of his face lay against the cool arm of the chair.

Vera laughed. "Let's hope so," she said. But now her face wasn't smiling. "What time is it?" she asked.

"I don't know how to tell time," Henry said.

"I know you don't know how to tell time," Vera said.

She carried Hazy past him to the kitchen, and Henry could hear her open the back door, and he could feel a blast of even colder air. Then Vera closed the door and said "Damn" again.

"Do you have any idea where she went?" Vera asked Henry.

"She went to get me Silly Putty," he said.

"Silly what?"

"Silly Putty," Henry said. "You can bend it and bounce it and you can use it to copy pictures."

"This is a toy or something?" Vera said.

Henry nodded, a little confused by Vera's confusion. Everyone he knew understood what Silly Putty was. Leo had some. The older brother of one of the babies at the nursery school had some.

"Do you really think she went to get you Silly Putty?" Vera asked.

Henry coughed again and nodded. "Do you want to play with it when I get it?" he asked.

Polio, Vera knew from her health class, could sometimes start with what seemed to be a simple cold or grippe. She'd learned, but now for the life of her couldn't remember, how to tell what the differences were.

Vera dialed the doctor's number, but his nurse said that he was out on house calls. He would certainly call in at some point, but she didn't know when. With rising panic, Vera put Hazel in the crib and, breaking one of Mrs. Gaines's cardinal rules, did not correct the baby when she put her thumb in her mouth.

This time Henry followed Vera into the kitchen, where she looked out the back door again, then picked up the telephone and dialed the zero and then asked for another number.

"Hello," she said. "I'm wondering if you can help me. Do you know Martha Gaines from the Wilton campus? Yes, the practice house, that's right. I'm wondering if you can tell me whether you've seen her today. Yes, has she been in the store? In the last hour or two? No? Would you have seen her? Yes, all right. Thanks very much. No, it's just that I haven't seen her for some time, and it's getting late."

Vera hung up, looking frantic.

Henry followed her back to the nursery.

"Maybe the grocery store?" Henry heard Vera ask, but by now he knew that she wasn't talking to him. He settled again into the rocking chair, his head back on its arm.

"Vera, I'm cold," he said, and she covered him with an extra blanket from the baby's drawer.

"I'm just going to check one more time, to see if Mrs. Gaines is coming," Vera told Henry.

He was watching Hazy in her crib when Vera left the room, and he was still in that position when he heard the wind slam the back door shut behind her.

MARTHA, MEANWHILE, was at neither the toy store nor the grocery store, but on her way back from the hardware store, where Arthur Hamilton had been recommending she buy an inhaler for Henry. She was halfway down Main Street, two blocks from the practice house, when she saw Vera running up the street in her direction. Vera was running, cold and coatless, with her arms crossed over her chest, the way shy girls did in gym class. Tiny white puffs of icy air formed in front of her open mouth.

"Vera!" Martha called.

"The key!" Vera called back.

"What? What are you doing here? Where's Henry? Where's the baby?" Martha shouted. A Pontiac sped by on the street in between them. Martha began to move faster than she had in years.

"They're in the house! I got locked out! I think Henry's got a fever! Do you have the key?"

By now, Martha was charging past Vera, her purse swinging back and forth on her wrist like a huge bell clapper.

A sense of panic—and a flurry of dead brown leaves—flew down the street behind them.

HENRY AND HAZEL HAD BEEN ALONE for only fifteen minutes, but word spread quickly that the practice house had been the scene of some sort of accident. In fact, there had been no damage.

With Vera first knocking, then pounding, on the back door, Henry had gone to the kitchen and found her face pressed against the glass. She had directed him to open the door, but he had simply not been able to do so; his hands, slick from the Vicks that he had somehow picked up from his own chest, had been too slippery to grasp the knob. Then he heard Hazy start to bawl, and despite Vera's protests, he turned to walk back to the nursery.

Hazy's face was bright red, her hair all matted and flouncy.

"Hazy," Henry said, but Hazy kept on crying. "Hazy," Henry said. "Be quiet, baby."

Finally, Vera stopped pounding on the door, and there was quiet. Through the slats of Hazy's crib, Henry eyed the baby, and she quieted down slightly. He was aware suddenly of the darkness in the hallway beyond the nursery.

Then he dragged over the rocking chair—a laborious process, especially because the gliders kept catching on the Oriental rug. In a moment, he had climbed up on its arm and, with surprisingly little hesitation, vaulted over the rail and into Hazy's crib.

THE PHONE RANG a good deal that evening. What Martha said varied little. Henry was fine. The baby was fine. Nothing had happened. Vera had been locked out for a few moments, that was all. No, of course Henry hadn't harmed the baby. In fact, Martha kept saying proudly, Henry had tried to calm her down. How many four-year-olds, Martha kept asking, would have had the sense and the sweetness to do for little Hazel what Henry had?

It was true that, when Martha and Vera had gotten back inside the practice house, they had found Henry sitting in the crib, with Hazel lying peacefully on his lap. An hour later, his fever—which turned out to be just the last vestige of a normal grippe—had passed, and he seemed and would prove to be entirely healthy. But that evening, between phone calls, Martha took Henry's temperature again and again, fussed and cried, and hugged him until he squirmed and pulled away.

Every time his temperature came up normal, she looked skeptical. She straightened his pillows. She gave him soup. She kissed him on his forehead, his hands.

"If anything happened to you—" she kept saying, but then she never finished the sentence, leaving Henry the not-unfamiliar impression that his well-being was somehow crucial to the progress of the world.

4

Miss Fancy and Mickey Mouse

There was a new girl in the nursery school the following fall. Her name was Annabel. Like Henry and Mary Jane, she was five. She wore her hair in braids and a headband. She wasn't as blond as Mary Jane. Her father didn't work for the college, but they lived somewhere in town.

For most of the first week, Annabel watched quietly as Mrs. Donovan, Mary Jane, Leo, and Henry went about their normal routines. Leo and Henry talked about some of the things they had seen on TV. Miss Fancy and Mickey Mouse got married again. Henry drew lots of pictures.

It wasn't until the second week that Annabel first spoke to Henry directly.

"Push me?" she asked while she hung motionless and timid on the swing in the backyard.

Boldly, Leo stepped in, palms up at his shoulders, ready to shove.

"No!" Annabel shouted, understandably alarmed by the seeming menace behind Leo's gesture.

"Leo, don't!" Mary Jane scolded. "She's scared!"

"I'll push you," Henry said. He stepped forward, leaving the concern for Annabel frozen on Mary Jane's face, where—with Henry standing behind Annabel to push her gently up into a rainy white sky—it quickly melted into something more like shock.

THE NEXT DAY, Henry pushed Annabel on the swing again, and after that was over, Mary Jane said she wanted a turn, too.

THE FOLLOWING MORNING, Mary Jane spent a long time drawing, and then she gave the picture to Henry.

"What's it of?" he asked her.

"A castle," she said. "It's where Miss Fancy and Mickey Mouse live."

"Who made you Miss Fancy?" Annabel asked.

"I did," Mary Jane said.

"Can I be someone?" Annabel asked.

"You're Annabel," Mary Jane said.

"Tag! You're it!" Leo shouted, and chased all three of them through the backyard, their Keds pounding the dry, cold dirt, their mouths open, their ears red.

Back inside, Henry drew a picture for Mary Jane and another one for Annabel, and so it went, on into the next weeks: Henry being entirely democratic with his attentions, a fairness that Mary Jane could not miss and in truth could hardly bear.

HE WOULD NOT MAKE a choice. At home, despite the drama he had shared with Vera, Henry had gone back to treating her no differently from the other practice mothers and Martha. At nursery school, he sat between Mary Jane and Annabel during lunch, tagged Mary Jane and Annabel equally often at tag, gave pictures to both of them now, and never said whose anything he liked better.

When he played in the block pile, he would not build his houses in the direction of anyone else's with the goal of joining them. Instead, he quite often would be happy just sorting the blocks, enjoying the pleasure of the semicircle fitting inside the arch, the sound the blocks made when he stacked them, like single claps of applause, the simple beauty of two quarters making a half, two halves making a whole. When he did construct buildings, he made sure to leave lots of space around them. That way, he explained to the others, if one of them toppled, it wouldn't knock the others down.

Outside, he could sit by himself for a long time, just noticing how some things looked like other things. Patches of light spotted the trees, as liquid and clear as puddles of paint. Five-fingered leaves fell down from the maple trees, open hand upon open hand.

ON THE LAST THURSDAY in October, Henry was in the playroom, building a tall tower from squares and cylinders. Annabel, stretched out on her stomach, regarded him through lazy, contented eyes.

For the fourth time in as many minutes, Mary Jane walked in from the kitchen, where Leo and she had been coloring. As nonchalantly as possible, she stepped over Annabel's legs, picked up a few blocks of her own, and settled down on the scratched wooden floor. Silently, she started to build, laying rectangle upon rectangle, as if she was bricking a wall up. She was careful not to encroach on Henry but eagerly went on building her wall, essentially making a barrier between Henry and Annabel. He didn't seem to notice. Annabel didn't seem to notice.

"Henry," Mary Jane said, and he didn't answer, too absorbed in his own construction project. "Henry," she said again.

She took a foot-long block and used it to sweep down the wall she had just made. Standing with the block in her hand, she sighed, exasperated and plaintive. "Henry, I'm trying to make a castle, you know," she said.

Henry nodded vaguely.

"It's where Miss Fancy and Mickey Mouse live."

"Okay," he said.

Tears filled her eyes. "Henry, don't you want to play Miss Fancy and Mickey Mouse?"

Annabel perked up at this. "We can both be Miss Fancy," she said.

"No," Mary Jane said. "You're not Miss Fancy."

Henry still hadn't looked up.

"I can be Miss Fancy, too," Annabel said, sitting up.

"No," Mary Jane said again. "Henry," she said, increasingly impatient.

"What?"

"Can we both be Miss Fancy?" Annabel said.

Henry, much to Mary Jane's astonishment, merely shrugged and again said "Okay."

Annabel stood up, radiant with bridal anticipation. Mary Jane turned red.

"No you can't!" Mary Jane shouted, loudly enough so that Leo emerged from the kitchen to see what was going on.

"Can't what?" Henry asked.

"She can't be Miss Fancy too!" she said to Henry. Nearly two months of pent-up jealousy and more than a year of pent-up love dissolved Mary Jane in that moment. She burst into tears but stayed on the spot, daring Henry to change his mind.

"Why not?" he asked.

"Because there can't be two."

"Why not?" Henry asked her.

"Because there can't!" Mary Jane shouted.

THE BUILDING BLOCK—one of the semicircles that fit so perfectly inside the arches—should not have done the damage it did. Having been handled by generations of children, plunged into water experiments, and left out in backyard soil and morning dew, it had no hard edges and not a hint of a splinter left. And yet, possibly the force with which it was thrown, or the angle at which the corner of its base entered the deep blue center of Mary Jane's left eye, made it an extraordinary weapon. At the moment Mary Jane started screaming—even before the blood began to stain her perfect face—Henry knew that by throwing the block, he had done the worst thing he'd ever done in his life. There would be days in Henry's future when the women who wanted his love would try to trace him back to this moment—like rings around a pebble in water trying to embrace their source.

THE BLOOD CAME OUT of Mary Jane's eye exactly the way that watercolors, if you used too much water, would rush down a page of paper and then pool in blotches rimmed by darker color. Blood flowed from the corner of Mary Jane's eye, descended the half globe of her cheek, slid past the side corner of her mouth and then down under her chin, finally settling onto the collar of her shirt, which it was immediately hard to remember as any color but red.

"Henry, what did you do?" Mrs. Donovan shouted, seemingly more eager to blame him than to help Mary Jane.

Henry, meanwhile, went to Mary Jane and did what he always did when Martha said she needed him. He tugged on one of his own ears—the ear with the little extra flap of skin—and he brought his face very close to Mary Jane's, so close that it startled her into a moment of quiet.

But then she started crying again, and she said: "I think you killed my eye!"

THE NEAREST HOSPITAL was in Titusville, which was about twenty miles northeast of Franklin. In the rush to get Mary Jane there, Mrs. Donovan pounded on the back door of the practice house and insisted that Martha take care of the children until their parents could come. Martha—almost as shocked by the sight of the little girl's face as she was by the thought that Henry was responsible for it—merely nodded, in uncharacteristic submissiveness, and went next door. Later, she would claim that she had never given Henry permission to go along to the hospital. Mrs. Donovan would always claim that Martha had actually told Henry to go.

In reality, neither case was true. Henry had simply decided that his place was beside Mary Jane.

Before she put Mary Jane in the car, Mrs. Donovan wrapped a wet dish towel around the girl's eyes, and in her plaid skirt, with her hands stretched out to feel for the car door in front of her, Mary Jane looked to Henry exactly like Jane playing Pin the Tail on the Donkey in one of the *Dick and Jane* books. Except that now there was blood on Mary Jane's collar, shirt, and hands.

———

AN INJURY TO THE EYE by blunt force—the doctor explained to Edith Donovan at the Titusville emergency room—will sometimes produce no more than a small bruise, a black eye, or dizziness and headaches. At the other extreme, he said, it can fracture the bones that surround the eye, force the bones' splinters to enter the cornea, and require immediate surgery. The latter was what happened to Mary Jane Harmon when Henry threw the block at her.

In the dim green corridor of the hospital, Henry stood by as Mrs. Donovan called Mary Jane's mother and told her what had happened. Meanwhile, two men wheeled away a small narrow bed with Mary Jane on it.

"Is she sleeping?" Henry asked Mrs. Donovan.

"Yes."

"How did they make her sleep?"

"They gave her medicine."

"Where are they taking her?" Henry asked Mrs. Donovan.

"They're taking her to fix her eye," she said.

"Are they going to operate on her?"

"Yes."

"You mean, cut her eye open?" Henry said, and he watched whatever color was left in his teacher's face drain away.

He tugged on his ear and brought his face close to hers, and then, with a gesture of infinite gentleness, he put his hand on her shoulder.

She hugged him so hard that he lost his balance and fell against her legs, and then she picked him up, and held him, just the way Martha sometimes did.

"WHY DID YOU DO IT?" Martha asked Henry that night, kneeling beside the bathtub as she took a washcloth and scrubbed his knuckles, scrubbed his kneecaps, scrubbed behind his ears.

"I don't know," Henry said.

"You have to know. You can tell me," Martha said.

Henry grabbed the bar of Ivory soap, then sank it under the water and watched as it popped back to the surface.

"Henry?" Martha said.

"What?"

"Why did you throw that block at Mary Jane Harmon?"

"I don't know why."

Martha's eyes narrowed, so that she looked a little bit like a fish. "Was she mean to you?" Martha asked. "Did she say or do something nasty?"

"No," Henry said.

"Because I know how little girls can be with little boys," Martha said.

Henry plunged the soap down again, this time with a bomber sound effect that he had learned from Leo.

"Don't do that," Martha said.

"Why not?"

"Because I'm talking to you."

Henry looked at her.

"Did she say something mean?"

Henry just shook his head and discovered, in his silence, a new form of escape.

FOR HER PART, Mary Jane woke the next morning to a room filled with flowers, drawings, and homemade cookies; to doctors and nurses saying how brave she was; to the strange, special self-esteem that can alight on a child in a hospital bed. It would take months for anyone to find out that the damage to Mary Jane's eye would be permanent, and it would take years for her to realize that what had so provoked Henry was her trying to force him to make a choice. She would, however, always remember the look on his face just before it turned to anger: a look that, even at five, she had recognized in some instinctive way as one of unspeakable helplessness and hurt.

MARTHA MADE HENRY WAIT a whole week before she would let him go visit Mary Jane.

"She'll think I don't love her," Henry protested as they sat upstairs Friday evening, Henry coloring while Martha pasted Green Stamps into her books.

"She'll know you love her," Martha said vaguely.

"No she won't!"

"Why don't you make her a card?"

"I've made her a card every day in school," he said.

"That's very nice of you."

"I never used red. I didn't want it to look like blood."

"We still can't go yet," Martha said.

"Why not?"

"Because."

"Because why?"

"Because her mother doesn't want us to," Martha finally said.

Henry looked disbelieving. "Is Mary Jane dead?" he asked.

"No, of course she's not dead," Martha said. Her face looked a little bit crumpled, as if there were words in her mouth but there was something stopping them up. "I'll see if we can go this weekend."

THERE WAS SOMETHING STRANGE, Henry thought, about how nervous Martha was when they were on their way to the hospital Saturday afternoon.

"She probably doesn't look scary or anything," Henry said to her.

Martha smiled a little. "I'm sure she's got a big bandage on by now," she said, trying to comfort the comforter. "You shouldn't worry."

"I'm not."

He did feel a little scared just before they opened the hospital room door, but Mary Jane was sitting up in her bed, eating what looked like chocolate pudding, and he went straight to the side with her normal eye, so she could see him.

"Hi," he said to her.

"Hi," she said. She smiled.

"Does it hurt?"

"Kind of," she said.

"I didn't mean to," he said.

"I know."

"You can hit my eye," he said.

"I don't want to."

"I have a joke," he told her.

"What?"

"What did the mushroom say to the carrot?"

Before Mary Jane could answer, a voice said coldly from behind him: "What are you doing here?"

Henry turned to see Mary Jane's mother, with a face like a pale stone.

"Well, we came to pay a visit to the patient," Martha said. Her voice was higher than usual.

"I was telling her a joke," Henry said.

"No," Mrs. Harmon said. "You are not to play with Mary Jane anymore."

Henry said: "I wasn't playing. I was telling a joke."

Mrs. Harmon said: "You are not allowed to play with Mary Jane anymore. I don't want you here. Don't you realize what you've done to her?"

Henry looked at Mary Jane, with the white bandage on her eye covering a fluffy wad of more white and, beneath that, who knew what, and his own two good eyes filled with tears.

"But I didn't mean to," he said.

"Henry didn't mean to," Mary Jane said.

"And you need to get some sleep now," Mrs. Harmon said to Mary Jane. "Mrs. Gaines, I'm sure you can understand. In fact, I thought I'd already made this absolutely clear to you."

Henry's face was wet now, and he used the back of his sleeve to wipe his eyes, but somehow that only made him cry more. It reminded Martha exactly of the way Betty had cried in the practice house kitchen, five years before, the day she had told Martha that Henry was her child.

"I didn't mean to," he said again, and Mary Jane said, "Henry didn't mean to, Mommy. He didn't."

"I don't care what he meant to do," Mrs. Harmon said, and with that she turned to Martha and said something the children were not supposed to hear but did: "Am I going to have to get one of the nurses to show you out?"

They didn't have time to say goodbye. Martha ushered Henry out into the cold, pointless, empty corridor; the cold, pointless, empty ride home; and the cold, pointless, empty nursery school, to which neither Mary Jane nor Henry would ever return.

5

Where's the Baby Going?

Henry had always asked questions, enchanting most people he met with an interest that seemed solicitous and loving: "What did you do today?" "Do you like apple juice?" "What's your favorite cookie?"

Some questions, however, were not aimed to charm: questions about God and Santa Claus, sex and death. These required answers that changed as Henry got older, answers that grew and broadened, rings on a tree.

"Where's the baby going?" was one such question. Henry was four the first time he asked it, and the baby was Herbert. Martha had said, "Baby's going to find his parents," which merely left Henry momentarily silent.

The second time, a year later, when Henry found a photo of Herbert, he asked, "Where is this baby?" and Martha had said, "He's with his parents."

"Who are his parents?" Henry had asked, but Martha hadn't answered him.

When Henry was six, the year after nursery school ended, he had come home one afternoon to find Hazel gone, and he had thrown himself facedown on the Oriental rug and cried. "Why couldn't we keep her?" he'd asked over and over. He had cried hard enough that afternoon to make himself sick. Martha had cleaned him up and cleaned up the rug but hadn't seemed to understand. Whether practice mothers or practice babies, everyone Henry loved eventually left, and Martha—in a way that it would take Henry years to see—seemed to gain strength from these departures and the role they gave her in his life.

THERE HAD NEVER BEEN REAL VACATIONS, but in August of 1954, Martha took Henry to the New Jersey shore for a belated eighth birthday present. He had never been to the beach. He had never worn a bathing suit. The flat, landlocked campus of Wilton College had provided the sole topography of his early life. Even the colors were exciting to Henry: the blue, green, and beige of the shoreline; the red, yellow, green, and turquoise of the beach balls and umbrellas, and the wild patchwork of blankets and towels that in some places nearly obscured the sand.

Martha spread out two beach towels from the hotel and settled in the sunshine while Henry walked down to the sea.

He had grown into a tall, extraordinarily handsome boy, with hair the color of mahogany and eyes still green with speckles of orange, eyes the color of autumn leaves. But he was skinny and pale, and he was sunburned before the first day was over. Freckles that Martha had never noticed sprang up on his nose and spread over his cheeks as if they'd been sprayed there by the waves.

She insisted he wade no deeper than his waist, a command that, given the fact that he couldn't swim, he couldn't really protest. But after he'd been knocked down a few times by the Atlantic, Martha ordered him out of the ocean completely.

Sulking beside her on his towel, Henry looked longingly down the beach at a family of five—a mother and father, two girls, and a boy about his age. They weren't markedly gleeful or giddy, not happy in any obvious way. But they all—even the mother and father—looked so much alike, as if they'd been carved from the same piece of driftwood, or painted with the same few colors of paint.

"Heidi is going to be gone when we get back, isn't she?" Henry asked.

Martha was proud of the shrewdness in Henry's question but

equally startled by the accusing tone with which he'd asked it. She hesitated a moment. "Yes, Henry," she said at last.

"Did Heidi go to find her parents, too?" Henry said. There was real bitterness in his voice, and it was clear to Martha that Henry had changed.

"Yes, Henry," she said.

"When do I get to go find *my* parents?"

The question stabbed Martha. Her answer stabbed him. "I am your parents," she said.

"Did you carry me in your stomach?" he asked.

"No," Martha said, feeling, nearly physically, the ache of her ancient loss.

"Then who did?" Henry demanded.

Martha picked up a nearly black mussel shell. The two halves were still joined, and when they were spread out, they made the shape of a heart. Martha dusted the sand from the shell. She said nothing but quietly realized the lie she was about to tell.

"Where is my father?" Henry asked.

"Your father is dead," Martha said.

"Dead?"

"Yes. He died in a train wreck a long time ago. He was working on the train."

Henry's eyes lit up for a moment. "Was he the conductor?" he asked.

Martha smiled at the familiar little-boy logic.

"No, I'm afraid not," she said. "He was just one of the men who painted the trains."

"Did you know him?"

Martha thought about the hospital bed, Tom's green checked shirt, the smell of shaving cream.

"Not very well," she said.

"What about my mother?" Henry asked.

The mussel shell broke into its two halves, their white-blue linings looking as if they'd been poured in with paint.

"Your mother."

"Did you know her, too?"

"She was a singer," Martha said. "She had a beautiful, deep alto voice, and she sang in the Christmas choir. That's where she met your father."

Henry squinted into the sunlight.

"Why didn't she want me?" he asked Martha.

"She *did* want you," Martha said, remembering what it had felt like to have a life inside her belly, inside her life. "She *did* want you, but she died the night you were born."

Henry looked down when he asked the next question.

"Did she ever even see me?" he asked.

"No," Martha said. "I heard that the last thing she said was 'Please, let me hold the baby.'"

IT WAS JUST OVER A YEAR LATER when Betty came back.

Neither she nor Dr. Gardner had called Martha to arrange this visit. Nor had they told Martha anything about Betty's intentions regarding Henry. After years of a silence that Martha had only gradually allowed herself to trust, she had received a postcard from Betty just the previous month. The postcard—featuring a cuddly-looking koala bear—said simply that Betty was planning to visit the States in the fall and was looking forward to seeing Henry, as well as to seeing Martha herself.

It had been eight years since Betty had left; seven since Martha had moved Henry upstairs; three since she had first enrolled him at the local public school, where people now knew him as Henry Gaines, never as Henry House.

Now Betty was standing beside her father in the rectangle of the doorway as if expecting a great welcome, and Henry, ever willing but completely uninformed about the significance of Dr. Gardner's companion, came over to the front door, produced a hand from his khakis pocket, and said, "I'm Henry Gaines. Nice to meet you. Why don't you come in?"

Thrown off balance, Martha quickly sent the current practice mother and the current practice baby on an unnecessary errand, and then she led the way to the living room. Unusually helpless, she was momentarily tongue-tied, so it was the affable Henry Gaines who remembered to ask the visitors if they cared for coffee or tea.

BETTY, NOW TWENTY-SEVEN YEARS OLD, looked shockingly older than she had when Martha had seen her last. It was not just that she had crossed that mysterious but permanent border from girlhood to womanhood, although in truth there was not a trace of innocence left in her face. There was also something desperate and dissolute about her, as if she had cried too much, or drunk too much, or possibly done too much of both.

She had, in any case, brought Henry a present. It was about the size of a *Life* magazine, only about eight times thicker, and it was wrapped in childish balloon wrapping paper that he did his best to ignore.

"This is for you," Betty said, and thrust the gift into Henry's hands, seeming nervous in a way that he did not yet understand.

"What do you say, Henry?" Martha asked too quickly.

"I was just about to say it," he said, looking up from the package. "Thank you. Thank you so much."

"Aren't you going to open it?" Martha asked.

Henry looked at Betty. "Should I?" he asked her.

"If you want to."

"Of course he wants to," Martha said impatiently. "Why wouldn't he want to?"

Beneath the silly balloon paper was a fine wooden box the color of Henry's hair. The box had a leather handle, and it opened like an attaché case, with two brass clasps on one side and two brass hinges on the other.

Henry paused, his thumbs on the two clasps.

"Go ahead," Martha said, as if she wanted to get something over with.

Henry flipped open the clasps. Inside the box was a wooden artist's palette, a curvy rectangle, like a face in profile, with an empty oval eye. Beneath this were three magnificently varied rainbows: fat, fresh metal tubes of paint; short, stubby sticks of Cray-Pas; tall lines of colored pencils. A fourth rainbow—entirely in shades of gray—was made of charcoals and pencils in different thicknesses. There was also a gray eraser wrapped in plastic, a silver pencil sharpener, and five paintbrushes in different sizes.

Henry thought he had never in his whole life seen anything as extraordinary.

Wonderingly, he ran his hands over the pencils, rolling them slightly, then regretting that he had disturbed the perfect alignment of their labels: Burnt Sienna, Red Paprika, Pea Green, Rust.

"I hope you still like to draw," Betty said.

"I *love* to draw," he said, wondering how she knew this, wondering why she'd said *still*. "I'm going to be an artist when I grow up."

"He spends hours," Martha said, somewhat grudgingly.

"Didn't I always say?" Betty asked.

"Always?" Henry asked.

Betty looked first at Dr. Gardner, then at Martha, who said: "You knew Mrs. Lodge when you were a baby."

"It's not Mrs. Lodge anymore. It's Miss Gardner again now," Betty said to Martha.

"Oh," Henry said brightly to Betty. "Were you one of my mothers?"

The color of Betty's face changed from Pale Apricot to Wild Rose. "Yes," she said, in a husky voice. "I was one of your mothers."

"You've seen Mrs. Lodge's—that is, Miss Gardner's—photographs in your baby journal, Hanky," Martha said.

"Henry," he said.

There was a moment of awkward silence. Then Betty asked: "Could I see some of your drawings?"

"Sure," Henry said. "They're upstairs. I'll show you."

As Betty stood, Henry reached out a hand for her, far less like a little boy than like an urbane gentleman, asking an unsure woman to dance.

———

"YOU DON'T NEED TO TAKE HER UPSTAIRS," Martha said quickly. "Why don't you go up and get your sketchbooks, Hanky?"

Together, then, she and Dr. Gardner and Betty listened to his footsteps as he went, obediently, up the stairs.

"I can't get over how big he's gotten," Betty said.

"Yes. Well," Martha said.

"I mean, he's a big, big boy now," Betty said, amazed. Her eyes filled with tears, and, impulsively, she threw her arms around Martha, who stiffened against the embrace.

"Oh, thank you, Mrs. Gaines," Betty said. "Thank you from the bottom of my heart for taking such good care of him. Truly. I can't—" And she started to weep again. "I can't believe he's so big."

"What did you expect, exactly?" Martha said, before she could edit herself.

"My guess is that Bettina didn't know what to expect," Dr. Gardner said drily.

"And what were you planning on telling the boy?" Martha asked.

"Nothing for the moment," Dr. Gardner said. "Bettina is, as far as anyone knows, just my daughter, home for a visit."

"Father, I've told you," Betty said, sounding exhausted. "I've left Fred, and I'm never going back."

"Bettina," he said in a warning voice that conveyed every ounce of his parental, institutional, and financial control.

"Here they are!" Henry said as he came into the room, carrying a sketchbook that nearly hid his torso, just as Betty added: "And I've come to get my son."

6

That Seems Perfectly Obvious

Martha stayed awake all night long, wondering what, if anything, Henry had heard and what, if anything, she had the power to do about it. At first, stretched out in her bed, she tried her hardest to sleep. But all the usual, comforting guideposts of her own surroundings seemed suspect, as if the entire tangible world was getting ready to turn against her. At one in the morning, resigned to sleeplessness, she switched on the lamp beside her bed, wrapped her chenille bathrobe around her, and walked over to the bookshelves. She took down Henry's baby book and turned the pages slowly, reading the captions, though she knew them by heart:

Who said I'd like applesauce?

Grace Winslow thinks I have a flair for music.

Lucky boy! Seven Mamas, seven Christmas presents!

Martha studied the few photographs in which Betty appeared, trying to discern if there really was a telltale pain or longing in her face—some sign of the biological parenthood that had then still been her special secret. In one picture, Betty was holding Henry on her lap in his first snowsuit; in another, she was lifting his chubby wrist to wave at the camera; in a third, she was laughing as he clutched the sides of his bath towel. She seemed no more possessive or passionate than the other women in the photos did, though that left plenty of room for both. But then there was the farewell sentence that Betty had written:

Goodbye, baby boy. I will never, ever, forget you.

Martha returned the journal to the shelf. She and two dozen practice mothers had filled four other books—for four different practice
house babies—during the years that had passed since Henry had come
upstairs to live with her. There had been Herbert, then Hazel, then
Heidi, then Hollis—and they had all been loved and patted and guided
through their large and little milestones. But Martha knew she would
find no comfort in looking at their photographs. She knew she
would only be looking for glimpses of Henry.

Martha walked into his bedroom, not exactly on tiptoe, because if
Henry had awakened, she wouldn't have minded in the least reaching
over to him and hugging him. She knew that he didn't like her to do
that so often in public anymore, but he would still allow it sometimes
when he was sleepy, or sick, or otherwise unfettered by the thoughts of
those boys and girls at school.

In truth, Martha longed to hold him now, but Henry, it seemed,
was fast asleep, his face turned away from the door.

AT FOUR IN THE MORNING, Martha tiptoed downstairs and, careful
not to wake the practice mother and baby, brought the iron and ironing board back up to her room. Her weekly ironing was still two days
away, but the task seemed to promise her some relief.

Not surprisingly, given her years of experience, Martha had always
been skilled with an iron—now, with the new Sunbeam she had
bought at Hamilton's, she was practically a virtuoso. She was not so
much aware of as offended by wrinkles, and she leaned her considerable weight into every crease, trying to tame the unstructured world
into something tidy and recognizable.

As she ironed, Martha thought about the night eight years before
when she had stacked her clothes, ready to take Henry away with her
if Dr. Gardner insisted he be sent back to the orphanage. She had felt
then, emphatically, that no one who wasn't Henry's flesh and blood
would ever have a better claim to him than she did. Now, unimagin-
ably, his flesh and blood had come to take him, but to Martha it
seemed entirely clear that Betty had become the stranger. Plus, the girl

had given him up. No matter the pressure placed on her and how difficult that had made things for her. She'd chosen to give him up. The small towns of this country were filled with other girls who'd gotten into trouble and made that decision, and then gone on with their lives. Of course, as Martha knew well from her dealings with the orphanage, all those girls had signed papers in which they'd made their choices official. Maybe that was the reason that Martha had never heard of one changing her mind.

"DR. GARDNER," she said out loud, trying to rehearse what her best argument would be. "Dr. Gardner," she repeated, but when she imagined what it would be like, standing before this man and trying to plead for his understanding—let alone for his grandson—she found herself choking and crying on the words. "Dr. Gardner," she began again. "Dr. Gardner."

Beyond the sweeping windows, she could just see a promise of morning.

"Dr. Gardner," she said out loud one more time, and through her tears she misjudged the geometry of the collar she was folding back, and she burned the part of her hand between her thumb and forefinger. It was a bad burn, she knew that immediately, but she was not entirely sorry it had happened. It snapped her back from her reverie into actual, present pain.

IN THE MORNING, when Martha asked him what he wanted for breakfast, Henry did not respond.

"Pancakes? Waffles? Frosted Flakes?" Martha asked. "You were so cute, the way you used to say that! 'Emem, they're g-r-r-reat!' "

And Martha chugged on and on—like a train conductor who doesn't know that the city he is steaming by has recently been firebombed.

"Don't you feel well?" she finally asked Henry when she'd realized he hadn't said anything.

He merely stared at her, speechless, his eyes momentarily more gray than green. Then the practice mother shouted for Martha to come, and so, while Martha had her back turned, Henry slipped out the door and disappeared, like a morning shadow.

MARTHA KNEW THAT she had to confront Dr. Gardner. In the end, she reasoned, it would not be Betty but her father who would make the decision about Henry's future. Betty was still, after all, an unwed mother. If Henry were younger, no doubt Betty could have moved with him to another town and told people that he had grown up in Australia, the child of a failed marriage. Divorce, while hardly smiled upon, didn't come with the stigma a bastard did. But Henry, thank God, was old enough to tell the tale of his upbringing all by himself. And even in 1955, unmarried middle-class women who had never worked a day in their lives did not live as single mothers unless their parents, for some reason, wanted them to. And good parents never wanted them to.

Martha sat at the kitchen table and took a sip of tea. Her sleepless night had left a foul taste in her mouth, but despite a few extra teaspoons of honey, the tea didn't help. It was bitter. She was sour. Her hand hurt. She was exhausted. She knew that she needed to compose herself, to arrange herself, but what she knew best had nothing to do with asking, let alone pleading, let alone threatening, to get what she wanted. What Martha knew best had to do with the tricks and illusions of self-sufficiency: with organization, planning, tidy corners, and well-followed rules.

Upstairs, she straightened her seams and swept up her hair and tied on her best silk scarf. But she looked like a woman unhinged, and she knew it, and finally she decided to give up trying to look composed.

"I need to see him," she told Dr. Gardner's secretary on the phone. "He'll know why."

"Will he?"

"He will," Martha said, and realized her voice was quavering.

She was fifty-seven years old, and there was no future for her without Henry. There was only her tiny world, bordered by practice walls and practice floors, and filled with practice people. If Henry left, Martha knew, he would eventually become only the practice son who'd come to give her a practice sense of purpose.

FIFTEEN MINUTES LATER, she was sitting in the anteroom in the president's office, using the forefinger of her unhurt hand to trace the inner embellishments of the gold Wilton College seal that adorned her black wooden chair. She knew that every form of security she had was tied to that seal, and yet she also knew—perhaps, she thought grandly, the way that heroes know before their last acts—that she would sacrifice it all in a moment in order to keep Henry by her side.

Inside Dr. Gardner's office, two other identical chairs stood across from his desk, and he motioned Martha into one of them.

"Mrs. Gaines," he said evenly, as if it was the beginning of an annual salary review.

"Did you know this was going to happen?" she asked him. She was aware that her tone was harsh and accusing, but she was unable to correct it.

"I beg your pardon?" Dr. Gardner asked.

"Forgive my informality, but I have to know. Is this why you've let me keep the boy all these years? Just in case your daughter came back?"

Dr. Gardner said nothing, but he seemed surprised by the question. Martha went on. "A real adoptive family would never let him go if his natural mother came back. Is that why you had *me* keep him instead?"

"Of course," Dr. Gardner said, which was both the least expected and the most honest answer Martha could have imagined.

He stood up and turned slightly away from her, appearing to examine the photographs on his credenza: pictures of him with national leaders, visiting scholars, former students. Pictures of Betty and his late wife, whom Martha had met only two or three times, all of them at Betty's birthday parties.

If Betty's mother had lived, Martha thought, maybe Betty would have had the sense not to marry the first boy who came along, and then get pregnant with someone else, and then give the baby up, and then want the baby back.

But then, of course, Henry wouldn't exist, and at the thought, Martha felt herself growing faded and immaterial.

"If you take him away from me," she said, "I will leave this institution."

"Well. Yes, that seems perfectly obvious," Dr. Gardner said coldly.

Martha stood on faltering legs. She could feel a flush spreading across her face, down her neck, her chest, and tingling in her legs. She hoped it didn't show. In the next minute, she realized she was feeling for the arm of the chair, ever so slightly toppling. It was not exactly faintness, but something more like vertigo, the sensation that the center had just lost its place: like the cylinder of a washing machine when it tries to spin too many heavy clothes.

The arm of the chair, however, steadied her, and she didn't lose a step.

"Well, Dr. Gardner, I suppose if you know that, then you know everything. Including where I'll be if you have any news to tell me."

She inhaled deeply and found that it helped to steady her more. Then she turned, as grandly as she could, to leave.

"Just a moment, Mrs. Gaines," Dr. Gardner said, and he waited until she had turned back to him. "I want to ask for your continued professionalism and patience while I resolve this situation. I am planning on discussing everything with Bettina, just as soon as she wakes up."

"Wakes up?" Martha said. "She's sleeping?" She looked at her watch, unnecessarily. Whatever time it was, it was too late in the morning for a grown woman to be sleeping.

Dr. Gardner nodded gravely, pushed his chair back, and sat up. "Mrs. Gaines," he said, "in addition to losing her husband in Australia, my daughter gained certain bad habits. Or rather, to be precise about it, failed to break them."

"I see," Martha said, though she didn't yet, entirely.

"Bad habits," Dr. Gardner continued, "unfortunately related to the consumption of alcohol. I tell you this because your history of discretion is well proven by now."

"I should think," Martha said drily.

"In any case, the combination of the circumstances, the long trip from Australia, and far too much wine with dinner have all contrived to keep her in bed this morning. Which has only confirmed my inclination," he added pointedly. "Because despite what you may think, I believe my daughter has handled her life thus far abominably, and I have absolutely no reason to think that if she took the young fellow with her, she would do anything but ruin his life as well."

7

You Must Want to Know

In fact, Betty had been awake for most of the night, and the young fellow was already with her. She had been standing by the bus stop when Henry got there, squinting into the morning sun, waiting for the next part of her life to begin.

Henry could tell that she was nervous, because she fiddled with the gold ring on her left hand.

"Can I talk to you a minute?" she asked him.

He shrugged.

"Did you hear what I said to Mrs. Gaines yesterday?"

"Uh-huh."

"That you're my son?"

"Uh-huh."

"I thought you had."

Henry tugged on his ear, the one with the extra teddy-bear flap. Betty reached out fondly to touch it, then drew her hand back when Henry recoiled.

"You are my son, you know," she said.

Henry didn't say anything—just strained to look over her shoulder to see if the school bus was in view.

"Do you understand that?" she asked him.

"You're my mother," he said, and though he tried to keep his face impassive, he felt something revving or roiling inside.

"Well, I thought you'd probably want to know why I left," Betty said.

No. What he wanted—what he had wanted all night, awake in his bed, feigning sleep when Martha looked in because he had known he could not feign sweetness—was merely for this Betty not to have come yesterday at all.

"You must want to know why I left," Betty said.

Henry pulled on his ear again, and at the exact same time, Betty pulled on her gold ring.

"Did my father give you that ring and then make you go away with him and did Emem hide me so I couldn't come too and now are you back to get me?" he asked.

Despite her worried look, Betty smiled. "Oh, Son," she said. "That's too many questions to answer at once."

The word *Son*, uttered with such apparent ease, floated up in the air, sweet and cozy, like a comic-strip thought, but then snaked its way into sibilance and evil. *Son*, a snake's hiss. Not even Martha had ever used the word *Son* as if it were his name.

"Did my father really die in a train wreck?" Henry asked.

Betty looked startled. "Who told you that?" she asked.

"Emem."

"Come on, let me take you to school," Betty said.

"I ride the bus."

"I know you ride the bus."

"Grown-ups don't ride the bus," Henry said, looking urgently toward the small yellow-orange rectangle, now in view but still blocks away.

"What if I told you that I rode this very same bus to your very same school when I was your age?"

So *what*, Henry thought. So what.

"I know every stop on the way," Betty said.

ON *GUNSMOKE* JUST THE WEEK BEFORE, Henry had heard Marshal Matt Dillon say straight out to some troublemaker: "All that is your business. I don't see as how that concerns me." That was what Henry wanted to say, but his throat felt hot and closed, as if the words would have to fight their way out.

Eventually, Henry would come to see Betty as the logical, nearly inevitable, means for escaping from Martha. For the moment, though, as he listened, his confusion gave way not to hope but to anger.

She talked her way onto the bus, this woman, and sat with him in the last row, where all the chewed-up gum spotted the floor. Henry studied the patterns of the pale beige splotches while Betty talked. He found two kitten faces and a Christmas tree; a fish, a snake, and a bottle. He tried to concentrate on arranging their shapes, figuring out how to fit them into one scene. A Christmas morning, maybe, with different presents under a tree.

IT WAS ONLY TEN MINUTES TO SCHOOL, but Henry's face burned hotter every time the bus made a stop and he had to see in surprise, then hear in giggles, the reactions of his classmates as they came aboard. He was most embarrassed when Mary Jane Harmon climbed onto the bus. She sat next to Henry every day, but her usual look of expectancy was dashed today in an instant of silvery surprise. Though their friendship had been rekindled in the relative protection that school gave them from their still-bitter mothers, they had few opportunities to talk. The currents of nine-year-old boys and girls had swept them into separate pools, and the morning bus was one of the only places where—perhaps just because their classmates were too preoccupied or too sleepy to care—they were free to defy the usual laws of fourth-grade conduct.

As Mary Jane found a different seat, Betty talked on about how cute Henry had been as a baby and how much she had hated to leave him. Betty was good enough to whisper all this—and in fact the bus noise was so loud that even Henry missed a few of her words. But what he experienced was a rage so deep that it seemed made up of colors, as if, in his mind, someone was riffling through sheaves of construction paper: red, orange, purple, black.

"So my father didn't die in a train wreck?" he finally whispered to her.

"No," Betty said.

"So where is he?"

"I don't know."

"Is he in Austria?"

"Australia."

"Is he in Australia?"

"No. The man in Australia was my husband. But he's not your father."

They were the last ones to get off the bus at the school. Henry thought about Father and Mother in the Dick and Jane books. Sure, there were times when Mother was in the kitchen without Father, and times when Father was in his basement workshop without Mother. But Father and Mother went together, just the way Dick and Jane did.

"When you learn about the birds and the bees," Betty said, "you'll learn that it's possible to make a baby without actually being married, and that's how your father and I made you, and then he disappeared, even before I knew I was expecting you."

"You could have told him," Henry said.

"No," Betty said. "I couldn't. Because I didn't know where he was."

"Why not?" Henry asked. It was almost a shout.

Betty sighed a little. She said: "He was just a nice guy who I went to the movies with, and I didn't know who he was, Henry."

"What was the movie?" Henry asked.

"What?"

"What was the movie?"

Betty smiled. "It was *A Tree Grows in Brooklyn*," she said.

"Where's Brooklyn?" he asked.

SHE DIDN'T CALL HIM HANKY. That was the only good thing about her, he thought, and, for this moment, the only thing that brought him even close to liking her.

Before he went into the school, she made him stop on the steps. She took out a camera, and she said, "Smile, Son." The hissing again. And then she took what seemed to be an entire roll of pictures. On purpose, he did not smile in a single one of them. The cluster of classmates who lined up behind Betty, making goofy faces and trying to get him to laugh, didn't alter the parade of crazy, furious colors in his mind. Only when Mary Jane stayed after the rest of them were inside—waiting for him, needing to know who this woman was, offering her one blue eye, and the smile he'd always known he could trust—only then did the mad parade come coolly to a stop.

AT NINE, MARY JANE WAS skinny and quick, both taller and more athletic than Henry. Her black eye patch was like a permanent bruise, a constant reminder of their long-lost days of nursery school, but she spent every single recess out in the play yard, jumping rope. She could do a can-can kick, a leg over, and a flying cross. As long as she led with her good eye, she could jump into a row of three jumpers, and—even more impressive—she could jump backward to get out again.

Henry, by social necessity, usually watched these feats from a distance, just as he watched her walk the hallways with her girlfriends, stopping to hitch up her sagging tights or giggling over mysterious things. This morning, however, Mary Jane broke the usual protocol and pulled Henry into the coatroom.

"Who was that?" she asked him. "Why was she on the bus? Why was she taking pictures of you? Do you know her?"

"Sort of," Henry said.

"Who is she?"

"She's President Gardner's daughter," Henry said.

Her eyes widened. "From the college?"

Henry nodded.

"Well, what's she doing here?"

Henry looked at the floor and tugged on his ear.

"Henry? Why was she here with you?"

Rupert Biggs ducked into the coatroom. "You're going to be late for homeroom," he said. He tore off his plaid jacket, jammed it onto an already full coat hook, and darted out again. The coat fell immediately to the floor, and Henry, moved by some primordial home economics instinct, bent to retrieve it and hang it up again.

"Henry," Mary Jane said again. This time the word was not a plea for an answer but rather a statement about Henry's ability to trust her with whatever that answer would be.

"You can't—you can't tell anyone," he said.

"I never would," she said, and he believed her utterly, but still hesitated, trying to find the right words.

She merely looked at him, waiting. He had noticed lately that she could convey with one eye a great deal more than most people could convey with two.

He glanced behind her toward the coatroom door, then turned back to her. "She says she's my real mother," he said.

"Your real mother."

"Yes."

"President Gardner's daughter is your real mother?"

"That's what she told me," Henry said.

"I thought your real mother was dead."

"So did I."

"So Mrs. Gaines—" Mary Jane began, as always following Henry to the first place he was likely to go.

"Yah."

"So Mrs. Gaines knew all along?"

"Yah."

"So Mrs. Gaines—"

"Is a big fat liar!" Henry shouted, bereft. He tried to say more, but he couldn't, and then he tried to swallow, but found he couldn't do that either. His eyes widened in panic.

"Henry?" Mary Jane said.

She took a step forward, as if to help, then looked back toward the hallway, trying to find a grown-up.

Henry managed to swallow, then catch his breath. But in his terror, he felt a shiver of nausea and dizziness. Instinctively, he turned away from Mary Jane, looking down at the ground and stuffing his hands into his pockets, as if trying to lessen the chance that any part of him would be touched.

8

Cheese!

Martha's sense of relief, meanwhile, had lasted only as far as the front porch of the president's house. Walking down the old wooden steps, she suddenly felt that she had to see Henry in order to know, really know, that he was going to stay safely with her. Not exactly intending to, she simply walked from the president's house and continued until she was entirely off the campus, disappearing into the town of Franklin, not even letting the week's practice mother know that she had gone.

It was easily three miles to the public elementary school that Henry attended. Every morning for three years—until this fall, in fact, when Henry had begged her to let him go to the bus stop by himself—Martha had walked him to the yellow school bus. All those mornings, he had found a seat by the window and had always remembered to turn and wave a shy but shining goodbye.

Twice a year, Martha had gone to Henry's school: the first time, on the first day, it was always to make sure he was registered; the second time, sometime in the late fall, it was for the parent-teacher meeting. She had never felt welcome. She had never felt relaxed. All around her were pairs of parents: the mothers in their pretty young dresses, the fathers in their suits and hats. Parents came in twos. That was the rule, and Martha had broken it, and only the fact that she had adopted this boy instead of birthing him out of wedlock kept Martha herself from being a total outcast in this world.

As it happened, Martha arrived today just as the children were being lined up on the basketball court for their yearly class pictures. Rows of slatted wooden folding chairs had been arranged next to one of the chain-link fences, and the children were shoving and teasing each other as the teachers tried to corral them into lines arranged by height. Martha searched for Henry's class and found it quickly. As a fourth-grader, he was in the oldest class. Most of the girls had white anklets and bangs or hair clips and were wearing Sunday dresses. Most of the boys were wearing button-down shirts instead of polo shirts, and some were wearing ties as well. Even through her worry, Martha frowned at the thought that Henry had not told her it was picture day. She didn't like the thought of Henry not telling her things.

She saw him file into his row in the middle of the line: neither the shortest nor the tallest but, as in most things, just right. He had his hands in his khakis pockets, as usual, and he was wearing a striped polo shirt. His Oxford shoes were dusty, and there was a fresh grass stain on one of the knees of his pants. Martha didn't know the boy to the left of him, but the girl to his right was that Mary Jane Harmon, with the eye patch and the cruel mother. Both children, Martha noted proudly, were trying to get Henry's attention. Her boy was popular, she knew that, and though it made her nervous, it also made her proud.

The photographer fussed and fooled with his tripod and his heavy blanket, readying one of his plates, and meanwhile the sun was in the children's eyes, and Martha could tell that they were hot and annoyed, and she remembered just how little real affection she felt for children in general. Only Henry truly appealed to her—squinting, serious, handsome, hers.

"Henry!" she shouted, waving a gloved hand. She said it exactly as the photographer said "Cheese, please!" and so, in the fourth-grade photograph for the Franklin Elementary School in 1955, the entire class seemed to be looking distractedly off to one side.

Henry scowled at her—a true scowl—as he slowly crossed the basketball court to see what it was that had brought her here.

She was not his real mother. That much he had known for as long as he could remember. But she had lied to him—actually lied—had told him his mother was dead, denying him, in the same moment, both hope and trust. He could see her, sitting in the New Jersey sand, holding that stupid heart-shaped shell and making him feel that she was all he had.

Henry sensed that fingers were being pointed at him and giggles suppressed. Betty's bus ride this morning had been bad enough. This visit was something it would take him months to live down, and he knew it.

"What are you doing here?" he asked Martha.

"That's not much of a greeting," she said, reaching out for him.

He looked behind him.

"Come on, give me a hug and I won't ask you for a kiss," she said.

"What are you doing here?" he asked again, ignoring her request.

"I just wanted to see you," she said, then added: "I was passing by."

"Why were you passing by?" Henry asked.

"I had an errand."

"What kind of errand?"

"An errand, Hanky," Martha said. "You don't need to know what errand."

"Henry," he said.

"Yes," she said. "Henry."

"I have to go to class now," he said, and he turned to walk away.

"Hanky!" she shouted. Then, desperately: "Henry!"

He turned back.

"Come straight home after school," Martha said.

His eyes narrowed slowly as he glared at her, as if his pale eyelids were a blanket of snow icing over the warm colors of the autumn earth.

THE PRACTICE HOUSE WAS often chaotic in the afternoons, when Henry came home from school. Martha was usually in the kitchen, cleaning or cooking while she kept an eye on the practice mother's preparations for the baby's dinner. Sometimes there was a wash going in the utility room as well, or some extra Household Equipment lesson in how to iron skirts with pleats, or how to treat blood and chocolate stains, or how to disguise small cigarette burns in polished wooden surfaces.

Then the baby would wake up, and there would be a bottle and a rush of activity to get him ready for his daily walk. Henry didn't mind the bustle, because it kept Martha's focus elsewhere. As soon as the practice mother left, Martha would find him, though. No matter what he was doing, she would greet him with that same look—part pleading, part searching—as if the affection she feared he might develop for someone or something else would be physically imprinted on and read in his eyes.

Today was more intense than usual. Henry was positive that, if Martha looked hard enough, she would find the reflection of Betty there. Apparently he was right.

"Did you see Betty today?" Martha asked him.

Henry shrugged.

"Did she talk to you?" Martha said.

He shrugged again.

"What did she say? Where did she talk to you?"

"On the way to school," Henry said.

Martha scowled. "On the bus?" she asked with evident horror.

"Yes."

"Your regular school bus?"

"Yes."

"And what did she say?"

He shrugged again. "I'll tell you later," he said, already knowing that he never would. "I'm missing the Mouseketeers."

HE KEPT THE SET ON AFTER *The Mickey Mouse Club*. He watched *Kukla, Fran & Ollie,* and after that *Sergeant Preston of the Yukon*. The Yukon, as usual, was covered in snow; the trees in the background were black and gray; Preston's Mounties uniform was gray and white; Yukon King was gray and black. As Henry watched, his mind wandered. He thought about Betty, wondering if he looked like her, wondering if

Australia looked like the Yukon, wondering what either place would look like in color. More darkly, he thought about Martha. He wondered what other secrets she'd kept, what other lies she had told him. He assumed that there had been many of both. Trust was not a muscle he knew how to use.

IT WAS AFTER DINNER that Betty showed up. Martha had known she would come again, but she had expected her earlier in the evening, and, washing the dishes and drying them, she had allowed herself to relax for the first time in two days. The ringing of the doorbell was a mild assault.

"Go wash up now," she told Henry.

He felt fairly certain that it would be Betty at the door, and also that it would be better not to talk to her with Martha there.

But he sat listening at the top of the landing, his hands around the spindles of the balustrade.

"What do you want?" Martha asked Betty.

Even given the circumstances, it surprised Henry to hear Martha's lack of civility.

"You know what I want," Betty said.

There were a few moments of whispering, and Henry clutched the spindles more tightly.

"You know," he heard Martha say. "You don't know anything about raising a child Henry's age."

"Neither do you," Betty said swiftly.

"I know this child," Martha said. "I know every single thing there is to know about this child. And I know he wants to be with me."

Henry could hear the hiss and strike of a match against a matchbook, and he could even hear Betty exhale. "Why would he want someone who lied?" she asked.

"Why," Martha replied, "would he want someone who left?"

THOSE WERE THE QUESTIONS. At the top of the stairs, Henry tried to answer them for himself. He tried to want someone. He couldn't. He tried to imagine something. He couldn't. If he wanted anything, it was to scream at Martha for lying, scream at Betty for leaving. He went to his room, sat at his desk, and stared at the shadows on the wall until he found shapes and patterns.

"ARE YOU TAKING ME WITH YOU?" Henry asked Betty when she met him at the bus stop the next afternoon. She seemed smaller than she had the night before. Her breath smelled sour and sharp, and he tried to keep away from it.

"No," Betty said. "Not yet."

"Then why did you come?"

Betty's eyes got wet, and she looked down to snap open her pocketbook. Henry thought she was reaching for a tissue, but instead she took out a photograph. She handed it to him proudly, wanting him to look at it.

"Why did you come," he asked her, not looking at the picture, "if you're not going to take me with you?"

"I'm going to tell you the truth," Betty said, with an emphasis on the first word. "I want to take you with me. My father won't give me the money, and I don't have enough of my own."

"We could get a job," Henry said.

"I *will* get a job," Betty said. "And I *will* come back for you," she said.

"What if I'm not here?" Henry asked.

"I'll find you."

A slow tear, like a drop of syrup, ran all the way down her nose. Henry thought maybe he didn't want to go with her after all.

"I want you to keep this picture of me," Betty said.

Henry looked down at it. It was black-and-white and had a generous crease in it, but Henry could tell that it was a picture of Betty, only when she was so much younger and prettier that it didn't matter to him at all. He looked back at Betty, and in what may have been his first completely intentional act of cruelty, he said: "You don't look anything like this anymore."

9

Eastern Standard Time

Only five days later, Betty Gardner boarded a train heading east, to New York City, where her father had decided that her unfortunate past might be less objectionable, or at least less noticed.

With the help of a former Wilton professor, Dr. Gardner had arranged to have Betty try out as a researcher at *Time* magazine. It would be a new start, he told her, insisting that she be grateful for the opportunity.

Until the moment Betty left, Martha felt as if she was virtually incapable of any emotion but fear. And even after Betty's departure, Martha couldn't help feeling that the visit had left a pall, a layer of emotional ash that had changed forever the way that Henry was going to look at things. Martha blamed this largely on Betty and even, to some extent, on Betty's father. It did not occur to her that there was any other blame to be assigned.

IN 1955, PASSENGERS ARRIVING at New York's Penn Station walked off their trains, up to the glorious concourse, and into a reality that rarely fell short of whatever superlatives they had heard in advance. The celestial ceiling, with its vaulted arches and its web of wrought-iron window frames, was churchlike and dizzying, fearsome and immense. Hanging in the smoky air between the ceiling and floor—like a man-made sun—was the famous clock, with its heavy Roman numerals, precisely squared-off minute marks, and, in capital letters, its nonnegotiable message: EASTERN STANDARD TIME. From tall white poles around the vast room, modern loudspeakers hung in clusters like giant, incongruous lilies of the valley. Thousands upon thousands of people strode through the concourse without hesitation or apparent fear.

Her two suitcases on either side of her, Betty stood for at least ten minutes, taking the whole panorama in. It occurred to her that she had not felt this much like a child since she had first arrived in Australia and gone looking for Fred's address at the Melbourne post office. Thank God she was not a child now, she thought: A few moments later, she had gathered her bags and taken a seat in an all-but-empty bar called Brown's.

An exhausted-looking waitress came over to take her order.

"Gin and tonic," Betty said.

"Any particular kind of gin?"

Despite her fear, her fatigue, and even her sadness, there was something to be said, Betty thought, for a city in which even a tired-looking waitress asked you what kind of gin you wanted.

SHE HAD LEARNED to drink gin in Australia. She had learned to drink everything there, discovering the sweet and sharp contradictions of booze: the cushiony insulation and the flat, hard taste. She had needed both the softness and the hardness for dealing with Fred, who drank even more than she did and with far less apparent consolation. Neither of them had had a clue about how to build a marriage, let alone a life. It became clear after a while that they would each protect their own secrets and garner more. What little they'd had in common before the war had long since been outgrown. Betty had become a mother and Fred a soldier, and both had been deserters. Yet neither of them could acknowledge just how useless with shame their hearts had grown.

"First time here?" the waitress asked as she brought Betty's drink.

Betty nodded and stirred the gin and tonic with a heavy plastic brown swizzle stick.

"Where're you from?" the waitress asked, apparently grateful to have some company.

Betty took a sip and welcomed the coldness and warmth, flowing simultaneously.

"I'm from Australia," Betty said.

"Australia? Well, you couldn't have taken the train from there."

Betty smiled. "No, I was visiting my son. In Pennsylvania."

"What's he doing there?"

"Damned if I know," Betty said, and drained her glass, feeling the ice cubes kiss her top lip. "Bring me another, okay?"

She studied the cocktail napkin, ate some peanuts, tried to get one more taste of gin from the still-large ice cubes. She thought for the first time about what she would say when people in New York asked her about her past. It struck her that she could lie and that there was almost no reason not to lie. But with this waitress, for some reason, it seemed even more tempting, almost exotic, to tell the truth. Looking into those tired, pale eyes, Betty had an instant and grateful under-standing of the freedom that would be granted her by the anonymous city.

"He came from a one-night stand, my son," Betty said after a long sip from the fresh drink.

The waitress looked over her shoulder carelessly, then sat down. "And they made you give him up?" she asked.

Betty nodded. "When he was just a year old," she said.

"You weren't married?" the waitress asked.

"I was. But not to the father."

"Oh."

The waitress leaned on her hand, a heavy elbow on the small table. "But you had the baby a whole year?" she asked.

"Well, I wasn't living with him, but I got to see him a lot."

"You're lucky," the waitress said. "My cousin had to give hers up before her milk was even dry."

Betty's impulse to share her story changed almost harshly into the need for her story to be understood.

"Lucky!" Betty said. "One night. One guy. And pregnant like that."

"Yeah," the waitress said.

Then Betty told her about Martha, the practice house, and Dr. Gardner. She told her about the long, pale Australian nights and the futility of Fred's attempts first to get, then to keep, a job.

"And did you ever tell him about your son?"

"No. Yes. No." Betty laughed at her own confusion. "At the very end I did," she said.

"Why?"

"Because we'd tried for eight goddamn years to have a baby of our own, and he kept saying I just wasn't made to be a mother."

FORTIFIED BY THE DRINKS and emboldened by her confessions, Betty left a large tip for the waitress and dragged her bags out onto the street. It was mild for October, sunny and clear. Graceful cane-shaped streetlamps arched along Fifth Avenue. A billboard several blocks away advertised Knickerbocker beer. Two-toned taxis in every color drove by, and it took Betty a while to realize that when the lozenge-shaped signs on top of them were lit up, that meant they were empty, not full.

The leather seat inside was soft and cool.

"Barbizon Hotel for Women," Betty said. "One forty East Sixty-third Street."

"What's the problem, you don't like men?" the cabbie asked.

Betty didn't answer, just sat back in the seat and sensed the energy beyond the window. After all the years of hearing about New York, she knew immediately that she would love the rhythm of the place: the peculiar set of expectations and flashing intensity, the steam coming from the backs of buses, the rounded streetlights, and the sense of power.

"FIRST TIME HERE?"

Now it was the red-haired clerk behind the check-in counter at the Barbizon Hotel.

Betty laughed again.

"I suppose that's 'yes,' " the redhead said.

"People keep asking me this," Betty said. "What is it, do I look that young?"

The redhead shook her head. "Just scared out of your mind," she said nastily. "Not young."

THERE WERE TWENTY-THREE FLOORS in the Barbizon Hotel, and on all but the first, no men were allowed. Looking at the clusters of single women in the lobby, and the prim, perfectly dressed elevator girl on the way up to Nine, Betty wondered if she was the only woman in the whole hotel who no longer owned a pair of gloves.

Her room, 903, was small and drab. The walls were pale yellow. A beige desk and a beige dresser stood awkwardly side by side. The beige striped fabric on the narrow bed and the draperies matched, except that the drapes had been faded by the sun. The rug was nondescript and industrial.

Betty unpacked, listening to the traffic noises rising from the street. Cars were honking and a man was cursing, and intermittently she heard what sounded like drilling. From higher up—presumably somewhere in the hotel—came the sound of a singer rehearsing, and from outside, in the hallway, there was occasional laughter and running.

At the bottom of one suitcase was the photograph of Henry that Ethel Neuholzer had taken nearly a decade before, and there was the yellow tin canister holding the roll of film that Betty had managed to take of him just this week.

Henry. The smell of his baby neck came to her, somehow. The nights in the rocking chair.

It was not as if she viewed her right to him as unequivocal.

She knew that she had left him, and under normal circumstances—if she had been like the dozen other girls in the Home, for example—she would have left the hospital a week after his birth and never seen him again. She knew, too, that if she and Fred had managed to have their own baby, she would never have come back—or, probably, ever wanted to.

"But I've seen him," she had said to the waitress at the bar that afternoon. "I know him. I helped take care of him when he was little. And I do know where he is."

BETTY'S IMMEDIATE GOAL, however, was to land the job at *Time*. Not even the best-educated women—the graduates who came directly from Wellesley or Smith or Cornell—were spared a six-month audition. And Betty—whose lack of formal education had been barely finessed (the former professor had said Betty came "well-recommended from Wilton College")—was certain to be no exception.

The tryout took place on the clip desk, which existed so that research files at *Time* could be kept current for the in-house library. Subjects ranged from the obvious—world leaders, movie stars, moguls—to the less predictable—maple syrup, shoemaking, children's toys. To work at the clip desk, you needed a soft green pencil, a sharp pair of scissors, a rubber date stamp, a stack of folders, and the ability to concentrate long past the hour when words began to fox-trot across the printed page.

Everyone worked hard. The magazine closed its pages in sections, so there was always a deadline looming, and the women—unfailingly cast into supporting roles—did more than their share of the heavy lifting. By her third week on the clip desk, Betty had already gotten the sense that if she was going to be hired full-time and, more important, if she was going to succeed once she was, then she was going to have to fake a lot of knowledge that she didn't have. Faking a past was the least of her worries. If anyone at the magazine had noticed her yet, they hadn't had time to let on.

THE RESIDENTS OF THE BARBIZON noticed her from the start. Not since her days at the practice house had Betty known more gossipy women. They rarely referred to each other by name. Whenever they talked about those not present—and that was the main staple of their conversation—they called them by room number.

"Have you seen 202's new pumps?"

"Who does 784 think she is?"

"I hear 420's got a new beau."

They were, for the most part, women in waiting: waiting for better jobs or better men or better clothes or better figures or better options. Most of the women Betty met there in her first few months in New York were working as salesgirls in department stores, or waitresses, or models. Most of them were younger than she: in their early twenties, just starting out. But Betty's age did not confer status in the Barbizon Hotel. On the contrary, some of the most vicious gossip was reserved for the older women—women in their thirties and forties—who glided through the lobby and restaurants like a ghostly Greek chorus: a future menacing any woman who didn't find a man.

In the evenings, some of the women who were dateless would gather in the lounge in front of the communal television set and watch the variety shows—Bob Hope, Ed Sullivan, Martha Raye—with their array of visiting stars: Janis Paige, Ezio Pinza, Marlon Brando, Douglas Fairbanks, Jr. From time to time, clusters of girls would start conversations, then be shushed by the others. The proper postures, trim clothing, and tidy language of daytime all went by the boards, and the women lounged and slouched and cursed and chewed gum.

Betty saw all this peripherally. Three months into her trial period at *Time*, she was no more sure than she'd been at the start that she'd end up being hired. So she was the first one at the clip desk in the morning and the last one there at night. She worked harder than she had ever worked—either as a homemaker in Australia or as a student in college or high school.

In the first few weeks, Betty had lived for the two gin and tonics that she had at the end of every day. By the fourth week, her loneliness honing her needs and dreams, she permitted herself only one. By the fifth week, before she let herself have even one sip, Betty would write down on a cocktail napkin the fifty states and their capitals, or the names of the NATO countries, or the members of Eisenhower's cabinet. Only after that—and only if she had remembered them all correctly—would she permit herself to have the drink, and mentally toast the little boy she was planning to rescue and reclaim.

Sometimes, coming home late from the office, she would pass the television room and see the silhouetted forms of girls who had fallen asleep in their chairs by the irrelevant light and noise of whatever late movie was playing, and she would shudder. Back in her room, she would bathe or shower, then wrap her flannel robe around her, set her alarm clock, turn off her lamp, and say good night to the photo of Henry. A lovely new frame for it, bought on Bendel's main floor, had been her only indulgence. Made of real red mahogany, it sat on her pale dresser in her pale Barbizon room like a tiny, personal hearth.

10

How Could I Not Like You Anymore?

By the spring of 1956, to his fourth-grade teachers, Henry Gaines had started to seem increasingly dull. Whereas once his hand had shot up in response to any question—whether or not he knew the answer, in fact—now he merely stared back, impassive. By midyear, to most of his classmates, Henry had become, to use their various terms, a goof, a nerd, a spaz, a freak.

Only in math class—when the students were routinely asked to come up to the blackboard in order to show, rather than recite, their work—did Henry reveal any willingness to participate. In front of the class, he would wield the white chalk like a conductor's baton, and he would usually write out the solution to the problem in numbers that were every bit as grand and confident as his personality now seemed small and hidden. Sometimes—especially when Mr. Gilder wasn't looking—Henry would step aside when he was done and wave his arm with a surprising flourish. And once, when Mr. Gilder left the room, Henry drew a comic-book lightning bolt, like the kind hurled by the Flash, and the lightning bolt, pointed at Mr. Gilder's desk, was trailed by whooshing lines of speed.

The buzz in the classroom blended awe with nervous worry. But just as Mr. Gilder's shadow appeared behind the mottled glass in the door's window panel, Henry used his entire right arm to erase what he had drawn, and then, returning to his seat, he used his left hand to wipe his sleeve.

It was a dazzling performance, by far the most appreciated by Mary Jane, sitting in the third row from the back. She was as careful—and clandestine—in watching Henry's artistry as he usually was in watching her.

Though they rarely talked now, she seemed to know—without his having to tell her, without, perhaps, his knowing himself—that what had changed was inside him and had nothing to do with her.

DURING RECESS, HENRY READ borrowed comic books: *The Flash, Superman, The Phantom.* Martha told him that studies showed they would poison his mind. In April, he traded his lunch so that he could own one of the books himself, and he brought it home concealed in his loose-leaf binder. Then he carried his illicit prize upstairs and shut his bedroom door.

Martha's appearance was entirely predictable. She could locate his private moments the way the Flash could find a criminal.

"Hanky?" she called. "Henry? Are you all right?"

Not waiting for an answer, she simply opened the door. There were no locks or latches on any of the doors in the practice house anymore. Years before, Martha had told Henry, he and some baby named Hazel had been locked inside by accident, and Martha had made certain that nothing like that could ever happen again.

Henry did not answer, even with Martha now standing behind him. She was a liar; it was a thought that was a reflex by now. He didn't have to answer her.

"Henry? Hanky! Why did you close this door?"

Henry did not look up from his desk until Martha had said his name two or three more times.

"Why can't I close my door?" he asked her.

"Why do you want to close your door?"

He stared at her hard. "Because I want to," he said.

He saw the redness begin in the tip of her nose, then spread to her cheeks. She pawed nervously at her silk scarf, and in the next moment he was overcome not by sympathy but by an inchoate instinct to forestall the confrontation he sensed he was not yet ready to have.

"Homework" was all he said.

She smiled, at first doubtfully, then with evident relief.

"Oh, Hanky," she said. "I was starting to think you didn't like me anymore."

"Oh, Emem," he said, though of course he knew the answer. "How could I not like you anymore?"

Tears fell down her flushed cheeks and into a pool of entirely unwarranted relief.

THOUGH MARTHA NOW usually knocked before she opened Henry's bedroom door, he took to reading his comic books in the closet anyway. It gave him a sense of added protection. But he did not simply read there. Rather, using a step stool as an easel and an overturned shoe rack as a desk, he would snap open the brass clasps on the art set that Betty had given him, and he would bask in the different rainbows, then carefully withdraw pencils, paints, or pastels. He would spend whatever time he could practicing his drawing by copying the pages of the comic books. Day by day, he drew with increasing confidence, mimicking perfectly the lines, shapes, and shadings, the tricks of crosshatched crescents for muscles, white swaths and ribbons for speed and light.

One spring day, by accident, Henry lost his balance somehow and toppled forward slightly, green Cray-Pas in hand, leaving a two-inch mark on the closet's baseboard that he decided not to clean.

The next day, quite intentionally, he retrieved the green Cray-Pas and drew another mark beside the first one, then another, and then another.

By the end of the evening, Henry had laid aside his copy of *The Flash* and had filled most of the bottom of one closet wall with a lovely, bucolic field of grass. In this field, there were blades of grass made with Cray-Pas, others with colored pencils, and others with paint. There was not a green in the entire art box that Henry didn't use, and the field that grew in his closet was, as a result, one of almost infinite depth and surprising realism. It was, Henry imagined, a place of deep colors, vast distances, and great possibilities. One day you might be swinging for the fences or digging for worms there, and the next you might be lying under an open sky, having a picnic with a mother who had always been your mother, and a father who wore a cardigan sweater and whose eyes were always twinkling with magic and mirth.

11

Silence

Whenever the doctors asked, it was difficult for Martha to pinpoint the exact month, let alone the exact day, when Henry had stopped speaking completely. Martha knew, because the school told her, that at the beginning of fifth grade he had still been talking occasionally to his classmates. But gradually a gray curtain seemed to descend on every side of him. In his increasing silence, he appeared to be frozen, like a character on a lunch box: something that was meant to be animated but no longer was.

Dr. Gardner still made seasonal visits to the practice house, always on academic pretexts and always with overtures to Henry that were simply too formal and stiff to be returned. Henry's silence appeared therefore to be part of a long-standing reticence. But Dr. Gardner did seem to notice that it was more intense than usual, and while he viewed Henry with increasing frustration, he looked on Martha with increasing doubt.

Martha, on her swift trip from embarrassment to fury, never seemed to pass through concern for Henry's well-being. She seemed to think his muteness was entirely within his control, merely a bit of pre-teenage rebellion he had cooked up in order to upset her or to make her look bad.

"Do you *want* them to take you away from me?" she asked Henry repeatedly. Ironically, it was the only question that tempted him to speak.

————

IN THE EVENINGS, especially when Martha was busy downstairs with the practice mothers and the newest baby, Henry would sit on the floor of his closet, painting or drawing on the walls. He blended copies of different superheroes into one of his own, whom he called the Ray. The Ray had no earthly ties. Like Henry, he had been born in 1946, but on a distant, dying star. He had come to earth in the spaceship that had crashed at Roswell, New Mexico, in 1947.

Like Superman, the Ray could fly and had enormous strength, but whereas Superman could only see through objects, the Ray could see through minds. He knew exactly what people were thinking and exactly what people had done. With this power to detect truth and falsehood, the Ray could isolate crimes of all kinds: even those that had not yet been committed.

Temporarily sweeping aside the long pairs of pants that formed a curtain over his canvas, Henry would use the colored pencils in his art box to draw picture after picture of the Ray on the side closet wall. Softening somewhat the angles and curves of the Flash's muscles and the shape of his face, Henry drew a superhero who had eyes like tunnels—deep and dark—with wavy lines of power emanating from their depths.

Henry drew the Ray flying like Superman, the beams of his special vision creating a swath of red light that illuminated the sinister city beneath him. Within that swath, he drew people engaged in terrible activities of all kinds: robbers holding up stores and gangsters shooting off guns and someone stuffing someone into a refrigerator.

Sometimes, Henry drew pictures of the Ray handing criminals over to the police, and sometimes he drew pictures of men and women looking afraid of the Ray, as if their crimes and lies would cost them a terrible price.

ONE DAY IN RECESS there was a cluster of fourth- and fifth-graders around Willard Estes, who was showing off a yellow-brown piece of paper with ornate writing on it that said DEED OF LAND. The deed, under the name of the Klondike Big Inch Land Company, had been offered on *Sergeant Preston* and was an official document stating that Willard was now the duly registered owner of a one-inch tract of land in the Yukon.

In Henry's mind, dreams of escape now mingled, and one form of exit did not contradict another. On one wall of the closet were his fantasies of power and effortless flight: the Ray, soaring over the dark city, seeking out evil intentions and lies. On the second wall was his original verdant field—now with a patch of Yukon land in the distance, glimmering like the image of a well in the desert. Another six months later, there was a third form of exit, namely the automobile. With intense precision, Henry had copied the latest model Lincoln from the pages of *Life:* its flamboyant green gleaming hubcaps like armored knees; its headlights nearly as wise and searching as the eyes of the Ray.

The ad said:

Why be tied down to yesterday? The one fine car designed for modern living. Powered to leave the past far behind.

AT SCHOOL, MARY JANE WAS the only one who talked to him now. All the others were tired of his not talking back.

"I know you can't help it, Henry," she said. "This is just who you have to be right now."

He nodded.

"But they don't understand you," she said.

He nodded.

"They don't understand anything."

He nodded.

"They could have turned out worse."

She had meant it as a compliment, and he understood that. Mary Jane at ten still wore her confidence the way she always had: frankly, beautifully. Her confidence was the first thing—after her eye patch—

that everyone noticed about her. It was as if the fact that she'd lost an eye entitled her to be more outspoken about what she could still see.

For his part, Henry knew that if he had absolutely had to talk—if, for example, his father suddenly appeared and asked him if he wanted to go have a catch—he could have talked. But there was nothing in his current life—not even Mary Jane's niceness or the other children's indifference—that made him feel he had to speak. And, quite to the contrary, his muteness gave him protection from Martha, a zone around him—like Superman's Fortress of Solitude. Little by little, Martha's questions decreased in number and intensity, as if she were some tentacled beast who'd been forced to retract and retreat. Henry's silence gave him a refuge, an excuse not to participate, but it was also a weapon for keeping Martha at bay. Occasionally, he would remember that his silence was a lie, and he might even start to feel guilty. But then Martha would speak with fondness about some aspect of his infancy, some wonderful moment they'd supposedly had, and he would remember all over again the lies she had told him.

From time to time, she would take him to see a new doctor, and after they left she would start to weep and to lecture Henry about how, if he didn't start speaking, the school would kick him out. Seeing Martha finger the edges of her scarf or twist a handkerchief in her hand, Henry was starting to think of that expulsion as a sublime promise.

PART THREE

Great Escapes

1

Mentally Defective

The Humphrey School had been established in the western part of Connecticut in 1858 for the purpose of housing—and, if possible, educating—boys and girls with problems ranging from mild tics and chronic inattentiveness to blindness and cerebral palsy.

The school's original name—as the current crop of students chose to remind each other whenever humanly possible—had been the Custodial Asylum for Unteachable Idiots. In the early part of the twentieth century, that had been changed to the Humphrey Asylum for the Feeble-Minded, and then, in the enlightened 1930s, to the Humphrey School for Mental Defectives.

By September of 1960, it was usually just called Humphrey. That was when Henry House—registered as Henry Gaines, fourteen years old, functionally mute—arrived for his freshman year, despite the panicked objections of Martha but on the insistence of Dr. Gardner and the advice of the public school. As far as anyone knew, Henry hadn't spoken a word since some time during the fifth grade. He was by now nearly six feet tall, skinny, stretched out, and, despite the season, already winter pale. His hair had grown somewhat darker, and its sharp contrast to his very light skin made it look as if he'd been sketched in ink but not yet colored in. He still wore khaki pants and still kept his hands tucked away in his pockets. He still had the kind of eyes that, even in silence—perhaps especially in silence—invited attention and evoked confidences.

———

THE SCHOOL HAD HIM EXAMINED by the campus doctor, who, like all the doctors back home, probed his throat, neck, and ears, and then said: "So you don't talk, eh?" as if that simple question—or perhaps the tone with which it was asked—would magically unlock the strongbox that had been holding his voice.

The headshrinkers had him do puzzles, matching words to pictures, matching blocks to shapes, matching definitions to words. They had him do computations, solve equations, and fill in missing numbers in murky, capricious sequences. All of the testers concluded that Henry was highly intelligent and that his muteness was in no way a physical symptom. Like the vast majority of students at Humphrey, Henry was, in the words of the final examiner, "either socially maladjusted or emotionally disturbed."

But he was free—if not from Martha's expectations, then at least from her ever-oppressive, ever-invasive presence. While most of the two hundred students at Humphrey arrived scared, lonely, or outright hostile, Henry coasted in on a giddy tide of liberation. While most of the others would ask, repeatedly, how long it would be before they could return home, Henry, in his silence, began immediately to calculate the number of days, weeks, months, and years that he might be able to stay. From his earliest days on the campus, he understood two things. The first was that if he ever started to speak again, he would automatically risk being deemed healthy and sent back to Martha. The second was that, until he found someplace better, he was not going to say a word.

THE HUMPHREY CAMPUS, spread over two hundred acres, had once been a working farm. The barn buildings remained, flanking the entrance on the top of a quad and housing a small gym, an art studio, an auditorium, and a dining hall. On the opposite side of the rectangle were the administration and classroom buildings, infirmary and rehabilitation center. The residential dorms ran along the connecting sides: boys' dorms on one end, girls' on the other.

Henry was assigned to Matthews, the freshman boys' dorm, which held three rooms of eight thirteen- and fourteen-year-olds, as well as a downstairs suite for the dorm parents. Henry's seven roommates were a varied lot. Three had flunked out of their schools; one was a juvenile delinquent who had been arrested three times; one was a spastic who needed help dressing and doing most things; one had had polio and was still partially paralyzed; and the last one seemed fairly normal but wispily thin in a frightening, sickish way.

It would take weeks before Henry could learn and keep straight the names and disabilities of the students in the other rooms—let alone in the other classes and dorms. But it was only a few days before Dave Epifano apparently stole the spastic boy's Parker pen; before Marc Forman and Bryan Enquist were sent to the dean's office for systematically cutting the tips off all their classmates' shoelaces; before it was apparent that Stu Stewart, the skinny one, never seemed to eat at all; and before Ben Terry, the polio victim, made it abundantly clear by night that neither his left hand nor its favorite instrument had been in the least bit affected by his illness.

At all this, Henry experienced a sort of bubbling elation. After eight years of public school, he was certainly used to being surrounded by boys with competing egos and quirks—even used to encountering, as he did in his classes, girls with differing expectations and levels of tolerance. What was new—and somewhat thrilling—was the sense that his own problems barely made an impression on anyone else. In a world where theft, indolence, shaking, paralysis, and chronic masturbation were the norm, how was a little muteness going to get in anyone's way?

"Hey, Gaines," Ben Terry said late one night that first week, when he sensed that Henry was still awake and listening in the darkness.

Henry flicked on his flashlight and looked at Ben expectantly.

Ben grinned at him nastily, pitching a wad of used tissue into the wastebasket nearby. "Hey, Gaines. Sometimes I do it five times a day. Even if you could talk, you wouldn't tell anyone, would you?"

THE PLACE WAS BEAUTIFUL. The trees on the hills in the distance were just beginning to change color, their fluffy shapes outlined vaguely in brown, as if they had somehow been dipped in tea. Fallen leaves paved the campus paths, a different-colored carpet to discover every morning, every afternoon. Martha's protectiveness had always made the Wilton campus a forbidden country for Henry. But Humphrey was immediately his to master: his in a way that no other place—except perhaps the green field in his bedroom closet—had yet been. Just having breakfast in the dining hall, then walking to a class, knowing that there was no one to avoid or to dread, was wonderful.

Henry was making exactly that trip when he first saw Charles Falk. At least six feet three, he stood in a noticeable slump, as if his body had permanently accommodated itself to the task of bending down to hear what his students were saying. His hair—wiry and black, like a Scottish terrier's—was long enough to seem like a matter of choice and not of neglect. His face—sallow but kind—reminded Henry of the scarecrow's in *The Wizard of Oz*.

When Henry first saw him, Mr. Falk had stopped on one of the paths to the dining hall, and a woman with an orange jacket and a long brown braid was balancing against him, emptying gravel from her shoe while she stood on one foot, laughing. It was September, but the light was still summer light, and Henry paused where he was walking, without really knowing he had, just staring at the way the couple's bodies leaned into each other, like trees that have grown side by side. All Henry could feel at that moment was longing, though whether it was for the woman, or simply for the chance to be part of something that intimate, was not clear even to him.

Conscious of Henry's glance, Mr. Falk looked back over the woman's brown head, slumping and smiling in such a friendly way that Henry had to turn around to see if there was someone behind him, and then he looked back, embarrassed.

———

A WEEK LATER, when the school's elective courses began, Henry discovered that Mr. Falk was going to be his art teacher.

"I'm not going to ask you to tell me why you don't talk," he said to Henry the first day. "I'm guessing everyone always asks you questions, and it must bug you like crazy."

Henry smiled, his eyes brimming with surprise and gratitude.

"I *will* ask you to tell me," Mr. Falk added. "But I'm going to ask you to draw the answer for me."

Henry hesitated. Mr. Falk handed him a set of charcoals and a thick, novel-size sketch pad.

"But not today," Mr. Falk added. "Today, we do lines and shading."

Mr. Falk turned toward the full class. "All right, everyone," he said gleefully. "Gather 'round and listen. Let me explain to you the laws of my classroom. They are few but they are essential, and woe to anyone who ignores them."

IT TURNED OUT THAT THE WOMAN with the long braid was Mr. Falk's wife, Karen. They had been married just the year before, and they did things in public—or at least on the paths of the campus—that were considered rather shocking in 1960. They held hands, sometimes kissed, referred to each other by first name, and insisted that the students do so, too—at least when no other teachers were around.

They were the dorm parents for Reynolds West, the sophomore girls' dorm, and, with Charlie at twenty-six and Karen at twenty-three, they were universally sought after by their nearly contemporary charges. From the start, Henry wished that he could wake up some morning to find the Falks having miraculously replaced the Gordons, the strict and ancient couple who were dorm parents at Matthews.

It was, for example, Dr. Gordon who stood at the entrance to Henry's dorm room nearly every afternoon and barked "Gaines! Mail!" with increasing exasperation as the rushing stream of letters from Martha showed no signs of slowing.

The envelopes gathered on Henry's desk like autumn leaves.

He opened perhaps one of every four. They seemed completely interchangeable. They all began in a similar way: "My darling Hanky." Or: "My sweet little boy." Inevitably, the first paragraph was about how much Martha missed him, how empty the practice house was without him, how she still thought it was a mistake for him to have been sent away, how no one would ever be able to help or understand him better than she.

There was always a passage to make him guilty. Veiled sometimes, but unmistakable:

"Some of the girls don't understand that it takes more than love to take care of a baby."

"Well, Tennyson said, 'Better to have loved and lost.'"

Or she would quote some popular song: "When each weary day is through, how I long to be with you."

The letters invariably ended with a plea for news.

"You have to tell me how you are."

"I don't ask for much, just a word or two from you."

"The school tells me nothing, just that you are fine."

"Why won't you write to me?"

And, most recently and darkly: "Maybe you'd rather I didn't write to you at all."

HENRY HOPED FOR A LETTER from Betty instead. In the first week, he had sent her a card—just so she would know where to write to him now. The truth was that it had been months since he had seen her New York postmark, an emblem that had always been both confusing and exciting to him. The last time had been in June, on his fourteenth birthday. For four years, Betty had sent him cards at the practice house and never stopped writing "someday" to him. As each year passed, however, Henry's wish to be rescued by his birth mother changed: sometimes it deepened; sometimes it paled. In her letters, she usually wrote bitterly about "the Wiltons," by whom she meant her father and Martha—and how they were keeping Henry from her; often she described how costly it was to live in New York, and again and again she explained how she couldn't afford to have Henry come and live with her just yet. But sometimes, too, she seemed to forget entirely that this was the plan, and she would write to Henry about how she had carelessly gone to see some Broadway show, or eaten in this or that restaurant, or shopped for shoes at Macy's. Henry's sense of his own future, consequently, had become no more comforting than his sense of the past. At times he even imagined that it would be better to have neither Martha nor Betty. How hard could it be, he often wondered, to graduate from high school and find a job and a life somewhere on his own?

In any case, the card to Betty had so far been the only piece of mail that Henry had sent. For three weeks, he ignored every one of Martha's letters. While the other boys spent their occasional free time writing to their parents or siblings—in the case of Stu Stewart, there even appeared to be a canine correspondent—Henry, after finishing his homework, would usually just sit at his desk, looking out at the courtyard and the paths of the campus below, or staring at the increasingly flamboyant Connecticut hills. His dorm-room desk was a large, heavy oak one, very old, and nearly as deep as it was wide. Sometimes Henry merely studied the patterns in the grains of its wood, trying as always to find shapes, and sometimes he reached into the bottom of its three drawers for his art supplies. The art set that Betty had given him still had most of its paints and pencils in their original sections, even in their original order; they had just been considerably shortened by use.

Decidedly newer, though prized nearly as much, was the sketch pad that Charlie had given him during the first class. "These are your Falk Books," he had told the class solemnly. In them, the students were expected to make one drawing a day.

One afternoon, while Henry was making his Falk Book sketch, Dr. Gordon materialized behind his chair, not one but three letters from Martha in his hand.

"Mr. Gaines," he said. "Doesn't the speed at which this correspondence is piling up seem a little alarming to you?"

Henry nodded in wry agreement.

"And yet my strong suspicion is that this will not change until you offer your mother some form of reply. The dean has had a complaint."

Henry raised his eyebrows.

"Yes. From your mother. She wants to know why she hasn't heard from you. She is blaming the school. She is saying she intends to come to the school in person if she doesn't hear from you within the week."

Dr. Gordon reached into Henry's art box and pried up a blue colored pencil. Henry flinched at the invasion.

"And so, Mr. Gaines," Dr. Gordon said, handing him the pencil. "I suggest that you write home."

HENRY WAITED ONE MORE DAY, and then he sat down to write.

"Dear Emem," he began.

Beyond his window, at the statue of Anderson Humphrey, Henry saw two upperclassmen standing together. The boy removed his own scarf with both hands and circled the girl's neck with it; he pulled her in close as if to kiss her, but then he did not. Something in that gesture felt satisfying to Henry.

He looked back at the page. "Dear Emem," he read, and then wrote:

I'm sorry I haven't written you sooner, but things have been very busy here. My dorm father told me that you have been calling the school, and I wish you would not do that, because it is a little bit embarrassing.

I live in a dorm with seven other boys. Some of them are very nice. I am very busy. I take English, Geometry, Biology, Art, Social Studies, and Phys Ed. My favorite subject is Art. My teacher is Mr. Falk and he is my favorite teacher.

I hope everything is all right back at Wilton, and that you have a
good group of new students starting at the practice house.
I will write to you again as soon as I can.

From,
Henry

He was particularly pleased with the sign-off. He thought the "From" offered, by omission of the more expected word, exactly as much as he wanted to give.

ONE DAY IN NOVEMBER, a letter arrived in a bright yellow envelope and the open, upright script that Henry immediately recognized as Mary Jane's.

She was still at their same public school, and she wrote with plenty of gossip, including updates on two of her closest girlfriends, who, it seemed, had taken turns wearing the same boy's pin.

"Henry," she wrote after delivering this bulletin. "Do you talk to anyone at all? I mean not just actually talk, because I know you can't yet. But is there anyone there you can really trust? Or even sort of like?"

She enclosed a photograph showing the freshman members of the high school newspaper staff. There was Mary Jane, along with Willard Estes and a few students Henry recognized, as well as some he didn't. They were mugging for the camera, wearing fedoras with cards that said PRESS.

"Thought you'd like to see the staff," Mary Jane wrote. But Henry was certain that she wouldn't have sent the photograph unless it showed her looking so unexpectedly pretty and newly mature. He wondered what the difference was. She was wearing a plaid skirt and one of those sweater sets she always liked, so it wasn't that, exactly. It took Henry a moment to realize that her hat, slanted on an angle, almost completely shadowed her eye patch—*his* eye patch, really, the proof of his monstrous nature, and the reason he'd never, until this moment, been able to look at her without guilt. Now, with half her face in shadow, he could see, as if for the first time, Mary Jane's breasts and hair and waist and, somehow most compellingly, the fullness of her innocent mouth.

AT FOURTEEN, HENRY WAS a mutiny of awkward contradictions. His cheeks were smooth, but his legs bristled with new hair. He had grown about six inches in the last eighteen months, but he had not yet begun to fill out. And his face—still lightly freckled, still dominated by his eyes—had only just started to develop angles, as if a sculptor was making his first, broad cuts in a rounded block of soft stone.

In short, Henry's body was not entirely at peace with itself, nor was he at peace with it. And though being silent saved him from some of the usual teenage embarrassments, it did not save him from the usual teenage impulses. It surprised him fiercely, furtively, nightly—and in this he felt a gleeful sense of his own potential. Sex, if he could ever achieve it, seemed to Henry the ultimate way to grow up.

Meanwhile, Ben Terry, having bowed somewhat to dorm-room pressure, had lately taken to waiting for all the boys to fall asleep before engaging in his pressing, nightly, private recreation. Tonight, Henry lay in bed, determined to outwait him. He listened as the other boys' bedside lights were clicked off one by one, and their pillow turning and sheet rustling stopped, and their breathing became even.

Eventually, in the darkness, Henry could hear the quiet flapping of Ben Terry's sheets; his soft, occasional moans; and finally his urgent, adenoidal breathing. Henry reached for the blue transistor radio that Martha had given him, and with the flesh-colored plastic earpiece providing at least one kind of privacy, he listened to music from a distant Hartford station and began to move his own hand. He was imagining Mary Jane's hair and her mouth, the smirk from the photograph, the tiny white flecks of light on her lips. He was listening to Nina Simone sing "I Loves You, Porgy," her voice hot and dusty, heavy and full. Henry looked down at the ridiculous cowboy sheets that Martha had sent with him, then closed his eyes so he wouldn't have to see them. "Don't let him handle me," Nina Simone sang, "with his hot hands." Henry heard the simple two-four beat, back and forth, up and down, like a musical seesaw, and then the spray of steel brushes on the tight tops of the drums. He heard Nina Simone sing, "Someday I know he's coming," and then four long extra beats before she sang the rest of the phrase ". . . to call me." And for every beat a stroke. "It's going to be like dying, Porgy." But it didn't feel like dying. It felt much more like life.

HE LEARNED ABOUT the Civil War in social studies, read *As You Like It* in English, sketched the cell in biology, attempted proofs in geometry, and, for the first time in his life, got to be a starting forward in basketball. Instead of languages—the school offered French and Latin for some students—Henry also spent three hours a week in Therapy, where a succession of doctors and caseworkers tried a succession of approaches that were, in 1960, considered to be advanced. They asked him to build houses on sand tables. They asked him to pick colors that went with certain feelings. Happily for him, they asked him, again and again, to draw. Draw your family. Draw your best friend. Draw yourself. Impressed by his evident talent, they failed to make much progress with their clinical interpretations. And though Henry had no problem with the art or the building or even with what he might somehow reveal about himself, he was resolute in his silence: cushioned and comforted by it.

The investigators were clearly somewhat frustrated. Finally, at the end of the first semester, they gave Henry his own tape recorder: a brand-new portable Ampro hi-fi two-speed reel-to-reel that weighed only thirty pounds and had a carrying handle on its case and a speaker built in. With this machine, they gave him a list of questions that he was supposed to try to answer daily: what had he eaten for breakfast and lunch, what were his homework assignments that night, what had he scored in the basketball game, what had he dreamed of the night before.

Dutifully, at least for the benefit of any nearby roommates, Henry would follow their instructions and unsnap the case each evening, lift off the lid, turn on the power, and push the piano-like key that said RECORD. Then he would watch the plastic reels turn, as pointless as the wheels of a stationary bicycle, and the skinny brown tape would transfer silence to silence. After ten minutes or so, Henry would push the key for STOP and then the key for REWIND, and then he would carefully place the cover back on and put the machine away.

One evening, when Henry opened the case, the take-up reel was not empty, so he pushed REWIND and then, somewhat warily, PLAY. As he suspected, the recorder had been used. The tape started with a variety of scatological songs, segued into a sweatily read passage from a well-known and much perused issue of *Playboy*, then featured someone saying "This is Henry Gaines" and then a gap, with a few staticky remnants, for what had clearly been an attempt at a monologue in Henry's voice. After that evident erasure, the tape ended with the unmistakable sounds of Ben Terry doing what Ben Terry did best.

The silence Henry's roommates had managed to maintain while they waited for him to listen to their masterwork devolved into great bursts of laughter and cursing, and Henry offered up his best wry smile. In truth, he was wounded, and he stayed behind when the others went off to dinner.

Alone in the room, he sat back down at his desk and looked at the list of the therapists' questions. All traces of the evening light had faded, and Henry for the first time found himself wondering if he might be able to protect himself better with a voice than without one. The last time he had allowed himself to speak to anyone, he had been a boy of ten. With determination born of betrayal and nurtured by adolescence, he had stayed silent while around him—first in Pennsylvania and now at Humphrey—his classmates' voices had broken and squeaked and slipped, bat- and birdlike, out of their throats. He wondered if he would sound anything like the deep baritone—he guessed it was Epifano—who had supposedly impersonated him on the tape.

With the unusual absence of chaos around him, Henry considered the first question.

What did you have for breakfast?

He pushed the RECORD button.

Eggs, he thought. The word first formed in his head, a capital *E* and two round *g*s and a sinuous *s*. The word took on the shape of an egg, encapsulated in an oval, clean and bold. *Eggs,* he thought. The word would require him to open his mouth as if he was trying to show all his front teeth. *Eggs,* he thought. He made his lips pull back. The brown tape spun around and around. The red power light flickered warmly. But much to Henry's intense surprise, he couldn't make a sound.

2

Attachment

Martha Gaines stood at the doorway of the practice house and expertly shifted the new baby to her left arm and opened the door with her right. It was September 1961, and the students would be arriving in an hour or so, and that would give her just enough time to record the baby's measurements in a brand-new practice house journal.

"Welcome home, Huck," she said to the baby as she stepped inside the house. She adjusted the baby's yellow cotton blanket, but then, instead of carrying him straight to the nursery, she veered off to the living room.

Martha's heart was broken, and her step was unsure.

Nothing was right. Heather, the previous year's newborn, had contracted an acute infection at only thirteen months and, after a four-week stay in the pediatric wing of the Titusville Hospital, had been returned to the Franklin Orphans' Home. Martha had had to wait until fall for a new baby, and even so, he was just as young as Henry had been.

Her jacket still on, her purse still slung over her left wrist, Martha sank into one of the armchairs and held the baby before her, in both hands, like an open book. The baby was asleep and showed no signs of stirring. Martha knew the immediate tasks, but for the moment they seemed impossible. Frozen in place, the baby before her, Martha stared ahead, transfixed by—but temporarily helpless before—what looked like a faint handprint on the living room wall.

By the time the students arrived half an hour later, Martha had pulled herself together enough to put the baby, unmeasured, into the crib, and to locate her attendance list. As they came to the door one and two at a time, Martha tried not to look as weary as she felt. The three returning students greeted her and each other with warm reunion hugs. The two new ones seemed polite enough, but it did not take Martha long to notice that one of them had a full cast on her arm.

"What happened to your arm?" Martha asked.

The girl giggled and, using the other hand to tuck some extra-long bangs behind her ear, said: "I was playing lacrosse."

"Lacrosse."

"I was trying out for the team. I wasn't *going* to try out for the team, but then this boy who was watching—he said he thought that I ran very well. And so I—"

"Excuse me," Martha said coldly. "What is your name?"

"It's Lila, Mrs. Gaines. Lila Watkins."

"Lila. And how were you thinking you would now handle this course?" Martha asked.

Lila's facial expression changed from amusement to confusion.

"This is why I'm here," she said. "This is what I signed up for, Home Ec. Right?" She looked around to the other girls, as if they could help her in some way.

Martha merely glared. Perhaps a decade ago she would still have had the patience for this. But patience was out of the question now.

The baby began to wail.

"Oh," Lila said. "Is the baby here already? Can we see her? I mean, see him? I mean, is it a girl or a boy?"

"His name is Huck," Martha said, "and his nap doesn't end until one o'clock."

"But he's crying," the other new girl said. "Shouldn't we pick him up?"

Martha exhaled audibly. "If you don't train him now, you can't train him later," she said.

Martha walked to the front door, opened it, and made a sweeping gesture with her hand.

"This isn't playtime," she said to Lila. "This course requires actual commitment and effort. Come back when you have two working arms." She shut the door before Lila could offer any reply.

IT HAD BEEN FIFTEEN YEARS since Martha had carried Henry, wrapped in his green cotton blanket, into the practice house; fifteen years since she had surprised herself by kissing his tiny, perfect face and feeling the beginnings of an ancient hunger appeased. It had been thirteen years since he had stayed as her own—and one since he had been ripped away from her.

Since then, Martha's days had been a study in self-discipline. There was almost nothing she did anymore that didn't demand an act of will. The problem was not only Henry's loss and the daily surprise of her loneliness. The problem was also physical. Whether it was rheumatism or arthritis Martha wasn't sure, and she hated seeing doctors because they always seemed so condescending. But whatever the cause, the reality was that Martha's body hurt. Sometimes it felt like her bones, and other times like her muscles. Sometimes it was her calves and shoulders, other times her back or feet. Movement, which had never been something she had achieved with grace, felt more and more difficult as the months and days went by. She was sixty-two years old now, and she would think twice before negotiating the stairs; then at the top, she would find herself winded. The bed seemed higher, the armchairs lower. Sometimes she would catch herself rubbing her hands, and only then would she realize how stiff and sore they were. Ache and exhaustion pervaded every part of her.

In growing measure, though, so did self-doubt. By 1961, Dr. Spock's had been the prevailing voice in American child rearing for fifteen years. Martha now kept her copy of his book in plain view and had ceased to argue—much—when students inevitably and reverently quoted him. Martha's original rules—the ones she had struggled so long to impart and enforce—had started to bend. She told herself that, like everyone else, she should be allowed to improve and refine her methods. But deep down, she was nagged by worry—a worry that had as many faces as there were practice house journals upstairs. If she had, in fact, been wrong in her methods, then what did it mean that she had sent sixteen babies raised by those methods—and dozens of would-be mothers—out into the world?

It wasn't just Spock. The winter before last, Martha had seen a documentary called *Mother Love* in which a psychologist named Harry Harlow stated his belief that touch was more important than food in the forming of early attachments. His experiments showed that rhesus monkey babies clearly preferred cloth surrogates they could cuddle to wire surrogates that gave milk. When they were frightened, the baby monkeys shook and shrieked if they had only wire surrogates, but they ran quickly to the cloth surrogates for what Harlow called "contact comfort."

Martha had tried to dismiss from her mind the images of those tiny baby monkeys, scrunched up on their terry-cloth surrogates, or straddling them in full-body hugs, or nuzzling their crude wood faces. She had spent two decades teaching that a baby needed to be fed and kept clean, not cuddled and coddled as if somehow just the state of being alive required some kind of sympathy.

But the notion that the attachments babies made in the first year of their lives could matter that much: this notion was starting to haunt her, especially with Henry having been shipped off to a special school. At one point Harlow had declared that a cuddly cloth surrogate could be every bit as comforting as an actual birth mother. But now, Martha read that even the cloth-mothered monkey babies had eventually gone mad. In the absence of a single, consistent, living mother, they rocked ceaselessly, banged their heads, and chewed off their own fingers. Some of them shrieked and shouted. But others simply fell silent.

3

Art Lessons

By the fall of 1961, the muteness that Henry had thought he was feigning had somehow become a real condition. Occasionally—if he was alone in the showers, or walking across an empty part of the campus—Henry would be able to whisper a word or two to himself. But in truth he had almost forgotten how it felt to form words anywhere but in his head, where they appeared, most often, as combinations of letters.

In the absence of expression, what Henry observed became more acute, and the natural world a perpetual crowd scene. Beak-nosed women appeared in cloud formations, and baby faces in dimpled potatoes. A stone kicked up in the road by a passing car revealed the profile of an old man, and, in the lines of cracked river ice, Henry saw a stick figure of himself.

Sometimes, Henry wasn't sure if he was seeing art in nature or nature in art. A straight but puffy line of clouds in the sky at dusk looked to him as if it had been painted on with a wet brush. The mountains looked sculpted. The pond looked glazed.

Whenever he had time between classes or after meals, he filled his Falk Book with these images, and his best days were the ones on which he had art class.

THE ASSIGNMENT HENRY CARED MOST ABOUT was the multipart one that Charlie announced during the very first class of sophomore year.

For what would be counted as the equivalent of a term paper and a final exam, the students were asked to create self-portraits using no fewer than five different perspectives, or "lenses," as Charlie called them. The obvious approach—the one that would quickly be adopted by most of the students—was to do a front, a back, and two side views, and, for the fifth panel, some less formal pose: playing soccer, say, or walking on a beach. Henry, after hearing the assignment, held up the five fingers of one hand with a questioning look.

"Yes, five," Charlie said.

Then Henry, to Charlie's evident delight, held up both hands.

"Yes, you can do ten if you like," he said.

Then Henry flashed both hands twice.

Charlie, smiling, said, "Why don't you see what you have time for?"

Henry spent that first class doing a detailed painting of his left eye. In patches of tempera, he laid out the bright fluidity, the orange-specked liveliness, the green serenity. In his next class, he focused on his bangs—the side-swept riot of browns and reds that, magnified on Henry's canvas, looked more like his closet's field of grass than it did like a partial self-portrait. So it went. A dozen eyelashes. The corner of his mouth. His eyes again: singly, in tandem.

Back in his room, in his Falk Book, Henry planned and sketched, rearranging the fragments of his self-portrait like the tiles in a sliding number puzzle, ordering and reordering them, trying to find the right sequence. In the studio, his paintings were multiplying much faster than the usual class times would have allowed, and Charlie knew that rules were being broken.

"When's he doing all this extra work?" Karen asked Charlie one morning when he showed her the pieces of Henry's self-portrait—at least a dozen of them, by now, propped up along the studio's back shelf.

"At night, I'm guessing," Charlie told her.

"You'll both get in trouble," Karen said.

Charlie grinned.

"You could get him expelled, you know—if he's out of bed after curfew."

"You know he was brought up by only women? Watching his every move and then handing him over again and again?"

He had told this to Karen before, and so she gave him a barely indulgent look.

"I'm not sure you'll be able to make that up to him, darling," Karen said.

"He hasn't spoken to anyone in *years*," Charlie said.

"I know."

Charlie held up one of Henry's paintings—the corner of a mouth.

"He's used to everyone watching him."

Charlie showed Karen another panel, no doubt intended as the central one. It showed a circle of faces, an audience of attentive eyes. "I could be the one he talks to," Charlie said.

More paintings appeared. Two or three nights a week, Henry was sneaking into the darkened art studio, working by a single lamp, making sure to clean his brushes even more thoroughly than he did in class. He loved the quiet, the sense that he was safe in some embryonic way, and he loved the exotic smells of the turpentine and paints, which forever after would fill him with a sense of freedom and hope.

A SOPHOMORE NAMED DAISY FALLOWS was waiting for Henry outside the art studio one night in October, her arms crossed, her red flannel shirt collar turned up, her red hair flying.

She was extremely small, and Henry had grown even taller since his freshman year, so it wasn't until she came up close to him that he really could see her eyes, which, it turned out, were flashing and filled with fun. She tilted her lips up just perceptibly, but he had absolutely no doubt what she wanted, and so he kissed her, feeling for the first time in his life the soft tumble of another person's tongue in his mouth.

It was more or less exactly the way he had imagined it would be, except for one surprise, which was Daisy taking his face in her scratchy gloved hands and saying, "I figured you were the safest, Henry, because

I can trust you." Then she looked back over her shoulder and giggled. "I mean, after all, it's not like you're going to *talk*."

IT WAS CLEAR TO HENRY that Charlie knew he was spending extra time in the art studio. Sometimes, Henry would find a box of Lorna Doones or a bag of potato chips. It was also clear that these gifts must not be acknowledged, but, in a completely surprising way, it now seemed to Henry that someone neither intrusive nor possessive was watching over him.

Nothing in Henry's upbringing had prepared him for the kindnesses that both Charlie and Karen Falk now regularly bestowed on him. To Henry, who was first invited to Reynolds West to have tea and to look at their prized Matisse lithograph, it had never seemed possible that home could be a place where one felt free.

Like the dorm parents in the other houses, the Falks had three small rooms on the first floor: living room, bedroom, and kitchen with dining alcove. To Henry, the apartment seemed palatial, partly because the Falks had emptied it of all the stodgy, traditional furniture that was standard in the other houses, and had instead surrounded themselves in a Bohemian blend of blond modern wood and light avocado fabrics, stacks and shelves of books and records, and different colors on every wall: black, brown, purple, and navy in the living room; red, orange, yellow, and rust in the kitchen; lavender, pink, mint, and robin's egg blue in the bedroom. To Henry, being in the Falks' home was like being inside his art box.

The traditional decoration was limited to just two objects. In the kitchen, there was an enormous campaign poster of John F. Kennedy that was red, white, and blue, under a black-and-white photo of Kennedy's face. Sometimes, when Henry sat in the kitchen with Charlie and Karen, he would stare up at the photograph, with Kennedy's white-white smile and his side part and poufy dark hair; and the face would splinter into shapes and planes and lines, until Kennedy became not a man but a collection of parts to draw.

The other piece of art in the Falks' apartment was the Matisse litho-graph: a wedding gift from some wealthy relative and clearly, without any doubt, their prized possession. It was not a large picture, not even a foot high and not even two feet wide, and it was not particularly colorful—at least not compared to the rest of the rooms and to Ma-tisse prints that Henry had seen in Charlie's art books. This one had only two colors: the mustard yellow of the flat background and the black of the lithographed lines depicting fourteen large-petaled blos-soms floating abstractly behind a robed woman who sat with a child on her lap. Apart from the fact that neither the woman nor the child had any facial features at all, what made the image unusual was that the child was holding its handless arms stretched out to either side.

The Matisse held the place of honor above the living room fire-place, in which the Falks, one autumn Sunday, were letting Henry help them paint a fire.

"It's called *La Vierge et l'Enfant*," Charlie said, gesturing up to the lithograph.

"That means 'The Virgin and Child,' " Karen chimed in, helpfully.

Henry blushed slightly at the word *virgin* and looked at the floor.

"Virgin, you idiot, like the Virgin Mary," Karen said.

Henry pantomimed the Christ figure.

"Exactly," Karen said. "That's why the baby is shaped like that."

Henry stared at the lithograph, then went back to painting the fire, making flames of red, orange, yellow, and purple, licking up at the back and sides of the brick.

ONE MONTH LATER, on a frigid November night, in the back corner of the art studio, Daisy Fallows took a pack of Viceroys from the waist-band of her pink denim slacks and gave Henry his first cigarette. Pre-tending he had smoked before, he nonetheless reeled from the assault on his throat and lungs, but he managed neither to cough nor to vomit, and instead concealed his imbalance by kissing Daisy and slid-ing a shaking hand under her sweater.

An hour after that kiss began, an hour during which they had explored, it seemed to Henry, every possible variation in the choreography of kissing, Daisy looked at her wristwatch and let out a little shriek when she saw that it was nearly two. Then she retied the shoelaces on her saddle shoes and went skipping out into the night, a burst of cold air rushing in behind her. Moments after that, a cigarette butt rolled into a puddle of turpentine, and a small excitement of flames leapt up toward a roll of canvas.

At least three minutes too late, Henry grabbed the first object he could find to try to smother the burning canvas, but what he found was a roll of newsprint, and that went up too.

EVEN AS HENRY WATCHED IN FEAR, he could not help noticing the extraordinary profusion of colors that the fire created. At each new cluster of supplies, there would be a hissing and popping, and then bright yellows, greens, and magentas would emerge from the flames, like overblown flowers. Then came the moment—Henry later would remember its details precisely—when he went from thinking that the path of the fire would stop to understanding that there was no way it could.

It was the moment when he realized that there were choices to be made. On the far counter of the room, and on the wall and shelves behind it, were most of the class's finished artwork: pinch pots left out, ironically, to dry; canvases not yet hung; the Falks' Matisse, surrounded by the copies and variations that Charlie had asked the class to make just this morning; panels of Henry's and his classmates' self-portraits, three months' worth of fragments not yet assembled in any permanent way.

Transfixed, Henry looked before him at the shelves of paints, Cray-Pas, and palettes; the glass-paned cabinets holding the empty pineapple juice cans with their bouquets of brushes; the rows of articulated figures, seeming to bow their heads now as the flames blackened their wooden backs.

He could feel the heat—not frightening, really, but strangely inviting. It occurred to him, passingly, not to fight it. He had a thought of being subsumed in all the colors. If he escaped the fire, he would have to face Charlie and Karen. And the guys. And no doubt be expelled. And be sent back to Martha. The eyes of the women in his central drawing stared at him from the back wall, daring him to become un-witnessed. Instead, he took a deep, smoky breath, grabbed what he could from the far wall and shelf, and then ran back toward the door. Out in the snow, he tried to say the word: *fire*. The sound didn't even catch in his throat. There really was no sound. But Henry knew he was the only possible siren. It was two o'clock in the morning, and the nearest dorm wasn't near enough for sleeping people to be awakened by smells of smoke or sounds of fire or sights of a palette, however sur-prising, of brilliantly colored flames. Then Henry dropped what he'd rescued on one of the benches in the yard, ran to Reynolds West, and pounded on the door. There was no response. Finally, what began as a whisper broke into an audible croak.

"Fire."

He said it again.

"Fire."

He said it loudly.

"Fire!"

Charlie started running as soon as he understood the word. Karen, with Charlie's winter coat in hand, loped after him awkwardly, trying to fling the coat over his shoulders while the slippers she was wearing made her slide in the snow.

By the time they arrived at the studio, the heat was too intense for them to get near the place. They ran to Reynolds East to call the fire department, and from then on, it was merely a question of waiting and watching while the red town fire truck, reminding Henry un-avoidably of the one he and Martha had played with when he was lit-tle, rushed in on the usually off-limits campus lanes.

The hoses were taken out even before the truck had come to a stop. But it was clear there would be no chance of salvage. Even as the front side of the studio began to resemble the alligatored skin of a log near embers, Henry again noticed the incredible profusion of colors and saw that the sky behind the studio looked yellow and green. As the right corner of the roof caved in, he couldn't help thinking that the building, still burning, looked as if its top corner was being erased.

Gradually, students and teachers began to gather, tumbling out of their dorms, pulling their bathrobe belts tight against the cold. Some wore slippers, others boots; some had thrown sweaters over their pajamas; a few were fully dressed. They formed a semicircle, no different from the ones they'd formed on the bonfire nights in the early fall, when they'd all roasted hot dogs, sung school songs, and put on skits.

By the time Daisy appeared in the circle, it seemed to Henry that it had been weeks or months since he had seen her last. Later, she would complain to him that his look was first angry, then blank, and he would pretend to be sorry for both, but in truth he would want to get as far away from her as he could. It would take him years to figure out that the intimacy of sharing a secret guilt was more than he could bear.

For the moment, his only thought was whether Charlie was going to turn him in and send him back to Martha.

WHEN THE SUN ROSE, it seemed there was no color left anywhere in the world, as if the fire had consumed not only the watercolors, oil paints, and acrylics in the studio but also all that they could have created. The gray of the smoke and the gray of the ash and the gray of the late autumn skyline all seemed to settle around the ground where the studio had been. The smell—throat-stinging, bitter—was of chemicals and ash.

At about seven in the morning, the dean climbed up onto one of the stone benches and announced that all classes would be canceled for the coming day, and that students should spend their time in their rooms, relaxing as they wished to, and making up for lost sleep. The dean suggested it wouldn't hurt if some students used the time to tidy their rooms, study for upcoming tests, and ponder whether they had any clues as to what or who might have started the fire. Then the dorm parents began to usher the students back to their rooms. The firemen stood ready for any last bursts of flame. But there was really nothing left to burn. All that remained of the studio was the soggy gray and brown earth, a few pieces of glass, and the metal file cabinets. Eventually, as students looked on from their windows, the firemen climbed into their truck and carefully—perhaps even somewhat abashedly—backed out of the quad.

Returning to their apartment after making sure that all their girls were accounted for in Reynolds West, the Falks settled into the kitchen, where Karen put up a kettle for tea and Charlie took out and filled a pipe.

After a long silence, she said: "It had to have been him."

Charlie barely nodded.

"Charlie. It had to."

"I know."

They sipped their tea.

"Want to eat something?" she asked him.

He shook his head.

"Do you think he did it on purpose?"

"Of course not."

"He was the one who yelled 'Fire,' though."

"I know."

"Do you think he could talk all along?"

"No. I don't know. No," Charlie said.

"What's upsetting you most? The Matisse? The studio? Or him?"

"What to do," Charlie said, and stood up, absentmindedly reaching for the cups and putting them in the kitchen sink, not quite realizing that his wife was still drinking her tea.

"Thanks," she said sarcastically.

"You're welcome," he said, missing her point completely.

It was not until they walked into the living room that they saw the Matisse hanging over the mantel, safely back where it belonged.

4

When It Comes to That

The photograph of Henry in the square frame—the personal hearth beside which Betty had warmed herself on so many lonely nights—remained, six years after she'd moved to New York, in its special place on her Barbizon Hotel dresser. Bare-bottomed and shiny-eyed, Henry still held his pose—just scarcely up on a chubby arm, turning back toward the women, the attention, the light. By now, however, in the fall of 1961, the photo had been joined by several others, in simpler frames. One was from the roll Betty had taken in Franklin that long-ago autumn, when Henry had squirmed on the school-yard steps, unwilling to offer a smile. Another—this one an eight-by-ten glossy—showed six laughing women, Betty among them, pretending to christen a copy machine in the new *Time* research library.

But the photograph that now sat in front of all the others was actually just the cover of a two-inch-square book of matches, one of those pricey, enforced souvenirs from a nightclub called the Latin Quarter. The photo, in black and white, showed Betty under the possessive arm of a man named Gregory J. Peterson. Peterson was editor of *Time*'s arts section, where Betty had been working since being hired as a full-time researcher. He was a tall man in his late forties with prematurely white hair that he swept away from his eyes at regular intervals with a grand, patrician hand. And he had become—despite his position, his wife, his three children, and his unpredictable, often unpleasant moods—the undisputed focus of Betty's life. So far, the only times she had sensed any interest from him had been on a few of the magazine's closing nights, when a bunch of writers and researchers would follow him to some loud, bright restaurant and compete to see who could make him laugh. The night at the Latin Quarter—the night of the matchbook—had been one of those nights when it seemed as if everything Betty said and did was delightful and full of meaning to Greg. He had looked at her with such intensity. A kind of appreciation, she thought.

And so on more and more evenings, rather than going to bed with dreams of reclaiming Henry in her head, she fell asleep replaying conversations she'd had with Greg, wondering at the things that had caught his attention, trying to find the pattern, the key. Sometimes she would wake from a dream and then lie very still in the dark, small room, allowing herself to imagine what it would be like to be with Greg always, nestled under his arm, having it understood that he'd chosen her—and not just for this meal or for that story.

Other times, turning on her bedside lamp, she would pick up the book of matches. The image of the two of them—spanning the shiny cover—was printed across the thick, wide cardboard matches inside as well, so that if one were to use any of the matches, it would be like ripping planks from a muraled fence. Betty knew that she would never light a single one.

SO IT WAS NOT FOCUSING on Henry that brought her any closer to her hope of reclaiming him. Nor was it continued discipline with her drinking, her study of current events, or even her habits at work. What pushed her closer to her dream of reclaiming Henry was the still formidable—and now more fashionable—presence of Ethel Neuholzer, the lively, snack-toting girl who had taken that first picture of Henry so long ago.

Ethel, it turned out, was working for *Life* magazine, *Time*'s popular sister publication, and it was after both magazines' move to their new building on Sixth Avenue that Betty first encountered—or re-encountered—her. A forty-foot-long bronze and glass geometric mural was being installed in the lobby, amid much confusion. When Betty first saw her, Ethel was standing at one of the steel-lined elevator banks. She was wearing black capri pants and a black turtleneck—like Audrey Hepburn in *Funny Face*, except about twice the width. Hanging across her chest was a pair of professional cameras, one with an enormous lens. At her feet was a large black equipment bag and what looked like a leopard-skin coat.

She was talking to a young man whom Betty took to be her assistant. "I want to find a way to get the sense of the scale," she was telling him.

Impulsively—perhaps a bit overdramatically—Ethel sprinted across the lobby and then squatted at the other end, making a frame with her hands, through which she looked intently. "Let's try this," she said, and then, through the pretend viewfinder she had created, she saw Betty looking on.

Ethel glanced away for a moment, then back, and then smiled and started walking quickly along the gleaming elevator bank toward Betty.

"I saw your name on the *Time* masthead," Ethel said wonderingly. "But I really couldn't imagine that it was the same Betty Gardner."

Betty shrugged, but before her shoulders had even lowered, Ethel had locked them in an exuberant embrace.

"I'm photographing this thing for the magazine," Ethel said, unnecessarily. "Do you like it? I don't think I get it."

"You work for *Time*?" Betty asked, confused.

"No. *Life*," Ethel said. "But don't be too impressed. This is just for the newsletter."

"Oh."

"They did actually make me a full photographer about five years ago," Ethel said. "But they still send me out to do the piddly stuff."

"Miss Neuholzer?" the assistant asked.

"I'm in your way," Betty said, and started to leave.

"No, listen, I'm sorry," Ethel said, and linked her arm through Betty's. For a moment, she looked exactly the way Betty had remembered her: soft, kind, and lively. Then, as if reading Betty's thoughts, Ethel reached down and rummaged in her big black purse to pull out a snack. But instead of a Clark Bar, she extracted a can of Metrecal.

"Metrecal?" Betty asked.

"Don't get me started," Ethel said. "But listen. Want to lunch sometime and eat real food?"

"That'd be nice."

"No, I really mean it. Better than that. Where are you living?"

"The Barbizon," Betty said. "Why?"

"The *Barbizon*?" Ethel said. "Might as well be the morgue."

"It's not that bad," Betty said.

"It's not? I heard that men can't take the elevators."

Betty nodded. "They can't," she said.

"We've got to get you out of there. Look. I'm semi-serious about this. Move in with me."

Betty laughed. "What?" she said.

"I'm living on Forty-eighth Street, and I can't afford the rent, and I'm never there anyway."

She said all this while walking away, toward her assistant, so it was nearly impossible for Betty to judge if there was any meaning behind her words. "Wait," Ethel added. "I have something for you."

She dashed over to her bag, reached in, and pulled out a pair of blue sparkle sunglasses.

"Someone gave me these. They look terrible on me. But they'll look great on you," she said.

With terrific deftness, she placed the glasses over Betty's startled eyes and waltzed around one more time, waving a hand behind her back.

Out on the street, in one of the huge plate-glass windows of the new building, Betty caught her reflection with the sunglasses on. Almost glamorous, she thought.

BETTY MOVED IN WITH ETHEL a few weeks later, exulting in the promise of freedom from the Barbizon women, of proximity to Ethel's exuberance, and, finally, of a place where a teenage boy would be, if not easily accommodated, at least not forbidden to enter. But in the meantime, the focus under Ethel's tutelage was strictly confined to fully grown men: to Greg Peterson, in Betty's case, and to a *Life* sales manager named Tripp Whitehouse in Ethel's. Ethel had been sleeping with Tripp Whitehouse for three years now. In private, she referred to him as "my lover," which almost made Betty long for the Barbizon. Tripp was, inch for inch, one of the least impressive men Betty had ever met. Red-nosed, prematurely balding, slow in both motion and apparent comprehension, Tripp was nonetheless to Ethel the epitome of glamour and, like Greg for Betty, the main player in the ongoing narrative of her life. Ethel spent a good deal of her time with him in one of the hotel suites that Time-Life kept for visiting staff and guests. Betty was never sure how they arranged that, but two or three nights out of every seven, Ethel did not come home.

There was so much about Ethel that seemed to promise glamour. Ethel owned her own china set. She had a pink Lady Sunbeam that dried her hair in a vinyl cap. The furniture in her apartment was all low and lean and modern, made of walnut with canvas webbing, as if at any moment someone might have to lie down, or neck. True, she had never married, and she was childless and living alone at the end of a decade during which most people in their twenties had paired up as if they were Ark-bound. True, Ethel was, like Betty, working absurdly long hours and earning absurdly little pay. But she made these things seem like choices: the preferences of a career woman hitting her stride in mid-century.

It would take Betty months—months of actually living with Ethel and watching her journalistically—before she realized just how much of her time Ethel spent yearning to be someone else. This was the reason for the leopard-skin coat and the sparkle sunglasses and the stack of magazines constantly rising on and beside her night table: *House & Garden, Architectural Digest, Esquire, Vogue, Bazaar.* It was not until later that Betty realized that Ethel actually used Lustre-Creme shampoo because Elizabeth Taylor advertised it, and Lux soap because Kim Novak did. But Ethel's relative naïveté in such matters underscored her optimism, and Betty found herself hoping that some of that would rub off on her.

THERE WERE DAYS at the office when Greg left long before Betty did, and it would strike her—in the vacuum created by his absence—that work meant virtually nothing to her without him to see her do it. She was fighting off just this lost sense on an early December evening when most of the offices were already empty and dark. The bullpen, where Betty worked, had taken on a sort of fragmented appearance, with selected desks lit up like panels of a dark comic strip. Betty was working on a story about a voice instructor who believed he had discovered a way to teach people to sing in all ranges. Apart from checking the usual spellings and dates, she was supposed to find out the notes of Maria Callas's singing range, the year in which the practice of castrating tenors had been ruled illegal, the names of Mozart's sisters-in-law, and the name of Giuseppe Colla's fiancée. And since Betty had begun the day not having heard any of the names in the story except Mozart's, it had definitely been an uphill slog.

She heard Greg's voice before she saw him. She was used to listening for that voice, and then, in the sixty to ninety seconds it took for him to get from the hallway to the bullpen, she would always wet her lips, smooth her hair, and pinch her cheeks. Tonight she was so tired that she thought for a moment she'd imagined his presence, and before she realized that she wasn't imagining him, it was too late, and he was standing in front of her desk. He was drunk. The hum of the cleaning woman's vacuum came nearer and nearer as she made her way up the hall. Greg insisted Betty leave the story, and he took her downstairs to La Fonda del Sol, the restaurant on the main floor of the Time-Life Building. It had been designed by someone famous—not just the room but the plates and napkins, the menus, matchbooks, and cigarette holders. Whenever Betty went there, she felt the tingly sensation that she was immersed in a metropolitan life that almost anyone would have envied. The ice in the glasses was rounded and clear, the conversation was newsy, and everything felt sophisticated, classy, and urbane.

For months, the papers had been filled with reports on the trial of Adolf Eichmann, and although Betty still had at best only a vague understanding of the legal intricacies and issues involved, she had learned in her years at *Time* how to nod intelligently and listen intently, and she had learned how to ask questions that seemed to demand intelligent answers. Tonight, as she heard Greg go on about the likelihood of a verdict this week, she tightened her lips into a concerned pout. In truth, she could not have felt less about the prospect of a verdict this week. But she was enjoying the idea of being someone who could lean forward into the light of a candle and look as if she cared.

"Will it come to that?" she asked Greg. She opened her eyes wide, knowing her eyes could pull him in. She took a sip of her white wine. Just her first glass of the evening. Just a glass of white wine. Elegant and ladylike and smooth. She played with a book of matches that had the cheerful face of the sun on it, giving her a benediction. She already knew she would put this matchbook next to the one on her dresser.

"WILL IT COME TO THAT?" Betty asked Greg again an hour later. They were on their desserts, and it was Betty's fourth glass of wine. She had forgotten that this was the question she'd asked him about Eichmann. Now she was asking it about the cover story, which Greg was saying probably wouldn't be finished until Thursday or Friday, and he might have to edit it, and Betty might have to help check it, depending on the schedule of the medical editor and his team.

"Will it come to that?"

"You're repeating yourself, honey," Greg said.

"What'd I say?"

"You said, 'Will it come to that?' " Greg said.

"I did?"

"Several times," Greg said. "But that's all right." He patted her hand with his own. "I have a question for you, too."

"What is that?"

He leaned in close, so close that she could see the yellow stains on the edges of his canine teeth. "Tell me," he whispered with unmistakable innuendo. "What would you like it to come to?"

THEIR FIRST KISS was in the elevator—silver and cold—on the way back up to the magazine. Their second was half an hour later, after Greg had taken her to the Waldorf, which was twelve short blocks and a large decision away from her apartment.

Not counting her years at the Barbizon, the only other time that Betty had been in a hotel room had been on her way home from Australia. Then she had been on a mission to reclaim her son. Now she had no mission, or in any case chose to pretend she had none. She pretended instead to be Greg's mission, because that was the best way to arrange things in her mind.

Up until the kisses, he had been a man with a certain kind of power, and after the kisses, he was a man with a different kind of power, but now she had power as well.

There was a marble fireplace with overflowing planters of ivy, and there was a vase of lonely roses on a side table. Beside that were two striped, silk-covered chairs, and across from them an ebony cabinet holding a fancy hi-fi. The ceilings were high and the drapes heavy. Greg's breath smelled of gin and his neck of cologne. He had a cotton handkerchief in his breast pocket, and an elegant pair of shoes that hit the thick carpet silently as he pulled off first one and then the other.

Betty stood by the window, wondering if sex would finally move her—as it hadn't, in truth, with Fred and as it hadn't, in truth, with Henry's father. She could not remember his face now, only the movie they'd seen together that night in Pittsburgh so long ago now: *A Tree Grows in Brooklyn*. In those days, she had wanted to be more like the hardworking, future-planning mother in that film than the drink-loving, flighty father. Now she wasn't sure. He did have a lot of fun, that father.

Greg was rough with her—from his cheek, which was stubbly with midnight, to his hands, which grasped her wrists and lifted them over her head, to the rest of him pushing in and against her. She tried to feel something good, to be swept up the way she had read that women could be. Only at the last moment, as he shouted and then sighed, did she feel some sort of pull, a shudder, something that wanted or needed more.

5

Henry and the Falks

Back in her spot over the mantel, the Mary in the rescued Matisse seemed to offer a peaceful benediction, perhaps a thanks for her safe return. Henry looked up at her, waiting for some freshman girls to leave before he joined the Falks in their kitchen and said out loud the sentence he'd been rehearsing since the fire, three days before.

Finally, the door closed and Henry sat down at the kitchen table.

"I can talk," he said.

The Falks looked at each other before they looked at him.

"Yeah," Charlie said. "We kind of figured that out when we heard you yell 'Fire.' "

"Did anyone else hear me?" Henry asked. He looked down at the table and drew patterns from the water rings. He was doing his best to seem casual, though the sound of his own voice was nearly as foreign to him as it was to the Falks.

"Apparently not," Charlie said.

"We don't know yet," Karen said at the same moment.

Henry glanced up, scanning each of their faces, trying to parse the difference between their responses.

Charlie puffed on his pipe unsuccessfully, then pulled an ashtray across the kitchen counter and tapped the pipe's bowl, hard, against the palm of his hand. While he did so, he shook his head.

"Karen?" Henry said. It was the first time he had ever said her name.

She was wearing a peasant blouse, white with red stitching, and she pushed the sleeves up to her elbows, then plunged her hands into the salad bowl and started to toss the leaves and tomatoes.

"Are you mad at me?" Henry asked.

"Mad?" she said.

"Not so much mad," Charlie said. "More like—"

"Like what?"

"Tell him, Charlie."

"Confused, I guess," Charlie said. From his back pocket he produced a packet of pipe cleaners. Henry watched as Charlie withdrew one stalk and placed it inside the stem of his pipe.

"I used to think those were just made for arts and crafts," Henry said.

Despite himself, Charlie looked at him and laughed. "Then why did you think they were called pipe cleaners?" he asked.

Henry shrugged and smiled, and Karen laughed out loud, and then all three of them laughed, another first.

Karen put the salad bowl on the kitchen table, then picked up Charlie's used pipe cleaner and tossed it into the trash.

"What are you confused about?" Henry asked Charlie.

"Did you just get your voice back the night of the fire?"

"Or have you been faking all along?" Karen added.

"And would you tell us if you were?" Charlie asked. "Do you know that you can trust us?"

So he told them. He looked at Karen—picking a heel of a cucumber from the salad to pop into Charlie's mouth; and he looked at Charlie—tamping the new tobacco into his pipe, his pant legs splotched with paint—and he told them the truth. He told them how his silence had started in anger, then changed to escape, and then, terrifyingly, become real. *Fire,* he explained to them, had been the only word he'd been able to speak for months, even to himself. He begged them not to tell anyone. Tacitly, they agreed. He had told them just enough to make his being sent home seem too punishing an option.

———

APART FROM THE FREEDOM he now enjoyed with the Falks, Henry found other benefits to spending so much time in and around a girls' dorm. On his way to the Falks' apartment one spring afternoon for example, Henry looked diagonally through the two corner windows of the downstairs living room and saw that Sheila Martinson was waiting around the corner. She was standing under a shower of apple blossom petals, holding her books, and when she walked by—pretending that she was just coming back from the dining room—Henry knew that she had been waiting for him.

He knew this in the same way he had known that Daisy wanted him to kiss her, and that she still wanted him to kiss her, even though he had been avoiding her ever since the night of the fire. If he had stopped to ask himself why he had such faith in his attractiveness, he might have traced it back to his days in the practice house; to his primal skill in discerning women's longings and fitting himself, puzzle-piece-like, into the rounded clutch of those needs. But he hadn't yet stopped to examine it. He merely enjoyed his power.

"Hi, Henry," Sheila said, with her best attempt at casualness. Sheila was known to be what at Humphrey and other places was simply called *slow*.

Henry gave her one of his best, most inviting smiles.

"Have you done your chemistry yet?" she asked him. She said *chemistry* as if she was proud that she knew the word.

He shook his head no.

"Do you want to do it together?"

He knelt down unexpectedly and brushed a petal from her brown-and-white saddle shoe. Then he glanced up and behind her, in the direction of the apple trees where she had been waiting for him. He grinned knowingly—almost cruelly—but rather than being embarrassed or defensive, Sheila grinned, too, as if relieved to have been discovered in the perfectly understandable act of wanting to be with him.

He took her hand, grabbed her books, led her around the corner of the house and back under the apple tree. He kissed her, tasting the minty gum that she had no doubt just discarded; chewing it was probably the most serious crime she had yet committed. He was confident there would be others. He felt sure, just as he had with Daisy, that nothing could stop Sheila from loving him, just as nothing could make him love her.

Through the spring, he ate dinner many nights with Karen and Charlie, and not only Sheila but lots of the other girls stopped by frequently, looking for homework help, dimes for the laundry, schedules—and, he thought, for him. He continued to avoid Daisy. He flirted with two juniors at the beginning of April, and a few weeks later he drew a portrait of a senior named Beth while she posed in a cone of sunlight. Every time that spring that Sheila asked him if he still wanted her to be his girlfriend, he would take her to the apple trees and kiss her again. Once he just gave her a drawing of an apple with a smiling face, and it seemed, quite clearly, to please her.

ON A MONDAY AFTERNOON IN MAY, Henry sat doing his homework at the Falks' kitchen table, trying to figure the square footage in the part of a field that a cow could circumscribe if it was tied to a post. In front of him—directly in front of him—Karen was chopping vegetables, her hips swaying just slightly as she sang along with Barry Mann:

> *Who put the bomp*
> *In the bomp bah bomp bah bomp?*

She was wearing a pair of tight slacks with a kind of Indian paisley fabric, all dark blues and reds. She was wearing a dark blue V-necked sweater that was just tight enough to show the straps of her brassiere.

> *Who put the dip*
> *In the dip da dip da dip?*

Sometimes, these days, when Sheila and Henry made out in the laundry room in the Reynolds West basement, he would imagine that it was Karen he was kissing. Less frequent—but just as powerful—were the moments like this, when being alone with Karen made him think of things that he wanted to do with Sheila. He had reached the point where he was starting to think that kissing and stroking might not be enough.

Back in the boys' dorm, Stu Stewart, originally so silent and skinny, had matured into the sophomore class's aspiring Hugh Hefner. As Hugh was reported to, Stu kept a little black book with him at all times, though in Stu's case, the book had a cardboard cover and no phone numbers next to the names of the girls, because they all lived in the freshman or sophomore dorms. Still, Stu claimed to have had his conquests, including, he said, a blow job in the empty chem lab.

"Who was it?" Epifano asked one night.

"Yeah, who?" Enquist echoed.

"A gentleman wouldn't tell," Stu replied.

"Yeah, he's bullshitting," Epifano said.

"This from the king of bullshit?" Stu said.

"So who was she?" Enquist asked.

There was a pause, then a whispered answer. "Daisy Fallows," Stu Stewart said.

"You mean Daisy *Swallows*," Epifano said.

In the darkness, Henry heard, and pictured:

Daisy Fallows, red hair flying, tilting her freckled nose upward and literally burning down a barn.

Henry knew that the thought of Stu Stewart putting his naked self anywhere near that perfect face should have made him ache with pain and jealousy, even question whether he should have kept her, or whether he should get her back.

Instead—and for the first of many times to come—he simply decided to erase the troublesome image from his head. In his mind, he unwrapped a fresh new gray eraser—like the one that had come in his art kit from Betty—and molded it into a ball. Then, having summoned a perfect picture of Daisy as she had looked the night of the fire, he started with the toes of her sassy saddle shoes and worked his way, rubbing furiously, up to the top of her flaming red hair. Several times, in his mind, he paused to blow away the eraser dust and smooth the now-white portion of the page with the side of his hand.

IN THOSE WARMING SPRING NIGHTS, there was other mental art as well. Henry had swiped a copy of *Playboy* from Stu Stewart and kept it hidden in his sheets at the foot of his bed. Night after night—after the others had gone to sleep—Henry would turn the pages, learning the considerable pleasures of two-dimensional women. The language of sex seemed to echo with Shop: as a Playboy, apparently, you got hammered or plastered, then you nailed or screwed or drilled a woman who was built, or had a rack.

The issue of the magazine was more than a year old, and extremely well worn. In addition to the centerfold, with its naked Playmate's breasts aloft, it offered five Christmas Playmates, four pages of Marilyn Monroe, and a cover of a Playmate in a red, ermine-trimmed leotard. Under his blanket, Henry held the magazine and a flashlight, memorizing each image, so that when, inevitably, he needed at least one hand free, he could put down the flashlight, put down the magazine, close his eyes, and use every power he had to draw and redraw, see and resee, the women in his mind.

STRANGELY, WHEN STU RECLAIMED his copy of the magazine and Henry tried to re-create one of the women on actual paper, he found the results uniformly awful. He remained, even after nearly two years in Charlie's class, much better at drawing things that he could actually copy. That was the way he had first drawn the Ray, from purloined drawings of Superman and the Flash. The car in his closet had been copied from an ad, and even his self-portraits had come directly from the mirror before him. He was an extraordinary mimic when it came to art, and as he did with girls, he employed the chameleon gifts he had learned as a practice baby. When they studied Monet, he could paint like Monet. He could copy van Gogh, Picasso. When friends faltered on their daily Falk Book assignments, Henry could whip off sketches for them, reproducing their fledgling styles. It was only when

Henry sought a style of his own—or tried to imagine, rather than re-call or re-create—that he would start to falter.

PARTIALLY BECAUSE OF his newfound success with girls, however, spring felt open, free, and unburdened. Summer, inevitably, loomed. While Henry had stayed the extra three months at Humphrey the summer before, and though the school often advised that students who stayed through vacations would fare better, Martha had insisted that Henry come home this June. He felt vaguely intrigued by the prospect of encountering Mary Jane, but a reunion with Martha seemed more consequential.

"Take me with you instead," he said to Karen one afternoon in the Falks' kitchen.

"Take you with us? Where?"

"To Spain," he said. "This summer."

She laughed, but then instantly realized that Henry was serious.

"Oh, Hen," she said. "I wish we could."

"Why can't you, then?"

"You've got to go home to your mother."

"You mean Martha."

"I know. Right. To Martha, then."

"You know what that means."

Karen winced visibly, but mainly as a sign that she sympathized. She had once told Henry, however, that she wasn't sure she did under-stand what had been so bad about having all that love.

"I wish I could meet her," Karen said. "Why don't you let her come visit sometime?"

"Never," Henry said, with surprising force.

"Never what?" Charlie said as he walked through the door. He threw his jacket on the kitchen counter, nearly knocking over Karen's wineglass. Noisily, he pulled out a chair, sat down, and took his pipe from his pocket. He was wearing a green felt hunting hat, on which he had affixed a number of colorful tin bird pins. Every semester, it seemed, he added something to his repertoire to annoy the Humphrey administration. The paint-spattered blue jeans had come the year before.

"Never let Martha visit," Henry said.

"Didn't Karen tell you? She's coming next week," Charlie said, tamping the tobacco into his pipe.

"Very funny," Henry said, but he was not happy to realize that what to him would have been an unprecedented calamity could provoke amusement in Charlie and Karen.

"PLEASE TELL ME YOU'LL BE HOME for the summer," Henry wrote to Mary Jane that night. "I just don't think I could handle being at Wilton without having you around."

"I have a boyfriend," she wrote back. "So I don't know how much time I'll get to spend with you, but I'll be home."

"I don't care about your boyfriend," Henry wrote back. "I just don't want to have to be home every single minute of every single day."

"I'll be working at the Press," Mary Jane wrote back. "It might not be so bad to see your face."

The night Henry received this letter, he drew the first of what would be thirty postcard-size self-portraits—all identical, except for the lines around his mouth and eyes, which changed just perceptibly from day to day, ever so gradually tweaking up the corners of his smile, creasing the corners of his eyes until, when the pages were riffled, it was clear that Henry was smiling, then, inverted over the next many days, frowning again.

He sent the entire set to Mary Jane. "Here's my face," he wrote her. "Where's yours?"

6

The Summer of '62

On the day that Henry left for home, Charlie drove him to the bus station in a red Ford pickup that he had borrowed from the groundskeeper. The sky was nearly a denim blue, and the sun was hot: a June sun, early but strong. Henry felt his throat tighten as he stood beside Charlie and waited for the bus.

When it pulled up—muddy but silver, like a coin in the dirt—Henry had to look away from Charlie, and then he had to stuff both his hands into his pockets when he felt Charlie's arm go around his shoulders. Charlie handed him a pocket-size sketch pad.

"Mini Falk Book," he said gruffly. "Draw something every day. I'll be looking for this when you get back."

Then the doors of the bus swung open with a hydraulic hiss, and Henry climbed into the relative darkness, his feet making sticking sounds on the rubber-ridged floor, his hands reaching from seat rest to seat rest. He chose a place near the back, where the seats behind and in front of him were empty, and an old woman was sleeping in the seat across the aisle. The bus was hot, but the windows were closed, presumably for air-conditioning, and after only fifteen minutes or so, Henry put his head against the glass, feeling just a hint of air, as if someone was blowing gently on the crest of his forehead.

The bus trip to Franklin took more than six hours, and Henry slept for nearly four of them. At one point, he dreamed, though when he woke—hard and embarrassed and then relieved to see that he was alone—he could not recall exactly who or what had been in the dream. Some combination of girls, of course. Daisy or Beth or Mary Jane or Sheila or Karen. It didn't matter.

MARTHA WAS AT THE BUS STATION. Henry saw her from the window, standing stiff and pale, like one of the columns supporting the old station roof. It was strange to see her in this place, and Henry realized how rarely they had spent time beyond the confines of the practice house. That was another thing for which he blamed her now. Not only the pretense of his past but also the pretense of a normal life.

Just before the bus doors opened into the sunshine and the dreaded embrace, Henry felt a stab of longing for Charlie and Karen and their own routine. Perhaps it was just as insular a world, but it didn't feel as frightened. Then Henry stepped off the bus, misjudging the height of the last step and nearly falling onto the pavement, falling back into the smallness of childhood.

"Oh, Hanky," Martha said, and even Henry could see how much she had aged. He did not speak to her, naturally, but he did let her hug him hello.

The lines on her face had deepened, as if what had originally been drawn in pencil had now been traced over in dark charcoal. Her hair had thinned and grayed. She was every bit as heavy, though, still wearing a silk scarf around her neck, still wearing her Omicron Nu gold pin. He could feel the need in her arms, and in the way her chin fell on his shoulder.

"I can't believe you've gotten so tall," she said.

He shrugged guiltily.

Absurdly, she tried to take the suitcase from the belly of the bus for him, but he grabbed the handle from her.

"You've gotten so strong," she said.

They took a taxi to the Wilton campus.

"How are your classes?" she asked him, and "Who are your friends?" and "Are you hungry?" and "What shall I make you for dinner?" as if she'd forgotten why he had had to go away in the first place.

"Not even a hello?" she whispered to him. "A hello for Emem?"

He felt sad enough for her that he almost wanted to speak. But then her eyes filled with tears: glassy, deep, and dangerous, and ever so slightly, he leaned back away from her, watching the campus come into view and feeling his mouth grow tighter.

EVEN AGAINST THE still-June-blue sky, the practice house looked gray. The paint on the siding in front was peeling. Some of the green shutters looked unhinged. "I haven't had the help," Martha said in answer to Henry's unasked question. "You know, I used to have girls who could have painted this house in a weekend. But really. What a bunch! The one who's on this week showed up last fall with a broken arm. Honestly. I need to tell this group to come in out of the rain. I—"

At that moment, the front door was opened by the contradictorily helpful hand of one of the practice mothers.

"Ah, Lila," Martha said, obviously flustered, perhaps hoping the girl hadn't heard. "How nice of you to get the door for us. Lila, this is my son, Henry. Henry, this is Lila Watkins. She is one of our practice mothers."

No. The practice mothers in Henry's memory had, of course, all been adults. But the person to whom Martha was now introducing Henry was a nineteen-year-old blond girl wearing pale yellow Levi's, penny loafers, and a short, sleeveless yellow shirt with a large white daisy across the chest. Her eyes were blue, but not as blue as Mary Jane's.

Lila smiled as if Henry was a second helping of something.

"What's happening?" she asked him softly as they stepped inside.

He smiled back at her.

"Henry doesn't talk," Martha said quickly.

"Doesn't talk?" Lila repeated.

Henry shook his head no, an ambiguous gesture that could have been either a contradiction or a confirmation of what Martha had just said.

"Your room's exactly the way you left it," Martha told him.

To his great relief, she didn't follow him upstairs.

THE BLANDNESS OF THE ROOM shocked him. Apart from the cowboy lampshades and cowboy bedspread, there was no source of color in the room at all. The walls were not only beige but dingy and cracked. Henry was startled, and almost embarrassed for Martha, to see that along the baseboards there was an unmistakable line of dust.

He tipped his suitcase over with one foot, unzipped it in order to unpack, but then, overcome by exhaustion, threw himself onto the bed instead.

In addition to being colorless, everything in the room seemed shrunken. Henry tried to remember what it had been like to do his homework at this desk, to sit in that spindle-backed chair, to pin things on this bulletin board. Even the window frames seemed small, keeping the world outside in check.

From his bed, Henry stared at the closet while listening to the downstairs sounds—so familiar and yet so unexpected—of Huck, the practice baby: the crying and soothing, the kettle boiling, the lilt and singing, and then the silence. Finally, after nearly an hour, Henry fought off his inertia, stood up, and opened the closet door. It was clear that Martha had been here at some point: Most of the clothes Henry had left—and doubtless outgrown—were gone, as well as his old shoes and boots. But if Martha had been tempted to question—or conceal—his drawings and paintings, she had overcome the impulses. Like frescoes, they remained intact, their vividness slightly faded, as if the beigeness of the house had seeped in and paled the colors he'd left behind.

GROWING UP IN THE PRACTICE HOUSE, Henry had already absorbed a great deal of hands-on knowledge about the care and keeping of a household. Even at ten or eleven, he had been perfectly capable of cooking a meal, scrubbing a bathroom, helping to drape a curtain. He had helped Martha polish furniture, clean ovens, and rewire lamps. He had never plastered and painted a room, but after all the work in Charlie's class, he had gained a deeper confidence about what his own hands could do.

At dinner, as he watched Martha go from prattling questions to seething silence, he pondered the state of the walls behind her, the baseboards below, the ceilings above. He thought about the Falks' rooms, with their artist-palette walls, and he tried to decide, even as Martha kept talking—telling him campus news, telling him how she'd missed him, telling him about the conference she had to attend the following week—what colors would work best in each of the practice house rooms. Each image was nearly subversive, with the power to push out against the ancient, stifling blandness around him.

"That's a funny look," Lila said when Henry brought his dinner dish to the kitchen and rinsed it in the sink.

He raised an eyebrow in her direction.

"The way you're looking around," she said. "As if you're planning a getaway."

There was something flirty, sexy, and knowing in nearly everything she said, and he resolved that, before the summer was over, he would be making love to her in a room that was every bit as colorful as her clothes.

MARY JANE'S SUMMER JOB was in the office of the Wilton College Press, which published only the occasional book but distributed articles by faculty members, wrote and printed a monthly newsletter, and sent out whatever announcements the alumnae stirred themselves to write.

The press building was on the farthest end of the Wilton campus— past even the president's house, with an impressive view of the large pond, compensation for its lack of proximity to everything else.

Mary Jane had written to Henry that she would be starting her job the week after graduation, and so, after his first full day back home,

Henry walked across the once forbidden campus to meet her. The campus was green and manicured, well dressed from its recent commencement day, but there was the lazy, suspended feeling of work just done. Everyone seemed to be finished with something, and even the people who thought they recognized Henry seemed to turn only slowly toward him, as if the act of recognition itself required more energy than they could spare.

By six o'clock, Henry was sitting on one of the stone benches overlooking the lake just a few yards from the press building's front door. Waiting for Mary Jane, Henry pondered the summer months stretching before him, and the silence he would have to impose on himself all over again. He wondered if he should speak to Mary Jane, just as he'd spoken to Karen and Charlie. He knew he could trust her to keep his secret. He didn't know if he wanted to. A breeze blew up, and the latish sun hit the water, making the surface look like crumpled wax paper. In his mind's eye, Henry tried different colors on the walls of the practice house, divvying up the rainbow. He thought about Lila Watkins, with the daisy across her chest.

When, just a little past six, Mary Jane finally emerged, it was almost shocking to see her in three dimensions. At sixteen, she was stunning. Her hair, which had always been so remarkably white-blond, had deepened into a more predictable, but no less beautiful, yellow, and its straightness and length made it seem to move over her shoulders like a well-ironed piece of satin. To paint it, Henry thought instinctively, you would need a kind of watercolor that looked as if it never dried. Her face, like his, was pale, as it always had been; like his, too, it had become more angular.

She stopped at the foot of the steps, rummaging in a large beige macramé bag. She was wearing white capri pants and an oversize, man-tailored shirt. She looked like a woman, not like a girl. She hadn't seen him yet, and for a moment, he felt overwhelmed with the sense of coming home.

When she saw him, she let out a little yelp, leapt from the third to the last step, and rushed toward him, her arms outspread. Awkwardly, he hugged her, and as he did, his cheek brushed against the rim of her eye patch.

There was nothing awkward about her. She was filled with the same kind of confidence that had led them through so many games of make-believe, so many school-yard negotiations, so many one-sided conversations. Without thinking, he bent down to kiss her, forgetting every girl from Humphrey, forgetting Lila, forgetting, apparently, everything except the need to win her, too. Mary Jane accepted his lips curtly, with a brief, authoritative smack.

She reached into her bag and took out a white tin box with black writing on it and six unfiltered cigarettes inside, lined up like pieces of chalk. She lit two of them with a single match, expertly extracting one from between her lips and handing it over.

Henry took the cigarette and, as he did so, noticed a silver ring with embossed hearts on Mary Jane's right ring finger.

"George gave it to me," she said, following Henry's glance. "George. Remember? My boyfriend? He's spending most of the summer with his parents on Cape Cod," she said. "He's a poet. He wants to be a journalist, like me." She looked at Henry slyly. "But I think he might just be saying that because he really loves me."

Henry studied Mary Jane's face for signs that she was boasting—or trying to make him jealous. But her tone and face were just neutral enough to make him think she had nothing like that in mind.

Henry nodded, as if the truth of who loved Mary Jane wouldn't matter to him one way or the other, as if he hadn't wanted to kiss her just a moment before, and been tempted to tell her his secret. In truth, the talk of her boyfriend didn't matter to him as much as he suspected it should—and certainly not as much as he guessed she wanted it to. The most he was aware of feeling was a combination of curiosity and annoyance.

They sat side by side on the stone bench. She talked about her school, her job, his letters and drawings. She showed him a poem that the boyfriend had written to her. It was sappy, but Henry could see how she might think that it was deep. All the lines began with lower-case letters, and ended without punctuation.

"Have you ever written a girl a poem, Henry?" Mary Jane asked.

He shook his head no.

She tried not to smile, but this time, she gave a little something of her feelings away. Her mouth turned up just slightly, like a growing thing.

The smoke from her cigarette fled behind her.

"Raise your hand if you're glad to see me," she said.

THE NEXT MORNING, Henry walked through the campus and down Main Street to Hamilton's Hardware.

"Home for the summer, then?"

Arthur Hamilton called out the question from a tall, library-style ladder, where he was fetching some kind of copper pipe for another customer.

It took Henry a moment to locate the origin of the voice. He sighed inwardly. After two years in a place where everyone by now knew him as mute, he found it exhausting to have to have people discover—in Arthur's case, rediscover—that he didn't ever speak.

"First time you've been home in a few years, isn't it?"

Henry nodded.

"Yes, I know you. You're Martha Gaines's son," Arthur said warningly. "The mute."

Henry winced more at the word *son* than at the word *mute*.

"She hasn't been well, you know," Arthur said, and waited for Henry to look up at him before he descended the ladder.

"You didn't know that, did you? No, you wouldn't have known that. She's not the type to burden you with her needs."

Stung by the accusation, Henry was equally stung by the absurdity of the statement. What had Martha's treatment of him ever been but a bargain to ease the burden of her needs?

———

WHEN HENRY RETURNED from the hardware store, he lifted the cans of paint into Martha's view.

"Really?" she asked him gratefully. "Are you really going to paint? The place needs it so badly, and it's always last on everyone's list. Of course, I would have done it myself if I'd had the time . . ."

He walked past her.

"Where will you start?" she asked. "In your bedroom? Oh! In the upstairs parlor? Would you do that? It's so dingy in there!"

Fine, he thought. Let it not be dingy in there. He carried the cans of paint up the stairs, one on either side of him, like suitcases. It was still not yet noon, and so he began, first pushing the chairs off the carpet, then rolling it up, then pulling the furniture back into a forced grouping in the middle of the room.

Martha's desk, all pigeonholes and bills and receipts, was surprisingly easy to move, and it took no time at all to take down her pictures and memorabilia. More difficult was the bookcase, which Henry knew he would have to empty before he could try to move it.

He took the books off the shelf by fours and fives, whatever could fit in his grasp: books on household equipment, child rearing, psychology, different editions of Spock and Gesell, Wilton College handbooks, directories of women's colleges, books about health and hygiene, all coming off the shelves with dust flying—even, ironically, a whole series about cleaning. He carried the baby journals two by two, then stacked them more neatly and carefully, even though the parade of names—Helen, Harold, Hannah, Hope—made him feel something sick and terrible.

Where were they, the other House babies? Did they know how their lives had begun? Had anyone ever told them that they had been laboratory animals? Or had they, by leaving at the age of two or younger, been spared the necessity of that revelation?

Harvey, Holly, Hugh, Harriet—and then Henry stopped stacking the journals, because he had come to a name he knew—Herbert—and then to one that went with a face he vaguely recalled. Hazel. Hazy. The baby he'd been told he'd rescued. Henry looked back a second time. But no, his own journal was missing. Then he looked on, down the rest of the shelf: Heidi, Hollis, Herman, Hardy, Heather. No, his wasn't there.

HENRY WANTED TO PAINT, but he made himself focus on repairing the walls, pushing spackle into the pockmarks and cracks, leveling the to-pography.

At five in the afternoon, exhausted, he knew that even the sanding would probably have to wait until the next day, and so he put away his spackle, washed his hands upstairs, and was on his way out to meet Mary Jane when a strange sound from the kitchen made him stop. At first he thought it was the baby, because the sound was fretful and rhythmic, not unlike a baby's cry. But that was really a trick of his senses, because he had just walked past the living room and seen Lila on the rug with the baby, rolling a ball back and forth, both of them quiet and content.

The sound was of Martha crying. Little gasps and hiccups, little sniffles and whimpers of pain. All that kept Henry rooted to the spot was the knowledge that her crying was real, that she could not have planned it for him, could not have known what time he'd descend to pity and protect her.

He took a breath and stepped into the kitchen. She had actually put her head on her arm, and her chin, which had grown more slack in the two years of his absence, rested loosely on one sweatered fore-arm.

She looked up when she heard him step in and either was or pre-tended to be embarrassed by his seeing her.

She fingered the hem of her cotton handkerchief, turning it by the corners, presumably looking for a dry spot.

"Oh," she said. "I didn't mean for you to hear me."

He sat down across from her, understanding almost without car-ing that he was the reason for her tears.

"It's just—" she started. But the thought of whatever it was that was making her sad overcame her, and he watched her face flush from the dark brown spots at the top of her brow to the base of her double chin.

"It's not you," she said after she'd composed herself again. "It's this child-care conference," she said. "I've been to them before. A total waste of time, trust me. Lots of silly women standing around and talking about their theories when the child I'm supposed to care for—" Here she trailed off, because clearly there was a memory attached to this pain, and Henry didn't know what it was and didn't care.

"I don't want to leave," Martha said. "I haven't seen my son for two years, and I don't want to leave you now."

HENRY STOOD MARY JANE UP that evening. He stayed home, watching Martha direct Lila in the kitchen. He watched her using the carpet sweeper, ironing, cooking, climbing the stairs. He saw that she was slower, less accurate—less obvious in her attempts to tame and manage the world. *She hasn't been well,* Arthur had said, and Henry rehearsed the line in his mind, seeking sympathy in himself, or at least a fear of being alone. He was quite certain that he felt neither.

For the first time in his life, he allowed himself to imagine her dying. He found the thought almost giddily freeing. Her face would be wiped of its redness; her eyes would no longer be pleading, watching, looking for signs of love, or betrayal: whatever it was she expected. He saw himself living with Betty in New York or, better, back with Karen and Charlie, in a real family, in a real house, where he could trust that what people told him one day would still be true the next.

At her funeral, he imagined, he would be dry-eyed and stoic, and then he would stand up at the podium, and, for the first time in years, he would speak so that absolutely everyone could hear what he wanted to say.

7

I Know About My Mother

Henry was counting down the days until Martha left for her conference. Lila had rotated off duty and wasn't expected to return until the middle of the month. In her place there was Susan Steele, who wore striped shirts that made him think of sailors, and Carol something—she lisped her last name—who was remarkably loud and bossy.

By now, he had painted the parlor upstairs, as well as his own bedroom and the bathroom, each with two coats of primer and a coat of white. Martha kept asking him why he didn't move the furniture back in those rooms, and he had taken to writing her notes on his progress:

One more coat on the baseboards in the parlor.

and

Should be moving things back in a day or two.

He wrote notes more often than he'd had to at Humphrey; in fact, it seemed he was always tearing pages out of his Mini Falk Book, and by now the sheets of paper sometimes popped off, like overripe leaves, because he had pulled out so many before.

Two rooms back to normal by the time you return.

MARTHA LEFT, FORTUNATELY, in the morning, while Henry was still asleep, thus preventing any chance of an embarrassing goodbye scene. Carol was in the kitchen, smoking, when he came downstairs. Huck, nine months old, was in his high chair, kicking his feet, and Henry bent down to look at him.

"Hie!" the baby said.

Henry smiled at Huck, then at Carol, and opened the refrigerator. Martha had left him pancake batter, which he delighted in ignoring. Instead he took out three eggs and some butter and the old heavy black skillet. He stood by the stove, barefooted, in his khaki shorts and T-shirt, cooking. He toasted two slices of Wonder bread, and as he ate, he looked out the window, thinking about Mary Jane, who had been ignoring him, and about Lila, who had been sending him notes by way of Susan and Carol. Then he thought about the color tangerine, which was what he had chosen for the parlor upstairs, and the color maroon, which he had chosen for his bedroom. He had decided to leave the moldings and the ceilings white, at least for now, and the thought of the day stretching in front of him, with a paintbrush in his hand and no interference from Martha, filled him with joy.

"Favor?" he wrote on Falk Book paper, then handed the note to Carol.

"What favor?" she asked suspiciously.

Go to Hamilton's Hardware and buy me two gallons of paint.

"Buy you? With what money?"

We have an account there.

"Why can't you do it?" Carol asked him.

Mr. Hamilton always makes me try to talk.

Her eyes softened with the expected sympathy.

"If I go, will you watch the baby?" she asked.

He nodded, and shrugged an "of course."

"No, I mean *really* watch the baby, because your mother would *kill* me if I let anything happen to him," she said.

Another page from the Falk Book flaked off gently into Henry's hand. He wrote:

I know about my mother.

Carol stood up and put out her cigarette. "Okay, well, what color paint do you want?" she asked.

Upstairs, Henry fumbled under drop cloths in his bedroom to retrieve an old set of crayons, and, after several attempts, he drew a sample of each of the colors he wanted and brought them back down to Carol.

"Will Hamilton know what to do with these?" she asked.

Henry nodded.

"All right, then. I'll be back soon."

She handed Huck to Henry, and, with a wary glance or two backward, she stepped out into the sunshine.

Henry waited until Carol was completely out of sight, and then he lifted the baby high in the air.

"Hey, Bruiser," he said out loud. They were the first words he'd spoken since the goodbye he had whispered to Charlie.

HENRY CARRIED THE BABY into the living room and carefully leaned down to turn on the old Zenith. For a moment there was silence, and Henry felt a surge of nostalgia and sadness, but then, hesitant and sketchy, the sound began to come through the yellow-gold cloth of the old speaker grille.

Henry turned the scratched Bakelite knob away from the classical station until he found the beat he was seeking.

"How're you doing, Huck?" he asked the baby. "Do you do the Practice House Polka?"

I'm a-walkin' in the rain.
Tears are fallin' and I feel the pain . . .

Henry started dancing, keeping the baby's chin on his shoulder and singing along at the top of his hoarse, unused voice:

And I wonder
I wa wa wa wonder
Why, why why why why why she ran away . . .

Henry twirled and spun around the living room, the same room in which he had crawled and opened Christmas presents and curled up like a puppy in the sun, the room in which he'd been handed, like an hors d'oeuvre, from mother to mother.

In a scratchy falsetto, Henry sang on. "I wa wa wa wa wonder . . ." And Huck laughed and said "Wa wa wa!"

Henry was sweating when the song stopped, and he was happy to rest during the next number, a sappy Pat Boone tune. Henry stopped singing, and Huck reached up and grabbed Henry's bangs.

"Ouch!" Henry said, and that made Huck laugh.

"No, really! Ouch!" Henry said again.

Huck pulled on Henry's bangs again.

"Cut it out!" Henry said, and he fought the impulse to drop the baby onto the couch—just to get away from those small, grabby hands. How odd, he thought, to have to protect something that he wouldn't have minded hurting. And what was it, he wondered, that was giving him this self-control?

The glee on Huck's face turned into fear, and he squirmed, surprising Henry with his strength.

"It's okay, Bruiser," Henry said. "It's okay."

Huck still looked scared.

"It's okay," Henry said again.

Then the music changed, and Henry started to dance again, to the new song on the radio, and it was only after he had made Huck laugh again that he stopped and heard the words of the song:

> Well, just because I'm in my teens
> And I still go to school
> Don't think that I dream childish dreams
> I'm nobody's fool.
> Don't mother me, that makes me wild
> And please don't treat me like a child.

———

HENRY WAS ON THE TOP STEP of the ladder when the phone rang. It was just before noon. He had caught a tangerine drip with the side of his paintbrush, and he was smoothing it into a downward stroke.

He couldn't answer the phone. He knew that. A mute couldn't answer a telephone.

He redipped his paintbrush, and the phone stopped ringing. He loved the hum of the silence, amid the blast of tangerine.

Ten minutes later, the phone rang again.

"Damn," he whispered to himself. "What the hell does she want from me?"

It had to be Martha, he thought. Who else would be so relentless, so droningly intrusive? And where the hell was Carol?

Ten minutes later, he heard Carol come in, then the sound of her fussing with Huck, and then the downstairs bathtub running.

When the phone started ringing for the third time, he threw the brush onto the newspapers below the ladder.

On the fifth ring, he picked up the telephone and merely waited, expecting to hear Martha's voice coming through. There was a long silence, though, and then a man's voice.

"Hello?" the voice said. Silence. "Hello?"

Henry started to hang up, but there was something—possibly just the tone of worry—in the man's voice that he felt he recognized.

"Don't hang up," the man said. "Henry. Is that you?" Silence. "Yes, of course. You don't speak. Henry, if that's you, just tap the receiver with your finger."

Henry did.

"Good. Yes. All right. Well, this is your— This is Dr. Gardner."

It took Henry a moment or two: Dr. Gardner. The head of the college. Betty's father. Henry's grandfather.

"Are you there?"

Henry tapped on the phone again.

"There's something I need to say to you."

Henry could hear Dr. Gardner breathing: heavy, moist, old-man breaths.

"It's your mother. That is, it's Mrs. Gaines. She's had some sort of fainting spell. She's completely fine. But she's going to stay in Boston at least for the night. Henry? Tap if you understand me."

Henry tapped.

"Tap if you're going to be all right there at the practice house."

Henry tapped.

"I know that Nurse Peabody has been overseeing the practice house students, as usual . . ."

Hah, Henry thought. Nurse Peabody had apparently run into Carol on her way back from town, asked if she needed anything, and then said: *Fine, call me if you do.* If Henry had cared to make Martha happy, he knew he'd be able to delight her by telling her just how useless Nurse Peabody had been.

"But if you'd feel better with her staying there, just tap the phone."

Henry let there be silence.

"You're all right, then?" Dr. Gardner asked.

Henry tapped the phone.

"Good. I'll see you soon, then," Dr. Gardner said vaguely, and then he hung up.

Dear old Grandpa, Henry thought wryly. In truth Henry had never thought of Dr. Gardner as anyone other than a distant, awkward figure of vague and pointless authority.

AT LEAST ONE EXTRA NIGHT without Martha in the house. There was no doubt in Henry's mind about how he wanted to spend it.

Henry had kissed girls. He had held them, hugged them, smiled into their eyes. He'd tied their shoelaces, fixed their scarves, stroked their hair, and cupped their breasts. But he had not yet scored. Screwed. Nailed. Ridden. Drilled. All those *Playboy* carpenter verbs that confounded him with their apparent contradictions. Apart from his beloved centerfold, the only naked women he'd even seen were in art books.

He knew that Lila would be coming over the next day for the usual weekend baby visit, but he felt certain that he would be able to get her over tonight, especially if she knew that Martha was still away. He thought about asking Carol if she would bring a note to Lila, but he didn't think it too likely that one girl would want to fetch him another. He dismissed, for obvious reasons, the use of the phone, but then he thought again. What if he called her and simply said nothing? Surely she'd know who was calling.

Still upstairs, at Martha's desk, he rummaged through her papers until he found her attendance sheet. When she wasn't taking her turn at the practice house, Lila Watkins lived in a dorm called Stanton. When Henry dialed the number, he expected to hear her voice, and he was actually surprised by the way that her phone kept ringing, unanswered.

Frustrated, he went downstairs, got himself a peach, then came back up to the parlor, where he sat, knees up, on the newspaper-covered floor, leaning against an unpainted wall and surveying his work. He had done only two and a half of the walls and felt suddenly exhausted by the prospect of finishing. He ate his peach, allowing the juice to drip down his arm and mingle with the drips of the tangerine paint.

Vaguely, he wondered why Martha hadn't called him herself. Once again, he knew what he was supposed to be feeling about her. Worry, concern, fear of her dying. Once again, he felt only relief at her absence. Perhaps she was expecting him to try to track her down, her absence provoking the miraculous recovery of his voice. He wished that he could forgive her. He sucked on his peach pit, wrapping his tongue around it, feeling its hard, porous surface and wanting a softer surface to mine. Lila, he thought. He had to find Lila. Hurriedly, he stood up, pounded the lid back onto the paint can, and twisted his brushes into plastic wrap, the way he'd been taught to do by Charlie. He knew he had to find Lila, and he knew if he couldn't find Lila, then he would have to find someone else.

———

WHEN HE SAW HER, the sun was still high in the sky, but it was nearly eight. She was walking across the campus with a girl on either side of her and a stack of textbooks in her arms.

"Henry," she said. "You know Henry, don't you, Alice? Don't you, Melissa?"

They shook their heads no.

He nodded, smiling into their eyes, which caught the evening light.

"Oh, come on. He's famous. Henry Gaines. He's Mrs. Gaines's son," Lila said.

"Oh, wow," Alice said. "What did you do to deserve that?"

What, indeed, Henry thought grimly, but he smiled anyway.

"Henry doesn't talk," Lila said, and then she grinned. "At least nobody's heard him yet." She giggled and reached out to tickle the side of his neck.

He managed not to exclaim, and he caught her hand with his own. He held it tightly, the way he imagined a man would hold a woman's hand, and he watched with satisfaction as the surprise colored Lila's face.

"How old is he?" Alice asked.

"I don't know," Lila said, looking straight at Henry. "How old is he?"

HE HAD IMAGINED it would be in his bedroom, but as it happened, Lila seemed more inspired by the parlor, despite its mess of paint cans and papers, its smell of paint thinner and plaster.

It was difficult. It was his first time, and though Lila tried to seem older and more experienced, Henry suspected that it was her first time, too. They were on the newspaper-covered floor, but every time he pushed his way into her, she slid a little away from him, and papers flew up around their ankles. He tried gripping her shoulders, but that seemed to make no difference, only made him slide along with her. They were a boat in choppy water, leaving a wake of paint-spotted newsprint. He had always imagined that the girl would be rooted in place, wrapping her legs around him and moving up as he moved down. The action would be vertical—hammer and nail—not diagonal or horizontal, not something slipping, quite literally, out of control. In fact, it was the lack of control—over Lila's position, her pleasure, his own—that was the biggest surprise of sex. By the end, he had unintentionally steered them up against the closet door, and everything he was feeling escaped from him in sighs and breaths, and, finally, something close to a groan.

IT SEEMED A LONG TIME LATER when Lila stood up and walked across the room to retrieve her panties and light a cigarette. It took a while for Henry to identify what it was that seemed strange about her. Then he realized that she had newspaper ink on her backside. It was exactly like a comic strip that you picked up with Silly Putty and stretched.

In all the time he'd been mute, Henry hadn't once found anything so funny that he had absolutely had to laugh out loud at it. But this was his undoing. The giddiness from the whole day, the joyful relief in knowing that he'd finally gotten laid, and then the thought of reading Joe Palooka upside down and backward on Lila's rear . . .Whatever the reason, Henry started laughing.

Lila wheeled around, reacting first to being laughed at, and only second to the realization that Henry was making sounds.

"What are you laughing at?" she said accusingly, then: "Oh my God, I *knew* you weren't mute!"

"You have Joe Palooka on your ass," Henry said hoarsely.

"I have what?"

Henry walked toward Lila on his knees, then put a hand on her backside.

"Look," he said, and she torqued her head over her shoulder to see what she could.

"Oh, wonderful," she said.

"It is!" he told her.

She pulled her panties up.

"I wonder how long it'll stay there," Henry said.

"Well, I suppose you can find out if you want," Lila said.

"How about tomorrow?" he asked, grinning.

She smiled, too, rather softly.

"It was your first time, too, wasn't it?" he asked.

She grimaced. "Now that I know you can talk," she said, "that's all you want to say?"

Henry knew it was a test of some kind, but all he could think of was *thank you.*

"Thank you," he said.

"Thank you? For what?"

"For—I don't know."

"For being *your* first?"

"Yes. Thank you for being my first."

"Was it what you thought it would be?"

It had been so much worse, Henry thought.

"It was so much better," he said.

WHATEVER MENTAL PICTURE Henry had kept of Dr. Gardner in the last few years, it certainly bore no resemblance to the man who walked into the practice house the next morning and found Henry and Lila necking at the kitchen table. Apart from the expression on the old man's face—suitably horrified, with what looked like a touch of nausea thrown in—Henry had not remembered him being so small.

"Who are you?" Dr. Gardner asked immediately. "What's the meaning of this?"

Lila looked at Henry, and Henry looked back at Lila.

"Well, aren't you going to say something?" Lila asked Henry.

Henry gave her a warning glare.

"Henry?" she said. "Aren't you going to tell Dr. Gardner who you are?"

"Henry?" Dr. Gardner said, but then Henry could see him fighting through his confusion. "Henry," he said again, more softly this time. "I'm sorry, I—I hadn't expected to see you so— It's been quite a few years, hasn't it?"

"Answer him, Henry," Lila said.

Dr. Gardner turned icily toward Lila. "Are you a student in this house?" he asked her.

Henry could tell that she was intimidated, but that she was trying not to show it. "Yes, Dr. Gardner. I'm Lila Watkins," she said.

"Well, to begin with, Miss Watkins, where is the baby for whom you're supposed to be caring?"

Lila smiled like a contestant on a quiz show who knows that she knows the answer. "He's out with Carol for a walk. It's not my week on duty, Dr. Gardner," she said proudly, and Henry—despite his youth, his inexperience, and above all his profound gratitude for having just lost his virginity—made a mental note that this girl Lila was something of an idiot.

"Then, Miss Watkins, unless the rules of the practice house have changed without my knowledge, you have no business being here."

Caught, she looked down. "Yes, sir," she said.

"Miss Watkins," Dr. Gardner said.

"Yes, sir."

"Is it your usual practice to seduce young boys?"

"Me? Seduce *him*?" Lila said.

"What other word would you suggest to describe this kind of activity between a college student and a mentally defective high school boy?"

"Mentally defective!" Lila said with outrage completely suitable to the recent events. But even as she spoke, she was looking around the kitchen—perhaps for her purse, certainly for an exit. Henry considered speaking up. He ruled it out almost immediately. Later he would soothe himself somewhat by recalling that he had at least had the *impulse* to defend Lila. For now, his sense of the practical easily outweighed any urge toward chivalry.

"Mrs. Gaines will hear about this from me," Dr. Gardner told Lila. "I can assure you, Miss Watkins."

"Dr. Gardner, I—" Lila said, then halted immediately and merely directed whatever energy she had left into a long, low, X-ray-vision stare at Henry. It was the kind of look that the Ray would have given, with a wash of powerful yellow light.

"Henry, I am not happy with you, either," Dr. Gardner said, and Henry—silent, of course—decided not to hang his head but to look frankly at Dr. Gardner. Frankly, as if they were both men of the world, but apologetically, too, as if Dr. Gardner would understand completely, if only Henry had the voice to explain it to him.

IT WAS EXACTLY THE WAY it had been after the fire at Humphrey. There was a girl who knew the truth about something Henry had done, and whom he would have to trust to tell no one. The difference, however, between Daisy knowing that Henry had started the fire and Lila knowing that Henry could talk, was that Lila did tell. First she told Dr. Gardner. Then she told the other girls in the practice house program. They, in turn, told anyone and everyone they saw. So when Henry, seeking solace—and perhaps even more—from Mary Jane, found her outside the press building the next afternoon, her usual look of pleasure had already turned into something sour and disdainful.

"So I guess you heard," Henry finally said, hands in his pockets.

"Yeah. I heard," Mary Jane answered. She stared at him, seething, for a long time. Finally, she said: "So this is what your voice sounds like."

"What were you expecting?" he asked her. "Hissing and snarling?"

She didn't smile. "I really don't want to look at you right now," she said. She tossed her hair over one shoulder as she pulled her macramé bag up on the other.

"You're mad," he said to her.

"Shucks," she said. "What gave me away?"

"I'm sorry," he said.

She bent to tie a shoelace, but ended up swatting away a bee instead.

"It really wasn't that big a deal," Henry said.

She looked startled. "What wasn't?" she asked.

"Lila," he said.

"Lila! You think I'm mad because you had sex with *Lila*?"

"I *know* you're mad because I had sex with Lila."

"I am not."

"Oh, please," Henry said. "That's such bullshit."

"I couldn't care less that you had sex with Lila. Do you care that I've had sex with George?"

"Who's George?" Henry asked.

It struck him again as quite impressive that, even with only one good eye, she could convey a full spectrum of disdain, frustration, and outrage.

"Okay, I know who George is," Henry said.

"And?"

"And have you really had sex with him?"

"So you *do* care," Mary Jane said.

At that moment, Henry realized not only that he did care but that he cared enormously. Mary Jane, who had until this moment been the object of only his casual, even lazy desire, suddenly became the focal point of an obdurate need. Walking beside her in the moist July heat, Henry almost wished he had not been with Lila the day before—and not because of the trouble it was causing him but because he wished that Mary Jane had been his first. He stopped walking at that moment, directly beside an oak tree whose two main branches were splayed like a woman's thighs.

"I wish you had been my first," he told her. "And that I had been yours."

She looked at him warily. "Maybe that's half true," she said.

He tried to grab her shoulders, but finding them through the silk strands of her hair was oddly difficult. Mary Jane neatly shook him off, the hill rejecting the climber.

"So you're not mad about Lila," Henry said.

"You jerk. There's just this little lie you've been telling me for the last three hundred years," she said.

"Could you just stop walking a minute?"

Mary Jane stopped.

"Seriously, would it have made any difference if you'd known I could talk? It's not like we've seen each other. I wouldn't have written to you more often."

"That's not the point."

"What's the point, then?"

"The point is, I thought I could trust you," she said. "I thought we could tell each other anything."

"You *can* tell me anything," Henry insisted.

"Oh, I see," she said acidly. "Then it's just that you can't tell *me*."

Her one good eye looked sad, so Henry pulled her in and kissed her, hard.

"I love you," he said.

"No," Mary Jane said. "You don't."

MARTHA WAS EVEN MORE punishing when she heard about Henry's two deadly sins: sex and speech. Having recovered from her illness at the conference, she returned to a whirl of gossip and—somewhat mercifully—decided to dole out a silent treatment of her own. The sultry days passed little differently from the days before, except that it was now Martha who seemed unreachable.

By the middle of August, Henry had finished painting the upstairs rooms, and one evening, after he had moved everything back into place in the parlor, he walked up behind Martha in the kitchen, where she was stirring a stew. He put his arm around her shoulders, gently, the way that used to make her lean back against him and sigh.

"Come with me, Emem," he said.

She looked up wearily, warily, and turned down the flame. Heavily, sighing at least once, she followed him up the stairs.

With a flourish, he swung open the door to reveal the finished parlor.

"Do you like it?" he asked her.

She shrugged and gave him a half smile: a hurt, slight twitch of a half smile.

"Oh, come on, Emem, I know you like it," he said.

"It's very nice," she said tautly, as if she didn't think it was.

JUST A FEW DAYS LATER, he had grown tired of trying to appease her, and he persuaded Mary Jane—despite her own continuing iciness—to talk to the head of the Wilton Press. The result was a job painting all the trim on the building: grueling work that involved not only stripping but sanding the woodwork before he could even prime it.

In the sun, Henry worked in khaki shorts and white T-shirts and sometimes in no shirt at all. His shoulders became brown as mushrooms, warm to the touch the one time Mary Jane accidentally brushed a hand across them.

Lila subsided into the traffic of the practice house. The anger Henry felt at her having given away his secret averaged out with the gratitude he felt for her having slept with him. The result was that he ended up neither favoring nor ignoring her. She became, as August passed, just another practice house mother, another soft-smelling creature who would leave and probably never look back.

Throughout August, Henry painted the Wilton Press building, lavished attention on a slowly thawing Mary Jane, and waited uneasily for the other shoe to drop: either an encounter with Dr. Gardner or a lecture, with tears, from Martha. The closest she came to that was one evening when he came in after dinner to find her sitting in the kitchen, inexplicably holding a sleeping Huck.

"So," she said, "it was all so you could get away from me?"

Henry merely looked back at her, not trusting himself to answer without his long-ago-lit anger engulfing him.

But she was the one who shouted. "And everything was a lie!"

He stared at her for a long moment. "I learned from the best," he said acidly.

He walked out before she could answer him. The baby started to cry.

HENRY NOW ASSUMED that she would forbid him from going back to Humphrey, and he began to imagine running away to join Betty in

New York. Surreptitiously one night, he filched a stack of Martha's Green Stamps booklets and the Ideabook catalogue with Dinah Shore on the cover. After Martha had gone to sleep, Henry browsed through the book, trying to imagine what necessities for a trip to New York City could be cobbled together from its pages. He saw place settings in silver, silver plate, and stainless steel; china, crystal, everyday glasses; living rooms with fireplaces, televisions, and radios, where Dick-and-Jane children stretched out on cozy carpets; lamps and clocks and sports equipment; one happy family after another. And other than the suitcases on pages nine and ten, there was really nothing that would help Henry get to New York—unless he could go by sailboat, wheel-barrow, or lawn mower.

It turned out, however, that he would get to go back to Humphrey after all. Three weeks into August, Martha eyed him wearily one after-noon and said more words than she had said to him in weeks. "We'd better check through your clothes, don't you think? In case you need anything new for school?"

SHE SHOWED A SURPRISING STOICISM—or perhaps it was merely exhaustion—when it came time for the actual departure, and aside from her usual searching look—that familiar attempt to find some-thing essential, reassuring, grateful, and loving in Henry's eyes—she let him go without too much fuss or bother. In a stern lecture, Dr. Gardner explained that, while he realized Henry's newly recovered voice could qualify him for a place back home, Dr. Gardner himself had no interest in watching what he called Henry's "stabs at maturity" take place on his campus and with his students.

Henry's interest in their reasoning was casual at best. The impor-tant thing was the liberation and, after all the weeks of worrying, the knowledge that he could be safely ensconced with Charlie and Karen for another year.

On the morning of his departure, he walked over to the Wilton Press, the early sun showing the flaws in his recent paint job and then, by contrast, the near perfection of Mary Jane's face.

"So?" she said to him, a hand on her hip. He looked into her one blue eye, cold and serene and implausibly bright.

"Raise your hand if you're really going to be glad to see me go," he said.

Mary Jane smirked, then started to lift her arm, but Henry caught it in midair. He wanted to kiss her but stopped himself. She had closed her eye now, whether flinching from him or hoping for him Henry couldn't tell, but he didn't want to risk being wrong. Like her eye patch, her eyelid was a window shade, and Henry knew it would be a while before he would be allowed to see, let alone to share, the world behind it.

8

Not Henry's Anything

The bus trip back to Humphrey was for Henry as joyous and filled with giddy expectation as the trip to Wilton, two and a half months before, had been sleepy and filled with dread. There was no air-conditioning this time, but there was no need of it. The windows were all half open, and the crispness of the air and the sense of expectancy kept Henry wide awake. The bus smelled surprisingly of fresh oranges and spearmint gum. Henry looked up from his reading to see the lawns and houses flying past.

He had imagined that Charlie and Karen might be waiting for him at the bus station. It wasn't that he had told them when he was coming, or even how. It was just part of his fantasy of absolute belonging. In reality, he saw no one even vaguely familiar when his bus pulled in. The empty road vibrated with silence, car doors slammed, and a bird shrieked. Sheepishly, Henry dragged his suitcase to one of the taxis that sat, indolent and burning, in the late afternoon sun.

Despite his obvious wishes, his first stop on the campus was not Reynolds West but rather the main floor of Canfield, the junior dorm. His intention was merely to drop his bags before going on to Charlie and Karen's, but the double takes from his classmates proved to be both grand and gratifying. A simple "hi" from Henry, and the reactions ranged from "Say that again" to "Hey, guys, Gaines is talking!" He unpacked, listening while one boy would ask a question and then the others, by force of habit, would try to answer it in Henry's place.

"Are they going to let you stay?"

"Of course. Why wouldn't they let him stay?"

"Because he's got his voice back, asshole."

"Yeah, but they probably don't know that yet."

"You know, you can ask me," Henry said.

"Do they know, Gaines?"

"Yes," he said.

"So why are they letting you stay?"

"Aw, he's probably screwed up in other ways."

IT WAS NEARLY DINNERTIME when Henry finally managed to arrive at the Falks' doorstep, where they were welcoming a new set of sophomore girls: fluttery in the cool evening, wearing pale pink lipstick and sleeveless shirts, their hairstyles wide, short, and obviously new.

"Henry!" Karen shouted when she saw him, and in a moment she was hugging him while at the same time slapping Charlie's arm to get his attention.

"Hey!" Charlie said, transferring the slap to Henry's back. "You look like you've grown another foot."

"You're nearly as tall as Charlie now," Karen said, but Henry could tell that she was distracted.

Charlie picked up one end of a girl's steamer trunk; her father picked up the other.

"You all settled in Canfield?" Charlie asked before disappearing into the house, not awaiting an answer.

Karen must have seen Henry's face fall.

"We'll have a good catch-up later," she whispered. "I gather you've got a lot to tell."

"How do you gather that?" he asked her softly.

"Word travels fast 'round these here parts."

She smiled—wide and open and ever-embracing—but Henry couldn't help feeling chilled as he turned to go on to dinner, the sketches in his Mini Falk Book still sheathed in his back blue jeans pocket.

———

THE HUMPHREY DOCTORS were thrilled with Henry and took his apparent progress as proof that their methods—such as they were—had worked to restore his voice. His former three hours a week in Therapy would be reduced to two, they told him.

"Two?" Henry asked, using the somewhat softer voice that instinct told him would help him keep his place in the school while not impeding his social life.

"Well, we'll need to bring you along slowly," the older of the two doctors said. "We need to know what's unlocked this voice so that it doesn't lock up again. And now that you can talk, you can be a much more active participant in your cure."

Within the motley company of his fellow classmates, Henry's improvement now conferred upon him an added status. Marc Forman asked him to shoot hoops with him one day, and Bryan Enquist asked him to wait so they could walk to the science building. The oddest part of this was that none of these activities required much conversation, and rarely included any. But somehow the fact that Henry *could* speak now seemed to make him more approachable.

Just how approachable became clear two weeks after the start of school, when Dave Epifano, in a move as shocking as it was brief, reached down and cupped Henry's ass one morning at the precise moment that Henry put his towel on the hook in the shower room.

"What?" Henry said, as if he'd been asked a question.

"What what?" Epifano said.

Henry looked around as if Epifano's hand was still there.

"What the fuck are you doing?" Henry said.

"What," Epifano said, as if nothing at all had happened.

YOU COULD NOT LIVE WITH a pack of adolescent males and not know about this. *Homo, faggot, pansy,* and *queer* were all words that had been bandied about the dorm from the very first day of school two years before. Back in the spring, Henry had also read a long, serious article about it in *Playboy,* and just last month he had heard two of the practice house mothers speculating about whether one of their boyfriends had secret, unfortunate leanings. It was one thing to think about it generally, however, and another to be confronted by it in the humid, slightly mossy environment of the Humphrey School shower stalls.

Mary Jane wrote to tell him that she was applying to boarding schools for the following fall. "I'm not wigged out enough for Humphrey. At least not yet," she wrote, explaining that she was looking at several places in New England. Pointedly, she mentioned George, the lowercase poet, several times. At the end of the letter, she added, as if she was asking about the weather: "I assume you've had fifteen or sixteen new conquests since the summer. Why don't you tell me about the latest?"

In response, Henry drew a caricature of a lascivious-looking Dave Epifano.

"What can I tell you?" he wrote to Mary Jane. "I'm universally irresistible."

IT WAS NOT REMOTELY WHAT HENRY WANTED. What he had discovered he liked about girls was how he could make things happen with them. Whether it was sex with Lila, or kisses with Daisy, or even the original nonsexual favors he had extracted from his many practice mothers, what happened had always started with Henry's decision, Henry's idea. Then it was his charm and the skill he had: the skill to promise whatever was needed—flattery, interest, humor, apparent love—until the moment, inevitable as morning, when everything he wanted would be apparent in her eyes. The flash and sparkle. The meeting. A shared decision about a kind of adventure. He didn't know what he liked less—that Epifano was a guy or that Epifano thought *he* could make things happen.

HE HAD JOKED ABOUT IT WITH MARY JANE, but for the next week, Henry sought refuge in Karen and Charlie's apartment, debating internally whether to tell them what Dave had done, longing to ask for their advice. They seemed, in any case, surprisingly distracted. Perhaps it was the beginning of the term, Henry thought, and the Falks' usual efforts to make their new girls feel at home in Reynolds West. Perhaps Henry had angered them in some way they hadn't explained to him. Perhaps even they—despite their modern views and their blue jeans and youth—thought it somehow wrong that he had been kissing a girl at Wilton and had been rumored to have done much more.

Sitting at their kitchen table under the poster of John F. Kennedy, Henry tried to concentrate on his English essay, but as he watched and waited for Karen to start cooking dinner, he couldn't help noticing that her hips, like the base of a tulip, were rounder than he had re-membered.

"Stop looking at my wife's ass," Charlie said as he entered the kitchen, pipe in hand.

Karen waved the smoke away, feigning annoyance, then kissed Charlie on the lips.

IT TOOK A LITTLE LONGER than perhaps it should have for Henry to re-alize what was about to happen. His first reaction was to think of this as something that he and the Falks would share, like the fireplace they had painted together, or the secret they had kept. Only after a day or two did it begin to sink in that of course the Falks' baby would not be Henry's anything. Not his brother or sister. Not even his own practice baby. Only perhaps his rival, his replacement.

"When?" he asked Charlie.

"In about four months," Charlie said.

They were in the new art studio, cleaning brushes in the palms of their hands, making clouds of soapy colors.

"January," Henry said.

"That's right," Charlie said. "January. Karen's hoping it's born on New Year's Day."

"January first," Henry said, knowing that his reactions were slow and strange.

Charlie hit the back of Henry's hand with the paintbrush he had been cleaning. "Wake up," he said affectionately.

The world, however, had changed again, and when, four months later, Charlie and Karen disappeared one weekend and came home after six days with their newborn baby, Henry knew enough about babies and parents to know that Charlie and Karen would never treat him the same way again.

IT'S A GIRL!

Charlie had scrawled the sign in Cray-Pas, along with a hasty but winning drawing of a smiling baby, and taped it to the art studio door. On the morning in January after the Falks' daughter was born, Henry paused in front of the sign, staring into the simple circles of the baby's eyes, as if expecting to see a reaction.

On the following Monday, when the Falks were set to bring the baby home, Henry let himself into their apartment, only to find that a small cotillion of sophomores had already had the same idea.

WELCOME HOME, BABY!

They had painted the words in pale pink on a banner that draped from window to window. The letters barely showed up on the beige canvas cloth, a circumstance that annoyed Henry nearly as much as the fact that he'd been usurped in his role as chief decorator and Welcome Wagon. There were fresh flowers in paint cans and vases, and in the crib an assortment of bunnies and bears that would leave little room for the baby and in at least one case would outweigh her.

Most of the girls knew Henry already and were not overly surprised to see him come in. Two younger classmates were hastily informed about his identity.

"So what are you doing here?" one of them asked him flirtatiously.

"Came to bake a birthday cake," he said, smoothly switching plans. He made his way to the kitchen, leaving a modest trail of amusement, attraction, and skepticism behind him.

He knew, of course, where everything in the kitchen was, and he certainly knew how to bake a cake. In the practice house, he had helped to bake cakes as soon as he could hold a spoon.

"He's baking a cake."

"A cake."

"What's he doing?"

"He says he's baking a cake."

Henry enjoyed the fuss, the little echoed rivulets of female surprise and female condescension. He enjoyed the knowledge that there was actually no chance that any one of them could outbake him, or would fail to be intrigued by his display of skill. The last thing he would ever need from a girl, Henry thought, would be instruction. Certainly not in this; probably not in anything.

With Karen's radio on, he measured out the flour, the baking powder, the milk. He stirred the batter briskly, holding the bowl down low with his left hand, largely to impress the audience of sophomores watching him from the doorway. And though he had never tried it before, he showily—and successfully—cracked the eggs with one hand, on the rim of the bowl, just the way Martha used to do.

The girls left while the cake was in the oven. Henry was glad to outlast them. He made frosting from butter and confectioners' sugar, then put portions into smaller bowls to mix with food coloring. He knew exactly how he wanted to decorate the cake, and once it had cooled, he used an assortment of knives and spoons and the one new paintbrush he could find to create an exultant baby in the style of the Falks' Matisse, dancing ecstatically across the sweet canvas of the cake, its arms—with proper hands—outstretched.

IT WAS NOT AS IF HENRY had forgotten everything about what it meant to have a baby nearby. His first two years at Humphrey had been the only time in his life when he hadn't lived with one. He had forgotten, however, what it was like when the babies first arrived—the extraordinary focus, the sense that nothing as wonderful, demanding, or frightening had ever happened or was likely to happen ever again. A newborn made it all the more dramatic. The baby fit snugly in the crook of Karen's arm. It was extraordinary to Henry that anyone so tiny could have so much power.

The girls who had stayed were drawn to the sides of her crib as if by a physical, intractable force. There were five of them that first day, and they each managed to find a place around the little rectangle—their hands on the crib railing, their eyes looking down, identical with wonder, curiosity, delight.

Her name was Mabel. As she slept in the Falks' bedroom, the last of the girls departed, and Henry followed Charlie and Karen into the kitchen, where they began to unpack the gift baskets they had been sent at the hospital. Henry waited for them to notice his cake, which he had placed on the counter beside the stove. Charlie swung the fridge door open. Karen tossed him apples and pears. Charlie caught them, dropping them carefully into a drawer. There were candies and cookies, dates and figs, chocolate-covered raisins. Shredded green cellophane, like the kind that filled Easter baskets, fell to the floor like cut grass.

"Hungry, sweetheart?" Karen asked Charlie.

"I should be asking you," Charlie said. "Come to think of it, you should be sitting down. Come to think of it, *I* should be sitting down. Henry, make yourself useful. Finish unpacking," Charlie said. "You should be taking care of us."

"You're so right," Henry said. He lifted the cake from the counter and placed it before them on the kitchen table.

"Henry!" they both exclaimed, but at the exact moment they did, Mabel let out a cry. It was full-throated, and Karen sprang up automatically, looking both happy and panicked, a combination Henry recognized from the many practice mothers he'd seen.

"It's all right," he heard himself say. "You can't pick a baby up every time he cries."

Karen laughed, and Charlie smiled, and Henry felt rage.

"I'm serious," Henry said.

Small circles of darkness had appeared on Karen's shirt. She looked down and grinned, embarrassed but pleased.

"Thanks for the cake, sweetie," she said to Henry, and slipped out of the room.

Charlie managed, with apparent difficulty, not to follow her.

"Great cake," he said, and the artist in Henry suddenly wondered what it was about Charlie's face that gave away his insincerity. Something about the eyes, Henry thought: The look had been too fast to capture, but Henry sensed that Charlie's eyes had narrowed, and his whole face had jutted forward as if to compensate for an actual lack of interest.

"Listen," Henry said. "This may be the only thing I actually have had more experience with than you, and if you don't train the baby now, you can't train her later."

Charlie stopped smiling. "Are you kidding?" he asked.

"No."

"Train her? What would we train her to do?"

"Everything," Henry said. "Anything."

"Listen to me, pal," Charlie said. "I'm going to go in there now, so this probably isn't the time to talk. But it seems to me that when a doorbell rings, you answer it, and when a baby cries, you pick her up."

"Then that's what she'll always expect," Henry said, marveling at the realization that his saying this would be, if Martha could only hear it, the best gift he'd ever given her.

"Then that's what she'll always get," Charlie said.

AT FIRST, BEING ALONE WITH MABEL was an extraordinarily heady experience. For all his time in the practice house helping out with the practice babies, Henry could count on only one hand the times he had been left completely in charge of an infant, without Martha or a practice mother nearby. Mabel, in any case, was smaller than any baby Henry had ever held—smaller than any baby he had ever imagined. When Henry held her, even with his hand behind her neck for support, he could feel the shifting fragility of her, the fragmented mobility, of a body that seemed still to be in the process of being formed, not yet knit together.

Despite what Henry had told the Falks, he picked her up every time she cried. It was not out of sympathy, empathy, or respect for the Falks' views but rather because experience quickly taught him that the girls in Reynolds West would descend from all corners at even the faintest hint of the baby's distress. He didn't want interruptions. He wanted to be the one in charge.

In a moment, Mabel's face could turn primal, wrathful, purple, murderous—her tiny mouth stretched into an ageless anguish. A moment later, the comfort of Henry's arms or the rhythm of his walk or the chant of his voice could wipe all traces of pain away. Mabel looked up at him, her eyelids as pink as the inside of a shell, her tiny lashes like an insect's legs. He had never in his whole life been more aware or more afraid of the harm that he could do.

THE FALKS CAME BACK FROM a staff meeting at eleven o'clock on a morning in February, shaking the snow from their hats and boots, laughing at something, happy and eager.

"Where's that little girl?" Charlie said. Even his cheeks—usually so pale—were tipped red with the cold. The shoulders of his winter coat were mottled with melting snow, and he held at least five logs in his arms.

"What's the wood for?" Henry asked.

"I'm building a boat," Charlie said. "What do you think the wood's for?"

Karen, smiling, took off her coat, and Charlie carried the wood into the living room, where he dropped it before the fireplace. At the sound, Mabel woke and started to cry. Without apparent hesitation, fatigue, or even annoyance—with an expression that instead suggested eagerness—Karen strode into the bedroom to pick the baby up.

Charlie, meanwhile, took off his coat, and Henry stared into the fireplace, where the bricks he had painted with logs and flames had long since been taken for granted as a quirky fixture in a quirky place.

"Why don't you get us some kindling?" Charlie asked.

"Kindling?"

"Kindling. You know. Small sticks that make the bigger sticks burn?"

Henry said nothing.

"Tell me that, in the vast expanse of your home economics training, you were never taught how to build a fire."

Henry knew that Charlie had meant this to sound affectionate, but to Henry it just sounded mean.

Outside, he walked around to the back of the dorm. The snow was already melting, and his feet were wet within minutes. What was the point of gathering sticks if they were soft and wet?

Nevertheless he found a few fallen branches on the path that were not entirely soaked, and a dozen more by the apple trees. He brought them back inside.

Charlie was kneeling by the fireplace, his mustard-colored corduroys perfectly matching the background in the Matisse. He had already used some bricks to form makeshift andirons, and he was rolling up newspapers and wedging them between and around the logs.

Henry dropped his armful of kindling, then sat in the armchair beside the growing fire.

AN HOUR PASSED IN SILENCE, an hour in which Karen nursed the baby and Charlie and Henry stared into the fire. No one asked Henry a question. No one acknowledged that he was there.

A space had formed between the bottom log and the ashes below it, a space that was a long, down-turning arc filled in by embers, an orange frown. Flames rose between that log and the two or three in back, drawn upward by the draft from the flue—yellow with brown and blue licks.

While Mabel dozed, the Falks sat by the fire, alternately entranced by it and by her. Henry stood up and took a step back from the tableau, then another, then another—daring the Falks to notice that he'd left their charmed circle. But it was not until he opened the door, and the cold wind blew onto Charlie's and Karen's backs, that they noticed where Henry was standing.

"What the hell are you doing?" Charlie asked.

"Henry! The baby!" Karen said, holding Mabel closer, as if the wind was a weapon.

"I'm leaving," Henry said, in answer to Charlie's question.

"Well, you might consider putting your coat and scarf on first," Charlie said.

"No, I mean I'm leaving," Henry said.

"To go where?" Karen asked.

"To New York. To be with my mother."

For a moment, they both looked at him, their warm threesome temporarily frozen.

"You are not," Karen said.

"Trust me," Henry said.

Charlie stood up, almost wearily, and took a step toward Henry.

"I thought you were going to be my family," Henry said.

IN SOME PLACES, the snow was turned up and bumpy, the texture like a stucco wall's. In others, where it had been flattened and raked, it looked like the sides of the cake that Henry had made for the Falks, the white icing he had spread so artfully, using the edge of the serrated knife.

On the way to the bus station, Henry walked through the snow, leaving footprints he imagined as a dotted line that Karen and Charlie could trace, if they wanted to follow or find him. A lone brown mitten was fitted over an icy fence post, some passerby's helpful gesture but an apparently unnoticed one.

He caught the bus to Hartford at two o'clock, the whiteness of the world for once seeming not like a canvas on which he could paint things but rather like a heavy curtain obliterating all color and most life.

On the bus, Henry drew with his finger in the fog of the window, making lucid paths through the sheet of white. First he drew a random line, then its parallel, then its perpendicular. Circles, diagonals, triangles. Charlie had taught him once that if he lacked inspiration, he should start with simple shapes, then close his eyes and open them and try again.

He closed his eyes and saw only the drawing of the Matisse baby: the drawing he had saved from the fire, then copied so lovingly onto a cake for the parents in the house that had never been his and now, unmistakably, never would.

HENRY KNEW BETTY'S ADDRESS, and he knew that she worked for *Time* magazine, which he rarely if ever read, though Karen and Charlie did subscribe to it. Occasionally he had consoled himself by finding Betty's name on the masthead, knowing that as long as her name was there, he would be able to find her. The last he had heard from her had been just after Thanksgiving, when she'd sent him a postcard from some ski place in Vermont. She'd written that she was researching a story about the new trend in college vacations. Nothing personal. Nothing promising. But she had remembered to write to him—and that still meant something to him.

The train from Hartford to New York left at four-thirty, and it was not until Henry was sitting onboard that he truly realized what he had done. Somehow the train—straining forward into the deepening darkness, the last winter light sinking around it—made a sound that wasn't the clickety-clack he had always read about but rather a high-pitched, incessant, frightened whine.

PART FOUR

The Wonderful World of Color

1

New York

Exhausted from the week's closing, tight from the martinis she'd had with Greg and a few other editors and researchers, Betty came home just after one in the morning, climbed the five flights to the apartment, stepped into her entryway, and found Henry, literally, lying at her doorstep.

She didn't exactly scream, but she shouted.

She had no idea that it was Henry. There was simply a large, sleeping bum before her. But even as she shouted, she registered that there was a bunch of flowers, wrapped in florist's paper and wilting across the bum's lap, and she knew—the way you could know when a song was ending, even if you'd never heard the song before—that finally the past had caught up with her.

It had been seven years since Betty had been in the same room with Henry. The tone of her letters and postcards during that time had changed from eager and preparatory to something more formal and far less concrete. Promises and plans had faded and then dwindled. The once-monthly letters now were sent out once a season, more focused on the present than on a blurry past or a vivid future.

Henry had remembered Betty as a beautiful, petite blonde, a grown-up version of Mary Jane, with a sunny, open face. The reality of seeing her was somewhat shocking. Betty was, for one thing, a lot older. What had been in Henry's memory a warm, quick smile now

seemed a kind of twisted reflex, a squiggly line, like the type cartoon-
ists draw to portray confusion, intoxication, or dizziness.

For Betty, the shock was greater. The boy she had last seen was the
well-groomed nine-year-old, hands in khakis pockets, all tucked in
and polished. Now she was facing a teenager who looked as if he had
been stuffed, somewhat hastily, into his own skin. Everything about
him seemed somehow ready to burst. Even his lips seemed too full
somehow. His pants looked too short, or his feet too big; though his
shirt was tucked in, it was coming undone. He was still extraordinarily handsome, but there was a large, painful-looking pimple on his
forehead. Only his eyes—greenish gold, almost orange, she thought—
were truly familiar to her: the warm, soft, eager eyes that she remembered. She tried to focus on them, even as the martinis she'd had were
keeping her fuzzy, at best.

"Oh my God" was all she could say, and she repeated it several
times.

"Hi, Mom," he said, with just enough irony to make her smile. He
pretended to brandish the flowers, like a magician pulling them from
a sleeve. "These are for you," he said.

Awkwardly, they embraced. He smelled of sweat and Aqua Velva.
She fumbled with her keys, her eyes filling with tears, until he took the
keys from her, gently, and opened the door for her. How had he
learned that grace, she wondered, at a school for mental cases?

"Why didn't you ring the bell?" she asked him.

"I did. No one answered," Henry said, and then, foggily, Betty remembered that Ethel was overseas this week, shooting some corona-
tion for *Life*.

Betty stepped into the apartment first, but it was Henry who
turned on the lights and led the way into the living room. His calm-
ness overwhelmed her.

"Henry," she said. "My God, I thought I was having a heart attack."

"Sorry," he said.

"Why didn't you call?"

"I wanted to surprise you," he said.

"Does Mrs. Gaines know you're here?" she asked him.

"She thinks I'm still at Humphrey."

"And why aren't you still at Humphrey?"

"It's kind of a long story," he said. "But one thing. I'm not going back."

Her eyes narrowed.

"Trust me. They won't believe I'm gone until morning," he said. "I promise I'll tell you the whole thing. But not right now. You look tired."

"I was going to say the same to you."

She was equally touched and mystified by the way he seemed to want to take control of the situation. Could he be only sixteen? He seemed much older, as if he was ready to take charge not only of his life but of hers.

NEVERTHELESS, SHE WAS THE MOTHER. This was the chance she had always said she wanted, and after she set Henry up in Ethel's room, she stretched out on her own bed, too scared, excited, and tipsy to sleep. She tried to think. She was used to thinking from deadline to deadline—a week or two ahead at best. How long was Henry going to stay? Was this an episode or was it supposed to be a life? Betty got up to look at her checkbook. No surprise there: She had almost nothing to show for her seven years in New York. Had she been so extravagant? Would someone else have done better? At what point, she wondered, had she stopped feeling the urgency of getting Henry back, or stopped believing she could?

Betty dropped the checkbook into her purse and climbed back into bed. Having Henry here would mean more problems than just the money. She would have to break things off with Greg. She would have to go back on the wagon. She would have to start cooking real meals. She would have to find her own apartment, or hope Ethel wouldn't mind sharing this one—or maybe just staying away for a while. First and foremost, however, Betty would have to find Henry a school, so that no one—not her father, not Martha, not any official whom they might call—would be able to say that she wasn't being a good and responsible parent. Betty fell asleep fully dressed, as if some part of her was expecting to be needed during the night.

SHE WOKE IN THE MORNING to a blazing headache and the mild hope that she had been dreaming. But when she walked past Ethel's bedroom, she saw Henry lying with his back toward her in a tumble of Ethel's pale pink sheets. Her little boy, she thought, vaguely amused. There was nothing little about him, and almost nothing boyish.

"So does anyone know you're here?" Betty asked him, then waited while he turned toward the sound of her voice.

He stretched. His hair was tousled, and despite his being a virtual stranger, she felt the instinct to smooth it.

He told her a story. It was not completely a lie. It didn't include Charlie and Karen, or the child they'd just had. It didn't include his disappointment, or their new indifference to him, or the depth of the rage that had compelled him to leave. Henry told Betty instead that the doctors said he was cured and so they wanted to send him back to Martha.

"Won't she expect you to come home?" Betty asked.

"That's not home," Henry answered with a coldness that Betty found frightening. He sat up straight for the first time, as if he was being dared.

"So you're not planning to call her," Betty said.

"I was thinking you could call her," Henry said.

"And tell her what?"

"Tell her it's your turn to have me," he said. "And be my mother," he added.

Betty looked at Henry doubtfully.

"If you make me go back there," Henry said, "I'll just run away again. And then neither of you will ever know where I am."

They stared at each other. Betty's head felt heavy, her stomach empty, her heart suspended.

Henry's eyes softened again, then flashed with his spark. Orange magic. Fire.

"This is what we've wanted, right?" he asked his mother gently.

BETTY HAD NOT SPOKEN once to Martha Gaines since moving to New York City. Apart from Henry's own letters, Betty's few updates about him had come not from Martha but from Dr. Gardner, and those had been vague at best. Betty knew that she had to call Martha now, and also that in order to do so, she would need to be well fortified.

"You'll probably want to freshen up," she said to Henry.

He looked at her, untrusting, the whole broken past behind them, like a rutted road. But he asked her for a towel, and he said thank you and shut the bathroom door. When she heard the water running, Betty walked into the kitchen and reached for the bottle of vodka that she kept in the cabinet above the stove. She looked at the clock. It was just past nine, and she knew that if the school had called Martha, she would be frantic by now.

Nonetheless, she opened a can of frozen orange juice, spooned out its gummy cylinder, and meditatively watched it dissolve as she stirred it into a pitcher of water. When it looked like orange juice, she poured herself half a glass and filled the rest with vodka, not bothering to stir that. Then she downed most of it in one gulp and reached for the telephone.

HENRY HAD BEEN RIGHT about Humphrey. Martha had only just received the call, saying that he had gone missing.

"I was about to phone you," she told Betty. "I wanted you to be on the lookout for him. Just in case he decided to come to you. But I realized I didn't have your number. I called your father to get it, but he didn't answer. I was going to walk over to his house, but—"

Even through the haze of her own emotions, Betty could hear an added quaver in Martha's voice, a change not of octave but of tenor, a new kind of hesitation. Betty realized what the difference was. Martha sounded like an old woman.

"He's here," Betty finally said flatly. "Henry's here. He's already here in New York." She intentionally didn't say *here with me*, but she knew it would make no difference. If Martha hadn't hated Betty before, she would hate her forever now.

Waiting for Martha to speak, Betty remembered the day she had wept in the practice house kitchen after hearing that Fred was alive. She remembered those many cups of tea, the odd lack of sweetness in everything. With a chance, what would she do differently now? What wouldn't she?

"There?" Martha said. "He's there? How did he get there?"

"I think he took a train," Betty said. "He was here late last night when I came home from work." She added, as if it was consolation: "I didn't ask him to come."

"Let me talk to him."

"He can't right now," Betty said.

"Why not? And don't tell me he's lost his voice again, because I'm not going to believe you."

"No, he's got his voice," Betty said. "It's just that right now he's in the shower. And he told me he'd rather have me call you."

There was another, even longer, silence, and Betty knew that Martha was either crying or fighting back her tears. Betty topped off her screwdriver with another shot of vodka.

"Why?" Martha finally asked.

"Why what?"

"What did he say?" she asked.

"He said not to send him back to you, because he'd just run away again."

Betty could hear, on Martha's end, a baby crying in the background, and she could see the practice house walls, could smell talcum powder and baby formula, could feel the softness of Henry's neck, and the moist closeness of him on her shoulder, rocking to sleep at night. She sipped her drink, waiting, then put the cold glass to her forehead.

"Why?" Martha said several times again, and yes, she was crying now. "Why?" she said one final time. "Why would he choose you?"

HENRY TURNED OFF THE SHOWER, and Betty could hear the riffle of the curtain rings as they were swept back along the rod. She chucked the remainder of her drink down the sink, and then, thinking better of it, refilled her glass with orange juice. She filled a second one for Henry. Then she reached one more time for the vodka, adding just one last dash to her juice, which concealed it completely. She would give Henry juice and toast for breakfast. They would get groceries later. She would do the best she could.

Betty opened the stainless-steel bread box, flipping the curved cover back and watching the reflection of her face disappear.

HENRY HAD NEVER LIVED in a place where the buildings were taller than four stories. But Betty's apartment was in a five-story walk-up, and Haaren High School was actually seven stories tall. It had roughly a thousand students, more than seventy classrooms, a dozen labs, and two gyms. From the start, there was nothing Henry liked about it. The classes were large and noisy, and the students moved together in groups delineated by clothing style, hairstyle, and, most clearly, by background and race.

Ironically, Henry spent his first week at Haaren in virtual silence, moving wordlessly from classroom to classroom as if he was still mute. As he always had, he picked up shreds of important information this way: that math teacher was queer; that classroom was where a kid had been stabbed; that girl had fake tits.

The last piece of wisdom notwithstanding, the girls seemed astonishingly mature and confident to Henry, much more like college than high school students. But he tried not to notice anyone in particular, and he ignored the ones who noticed him. Occasionally, he felt the temptation to flirt. Occasionally, too, he felt a pang of curiosity about Lila, or a pang of regret about Mary Jane. But for now, he felt certain that a girl—any girl—would only make Betty's getting used to him more difficult. If he'd learned nothing else from his summer at Wilton, it was that a girl could cause complete havoc.

During lunchtimes, instead of playing handball in the courtyard or chatting up the girls on the front steps, Henry would sit in the cafeteria by the gleaming stainless-steel milk machine and sketch. He had nearly reached the end of his Mini Falk Book, which was now bent at the cover corners and held together principally by a number of dirty tan rubber bands. Turning its pages, he could see sketches of his roommates; practice drawings of spheres and cubes; the Humphrey campus and hills at sundown, in the morning, at dawn, in snow. He found the faces of Charlie and Karen: the serious portraits and the caricatures. He wondered if they missed him. He wondered if he missed them. They were receding into the horizon of his mental landscape: smaller and smaller as the city's buildings, and the city's people, rose. He wondered if he had ever truly missed anyone, or ever would.

IT TURNED OUT THAT for a grown woman, Betty was a fairly poor housekeeper, a terrible laundress, and a dangerously bad cook. Delighting in his ability to tease her and to win her, Henry quickly took to preparing dinner for both of them in the evenings, doing the laundry on the weekends, and generally tidying the place up.

"And you call yourself a Wilton practice mother," Henry said, which made them both laugh the first time, then feign laughter every time after that.

He asked her when Ethel was getting back from her assignment. He asked her whether, if he got a job, they would be able to afford their own place. He was the one saying *when will you be home* and making the grocery lists. He enjoyed the surprise on her face when she saw that he could do these things, and somehow the chores that had been chores at Wilton and Humphrey seemed more like talents now. He questioned whether they would win for him a permanent place in Betty's life, and he waited to be sure it was a place he truly wanted.

————

IT SNOWED ON AND OFF throughout February, and every time it did, a period of mourning seemed to descend on the city. People walked the streets rigid with cold and apparent disappointment. Bums and beggars appeared with cups or hands outstretched, then disappeared behind the breath clouds formed by their shouts and questions.

All of this baffled Henry. But in some ways, the snow kept New York simple for him: muffled and plain, its landscape like the ones he'd known. It was only when the snow melted that the hard geometry of the city was revealed: rectangles, squares, and cubes abounded: hard-edged, glassed-in, everything perpendicular. He could stand on any street on any avenue, looking north or south, and, with the exception of wheels, lights, human beings, and occasional trees, find nothing arced or curved, nothing sinuous or soft.

Just a little over a month into their new life together—the life Betty had supposedly wanted so much—Henry found himself on a Tuesday night in April alone in the apartment, not having any idea where she was. He had already gotten used to her coming home very late on the magazine's weekly closing nights. But this was still early in the week. He did his homework: geometry, history, English. At seven, he watched Walter Cronkite on the evening news. At nine, he opened a can of tuna and mixed it, as Martha had long ago taught him to, with mayonnaise, mustard, salt and pepper, a pinch of sugar, and a dash of vinegar. He toasted four slices of bread, so that he'd be ready to make Betty a sandwich as soon as she walked in. She didn't.

At ten o'clock, Henry called the *Time* switchboard and asked for the research department.

A tired male voice answered. "No. No, the girls all went home hours ago."

Restless and somewhat worried, Henry prowled the apartment with special curiosity, as if the search would yield clues to Betty's whereabouts. In the kitchen, he found two extra bottles of vodka above the stove and a tin of smoked oysters pushed back behind the peas and carrots. On a high bathroom shelf that he'd never explored, Henry saw a bottle of diet pills, a half dozen contradictory hair dyes, an assortment of stomach medicines, and three different hangover remedies. In Betty's bedroom, he studied his baby photograph in its red mahogany frame, and on a low shelf next to her bed he found current books—*Sex and the Single Girl, Silent Spring, The Feminine Mystique*—as well as stacks of old *Time* magazines, and one large book that he recognized immediately.

He opened it expectantly, and indeed, there on the first page was the same photograph of himself that was in the wood frame. Beneath the picture was an old, wrinkled piece of paper with the words "The Franklin Orphans' Home" printed on top and the date "June 12, 1946" written below it in a flowing, flowery script. With mixed excitement and trepidation, Henry sat in Betty's small rocking chair and turned to the next page, which was labeled HENRY HOUSE. The first photograph was of Henry sleeping, and beneath it, in Martha's unmistakable handwriting, was the caption: "What a dream!" As Henry turned more pages, he found photos of himself at five months, six months, seven and a half months, eight months and three weeks; he saw all the different practice mothers' handwriting; the little celebrations, the sharp reportorial squabbles over the tiniest of his milestones. He saw a life so acutely observed that it wouldn't have been clear to anyone if the center of all that attention had been a person or a thing.

WHEN THE KEY TURNED in the lock, Henry was too absorbed to react quickly enough. He slammed the book shut, but he didn't have time to put it back on the shelf. In the split second before Betty walked in, he let the book drop to the side of the chair.

But it wasn't Betty. Instead, posing in the doorway was a tall, dark-haired, overweight woman wearing too much makeup and an exhausted expression.

"Hey, kid," she said.

Henry sat up straighter, then stood.

"Henry Gaines," he said, sticking out his hand.

"No shit," she said, and she pulled against his outstretched hand as if inside a dance move. She bumped him toward her and kissed his cheek. He laughed.

"And you are . . . ," he said, and she smiled.

"Who the hell do you think I am? I'm Ethel. Christ," she said. "Tell me Betty didn't tell you about me. I live here, for Christ's sake."

"I know that. But she told me you were away on some assignment."

"Guess what, genius. I'm back. Where is she, anyway?"

Henry shrugged.

"Great," she said sarcastically. "That's just great."

Ethel walked into her bedroom—the room Henry had been using—and Henry followed her.

"What are you, some kind of neat freak?" she asked. "My room's never looked this good."

"Sorry."

She laughed and swept her hair up off the back of her neck, then used her evening bag to fan under her arms.

"God, I'm roasting," she said. "Are you roasting?"

"It's warm," Henry said.

"Warm. It's a fucking furnace. Close your eyes for a minute. I want to change out of this, and I don't want to scar you for life. And no peeking."

Henry closed his eyes, not remotely tempted to peek. "So I guess I'll be moving out to the couch," he said.

"Aww, we can share the bed," Ethel said.

Startled, Henry opened his eyes. She was standing there in a bra and girdle.

"Hey! Shut 'em," she barked. "Don't panic. I was only fooling."

"I knew that," Henry said.

"Anyway, I spend a lot of nights with my boyfriend."

"Really?"

"Don't worry. I'm a big girl," Ethel said. "Okay. You can open your eyes now."

She had changed into a white blouse, navy slacks, and a pair of flats.

"Come on," Ethel said. "Let's have a snack. Is there any food in here?"

"We went shopping last week," Henry said, feeling a bit protective.

He followed Ethel into the kitchen, where she swung open the refrigerator door, then looked in, absentmindedly adjusting her bra in back. "Ketchup, mustard, mayo, ancient tomato paste, lemon juice," she reported. "Some shopping trip."

"Try the cabinet," Henry said. "Want some cereal? We do have milk."

"We do, huh?"

Ethel took out the box of Kellogg's Frosted Flakes, then exchanged it for Special K.

"You're a photographer, right?" Henry asked.

Ethel looked at him a bit oddly.

"Didn't she tell you anything about me?" Ethel asked.

"That you're a photographer," he said.

She put down her cereal bowl on the dining room table and steered him by the shoulder back into Betty's room. She pointed to Betty's dresser.

"I took that one," she said, indicating the picture of Henry. "I'm not just any photographer, kid. I'm one of your goddamn mothers."

THEY STAYED UP TALKING. He asked her all about the practice house, about the other mothers, about Betty, about himself. Ethel was vague and jokey, until finally, Henry said: "You're not telling me anything!"

"What is it you want to know, pal? How screwed up it was? It was plenty screwed up."

IT WAS PAST ONE when Betty walked in the front door. She was clearly trying hard to make her movements intentional and sober. Ethel seemed embarrassed for her and trailed Betty into her bedroom.

Henry took the opportunity to reach into Betty's purse and take a cigarette from her pack.

Then the argument from the next room began, a marvel of ineffective whispering and unconcealed anger. What did Betty think she was doing? Wasn't this the kid she'd been waiting for all these years? Here she was, falling down drunk. No, Betty said, not falling down.

"Were you with Greg?" Ethel hissed.

Henry couldn't hear the answer. He didn't have a match, and he started looking around the living room. There was a lighter on the desk, but it didn't work. There was an empty book of matches on the side table with the lamp. Finally, Henry found a fresh pack of matches in Betty's purse, lit his cigarette, and then sat on the side of the bed, listening with mixed emotions as Ethel scolded Betty.

THE DRAWING ON THE BACK of the matchbook was of a baby deer: its eyes were enormous, with eyelashes that swept up like delicate branches. It had dappled skin, a turned-up button nose, and a ripple of fur scaling upward from its nose to the space between its eyes. It looked like Bambi, but the slogan underneath said nothing about Bambi. Instead, it declared:

"DRAW ME!" On the inside over, the message was clear: "If you can draw Winky, you might have a career as a professional artist!"

The instructions said entrants were to make a copy of the drawing—no tracing allowed—and mail it with a stamped, self-addressed return envelope to the Art Instruction Schools. There, a panel of judges made up of professional artists would review the submitted artwork. If they saw promise in the work, they would allow you to participate in a correspondence course. A series of books—each containing twenty-four lessons—would begin arriving within the month. The graduates of the school, the matchbook writing said, included famous illustrators and artists who had gone on to careers in advertising, cartoon making, and the fine arts.

BY THE MIDDLE OF APRIL, the city had warmed to a pleasant, breezy spring. At the playground, chain-link fences kept the children in: Girls with straight bangs and boys with sharp side parts ran from the seesaws, ran to the sandbox; on the weekends, women wore shirtwaist dresses and tourists wore hats, leading their children through Central Park, posing them for snapshots at the zoo or on the Shetland pony.

By day, Henry trudged through his classes, pretending to take notes but more often sketching. At night, after his homework and his housework were done, he would kneel at the coffee table, making sketch after sketch of Winky. The slope of his snout, like a gentle mountain; the dark patch of his nose, not completely filled in; the ragged staircase of fur that scraggled upward toward his ears.

From Betty's purse, Henry swiped other matchbooks, featuring "the Pirate," "Tippy the Turtle," and President Lincoln. On one cover, a steamy brunette in a backless evening gown posed for a man with a sketch pad. Above them were the encouraging words: "You are in demand if you can draw!"

Relentlessly, Henry practiced. Tippy the Turtle wore a turtleneck, which was reasonably funny. The Pirate had a scowl and a mustache, but he also wore an eye patch that made Henry think of Mary Jane. It occurred to him that she had not really been happy with him since he'd started talking again. He did feel chagrin about this, but no pressing concern. In his experience, Mary Jane had always returned to him in her enthusiasm and loyalty, no matter what his actual or perceived crimes had been. But sometimes, almost missing her, he altered the lines of the Pirate and tried to draw Mary Jane instead.

"Dear Mary Jane," Henry wrote in early May:

> I'm sorry I haven't written you sooner. Things have been very busy here.
>
> But dig the return address! I've left the Loony Bin and I've moved to New York. I'm living with my mother (my real mother) and going to a regular high school, where I talk like a (fairly) regular person, have no (regular) girlfriends, and—I know you'll say I deserve this—no real friends, either!
>
> Why don't you decide not to be angry at me anymore, and come visit me in the Big Bad City this summer?

Weeks went by, and there was no reply. Henry's drawings took on a larger life. If he was still sketching when he heard Betty's or Ethel's key turn in the lock, he would stuff his drawings under the couch, then dive beneath his blanket. Some instinct kept him from wanting to share his hopes. It was easier, and somehow less intimate, to share the laundry, the closet, the soap.

Sometimes Betty stood over him while he pretended to sleep. Martha had done that too, long ago—waiting for him to wake up and talk. Under Betty's gaze, he would keep his eyes closed, and eventually she would leave, and he would hear her wash off her makeup and jangle her jewelry into her jewelry box, or sometimes make a late, whispered phone call. In the mornings, while she was still sleeping, he swiped cash and loose change from her pockets and purse. Adding it to the leftover grocery money he'd been saving, he would have just enough for the art school entry fee. Taking a deep breath one May morning, he sent his drawings and the money out into the new spring world.

TWO WEEKS LATER, Henry received a letter of congratulations and, a week after that, the first book in the series. It was seventy-two pages long and had a black and green cover with silver lettering that said MODERN ILLUSTRATING INCLUDING CARTOONING and, underneath the title, a promising "Division I." Henry opened the book gently, as if he was trying not to disturb its contents.

HOW TO START, it said on the first page, and gave instructions for the kinds of drawings Henry was supposed to create and submit. On one sheet, he had to draw a barrel and a side table; on another, he had to draw a chair and wheels in perspective; others required a horse, a teakettle, a man carrying a basket. There were instructions on what paper to use, what pencil to use, how to fold the drawings, and where to leave space for criticism. The tone of the instructions was steady and slightly scolding. "Remember, you are not to draw the clothed figure of the man in overalls yet." But Henry found the clarity reassuring, and he raced through his homework that night in order to get to his drawing. He liked the portraits, and he liked perspective. But he liked animation best by far, the license it gave him to copy. He learned that Mickey Mouse was drawn from a series of basic shapes: circles for the ears, the head, the belly, the buttons on his pants; ovals for his eyes, nose, and shoes; triangles for his eyes when they were focused on something; and a heart for the shape of his tongue when he was smiling.

ON HENRY'S SEVENTEENTH BIRTHDAY, Betty brought home a bottle of champagne and drank half a glass for every sip that Henry took. He knew she was unusually upset. He suspected she had something to tell him. It was not until she had finished the bottle, however, and said, "We should probably have eaten something with this, I guess," that Henry asked her, straight out, what was on her mind.

"Let's wait for Ethel to get here," she said.

They waited. They watched Walter Cronkite. Medgar Evers, a black leader, had been assassinated in Mississippi, a day after JFK's civil rights speech. There had been some sort of attack in British Guiana. And the American Academy of Pediatrics was demanding that children be taught to view smoking cigarettes as immature and silly.

"Toss me a cig, won't you?" Betty asked.

Sometimes he liked her, despite her childishness. This was one of those times.

The news ended. There was a new show on called *Drawing from Scratch,* and Henry watched it while trying to pretend he didn't see how nervous Betty was.

Ethel came in just before nine—chaotic as always, her handbag unintentionally open, one of her stockings snagged, and a large package in her hands.

"Hey, kid!" she said. "Happy birthday."

She reached into her open purse and fished out two packages of slightly smushed Hostess cupcakes and a small box of candles. "Never say I don't know how to celebrate. And I've got a present for you, too. A real one," she added.

"I've got one, too," Betty said, obviously flustered. "Only I didn't wrap it."

She disappeared into her bedroom while Ethel put the four cup-cakes on three plates.

"The plate with the two better be for me," Henry said.

She laughed.

"What's with Betty?" he asked her.

Ethel shrugged, unconvincingly. "Where *are* you?" she shouted to Betty.

"I'm here," Betty said, and started singing "Happy Birthday." In her hands was the practice house journal, and when they were finished with the song, Henry blew out the candle that Ethel had put in one of his cupcakes, and Betty said, "This is for you, Henry. I think it's time you have it."

"Thank you," he said, confused. "What is it, you've run out of shelf space? And you want this in my room now?"

"I'm going to Paris," she blurted out.

"You're—"

"They've offered me a job in the Paris bureau. I can't turn it down. I think you should go back home to Martha and finish school there. You just have one more year. And then you can go to college. Maybe even back here, at NYU. And Ethel can maybe look out for you—" Betty sank into the dining room chair and gently removed the candle from Henry's Hostess cupcake.

He stared at her, mute. But this was it. This was all she had left. It was clear that she, too, couldn't speak another word. Years later, he would remember this as the moment his childhood ended.

HIS BIRTHDAY PRESENT FROM ETHEL had been six ten-dollar bills and a real leather artist's portfolio. Henry spent long stretches of the hot summer nights filling its plastic sleeves with his drawings. Some of them dated back to Humphrey, others had been done during his recent summer at Wilton; most were products of the Art Instruction Schools lessons. Restlessly, he arranged and rearranged the pages, trying to distract from the imperfection in this landscape with the boldness of that portrait; to group these still lifes, those cartoons.

"Dear Silent One," he wrote to Mary Jane.

> *Clearly your lack of communication is intended and has succeeded as*
>
> *1. a punishment for me pretending I couldn't speak all that time, and*
>
> *2. a taste of my own medicine.*
>
> *So it's worked. I am now totally serious about trying to make it up to you. I will grovel.*

He drew a sketch of himself on his knees, a supplicant at Mary Jane's feet.

> *Seriously. New York is now over for me. Betty (I don't think I'll be calling her my mother again any time soon) is going to Paris for good and she wants me back with Martha for senior year. There's no way I'm doing that.*
>
> *I want to be an artist, and I mean for real, and I'm going to spend the summer earning some money so I can get the hell out of here, and in case this means anything to you at all, I want you to know that you're the only one I'm telling this to. Partly it's to PROVE I trust you, and partly it's because I want you to be part of my plan.*
>
> *Is that intriguing enough? Write to me!*

During the days, he worked—thanks to Ethel—as a messenger for *Life*, bicycling down Sixth Avenue or across Central Park in the moist, hot afternoons, sweating off his teenage weight through streets of softening tar. In August, both Ethel and Betty went to cover the March on Washington, and Henry sat in the apartment, watching the television coverage. He saw the massive statue of Lincoln, just one of the many American landmarks he had never seen in person; this huge white statue staring serenely down on the black-and-white world, with Martin Luther King, Jr., flanked by black men wearing white hats, and people in the crowd seemingly frozen in place, seemingly knowing that it was their job to form a black-and-white blanket over the world. He watched commercials for Crest and Barbie and the new Avanti automobile, aware as if for the first time of the hugeness of the world. He drank a screwdriver, then another. After the third one, he vomited and then fell asleep with his clothes on. The last thing he remembered was that the ceiling looked as if it was porcelain clay, spinning on a potter's wheel. He left in the morning.

LIKE VIRTUALLY EVERY OTHER PERSON of his age or close to it, Henry had read *The Catcher in the Rye* not once but several times. Unlike Ben Terry back at Humphrey, who had started calling everything "phony," or Bryan Enquist, who had started saying, "If you really want to hear about it" at the beginning of every sentence, or even Stu Stewart, who, while exhibiting a healthy immunity to Holden Caulfield's language, nonetheless embraced his academic, romantic, anarchic stance, Henry looked down on Holden. He thought he could easily have romanced Sally Hayes, not only off the Rockefeller Center ice-skating rink but also right out of her famous "butt-twitcher" of a skating dress. Holden had wrecked it with the girl—simply by being too uncertain. Henry would not make the same mistake. He would find Mary Jane at Wilton, and he would take her with him.

HE CALLED HER HOUSE from a pay phone at the station.

"Can I come see you?" he asked her.

"Well, sure," she said. "Or I'll swing by your place later."

"No," he said.

"No?"

"I'm not going home," he said.

"What?"

"I'm not here to go home."

THE TREES OUTSIDE MARY JANE'S HOUSE were dark and heavy with the lateness of summer leaves. No space opened up between them, and the small front lawn before her house was cool and shadowed.

Henry rang the doorbell, and Mary Jane opened the door and then stepped back inside, letting the screen door hiss back against his hands. She stood at the front hall mirror, putting on lipstick that was a light crayon color: something like Carnation Pink.

Her lips formed a smile, but there was a challenge apparent too.

THIS IS WHAT SHE DIDN'T TELL HIM, and what he wouldn't understand until much later: She still loved him. She loved his hair, the glint of the light in its layered strands, the darkness of his eyebrows next to the mild green of his eyes. She loved the quickness of his insights and humor, and the way that everyone who met him wanted at once to be the one who pleased him, the one he liked best. She loved how people loved him. But she believed, as perhaps no one else could, that he was incapable of rewarding any one person with the gift they sought from him. True, he might someday choose one of them for marriage. But that wouldn't change what he held back. What they wanted from him—what Mary Jane herself wanted—was the knowledge that they were different to him, providers of treats and provokers of feelings that no one else could provide or provoke. But Henry never asked for anything: never, apparently, needed any help or any one person.

Mary Jane knew that she held the place as his oldest friend. She suspected that, to others, he might even describe her sometimes as his best friend. The labyrinth of their past unwound behind her—not nearly as complicated as the average person meeting them would have assumed. "Oldest friend" and "best friend" were merely phrases that implied intimacy. They did not reveal how Henry's voice—easy, now that the muteness was over, affable and confident—remained the same no matter what the subject of the conversation, or to whom he was speaking.

Henry's world, in Mary Jane's view, was a democracy of charm, interest, humor, and appreciation. Occasionally, she wondered if it was possible that he actually loved everyone—or no one—equally.

"I'm going to California," he said. "Marry me and come with me."

The tiniest dots of perspiration had appeared above her upper lip—tiny and sweet as champagne bubbles.

"Don't be ridiculous," she said.

2

California

On a steamy September morning in 1963, at the Walt Disney Studio in Burbank, California, a seventeen-year-old Henry Gaines sat across a cluttered desk from a cheerful man named Phil Morrow and waited, trying not to let the depth of his nervousness betray him. Morrow flipped the pages of Henry's portfolio as if he were leafing through a magazine in a dentist's office. The shiny plastic pages caught reflections of the desk light, whipping past, image after image.

There were three clear steps to being hired as a Disney animator. The first was to have your work viewed, reviewed, and approved by Morrow. The second was to draw solutions to animation problems in a tryout book. And the third was a four-week audition, during which you were given modest assignments and schooled in the Disney methods. After that, you would either be dismissed or offered a job.

Morrow's office was air-conditioned, and Henry was dressed in a light shirt and khakis, but he could still feel the dampness on his back, as if somebody's hand was there.

"Nice lines," Morrow said.

"Thank you."

Henry straightened up in his chair and twisted slightly, hoping to unstick the shirt from his back. He pulled at the short, sparse hairs of the beard he had spent the last month coaxing into being. Everything of value to him was in this man's hands. Henry studied the wall behind Morrow's desk: cels and sketches from past Disney films; some drawings of non-cartoon animals; a set of Mickey Mouse ears sus-pended from a nail, with small models of other cartoon figures filling each ear, like tiny passengers in tiny twin boats.

"Any formal training?" Morrow said. He didn't look up as he asked the question, so Henry couldn't tell what answer he was expecting.

"Yes," Henry said.

"Any formal training not by mail?"

Henry looked down. "No," he said.

Morrow left the portfolio open on his desk, lit a cigarette, leaned back in his streamlined blue plastic chair, flapped his tie onto the cen-ter of his short-sleeved, buttoned shirt, and proceeded to tell Henry that he would never be getting this chance if it weren't for *Mary Pop-pins.* For the last decade or so, Morrow explained, Disney's films had been mostly live-action, and most of the studio's animators had been working for the Mouseketeers show, for Disneyland, or for the coming World's Fair.

Morrow took a long puff of his cigarette, then flicked his ash vaguely toward the garbage can beside his desk.

"But Walt's been trying to land *Mary Poppins*—as it were—for nearly two decades," he said. "And now he's finally got it, he wants to do it with live action *and* animation."

Without a hint of warning, Morrow dropped his cigarette into a frog-shaped ashtray and reached into his top desk drawer for a hard pink rubber ball. Grinning hugely, he bounced it with force and preci-sion on the floor beside Henry, up onto the office's rear wall, ceiling, and back into his hand.

Henry laughed in wonder. "How did you do that?"

"Years of practice."

There was a single, loud thud from the other side of the wall.

"And the deep desire to annoy the hell out of my neighbors."

"Clearly, that's working," Henry said.

Morrow repeated the trick gleefully, this time tipping his chair slightly as he reached to catch the ball.

"Right, then," he said, putting the ball back into his desk drawer.

"We're arranging a tryout class to start in a few weeks. There would be about ten of you. That's if you get past the tryout book. Are you game?"

Morrow asked the question casually—asked it as if its asking hadn't just conferred meaning on Henry's whole past and, equally, hope for his future.

"I made it?" Henry asked.

"You made it so far," Morrow said.

With a bit of a flourish, and a definite smile, he now reached onto the wall beside him for an old hand puppet of Pluto. From inside the hand puppet, Morrow withdrew a small key and, with it, unlocked a drawer of his oak file cabinet, from which he extracted a small booklet. He closed the drawer, locked it, and returned the key to the puppet with the same seriousness. Then he handed the booklet to Henry.

"The test is in here," he said. "I'll need this back before the end of the week."

"That's it?" Henry said.

"That's it."

"So I leave now?" Henry said.

Morrow shut Henry's portfolio with a snap and handed it back across the desk.

"You leave now."

FOR NEARLY TWO HOURS, Henry walked the paths of the studio, nervous but elated. The sky was a flat, almost heavy, blue, as if it had been painted. The sun was strong. He strolled down Mickey Avenue, turned back to Pluto's Corner, went the full length of Dopey Drive, then looked up at the Mickey Mouse ears on the top of the water tower, and felt that his real life had started.

"You look like the Goof," an older man said as he walked past Henry, notebook in hand.

Henry kept grinning. He had absolutely no idea what the man had meant, but he sensed it wasn't an insult, and that to ask would make him feel he was still an outsider. He never wanted to feel like an outsider here again.

"THE GOOF," HENRY WOULD eventually discover, was what the old-timers called Goofy. There would be hundreds of things like that to learn. The language, the pranks, the customs, the routine. Walt's cough. The goldfish in the watercooler. For now, it was merely enough to try to get a sense of the place. The studio was spread out over fifty acres: part factory, part film set, part playground. Walking through its clean, paved streets, Henry Gaines, with his Wilton upbringing, recognized it instinctively as a college campus. There was the same self-containment, the comfortable scale, the sense of leafy safety, and, quite apart from all the buildings where the movies and art were made, there was a commissary, a theater, a gas station, an infirmary, a softball field, and several restaurants.

Two guys he guessed were about his age hurried past him carrying three or four musical instruments apiece.

"You lost?" one of them shouted genially to Henry.

Henry took a deep breath and exhaled. "Nope," he said.

HE SLID INTO A BOOTH in the studio café. A waitress with cartoon breasts came to take his order. He had a hard time not staring at her.

"New mouse in town?" she asked him.

"Hope so. I'm doing a tryout."

"They give you the book?"

He showed it to her.

"You're not going to do it in here, are you?"

"Why not?"

"Well, don't order anything that squirts or drips," she said.

He grinned.

"How old are you?" she asked him.

"Almost twenty," he said.

"Hah."

"Not almost twenty?"

"You look like you drew that beard on," she said, and tapped the eraser of her pencil against his jawline, then back onto her order pad. "What'll you have?" she asked.

THE CHALLENGE OF THE TRYOUT BOOK was to move a cartoon character from one pose to another. In the first drawing, Donald Duck stood on a pitcher's mound. In the second, he watched a fly ball soar above his head. There might need to be as many as eight drawings in between, and in fact, the position for which Henry was applying was known as in-betweener. In-betweeners were considered animators, but just barely. They didn't invent characters or create backgrounds or come up with story points or even bits of business. Their job was merely to fill in: Donald eyes the hitter, then looks over his left shoulder. Donald raises his right leg, then lowers it. Donald torques his body, then releases the ball. Point A to Point B, Point B to Point C. Basic. An in-betweener's job would put Henry on the bottom of the ladder—just above the lowly inkers and painters who were known as "the girls."

Henry understood from the moment he picked up his pencil that he would have no problem with this. It took him only till dessert— a slice of warm apple pie with a scoop of vanilla ice cream—to decide on his strategy, and by the time the waitress brought him the check, he had made the first of his sketches and learned that her name was Cindy. Two hours later, he was back in Morrow's office, basking in Morrow's surprise at his speed; watching, this time with both pride and terror, as the pages of his work were turned.

"Natural-born Duck Man," Morrow said.

"I'm going to hope that's a good thing," Henry said.

Morrow smiled. "Well, you've got your tryout," he said—and for a moment, Henry thought he could almost see those words, soaring around the ceiling, not unlike a ribbon of Disney bluebirds.

———

HENRY FOUND A ROOM in a hotel apartment complex called the Tuxedo. It was located on the improbably named South Sparkle Street, which was ten long blocks from the studio. By bicycle, it took him fifteen minutes.

The Tuxedo had stucco walls, both inside and out, a number of large potted palm trees drooping slightly in the entryway, a pool that seemed never to be used or skimmed, and a faint but constant odor of raw fish. Henry's apartment was a poorly lighted studio, a box just thirty feet by thirty feet. It had a full-size bed, a desk chair, a desk, a bureau, and a kitchenette in which every appliance was at most half its customary size. There was one large and terrible landscape painting above the bed, which Henry took down and put at the back of the closet. Even with the bare walls, the dim light, and the briny smell, Henry considered it by far the best place he had ever lived.

Over that first weekend, he shaved his beard, bought ties and short-sleeved, button-down shirts, and the first pots, pans, dishes, towels, and sheets he'd ever gotten to choose for himself.

WORK HAD BEGUN ON *Mary Poppins* long before Henry arrived at Disney, so there was already the bustle and flow of a studio in full swing. Henry loved the way people were always rushing around with items that, juxtaposed in any other context, would have seemed totally perplexing: a cage full of rabbits, a rolling shelf of cymbals and drums, ballet skirts, large sheets of tin, a golf shoe. It was a world in which it seemed that the real purpose of all things was to be transformed into other things.

The live action for *Mary Poppins* was being filmed on every one of the studio's soundstages. The animation, as usual, was being done on the main floor of the Animation Building, a three-story, double-H-shaped mini-factory that could hold up to nine hundred artists at a time.

The more senior the animator, the closer he sat to a north-facing window and thus to the best available light. The room to which Henry was assigned was a large bullpen and had virtually no natural light at all. But every man had his own desk, complete with a strong lamp, a large wooden drawing board, and a mirror in which to pose the expressions that he was trying to capture. It was not unusual to walk into the room and encounter a row of mirrored faces trying out sadness, levity, shock, awe, confusion, rage: as distinctive and outlandish as a row of Snow White's dwarfs.

There were nine other men with Henry in this bullpen, and when they were not feigning cartoon emotions, they were trying to conceal their real ones. Some of them had professional experience; others had degrees from three-dimensional art schools; all of them wanted the job, and though they'd been told that in theory all of them might be hired, they understood how unlikely that was. They tried, despite this, to project a sense of calm. Much had been made to them, even on the first day, about the studio's spirit of collaboration, about how the Old Man couldn't stand petty politics and had always insisted the artists learn from one another. Henry figured there would be time for happy collaboration later. For now, even if quietly, he sought every advantage.

On his third evening of the tryout, for example, Henry decided to attend the weekly drawing class taught by a Disney veteran named Mark Harburg. The classes were three hours long and were open to all current animators and would-be in-betweeners. They were held in a vast, barnlike room, where easels, huge rolls of paper, and several alarming human skeletons stood in shadow around the periphery, and a model—waiting for the class to begin—stood on a raised, well-lighted platform in the middle, wearing nothing but a man's cardigan. Artists' benches, each made of smooth wood, formed a large square around her. Henry scanned the room and tried not to stare at the model for fear of seeming unprofessional. None of the other would-be in-betweeners had come. But he noticed a sort of swagger as the other men took their places; they came into the studio joking loudly, and they swung their legs over the benches, mounting them as if they were steeds.

"Five-minute poses," Harburg said. "This is Annie. Pencil or charcoal. Go."

Annie took the cardigan off and tossed it to Harburg. She had a pale, thin, but muscular body whose only apparent imperfection was a disparity in the size of her breasts. She was young, with short, fine auburn hair; blank, gray eyes; and an eerie, Sphinx-like face. Neither shy nor proud, she struck her first pose, putting her left hand on her left shoulder and her right hand on her right hip. Henry spent the first thirty seconds of the pose just trying to fight the enthusiastic chaos of longing that she had provoked in him. He tried to concentrate on her eyes for a moment, and then was flustered to realize that the artists on either side of him were drawing quick sketches of her body, ignoring her face completely.

Harburg, meanwhile, walked slowly around the benches, leaning in over one man's shoulder to point out something on his pad. His threatened approach only made Henry more nervous. But then Harburg looked at his watch.

"Next pose," he said, and Henry was relieved to turn to a fresh page.

Annie twisted her torso this time, as if she had just been startled by something behind her. Henry sketched. Four lines. Five. The arc of her back. Henry knew he could draw—as long as someone told him what to draw—and here was the assignment: Draw this woman; make her real. She bent her right knee. There was a dimple on her backside, where the buttock met the thigh. Henry sketched, and the familiar habit took over: the habit of putting one line after another, adding a shadow, shaping a curve, bringing this thing into being; there was the compulsion, once it was started, to finish—and this kept him from feeling intimidated by the other artists. He sketched. She bent over. He sketched. She reached up. It was apparent from this pose that she had a scar just under her left breast; it was a dime-size indentation that even at this distance seemed to radiate pain.

"Hey, Annie," one of the guys said. "Is that new?"

"No," she said, not changing her expression.

"How'd you get it?"

"Next pose," Harburg said.

Henry thought she would conceal the scar with her next pose, but she merely reached to her other side.

"Annie?"

"None of your business," she said, but sounded more playful than angry when she said it.

"I've got a scar like that," another man said. "I got it when I fell off Mr. Toad's Wild Ride."

Everybody laughed.

"I've got stitches on my arm," another man said.

"From what?"

"Broke it when I was a kid."

They went around the room, talking about their scars and imperfections, and all the while they looked up at Annie, then down at their drawings; up at Annie, then back down, as if they were following a vertical game of tennis.

By the time Harburg came around again, Henry had conquered his nervousness and desire, and he was solely bent on getting the lines right.

Harburg stood behind Henry's bench for a moment and watched him sketch.

"Too accurate," he finally said.

"What?"

"You're being too literal," Harburg said. "That looks exactly like her."

"I thought that was the point."

"I don't want you to copy her. I want you to extract the point of her. Come away with something you could give to Goofy. Or Donald. Do you see what I mean?"

Henry nodded.

"You have no idea what I mean," Harburg said.

"You want a caricature," Henry said.

"I want an essence," Harburg said. "What you're trying to draw here is the world going by."

"Going by," Henry repeated.

"Annie," Harburg said, without looking at her.

"Yes?"

"One-minute poses."

"One minute!" Henry said.

Her movements became almost fluid now, as she changed from pose to pose.

A dark, assertive charcoal in his hand, Harburg reached over Henry's shoulder and drew what he had in mind: bold, quick strokes that suggested a motion but not really a person. A lunge, a reach, a re-treat, a mood. Her gender became irrelevant; her age, her hair, her eyes. She became a body in motion, nothing more. As the pages and poses flew by, Henry drew with increasing speed and freedom. By the middle of the second hour, he had at least three sketches that, partly because of the speed with which he had drawn them, conveyed a sense of mo-tion that nothing he'd ever drawn had conveyed.

"That's more like it," Harburg said. He called for a break, draping his cardigan over Annie's shoulders again, patting her shoulders pa-ternally.

The men lit new cigarettes, stood up to stretch, sharpened their pencils with pocketknives.

Annie slowly walked around the drawing benches, seeing whatever images of her last pose were still uncovered. Her face remained impas-sive, almost shy. When she came to Henry's bench, he instinctively reached to flip to a fresh page and cover up his most recent drawing. She eyed him and smiled kindly.

"It's your first time here, isn't it," she said.

"Yes."

"And you're doing the tryout?"

"Yes."

"My name is Annie."

"I know. I'm Henry."

"Have *you* got any scars?" she asked.

He laughed. "They're all internal," he said.

Her eyes softened further. "Really? Your heart's already been broken?"

He thought of the look on Mary Jane's face when she told him no. "Don't be ridiculous," she had said. Henry looked at Annie, inviting her to find out more.

She touched his elbow. Just a tiny touch. A little gesture, far too quick to capture, not even the length of a one-second pose, but Henry felt sure that, later that night, he would have no trouble drawing it from memory.

IT WAS A WORLD OF MEN, a world of fathers, cousins, and brothers, as clearly male and paternal as the practice house had been its opposite. Though there were certainly women at the studio—secretaries, assistants, inkers, and painters—they were virtually banned from the Animation Building and thus irrelevant to the real work.

Henry saved thinking about the women for the nights. He had two of them already in his mind: Cindy, with her amazing balloon-shaped breasts and matching carnival spirit; and Annie, who seemed so much more fragile, and thus provoked in him an eager, protective urge.

At night, Henry watched *Jack Benny* or *The Fugitive* or *The Twilight Zone* on TV. He tried to imagine which of the two women would be better to invite over first. On the surface, Cindy seemed a surer bet. No work to get her at all, and probably not much more to keep her. But something about Annie held promise for him, too: he pictured her gripping him tightly, and the need he imagined in her was somehow more compelling than the need he felt in himself. He didn't know why he wanted it, but he let himself imagine that, for the first time, it might be nice to have a girlfriend whom he allowed to need him.

THE ONLY WOMAN HENRY THOUGHT ABOUT during the workday was Mary Poppins. Emem had read the book to Henry when he was six or seven. It was a strange book, Henry had thought even then. In it, four British children—Jane and Michael and a pair of twins—were tended to by a nanny who was blown onto their doorstep, took them on all sorts of magical adventures, and then—in chapter after chapter, with what Henry had sensed as increasing cruelty—simply pretended that nothing magical had happened after all.

Martha had kept the book among Henry's favorites, but she was the one who had liked it. The fact that the main character was a better mother to the children than their real mother was not something Henry would notice until later, and then he would find other similarities between Mary Poppins and Martha. Both of them were stern and precise, both of them were convinced they were right, and both of them were dishonest.

None of that mattered now. Henry would not have cared if the main character of this film was a phone book. But he gathered quickly that Disney's *Mary Poppins* was a different story entirely. In the movie, Mary Poppins was more predictable in her goal: She came to fix a family, and she left when the family was fixed. There was also a certain cuteness to things. For one thing, the waiter who in the book had tended to Mary and Bert had been replaced by a team of four cartoon penguins.

Among those overseeing the required animations were two of the legendary studio veterans whom Walt had dubbed "the nine old men" long before they were old. Henry was asked to report to Ollie Johnston, whom he found at a wooden drawing board in a private office.

"Penguins or horses?" Johnston asked, as if he were offering weapons in a duel.

"Whatever you need," Henry answered, as if he was sure he could do anything.

"Let's see your penguin," Ollie Johnston said.

Henry reached into his back pocket for his sketch pad and whipped the pencil from its spiral binding. Within seconds, he had drawn the beginnings of a cheerful penguin.

"No, no, not that way," Johnston said.

Mortified, Henry looked back at his drawing, trying to find the error.

"No. I mean your *penguin*," Johnston said and, cocking his hands at right angles to his sides, demonstrated for Henry the most ridiculous, the most graceful, the most convincing penguin dance it was possible to imagine.

Henry laughed. "Oh," he said. "My *penguin*."

"It's even better when Frank and I do it together," Johnston said.

He made one last little shuffle and glide, then sat back in his chair.

"Good luck, kid," he said. "See you around, maybe."

HENRY LOVED THE WARM, TROPICAL MAGIC of California: the strange, contradictory foliage, the odd quiet, the sameness of the sky. He loved the white, green, and rust of the landscape, the pink and beige houses, the surprise of the hills. Above all, he loved the distance he had come from every place he had ever lived and, with only one exception, every person he'd ever known.

He felt almost too free to be angry anymore. When he thought about Betty and Martha, it was mostly with grim satisfaction that he was no longer dependent on either of them. And when, exactly four weeks after Henry started his tryout, Morrow told him that he would be hired as a full-time Disney employee, it was the first time since his arrival that he had felt the impulse to share his news with someone from his former life. He was tempted by neither Martha nor Betty, and he was still too wounded by Mary Jane. But as he bicycled home from the studio late in the evening, he realized that he wanted Charlie and Karen to know.

There was a faint tone of retaliation in the letter he wrote that evening, a none-too-subtle suggestion that he didn't need them after all. He wrote the letter on Disney Studio stationery and punctuated it with details of the animation world and samples of drawings and many mentions of the "nine old men" and how some of them would be working on *Mary Poppins* and teaching him what they knew. *Teaching* was obviously a word that Henry chose with much precision and little subtlety.

He enclosed an old paper face mask of Donald Duck that he'd found in his bottom desk drawer, a souvenir of whatever in-betweener had had the desk before him.

"I know Mabel is still probably a little young for this," Henry wrote. "But maybe she will enjoy it when she gets a little older."

He closed by drawing a sketch of a plump diapered baby wearing the Donald Duck mask, with her arms outstretched in glee.

HE WANTED TO CELEBRATE getting the job, and he decided that he wanted the celebration to be with Annie. In the break during the next drawing class, while she circled the wooden benches, Henry quickly altered his drawing so that when she came over to look, she found a picture of herself, fully clothed, with a flower in one hand and a scrap of paper in the other. On the paper was Henry's phone number.

She laughed when she saw it.

"Really?" she said.

"Come out with me tonight," he said. He grinned. He gave her his best eyes: green and golden, sweetness and mischief, a promise of fun and attention.

The class ended at nine, and by nine-thirty they were riding their bikes, side by side, through the warm night, toward the Tuxedo.

"This is where you live?" she asked him as they pulled up. The oval swimming pool glowed green in the night, gaudy as a gem.

"It's called the Tuxedo," he said.

"I thought we were going to get something to eat." She was still straddling her bicycle.

"We're going to," he said.

She looked almost sorry for him. "You want to try to cook?" she said gently.

He grinned.

Upstairs, he gave her a glass of white wine, and while she sat sipping it at the small table, he made her a grilled cheese sandwich on perfectly toasted oatmeal bread, with thinly sliced tomatoes and, on the side, a salad with his best vinaigrette.

"Where did you learn to do this?" she asked him.

"Do what?" he asked her.

"Most men don't know how to do this."

He was so grateful not to have been called a boy. He was so grateful to be looking not across a room at her but across a table. He was so grateful to have been hired. To have escaped.

"This is absolutely delicious," Annie said. She was so sweet. He didn't make a move to touch her. He asked her about her past, how long she had worked at Disney, when she had started modeling, and what other kinds of modeling she had done. He asked her if she liked the class.

"Sometimes it's weird," she said. "You know, having all my clothes off and having these men staring at every corner of me."

"You know if we're doing it right, you kind of disappear," Henry said.

"I what?"

"You disappear. We're supposed to draw you in a way so that you don't have to be human. So you can be an animal."

"An animal?"

"You've heard him. Like Mickey Mouse. Or Donald Duck," Henry said.

"You could just draw animals," she said.

"I'm guessing it's harder to get them to pose."

She laughed. She told Henry about her cat. "His name is Greyhound," she said. "Maybe you'll meet him sometime. I found him in the bus station on the day I left Cedar Rapids, and I just decided to take him with me."

"They let you take him on the bus?"

"I put him in my hatbox, and I smushed a hole in it with my high heel. The whole way here, I could stroke him with one finger, and once he poked his little pink nose up through the hole."

Henry couldn't tell what he liked more: the fact that she'd had a hatbox or the fact that she'd ruined it for a cat.

———

SHE WAS LIVING ABOUT twenty minutes away—another twenty minutes south of the studio, almost as far as the Ventura Freeway—and the hills were fairly steep. Henry and Annie pedaled side by side but didn't talk. There were almost no cars on the road. The houses were quiet. The sky was clear. Henry could smell the prickly scent of the junipers, and his own sweat. He felt entirely liberated. The palm trees lined the road up ahead like kindly elders, bowing only slightly in their exotic coolness. They didn't intertwine and splay their branches out needily like the trees back east. They stood, single and strong.

At Annie's door, she looked up at him. "Do you want to come in and meet Greyhound?" she asked.

"Next week," he said, and he kissed her. "Is it a date?"

She looked into his eyes. "I think you're the only guy I've ever modeled for who hasn't assumed I'd go to bed with him."

He kissed her again, more deeply this time, and hopped back on his bike. "See you," he said, feeling gallant, and he pedaled away, into the comfortable solitude of his trip back home.

WHEN MARTHA CALLED HIM at the office the following week, it actually took him a few minutes before he could identify the exact nature of the unpleasantness he felt. He had been expecting a call from Phil Morrow, and for a moment, hearing Martha's voice, Henry didn't place her, only the feeling she engendered, like the rediscovery of a disagreeable taste, or a particular kind of weather.

"Hello," she said curtly, as if it was he who had called and interrupted her.

He adjusted his expectations but couldn't hide his dismay.

"How did you find me?" he asked her.

"That's not much of a greeting."

"Did you call Betty? Or Charlie? Did one of them call you?"

"What difference does it make? Why were you trying to hide?" she asked him.

"I wasn't trying to hide," he said. "I moved. I was getting a job."

He looked into his artist's mirror and saw too many emotions:

anger, worry, pride, dismay, fatigue, defeat, and shame. If he had been forced to choose one, that last would have been the one.

"It's not a good time for me to talk," he said. "I'm working right now."

There was silence, a punishing silence, and in it, Henry remembered the depths of her need, and her guilt, which made the need so impossible to assuage.

"So I'll call you a little later," he said.

Still silence.

"So goodbye," he said, and hung up, detachment overtaking all the emotions in the mirror.

THERE WAS AN EASY BANTER and warmth among the people on the soundstages where *Mary Poppins* was being filmed. At first glance, it seemed to Henry as though every person who wasn't an actor was attached to a piece of equipment, not only physically but emotionally: gently rolling their lights and cameras and ladders along like beloved pets.

Henry, along with an in-betweener named Christopher Cott, stood well behind the camera, in the dark pocket of Stage 2. Together, for most of their lunch break, Chris and Henry had been watching the filming. Dick Van Dyke, wearing a candy-stripe suit and assisted by wires, was doing take after take of a long slide on one heel. Other than the gaily painted raised platform on which he was sliding, the only three-dimensional things on the set were a table, a chair, and, occupying it, Julie Andrews. The background was a yellow screen, and the cartoon penguins would come later.

In between setups, Chris sketched—unnecessarily, Henry thought, unable to tell if Chris was being pretentious or merely shy.

"What was wrong with that take?" Henry whispered as the director yelled "Cut" again.

"I don't know," Chris whispered. "It looked fine to me."

"Are they going to set it up again?"

"I don't know."

"You know, fellas," a voice from behind them said, "you don't have to whisper."

Henry turned to see Walt Disney standing just a foot behind them, wearing a cardigan sweater exactly like the ones he wore on his TV show. His face looked somewhat more haggard; his hair seemed somewhat more gray, and a little greasy; the collar of his shirt looked strangely too large. But the Mickey Mouse hairline, with its widow's peak forming two arches, was the same as it always had been, and so was the twinkle in his eyes.

Henry felt something unfamiliar that he recognized immediately as awe. "Nice to meet you, Mr. Disney," he said.

"What's your name?"

"Henry Gaines."

"Henry," Disney said. "There is only one Mister in this studio, and he does our taxes. I'm Walt."

WALT DISNEY HAD NO SONS. He had two daughters, one of them adopted, and in some ancient, addled part of Henry's brain, he had always imagined this meeting would be the pinnacle of his life. He was far too old now to fantasize about Walt being—or even becoming—his actual father, but that didn't stop him from experiencing Walt's smile as a benediction.

"And you, pal?" Walt said to Chris.

"Yes, sir. Christopher Cott."

Chris reached to shake Walt's hand and nearly stabbed him with his drawing pencil. Walt chuckled.

"You know this scene is all being done to the song playback anyway," Walt said, with the same tone of voice Henry had heard him use on TV to explain, say, how *20,000 Leagues Under the Sea* had been filmed. "The only reason to be quiet is so you don't disturb the actors. But you really don't have to whisper."

As Walt talked, the playback started again, and Van Dyke, seemingly as game for this take as he had been ten takes before, let the wires carry him forward.

Chris went back to his sketching, and a minute later, when Henry next turned around, Walt was gone.

The scene was continuing now, with Julie Andrews looking demure, then surprised, pretending to react to the place where the penguins were going to appear.

Beneath the music of the playback, Henry was startled for a moment to hear what sounded like a baby crying.

"Did you hear that?" he whispered to Chris.

"You don't have to whisper," Chris reminded him, with a rather satisfied smile.

Henry listened for another moment or two, until he became convinced of the sound—a sound, after all, that he'd heard throughout his childhood—and then he tried to follow it, leaving his post at the back of the soundstage.

It was only a few bars later—at best a minute or so—when Henry found that the source of the crying baby sound was in truth a crying baby. She was being held by a woman who was walking her around and trying to bounce her into silence, much the same way he had often seen the practice mothers do with the practice babies. The walk this woman was doing was having absolutely no effect, though. Henry came up behind her and made a silly face at the baby over her shoulder. Just as the crying stopped, Julie Andrews appeared, removing her costume hat and, in one graceful motion, trading it for the baby, who grabbed for her nose.

"That was so kind of you," Andrews said to Henry in her lovely, perfect British voice.

"He was—she was—" Henry corrected himself as he focused on the baby's pink shirt.

"She," Julie Andrews said. "This is my daughter, Emma."

"Emem?" Henry said.

"Emma," Andrews corrected in a Mary Poppins voice.

"Emma, of course. Sorry," Henry said. "The woman who raised me was named Emem."

"Your nanny?" Andrews asked with a sweet but ironic smile.

"No. I was adopted."

Andrews nodded warmly. She mentioned Walt Disney's adopted daughter, and she told him that the son of Pamela Travers, the author of *Mary Poppins,* was adopted as well. Years later, Henry would learn that, while this was true, it was also true that the author of the beloved classic children's book had apparently never told her son either that he was adopted *or* that he was a twin, and Henry would find it fitting that the woman who had invented the Martha-like Mary would also have been capable of apparently Martha-like betrayal. For now, he merely nodded politely to Julie Andrews and marveled at the coincidence of these many adoptions. It was one of the slightly mysterious things that made him continue to feel that he had magically, and at long last, arrived in the right place.

WHEN HENRY GOT BACK TO his drawing board after lunch, he found a message scrawled by Phil Morrow.

See Me.

Martha, it seemed, had called while Henry was watching the filming. Joe Gatz, an unsuspecting in-betweener, had picked up the phone at first, but then she had talked him into finding Phil.

"She seemed concerned about you," Phil said. He had a pencil in one hand and an annoyed dorm-father expression on his face.

"I'm so sorry," Henry said.

"So you're a runaway or something?"

"Something like that," Henry said.

"Well, don't let me tell you your business, Henry," Phil said. "But this approach of hers is not likely to endear you to the members of the team here. Especially the ones who have to talk to her. You know what I mean? Do I have to draw you a picture?"

"Good one," Henry said.

"Seriously. You're a big boy now."

———

THERE WAS A DRAWING CLASS that night, and on their way back to the Animation Building, Chris asked Henry if he was planning to go again.

"You bet," Henry said. "And you really should, too."

"Who wants to sit around after work drawing a bunch of fruit?"

"Fruit?" Henry asked.

"You know. Still-life drawing?" Chris asked.

Henry had to explain to Chris the difference between a still life and a life drawing.

"You mean there are actual women?" Chris asked.

"Well, one woman."

"And what does she do?"

"She takes off all her clothes and poses."

"Nude?"

"That would be the word for it."

"No clothes at all?" Chris asked.

"Not a stitch."

DURING THE BREAK, Annie came up to Henry. Her crossed arms belted the teacher's cardigan, and one collar flapped gently over the other, curled like the outer edge of a shell. She had come to see his latest sketch, and he obliged her by drawing on a polka-dot dress and putting her up on roller skates.

But despite the prospect of lording it over Chris, Henry found that he had little desire to ask Annie to come home with him after class. He did not understand why—though he had looked forward to seeing her all week—he now didn't want her with him, why the very sweetness and softness he had enjoyed seemed suddenly unalluring. Instead, after class, Henry shuffled out with the other artists, then walked over to the diner, where he knew Cindy was working. He asked her when she was getting off.

"Getting off my shift or just getting off?" she asked with a smirk worthy of Ethel Neuholzer.

But on their way back to the Tuxedo—riding their bikes side by side, just as he had with Annie the previous week—Henry learned that, despite Cindy's somewhat superior air, she was only nineteen, a run-away herself and a Hollywood hopeful. He called her Cinderella and was disappointed when she told him that he was not the first to do so.

"And what do they call you?" she asked him as they lay back on his bed together, one hour at best after they'd opened his apartment door. He stared up at the ceiling, finding a squirrel-shaped blotch of damp-ness in the concrete.

"They call me Henry," he said.

"Ever Henny?"

"No."

"Hank?"

"No."

"Hanky?"

"Stop."

He looked to his side to find her face. The pillowcase was scratchy. Too much starch, he thought.

"Never," he said. "No people ever call me Hanky."

"I'm going to call you Hanky."

"No," he said. "You're not."

She laughed, and her breasts seemed to float, buoylike, over the top of the bedsheet.

He gave her a menacing look and could see that he'd scared her with it. He had learned to do that, and was almost sorry, but she was the one who apologized.

3

The Feminine Mystique

They wore their hair long and straight now, as if they had never bothered to have it styled and somehow were proud of that. They barely wore makeup. Sometimes they deigned to wear headbands, sometimes a ponytail pulled to one side, as if this bit of asymmetry was also a bit of rebellion.

There were only three practice house mothers in the fall of 1963. Two of them were named Barbara and one of them was named Diane, and Martha decided to call them all Barbara and wait for the Diane to speak up.

Martha had stopped believing that she was right—about thumb sucking, about sleep schedules, about child rearing in general. She had stopped believing that practice could be useful in an actual life, with all its sharp corners and unexpected vacancies. Most painfully of all, Martha had stopped believing that what she was doing at the practice house had any kind of future.

Unable to escape the wide, recent shadow of Betty Friedan and her *Feminine Mystique*, Martha understood that virtually everything that had gone on in the practice house for the last thirty years would now at best be misunderstood and, much more likely, reviled and revoked. Far from being proud of their places in the program, the Barbaras were clearly embarrassed that they had signed up for home economics at all.

Martha held the newest practice baby in her arms as she showed the Barbaras around. The baby had slept all the way home from the orphanage and seemed, wrapped in the usual blanket, to be in a larval state.

"Oh, precious," one of the Barbaras said. "What's its name?"

"Not *it*," Martha said with some of her old firmness. *"She."*

"Oh, I'm sorry, Mrs. Gaines. What's her name?"

Martha realized, with a wave of vertigo, that she had not yet named the baby.

She looked back at the girls, blinking.

"Oh," she said. Her mind raced with *H* girls' names. Helen. Harriet. Hope. They had all been used. Holly. Hannah. Hazel. She could think of nothing.

"Doesn't she have a name?" another Barbara asked.

"Of course she has a name," Martha said, and after another moment's hesitation, she said, "It's Henry. It's Henrietta."

THERE WAS STILL ONE FUTURE that Martha could imagine: a future in which she and Henry lived in a simple house somewhere, and he went to college, and she wrote a book, or helped in a nursery school, or gave lectures on child care. He could still go to college, Martha thought. There was bound to be a college somewhere that would ignore his lack of a high school diploma and focus instead on the fact that he'd held down a real job. He could still be a college graduate. And she could still be something other than the woman who used to run something that no one thought should exist.

Martha had a strong feeling that Henrietta would be her last practice baby. Partly because of that, and partly because the weather this autumn was so warm and beautiful, Martha assigned herself the daily job of taking Henrietta on the afternoon walk. The wheels of the carriage—once so white and buoyant—were now permanently gray. The navy blue sides had held up well, but the rim of the hood was tattered from a thousand little adjustments, and on this bright late October afternoon, Martha was glad to be able to push it back and let the baby see the sky.

IN CALIFORNIA, THE SKIES WERE SUNNY, too, but Henry was longing for rain. When it rained at the Disney Studio, employees in both the Animation Building and the Ink and Paint Building had an excuse to use the tunnel that connected the two. It had been built for the sole purpose of protecting artwork that had to pass between the two shops. Though extracurricular trips to the Ink and Paint Building—alternately known as the Rainbow Room for its splendid colors and the Nunnery for its splendid women—were made surreptitiously, rain allowed the trips to be legal, and therefore to last longer.

The first time Henry was asked to make a tunnel run, he didn't realize that someone from Ink and Paint would generally come down to meet him halfway, and instead he walked the whole length of the tunnel, with its clean, tiled floor, slightly arched ceiling, and dim overhead lights. People walked through it as if it were a train station. They stopped and smoked, they talked shop, they gossiped and they flirted.

When Henry stepped out at the other end of the tunnel, he felt he had emerged into a life-size paint box. Though most of the girls worked wearing white lab coats and white gloves, and though the walls were gray or white to prevent unintentional distortions, colors were omnipresent: in jars of paints, glass canisters of powdered pigments, centrifugal mixers, bowls, scales, beakers, test tubes, and rolling carts of coaster-size paint cups that were periodically offered to the painters, like snacks or sandwiches onboard a train. To Henry, the colors were as sensuous as food. That Disney mixed its own hues—as distinctive and immutable as the notes in the musical scale—increased the sense of rightness about the place: one right blue for the bluebirds; one right yellow for the tambourine.

There was also the unspeakable rightness of a girl named Fiona Coulson—tall, boyish, British, and apparently oddly disinclined to sit still long enough to be a good painter—who seemed to enjoy stepping away from her brushes to pick up the latest drawings or deliver the finished cels for checking. She happened to have a desk not far from the building's entrance, so by early November, at even the hint of rain, Henry made it a habit to check the Out basket and see if there were things to take over. The first time Fiona gave him cels to take back, she said "Carry on" to him, and seemed pleased by her wit. She was not a terribly bright girl. But her legs and her British accent more than made up for anything that she lacked.

She called him Gainesy. She was twenty-seven years old, unfazed by her unmarried state, and she seemed to enjoy treating Henry like a novice, in every way.

"Is it all right if I kiss you?" he asked her one morning. The tunnel was cool, damp, and dark, and Henry knew instinctively that Fiona would like his asking for permission.

"Yes," she said deliberately, as if she was talking to someone who'd never kissed a girl before. "It's all right if you kiss me."

She stood with exaggeratedly good posture, as if she had once been a dancer and still hoped to be confused for one. Everything about her seemed pushed forward and swaybacked.

A few people walked by them, and Henry waited for his moment.

He tried to remember kissing Daisy Fallows for the first time, thousands of days and nights ago now, when the challenge had been to pretend to be more experienced than he was. Now he faced the opposite task: to feign innocence he had long ago lost.

"That was nice, Gainesy," Fiona said.

He faked shy intensity, and kissed her again.

"Will you do the pickup tomorrow?" he asked her.

"Yes. Carry on," she said, amused with herself all over again.

HE AVOIDED THE COFFEE SHOP for several days and instead ate his lunch at the main commissary and, a few times, with Fiona at the Ink and Paint lunchroom, known to all as the Tea Room. He had not seen Annie for nearly two weeks; a male model had posed for them for the previous few classes. But Cindy caught up with him one evening just as he was starting home.

"Where've you been hiding?" she asked him.

"Behind a bunch of penguins," Henry said.

"We've hardly seen each other."

"I see you right now," Henry said.

"You know what I mean. I spent the night with you, Hanky. I'm not just some girl, you know," she said.

Some girl was exactly what she was, in Henry's opinion. She was some girl who happened to have been working at the restaurant the day he first stepped in. She was some girl who happened to have been the first girl at Disney he met. She was some girl who happened to have wanted him to want her.

They walked together toward the bicycle racks, then strolled on through the back lots. Side by side, with their bikes between them, they walked past the London rooftops where Bert and the chimney sweeps did their dance; past the park pavements where Mary, Bert, and the children popped into a chalk picture; and onto the set for Cherry Tree Lane. Behind the sweet whitewashed front of the Bankses' home, there was, of course, no home at all. It seemed as fitting a place as any to try to appease Cindy with a kiss.

"You're not a nice boy, are you?" she asked him.

"No. I'm not a nice boy," he said, though of course to Annie that was exactly what he was and was expected to be, and to Fiona—well, he tried not to think of Fiona while he was here with Cindy. And to Mary Jane—well, he tried not to think about Mary Jane at all.

IN ART CLASSES BACK IN HENRY'S DAYS at Humphrey, Charlie had talked a fair amount about how to see things not as symbols but as shapes in relation to one another. Charlie had told the students that whenever they were having trouble getting something right, they should turn the subject upside down. Then they could draw without their eyes tricking their minds into believing things were shaped and sized differently than they really were. Henry was good at this.

Apples were not circles; chair legs were almost never perfectly perpendicular to chair seats; it was the eyes, not the nose, that bisected a human face—and so on.

In this way, Henry eventually came to see the three current women in his California life as well. It was as if he had turned them all upside down, to study how they were in reality. He could see in each the relationship of beauty to personality, neediness to generosity, humor to brains, silliness to insecurity. He could see their mouths and hands, their hair and clothes. He could see their attraction to him, and—understanding every aspect of them individually—he could understand where he found beauty in them. But he never let his eye trick his mind into seeing them whole, as symbols of anything greater than their parts.

ON A LATE FRIDAY MORNING in November, Henry walked through the tunnel to the Nunnery with a small and barely legitimate stack of drawings and, much to his delight, managed to meet Fiona on the other side.

"Come down with me for a minute," he said to her loudly. "I need your help."

"We're fooling no one," she said as she followed him down the stairs. "And we're not the first, you know. They do call this the Tunnel of Love."

"I don't care," Henry said.

Henry put the drawings on the top rung of a work ladder and stood close to Fiona, smelling her lemony perfume.

"I do in fact have to get back to the shop," she said. The way she said it, *shop* almost rhymed with *hope*.

"You do in fact have to let me kiss you first," Henry said.

"They're going to miss me up there," she said. "It's not even raining out." *Not* sounded like *note*.

"Say *shop* again."

"Shope."

"Say *not*."

"Note."

He kissed her at length, moving a hand gingerly from the back of her head to the back of her neck, then across her shoulder and down to her breast, where he let it linger, as if he was nervous to do more.

The tunnel was cooler than usual somehow, emptier than usual, quieter than usual.

After a long time, Henry cupped Fiona's breast and pressed against her, kissing her, his other hand high on the cool wall.

"What do you suppose is the longest time anyone's ever stayed down here?" Fiona asked him.

"Not long enough," Henry said.

"Odd that no one's come through, though," Fiona said.

"Yes. Quite," Henry said, trying to mimic her accent. "Odd indeed. You sound exactly like Julie Andrews."

"Have you met her?"

"Yes. Say 'supercalifragilisticexpialidocious.' "

"Say goodbye for now," Fiona told him.

The corridor echoed with her laughter, and with the promise of more silent moments to come.

OF THE NINE OLD MEN, Milt Kahl was the most irascible, and it was commonly understood that around his office in D-Wing, silence was an absolute. So when Henry came back from the tunnel and heard loud radio noises, he couldn't fathom why anyone would risk inviting Kahl's wrath.

The noise of the radio, however, quickly resolved itself into words. Henry heard:

"The shots apparently came from the fifth floor of the Texas School Book Depository building, possibly from an automatic-type weapon."

He heard:

"Police were looking for a young white man dressed in a white shirt, with Levi's . . ."

Chris ran over to him, all pretense of coolness gone.

"He's been shot. Kennedy's been shot."

Chris pulled Henry toward the desk of an in-betweener who had a radio.

Into the utter blankness of Henry's mind there rose a single image: the black-and-white campaign poster from Charlie and Karen's kitchen. The promising eyes, the white teeth, the straw layers of hair.

Henry looked around the bullpen for a face—any face—that wasn't contorted in pain, shock, or grim concentration.

"Just a moment, just a moment. We have a bulletin coming in. We now switch you directly to Parkland Hospital."

Whatever conversation there had been beneath the radio now ceased. Henry heard:

"The president of the United States is dead. I have just talked to Father Oscar Hubert of the Holy Trinity Catholic Church. He and another priest tell me that the pair of men have just administered the last rites of the Catholic Church to President Kennedy. I asked the father, 'Is Mr. Kennedy dead?' And his quote, 'He's dead, all right.' "

Everything stopped. Office doors that were usually closed were opened. Everywhere—outside and in—people stood in clusters. The reason was the need to have proximity to the radios; the effect was the sense that no one could bear to be alone.

HENRY FOUGHT THE URGE to run back into the tunnel, as if that could reverse time. He wanted to talk to someone, but he didn't know to whom. Charlie and Karen came into his mind, no doubt because of the poster. But then he imagined their shock, and their need to comfort the students around them at Humphrey. He thought about Mary Jane, but in light of her "don't be ridiculous," she was the last person with whom he wanted to risk seeming in need.

Henry left the Animation Building and wandered over the studio grounds. He found himself hoping to see Annie. He didn't find her, nor did he find Cindy when he stopped at the coffee shop. Lots of people had gone home already. The front gate was deserted. There was a hush over the whole place, as if a director had just called

"Action!" But the only actions were listening, and crying, and comforting.

WHEN THE PHONE RANG THAT NIGHT, Henry knew that it would be Martha, but for some reason it didn't bother him.

"Oh, Hanky," he heard her say.

"Hi, Emem."

It had to have been years since he had called her that.

"Isn't it awful?" she said.

"How's everyone taking it there?"

"Oh, well, you know. These girls. Who knows what they think about?"

"They weren't upset?"

"Well, only one of them was around when it happened, and she hightailed it out of here pretty fast."

"So it's just been you and the baby?"

"The baby. Yes," Martha said.

To Henry, she sounded almost unbearably old. An old woman, sitting almost alone in an old, almost empty house.

"Is there something else, Emem?" he asked her.

There was a brief silence, which Henry knew could mean either surprise or calculation.

"I'm losing my job," she said.

"You're what?"

"I'm losing my job."

"My grandfather *fired* you?" Henry asked, incredulous.

"No."

"What then?"

"He's retiring. Well, no," she said bitterly. "He's being made to retire."

"What does that have to do with you?"

"The new president," Martha said. "She doesn't *believe* in home economics. She's one of *those* women."

"Have you talked to her?"

"She says I'm old-fashioned, and out of touch. As if it will ever be old-fashioned to know how to care for a baby!"

Henry had a mental image of the line of practice house baby journals, their pages of photographs fading.

Mildred Fairfax made me this hat!

He sank into one of the two chairs by the table, took a pad and paper, and started to sketch. As he listened to Martha, he drew simple shapes. Circles and squares, triangles and rectangles. A round hat. A rectangular crib.

"If only you could come home for Thanksgiving," Martha said.

He drew the Bird Woman from *Mary Poppins,* sitting on the steps of St. Paul's Cathedral, feeding the birds. The Bird Woman was Martha.

Listen, listen, she's calling to you.

CLOUDS CAME AND WENT, and on Saturday the wind blew up. Henry walked to the food market. Plants and shrubs bent and twisted and tried to dance, but the palm trees remained stoic. Behind every open door and window was a working radio or television. Several bags filled with old newspapers had tumbled over on one of the side streets, and beside them were a discarded, seatless chair and an old electric fan, whose blades rotated with furious fake life.

Like almost everyone else in the country, Henry spent the rest of the day, and the next day, watching television. The world had altered. Reporters kept speaking about Mrs. Kennedy's pink suit; the green, grassy knoll; the red roses; the blue sky; the blood. But the world once again was in black and white. There was the black of the two-inch-high newspaper headlines: KENNEDY SLAIN, KENNEDY DEAD, and, bizarrely, in the *Los Angeles Times:* ASSASSINATE KENNEDY. There was the black and white and gray of television, broadcasting continuously, with all entertainment programs canceled. Cameras showed crowds standing across the street from the Dallas County Jail, shades of gray under a gray sign for a restaurant speciously called Victoria's Purple Orchid. *Life* magazine published an issue with its famous red logo printed in black.

The assassin's name was Lee Harvey Oswald. Oswald, like Oswald the Lucky Rabbit, which was Walt Disney's first cartoon character, a forerunner of Mickey Mouse himself. Henry wondered where Walt was now, what he was thinking about his wonderful world. No one had seen him the day of the shooting; he was supposedly in Florida, checking out land for some new project.

On Sunday, Jack Ruby killed Lee Harvey Oswald on television. Kennedy was laid in state, saluted, prayed for, and walked to his grave with a skittish, riderless horse. On Monday, stores were closed, and businesses only limped back to life as the week went on. On Wednesday, Henry used approximately half of everything he'd ever saved to buy a plane ticket home.

THE MOMENT THAT HENRY SAW MARTHA, he knew that he shouldn't have come. He understood—from the force of her hug, the moistness in her eyes, the slight tremor in her hands as she brushed nothing from his shoulder—that there was no way to quiet her need. He had flown across the country—a grueling trip—and would have to return after only two days. But this was not a gift; instead it was an excuse, a platform from which she would ask him for more. On the phone, Martha had said *If only you could come home for Thanksgiving,* and the implied end of the sentence had been: *then I would be happy; then I would feel better; then I might have the strength to make things turn out all right.*

Instead, the real statement should have been: *If only you could come home for Thanksgiving, then I could show you in person how much I need you.*

She went through the motions of trying to treat him like a man. She didn't flinch when he lit a cigarette. She offered him wine with dinner.

"What's it like out there?" she asked him, but even that simple question seemed to Henry an imposition, an unexpected and unwanted insinuation of herself into his world. He thought of his palm trees, strong and solitary. He thought of his apartment.

"It's nice," he said.

"Do you have a lot of friends?" she asked.

"At work," he said. "Great bunch of guys."

"Any special girl?" she asked him, somewhat coquettishly.

He thought of Cindy's breasts, and Fiona's legs, and Annie's sweet-ness.

"No," he said. "No special girl."

"Maybe you'll want to see Mary Jane," Martha said.

"Maybe," he said, but he didn't realize how much he wanted to until she appeared the next morning at the back door.

SHE HAD GOTTEN SKINNY in the months since she'd called his pro-posal ridiculous. A pair of bell-bottom jeans sat low on her hips, held up by a wide leather belt. She had her hair in a kerchief.

"Happy Thanksgiving," she said ironically.

"Yah."

"Why'd you come?"

"Martha," he said.

"Are they canning her?"

"It looks that way."

"Good boy for coming, then. Are you going to talk to your grand-father?"

"He got canned too," Henry said. "It won't make any difference."

"You should do it anyway," Mary Jane said.

They stood awkwardly by the old tree swing.

"Where were you when you heard?" she asked him.

He could sense in her the pain that he knew he should have felt more deeply.

"At work," Henry said. "What about you?"

"I was on my way home."

"Home? From where?"

"From college."

"I thought you were going to college here."

"Why would I go to college here?"

"Well, where are you going to college?"

Mary Jane paused a moment, then quietly said: "Berkeley."

Henry tried to let this register. He stared into her one eye.

"Berkeley," he said. "You've been in California the whole time I've been in California?"

"Well, it's only been a few months for both of us," she said.

So it was not just that she hadn't wanted to marry him, he thought. She hadn't even wanted to see him, though she had been just a few hours away. Henry's face must have registered, equally, his hurt and his determination to conquer it.

"I didn't know how to reach you," Mary Jane said.

"You could have tried the studio."

"I didn't know if you'd gotten a job there."

That hadn't stopped Martha, Henry thought, but immediately was embarrassed by thinking it.

He left Mary Jane standing in the yard where they had met in their childhoods: ice blond hair, red Keds, blood, Miss Fancy and Mickey Mouse, when there could be only one Miss Fancy.

"Henry," she called after him. "Let's talk about it," she said, but he pretended not to hear her.

MARTHA HAD A PLAN. That fact did not surprise him, but the extent of its impracticality did.

Over turkey dinner that night—brilliantly cooked, he would always give her that—she told Henry that the new president was considering two possible uses for the practice house: a residence for visiting alumnae, and a new fund-raising office. But Martha had a third idea: to turn the place into an art studio.

"We could have a darkroom in the bathroom upstairs," she told Henry. "The kitchen would be perfect for all the paints and supplies. The light in the living room would be ideal for sketching and painting, and we could turn the baby's room into a studio for you."

"For me?" Henry asked.

"Yes. You see, if you ran the whole thing, then maybe we could go on living upstairs."

HENRY HAD NO MEMORY of his grandfather's residence. In the few times they had met outside the practice house, the location had always been Dr. Gardner's office, where the presence of his secretary had perhaps justified the formality of his tone.

Now Henry stood in the living room, unaware that it was the place where he had long ago served up make-believe cookies and drawn patterns in the beige carpet. Dr. Gardner was in the midst of packing his things to move out, however, so the carpet had been rolled up; and the floor, newly uncovered, looked fresher than anything else in the place. The walls were bare and pockmarked; the bookshelves were nearly empty.

He looked old and slightly translucent, but his appearance stirred no emotion in Henry, who had long since lost any hope or interest in following the connection that their bloodlines might have suggested. For his part, Dr. Gardner eyed Henry as he always had: with a strange, awkward mixture of curiosity and fear.

"You've come to talk with me about Mrs. Gaines, I assume," Dr. Gardner said.

"Yes."

"Have a seat. I'd offer you a cup of coffee, but I'm fairly sure the china has already been packed."

There were still two upholstered armchairs, one on either side of the fireplace, but neither man sat.

"What's going to happen to her?" Henry asked.

"You're concerned?"

"Of course I'm concerned," Henry said.

"I don't think you've ever expressed your concern before," Dr. Gardner said.

"She's never been about to lose her job before," Henry said.

Dr. Gardner walked over to one of the windows and thoughtfully, almost lovingly, ran a hand down one of the drapes. "I want to ask you a question before I answer yours," he said.

"What?"

"Are you concerned about Mrs. Gaines because you care about her, or because you don't want to have to care for her?"

"I want to know what's going to happen to her."

"I honestly don't know," the president said. "It's not up to me anymore."

"You're telling me you have absolutely no influence on the new administration? You can't help protect anyone?"

"Not even myself, apparently," he said with self-pity.

"So Martha is just going to be fired?" Henry asked.

"No one wants a practice house program," Dr. Gardner said impatiently. "This is 1963. Haven't you heard? Women want to be liberated from all that."

"She has this idea that she could go on living there if it became an art studio," Henry said.

Dr. Gardner shook his head. "That'll never fly," he said. "Never. The best I can do is to try to persuade them to let her keep a room upstairs. And I was planning on doing that anyway."

Dr. Gardner reached into his inside breast pocket for a leather case, from which he extracted a cigar. Henry noticed that his hand was shaking.

"One more thing," Dr. Gardner said, and Henry turned back to see him scratch at the corner of his mouth with a shaking index finger.

"What is it?" Henry asked.

"Your mother," he said. "Have you heard anything from your mother?"

"No," Henry said, immediately debating whether to ask the next question. "Have you?" he finally said.

"No," Dr. Gardner said, a pained look crossing his face. "I guess she's given us both up," he said, which was the closest he had ever come, or ever would, to acknowledging that Henry and he were related.

———

MARY JANE APPEARED on Saturday morning and insisted she drive Henry to the station.

"I've got a taxi coming," he said.

"Oh, Henry. Come on. So I didn't tell you I was going to Berkeley. Let's call it even, okay?"

"Okay," he said. "We're even."

She looked away, and when she looked back, Henry could see that she was crying. Her nose was red, and tears ran from her good eye.

"Does your other eye cry?" Henry asked her.

"What?"

"Does your other eye cry?"

The question was so ridiculous, so inappropriate to the moment, that Mary Jane stared at him, and then they both burst out laughing.

BACK AT THE STUDIO, there was a major push to complete *Mary Poppins*. The opening was supposed to be in August of 1964, and there was still far too much to be done. A new class of in-betweeners had been hired, and both Henry and Chris took deliberate pleasure in watching their relative inexperience. The hours of the working days changed, so that there were weekend and evening shifts as well. In February, Henry was switched from the penguin waiters to Jane's pink carousel horse, and then, in March, to the bouquet of Mary's flowers that turned into butterflies.

Throughout the spring, Henry worked longer hours than he ever had and spent less time with the women. Fiona understood, because at the Nunnery, she was equally busy. Annie was hurt, and Cindy was outright angry.

"You're not the guy I thought you were," she complained to him on a night in late May when they'd spent the evening in bed and he had gotten dressed to go home.

"I'm not the guy anyone thinks I am," he said.

———

HE HAD BEEN PRETENDING to be eighteen for more than a year, so as his actual birthday approached, Henry found he was less happy than relieved about its arrival. He did not particularly wish to celebrate, but with some bygone, formless longing, he felt the need for attention, too.

It was Fiona who took him to dinner that night. This was not because he had decided he liked her best, and he certainly didn't love her. It was simply because she'd been the first one to ask. He might have preferred to go with Annie or Cindy. He had even thought about taking out a girl named Coco, whom he had just met at the market. Annie, perhaps, knew enough not to ask him if he wasn't asking her. And Cindy did ask, but as soon as he said he couldn't, she said she'd forgotten that she had other plans as well.

All three of them gave him presents, though. Fiona's was the dinner, and a cel she had painted of her own design: a hideous abstraction that Henry knew he was supposed to find deep.

"Thanks," he said.

"You don't like it," she said.

"Of course I like it," he said. "And I like you for making it."

From Cindy he received a trio of sleazy paperbacks called *Sex Hop, Sex Atlas,* and *Sex Pack.* It was clear that she thought her boldness would delight and inspire him.

"Thanks," he said.

"You don't like them," she said.

"Of course I like them," he said. "And I like you for getting them."

For her part, Annie had knitted him a scarf.

"Thanks," he said.

"You don't like it," she said.

"Of course I like it."

"Then why do you look so annoyed?"

"Because you spent too much time on this," he said.

"But Henry. I wanted to."

"You have better things to do," he said.

The effect on her was as immediate as if Mark Harburg had just asked her to change poses. Her eyes narrowed; her shoulders sank—so much that he felt he had to do something to open her eyes again, lift her shoulders. He stood looking down at her, and then he used the scarf to circle her neck and bring her in close, just as he'd seen some student do at Humphrey so long ago. He kissed her.

"You don't love me, do you?" she asked him.

"I couldn't love anyone more," he said, which was not exactly a lie.

4

To Help the Medicine Go Down

By now, Henry had imagined the phone call many times, but in his imagination, it had always been Dr. Gardner calling to tell him that Martha was dead. Somehow, he had not counted on an illness, with all the attendant demands and the guilt and dread. And he had not counted on Martha herself being the one to deliver the news.

"It's cancer," she said to him on the phone. It was the evening of August 27, the evening of the *Mary Poppins* premiere. Her timing was perfect, he thought bitterly.

"What kind of cancer?"

"Does it matter?" Martha said.

"Yes it matters."

"It's everywhere, Hanky."

She sounded almost relieved, or perhaps that was only his imagination.

"Will you come see me? I'm going to die."

"Have you gotten a second opinion?"

"I don't need a second opinion."

"Have they told you how long you've got?"

"Not long."

"Have they told you?"

"Henry. Don't make this hard for me."

———

HE HUNG UP AND WAS somewhat surprised to discover that the office was nearly empty. He had been on the phone for only ten minutes, and almost everyone was gone—either off to dress for the premiere or to go home early.

Henry walked through the bullpen, hands in his pockets as always, proudly surveying the storyboards for some of the films that were being developed. He imagined for a moment what it would feel like to be Walt tonight, what it would feel like to be Walt on any night.

With the light coming in the windows where the shutters had not been drawn, Henry walked back to his own desk and saw that someone had left a present for him, a six-inch-long box wrapped in the Mickey Mouse paper that usually adorned all studio gifts.

Inside was a silver spoon with Mary Poppins and her umbrella engraved on the handle.

"Something to help the medicine go down," Walt had written on a slip of celluloid, above his famous signature.

For a moment—and it lasted only as long as it took Henry to walk once more around the bullpen—he inhabited a world in which his secrets, fears, and wishes were somehow magically understood. The moment ended when he passed Chris's desk and saw an identical box on it, and then on all the others.

The spoon, obviously, had nothing to do with the specific pain that Henry or anyone else was likely to go through, now or ever. And though each note was indeed hand-lettered and signed, Henry should have been the first to recognize that in a world of animators and in-betweeners, that meant absolutely nothing, either. It was an opening-night memento, lovely and kind, but produced in bulk for everyone who had had even the slightest thing to do with the film.

For those who had had more than slight things to do, there was, instead of a commemorative spoon, a coveted ticket to the old-fashioned gala opening at Grauman's Chinese Theatre, where giant Disney characters stood curbside, greeting guests in black tie and gowns. The festivities were being aired locally, so when Henry got home, he nursed a glass of wine and watched the broadcast on TV. A trainload of balloons was released into the night sky. Actors were dressed as British bobbies and English music-hall singers, and various Hollywood reporters milled about.

"They tell me this could be one of your biggest pictures, Mr. Disney," one interviewer said.

"Well, I haven't retired yet, you know," Disney said. "You never know what's coming."

THE THING WITH WOMEN had become so easy. It took remarkably little for Henry to figure out how to get them. Part of his success, he knew, was the certainty of success itself. It never occurred to him that any of them would be ungettable. It was merely a matter of working out the steps from *apart* to *together*—just like the steps in in-between-ing.

For all his facility, Henry was not exactly cynical, and his confidence was so justified that most of the time it readily passed for charisma instead of conceit.

Mary Jane was the notable exception to this pattern, and in the days following Henry's conversation with Martha, he realized how frequently he was thinking about her. He wasn't sure why. Perhaps they really had evened the score. Perhaps it was all their history: Other than Martha and, if you counted him, Dr. Gardner, Mary Jane had been the only person who had known him throughout his life.

As he flew east on the last day of August—this time it was Martha who had paid for his airfare—he thought about Mary Jane, seeing her in sequential, but recessive, snapshots: skinny and slim-hipped and piratelike, laughing in the car after his question about her uncrying eye; pudgy and square and brutal on the day he had asked her to marry him; sexy in the photograph she had sent him at Humphrey; earnest in their grade school coatroom, listening intently as he told her about his real mother; and then finally, unavoidably, the sight of her blindfolded and bloodied, feeling for the car door—and then giggling in her hospital bed, bound to him forever by how each had forever been harmed.

"I'M SORRY," HE SAID TO HER, walking through the campus at Wilton the morning after he landed.

"For what?" she asked.

"For your eye," he said.

"Oh. That. You mean the crying thing?"

"No. Not the crying thing. I mean, your eye."

"Oh."

"You know, I wasn't even really throwing the block at *you*."

"Yes you were, Henry."

"I think I was just mad."

"You didn't want to play castle."

"That's right."

"And you didn't want to have to choose between Annabel and me," she said.

"And you said there couldn't be more than one Miss Fancy," he said.

"Do you want to choose now?" Mary Jane asked.

"Sometimes."

"Anyone in particular?"

So he told her about his three women. About Annie's delicacy, Cindy's sass, and the haughtiness of Fiona's smile. He told her about his vague, distracted guilt and his annoyance—really unchanged since nursery school—whenever one of them tried to make a greater claim on him than the others.

Imparting this kind of information was new to Henry, a discovery as concrete and startling as if someone had just revealed for him a new room in the house he had lived in for years.

MARTHA, MEANWHILE, seemed to sag more noticeably when Henry walked into any room where she was. Henry knew that she hadn't invented her illness. Two mornings after his arrival at Wilton, he had gone with her to her doctor's appointment and heard firsthand the litany of her symptoms, tests, results, and the doctor's unequivocal conclusion. But the doctor had also given no hint of a time frame. In fact, he had repeated—not only for Martha's benefit but also when she was out of the room—that some people could live for years with her type of cancer, which he called Hodgkin's disease. He said Martha might easily have had it for years as well.

At the end of his first day home, Henry understood that Martha would die from this cancer and that, before she did, she would use it at every possible turn to keep him close to her side. The claim upon him was nearly as strong as the rage it inspired.

5

It's Called a Toke

Henry first called Mary Jane at Berkeley on a Friday in October, but he had to leave her ten messages before she called him back. It was early November by then, and she was breathless with tales of the Free Speech Movement and her own raging debate about whether to join in with the protesters or simply write about them. This was a topic that kept her occupied—and, to Henry, somewhat more remote than he wanted—throughout the rollicking fall of '64 and the winter of '65. Mary Jane organized and petitioned and took part in the campus sit-in and didn't actually ask Henry to visit her until the middle of March.

She was living on the northeast side of campus in a two-bedroom dorm suite, where the radiators were always on and the windows were always open. The floors were linoleum and elephant gray. Track marks, scuff marks, rust stains, and spills of all kinds and vintages had contributed to their texture, if not to their allure.

Mary Jane had a roommate named Alexa, who seemed to want to share nothing more than the living room and the bathroom—and those only reluctantly. Southern and square, she wore white blouses, slim kilts, and dark green cat-eye glasses. Her prized possession was a small, pale blue Samsonite train case, in which she kept her ample supply of makeup. When Henry first met Alexa, she was doing what she would do on nearly all their subsequent encounters: namely, sitting at the card table by a window, leaning into the slightly clouded mirror in the little suitcase, and daintily checking, patting, sponging, or outlining various parts of her face. Brush in hand and palette before her, she reminded Henry a bit of Fiona—in those rare moments when he had actually seen Fiona at her inking desk. But it was clear that Alexa wanted nothing at all to do with Henry—or with Mary Jane, for that matter.

On Henry's second visit to Berkeley—this one in early April—Mary Jane drove Alexa from her makeup table by relentlessly playing *The Beatles vs. The Four Seasons,* and when the door finally closed, Mary Jane rolled Henry his first joint. She used the crease of the double record album as a kind of funnel, taking out seeds and impurities, creating a tiny green-brown mound of marijuana, a miniature version of the leaf piles that Henry and she had sorted as children under the ancient autumn sky. With the little pile ready, Mary Jane took out a small white booklet that had the word *Zig-Zag* and a strange Arabian-looking man on the cover. Smiling, she opened the booklet and popped one sheet out, leaving another behind it, just like Kleenex.

"Zig-Zag?" Henry asked her.

"Rolling papers," she said.

Smiling, she placed the marijuana carefully on top of the rolling paper, twisted it into a tight stick, and licked the edge of the paper to seal it. Finally, ever so gently, she ran the whole joint lightly into and out of her mouth—a tiny, provocative gesture that Henry would always enjoy watching.

"Are you ready?" she asked him.

IT WAS AN INITIATION. They both knew it, and knew that it was a milestone in the making.

Henry inhaled, predictably coughed, and endured her equally predictable laughter.

"Try again," she said. "Only this time, breathe in a little less and hold it in a little longer."

He followed her instructions, allowing the woodsy, sweet-sour smoke to enter his lungs.

"You're going to love this," Mary Jane said, as if the few puffs she had taken had already endowed her with cosmic mind-reading abilities.

"Should I have another puff?" he asked her.

"Toke."

"What?"

"It's called a toke. With a cigarette you have a puff. With a joint, you have a toke."

"Toke," Henry repeated, sampling the word and then the joint. A bit of time and a few songs rolled past. "Toke," he said again, and again illustrated the word. Suddenly, giddily, he found the word itself ineffably hilarious.

"Towwwwwke," he intoned.

"Yes, Henry," Mary Jane said, watching his progress with some satisfaction and considerable superiority.

"Towwwwwke," he said again, laughing lightly.

Her couch was a seven-foot-long thrift-shop monstrosity, covered in a salmon-red fabric that was the color and nearly the texture of heavy-grade sandpaper. Henry lay back on it and watched the smoke marble the air.

On Mary Jane's record player, the Beatles sang:

Do you want to know a secret?
Do you promise not to tell?

Henry sang along, "Ooo-ah-ooh."

"Now," Mary Jane said. "That's more like it."

SUNSET HAD TINTED THE WINDOWS ORANGE, but now the sun was down, the panes showed fingerprints, dirt, and a series of white splotches in which Henry struggled to find patterns or meaning.

"What are you looking at?" Mary Jane asked him.

"Bird droppings, I think."

"Gross."

"Actually, they're kind of pretty."

"Henry. We're not *that* high."

THROUGHOUT THE SPARKLING SPRING OF 1965, Henry spent nearly every other weekend at Berkeley with Mary Jane. Sometimes they even left her suite to wander the campus or see a movie or—especially after they'd smoked her pot—grab a bite to eat. Now clearly in her element, she had gathered a group of friends and a style of living that Henry found compelling, especially because it was so different from the still relatively buttoned-down world of Disney. Everything in Mary Jane's Berkeley crowd was long hair, long skirts, and long, intense talks.

Henry would drive up on a Friday night and arrive at the dorm bringing wine, but not the Almadén or Lancers that the rest of the undergraduates drank. He would bring something French, with a nice-looking label, and Mary Jane would light candles, then cigarettes, then joints, and they would talk half the night. One weekend—by her design but with his help—they painted her bedroom entirely black, including the school-owned bed and dresser, even including the ceiling, which inspired her to rub his shoulders and neck, though at a speed that was almost aggressively platonic.

Usually—despite the dorm's rules against such visitors—Henry slept on the couch, feeling a fraternal protectiveness as both Mary Jane and Alexa retired to their rooms and he was left to turn out the lights and make sure the hot plate had been switched off.

One night in early June, Mary Jane fell asleep on the far end of the couch, and when Henry woke in the morning, he saw that both her madras shirt and her eye patch had been thrown askew during the night. Her bra—white, clean, more rounded than pointed—was clearly visible. But he found himself staring instead at her face. He had always wondered what Mary Jane's eye looked like under the patch. Over the years he had imagined all kinds of horrors—bruised flesh, missing flesh, a hole like the kind a doll's eye would leave. Instead, her bad eye—what he could see of it, anyway—looked not that different from her good eye. Both were pale, fragile, closed in sleep. Hidden from sun-light all these years, the skin around her bad eye was fishily paler, and Henry thought the eyelashes were a little more sparse. But otherwise, there seemed no difference, and Henry found himself slightly disap-pointed, as if he'd finally been told a secret, only to discover that it was something he'd known all along. Nevertheless, it was an intimacy that until now he hadn't known, and as Henry lazily watched Mary Jane sleep, he realized with satisfaction how much he knew about her. Her favorite color was still pink. She was still angry at her mother. She was still scared of heights. Nervous around babies. Dreaming of being a journalist and taking on the world.

He had never seen her naked. He had never been naked in front of her. There had been their one, long-ago-summer kiss and his even less plausible marriage proposal, and now, after the wild, precipitous ter-rain of adolescence, their friendship had returned to its natural path. Still, when she woke and saw him, she covered her eye before she cov-ered her breasts.

6

Talk About Disneyland!

The New York World's Fair ran from April to October in 1964 and again in 1965. During those twelve months, four enormous Disney exhibits had drawn nearly 50 million visitors—as well as Walt's exuberant attention. Meanwhile, despite the huge success of *Mary Poppins,* there had been a constant and deepening depression at the studio, where the pared-down ranks of animators worked desultorily on various shorts for television's *Wonderful World of Color,* made up storyboards for possible new features, and bemoaned their dwindling budgets and status. There had been some hope that when the fair ended, Walt's focus would return to the studio. But now, as the fair came to an end, and Disney looked for ways to relocate hundreds of small moving dolls and large moving cavemen, it was obvious that he was much more interested in his three-dimensional than his two-dimensional worlds. There were even rumors of something most people were calling "the Florida Project."

Martha phoned Henry in early November.

"I read that Mr. Disney is starting an East Coast operation," she said.

"I've heard that too," Henry said.

"Well, how far east? Could you work for that and then come back and be with me for a while?"

"I don't think so."

"Why not?"

"Because," Henry said. "It's in Florida, which is almost as far from you as L.A."

"I'd think you'd want to see me while you still can," Martha said.

"SHE'S NEVER GOING TO LET ME GO," Henry told Annie. It was Christmas Eve, and for Annie's sake, he had gone to her church on Hollywood Way to hear her sing. Now they were walking back to her place. The air was warm and heavy. Annie didn't say anything.

"Annie?" Henry said. "You know?"

He could hear both sets of their footsteps.

"I know," she said, somewhat carelessly.

"And nothing I ever do for her is going to be enough," Henry said.

Again, there was silence.

"Annie?" he said.

"Okay, look," she said. "I just don't get it."

"What don't you get?"

"Hey, I know she lied to you when you were growing up. But now it's just that—all she wants is for you to be her son. Why is that so terrible?"

"She doesn't just want me to be her son," Henry said. "She wants me to live with her, and need her, and love her. Love her more than I love anyone else."

"She cares about you," Annie said. "Does that have to be a bad thing?"

Henry asked: "Would you want me to love her more than I love you?"

"Well," Annie answered, in barely a whisper. "That wouldn't be saying much, would it?"

They had reached the steps of her house. Someone had draped a W-shaped garland of Christmas lights on the doorframe, incongruous as the December warmth.

Henry tucked a strand of Annie's hair behind her ear.

"Aren't you going to ask me up?" he said.

"No. Not tonight."

She might suddenly have been speaking a foreign language.

"What?" Henry asked.

"Not tonight," Annie said.

"YOU SHOULD LET HER GO," Mary Jane counseled in the first week of the new year, after Henry had told her about Christmas Eve. With her ever-growing political fervor, she had spent her winter vacation organizing for the Student Nonviolent Coordinating Committee. Now Henry was sitting beside her at a table in the Union, watching her fold flyers.

"What do you mean, let her go?" Henry asked.

"Annie. You should let her go. What's she ever done to you? Why keep her on the hook?"

"What makes you think she doesn't like the arrangement?" Henry asked.

"Come on, doofus. Who would like the arrangement?"

"What if I love her?"

"Bullshit, Henry."

"What do you mean, bullshit?"

"I mean bullshit. You don't love her."

"How do you know?"

"You love *you*. And barely," she said.

IT MIGHT HAVE BEEN Mary Jane scolding him, or maybe just Henry's own yearning. Whatever the reason, he left his desk on the evening after he returned from Berkeley and went eagerly to the art studio. His goal was to stop by and ask Annie to come over after the class, but once he was there, he found he wanted to stay. It delighted him how completely he now took for granted his place in a room that had once been so intimidating.

Annie was up on the platform, mid-pose—by the look of it a long one. Her right hand was on her left shoulder, and her face was turned in to her right one, like a bird seeking shelter under its own wing. Yet her body language suggested not fear or sorrow but coyness. As Henry straddled one of the smooth wooden benches and nodded hello to the other artists, he marveled at Annie's skill and also at her concentration, because she had to have heard the door open, had to have felt the outside air against her naked skin, maybe even wanted to turn her head to see who had just come in. It was not until Mark Harburg said "Next pose" that she looked up and met Henry's eyes. He gave her his best, most meaningful, most sincere smile. And it *was* sincere. He wanted, at that moment, to be the wing above her.

After an hour or so, Harburg called for a break. Annie, as usual, pulled on a sweater and made the rounds of the artists' benches, looking at their work. When she reached Henry's spot, she found that he had dressed her in her current sweater, put a rose in her hand, and drawn his own dining table before her.

She smiled when she saw the drawing, but in a pale sort of way.

"How about I cook for us tonight?" he asked.

"I don't think so," she said.

"Candles. Lava lamps. Wine. Sherry."

"Henry," she said. "I'm getting married."

THE GUY'S NAME WAS JIMMY OAKES. Annie had met him at an interview for a modeling job that she didn't get. He was a photographer's assistant, and he'd been up on a ladder, clamping a backdrop to a metal frame, when she walked into the studio. The ad was for a shampoo, and though the photographer found her face utterly enchanting, he thought her hair was too flat.

Jimmy Oakes, Henry thought, must have seen in Annie's eyes the same mixture of sweetness and sadness that he had always seen; must have seen in her beauty the same promise of hope and inspiration; must have wanted, too, to be the wing protecting her.

Or maybe he'd just liked her in bed.

THE WEDDING TOOK PLACE in the Lutheran church where Henry had heard Annie sing just a month before. Her mother, who looked not much older than Annie, sat nervously in the front row. Beside her,

Annie's sister awkwardly twisted a strand of her long hair around a long pale finger.

The music was the traditional wedding march. Annie entered beside her father. She wore a garland of tiny roses and a necklace of baby pearls. Her dress was short-sleeved and calf-length, the color of a blush, not quite white, not quite a wedding gown. She wore makeup, and her hair was in a hatlike pouf; she looked almost unlike herself, clearly the product of too much advice.

Henry stared at her, transfixed. She was, of all the women he'd wanted and dated since coming to California, the only one who'd ever rejected him.

He had never wanted anyone more.

"I'M SO GLAD YOU CAME," Annie said at the reception when it was Henry's turn to embrace her.

"I wouldn't have missed it," he said.

She looked around for the groom. "I want you to meet Jimmy," she said.

"I will."

"You'd like him, Henry."

"No," Henry said. "I wouldn't."

He realized immediately how wrong it had sounded, though he had meant it as a compliment.

Annie fidgeted with her new wedding ring. "You mean we're not going to stay friends?" she asked.

"No," Henry said. "I don't think we could stay friends."

He said it because, despite the ring on her finger and the exuberant first dance with her groom, Henry believed that Annie could still be his, and it wouldn't be fair to want her.

HENRY FOUND MARK HARBURG leaning against a wall, a gin and tonic in his hand.

"Gaines!" he cried with liquid conviviality.

Henry walked over to join him.

"Think of it," he said. "Our little Annie. Married off."

"Yes, sir."

"Bet you didn't think this day would come."

"Well," Henry said.

"Bet you thought you'd be the one," Harburg said.

"No, sir," he said with complete honesty. "I never did."

AT ANNIE'S WEDDING, Harburg, in his slightly oiled state, had told Henry that the studio was going to go ahead with making *The Jungle Book* as an animated feature. Henry immediately knew that it was what he wanted to do.

On the surface, *The Jungle Book* was a classic children's film, filled with light and lovable characters and songs. To Henry, however, it was—darkly and unavoidably—a story of betrayal and, inevitably, of loss. First the boy, Mowgli, is orphaned, then handed off from panther to wolves, from wolves to panther, from panther to bear, and, finally and most painfully, from bear to humans. All of the characters care for him. But everyone he trusts is replaced.

"Trust in me," the python sings to the boy.

"I don't trust anyone anymore," the boy says.

Henry asked Phil Morrow to assign him to the film.

"I've got you on *The Borrowers* instead," Morrow told him.

"I've worked here three years," Henry said. "Isn't it time I have a say in what I work on?"

"I'll think about it," Morrow said.

Now, as if he were wooing a girl, Henry started doing daily drawings and leaving them on Morrow's desk. He drew himself as Mowgli beseeching Morrow as Baloo the bear. He penned a plea on a ribbon and wrapped it around Morrow's pink rubber ball. He slipped toy snakes into jacket pockets, and finally one day snuck into Morrow's office and left a life-size drawing of Mowgli on the back of his door.

At last, in March, Morrow told him he had the assignment.

Throughout the spring he worked on *The Jungle Book,* making colorful cartoons out of hope, lies, trust, and sorrow. He met a woman named Maggie at the supermarket one afternoon, emptied her grocery cart into his own, brought her home, cooked her dinner, and went to bed with her. Another time, he asked a salesgirl at Woolworth's if she was ambidextrous, and somehow that led to a conversation about her father, and somehow that led to bed as well.

In June he was given an actual raise, and he moved into a slightly larger, slightly higher apartment in the Tuxedo. Someone in the building had persuaded management to clean the pool, and as the California summer unfolded in cartoon-background perfection, Henry took to spending weekends doing laps and reading or sunbathing. Two new tenants—sisters—had moved in, and Henry enjoyed their parade of poolside fashions: the large white-framed sunglasses, the little kerchiefs in their hair, the two-piece bathing suits that were more provocative than the sight of their fully nude bodies would have been. Sometimes he invited Cindy for a Sunday swim, enjoying her company almost as much as the consternation her presence inevitably provoked from the sisters.

By September, Mary Jane was back at Berkeley for her junior year, and Henry began once again to spend every few weekends with her. He liked the freedom the visits gave him to be a less conventional version of himself, but he also liked the freedom from all the women he knew, all their expectations and hurt feelings, even all their gifts.

One late October Friday, he arrived at Berkeley to find Mary Jane's room dark, her record player silent, and Mary Jane herself curled up on the sofa, an unfamiliar look on her face.

"What's happening?" she said, without getting up. Her voice, usually unremarkable to him, seemed softer and lighter, as if she was having trouble finding the breath or the energy to speak.

"Hey," Henry said. He kissed her cheek, inhaling the complementary smells of marijuana and herbal shampoo.

"Did you drive, drive, drive?" she asked him.

"What?"

"Did you drive?"

"Why didn't you wait for me?" he asked.

"Huh?"

"You're already stoned. Why didn't you wait for me?"

She smirked, a secret crimping her lips, then hidden by a toss of her hair.

Henry put down his overnight bag just as Alexa emerged from her bedroom, uncharacteristically free from her Samsonite case.

"Hey, Alexa," Henry said.

"Hey," she said, the openness of her Southern twang completely belied by her sour expression.

"Got a date?" he asked her.

She glared at him through her cat-eye glasses.

"What?" he asked her.

"Ask your friend," Alexa said, and slammed out the door.

Henry took off his jacket and hung it on one of the hooks he had put up some weeks before.

"What was that about?" he asked Mary Jane.

She shrugged.

"You're being weird," he said.

"You're being weird," she repeated.

"Let me at least catch up," Henry said. "Where's your stash?"

AN HOUR LATER, Mary Jane had pulled the crocheted afghan over her knees and was systematically sticking her fingers through its holes.

"Come on, let's go eat," Henry said.

Mary Jane ignored him.

"Mary Jane," he said.

"Did you know that Mary Jane *means* marijuana?" she said.

"What?"

"Mary Jane. Marijuana. Marijuana," she repeated, this time rolling her *r* and blowing out her *j*, Spanish style.

Henry just looked at her.

"You're not hungry? Come on. Munchies," he said.

"Not hungry."

"What's going on?"

She crossed her arms on top of her head, a model in a bathing suit pose.

"I dropped acid," she said.

"Where?"

"What?"

"What did you do?"

"I dropped acid," she said.

THERE WAS ACTION ALL OVER the campus that night: some kind of party at the Union, tryouts for the debate team and the university chorus, the usual fraternity and sorority things.

Mary Jane loped along beside Henry, the good-natured grin on her face occasionally giving way to openmouthed, full-out wonder.

"Talk about Disneyland!" she said. She had stopped under the main gate to the campus.

"What do you mean?"

"Colors," Mary Jane said. "And shapes. Everything has a tail."

"A tail like a dog?"

She giggled. "No, Henry. Not a tail like a dog."

Abruptly, she sat down in the middle of the path.

"Not a good idea," he said to her, and reached his hand down for hers.

She put her hand up, four inches away from his.

"Hey," he said to her. "Over here."

"I *am* over there."

Her depth perception was off, that had to be it, Henry thought. Odd, given that with only one good eye, she had effectively had to compensate all her life for just this problem. She had always been, by necessity, the one to see things flatly and without adornment.

Henry's mind leapt ahead with contingencies. So well trained by Martha, he searched for mental checklists of all the emergencies he knew how to handle: fainting and burns, rips and stains, gravy too thin and batter too thick; closed fireplace flue and leaking gas stove.

He did not even really know what acid was, let alone what it meant to have dropped it, or what to do with someone who had.

AT THE FOUNTAIN, yet another hour later, Mary Jane sat on the ground, leaned back, and simply refused to move.

"Come on now," he said to her.

"No!" she shouted. "Leave me alone! Don't ruin it, Henry. For once I can see things you can't!"

HE STAYED WITH HER. Whenever people came by, looking curious about her location by the fountain, he hovered closer to her, blocked their view, and said she was fine. At one in the morning, she started running across the campus, then collapsed, giggling, on a patch of lawn. He followed her. She lay on her back on the grass and moved her arms, as if making snow angels. The ground was cold, and somehow colder for being dark. Henry couldn't decide if he hated Mary Jane or hated acid or just hated the moment, but he was never unclear about his job, which was to get her back home, safely.

"Henry," she said. "You doofus."

"Come on, Miss Fancy," he said to her, and he picked her up on his back—her arms around his neck, her legs threaded through his arms—and carried her home.

BACK IN BURBANK, work continued on *The Jungle Book*. But Walt, fully immersed in planning for "the Florida Project," was rarely seen in the Animation Building. Circulating around the studio were maps and plans for Disney World, a far larger and far more ambitious counterpart to California's Disneyland. In Disney World, Walt explained in a new half-hour film, there would be not only a theme park and exhibits, but also an attempt to create an entire model city. Walt called it EPCOT, and he said it would use all the latest scientific methods to create a new way of life, a city free of slums; "We won't let them develop," Walt said. There would be fifty acres of climate-controlled streets for stores and theaters where pedestrians, according to the film, would "enjoy ideal weather conditions, protected day and night from rain, heat and cold, and humidity."

"It's not real life," Mary Jane said. It was November, just a month after her acid trip, and Henry was walking her back to her dorm from lunch. They walked side by side, hands in their pockets, only occasionally bumping against each other with a laugh or a gibe.

"What do you mean?"

"EPCOT. It's this totally pretend world he wants to create. Perfect little kitchens. Perfect little people. Perfect little streets. Just like the World's Fair."

"It's bigger than that," Henry said.

"Which makes it worse," Mary Jane said. "Don't you think it's kind of fascist? 'You will be happy, or else?'?"

"No war," Henry said. "Peace and harmony. Isn't that what you're always for? What's wrong with it?"

"Henry," she said to him witheringly. "Just tell me this. What does EPCOT stand for?"

"You know what EPCOT stands for."

"Say it."

Henry sighed. "It stands for 'Experimental Prototype Community Of Tomorrow.' "

"Right," she said.

"So?"

"So no wonder you like the stupid thing," she said. "It's just one big practice house."

SHE HAD BECOME AN ALMOST fanatically political animal. She claimed to have cared all along—about the rising threat of Vietnam, and the racial divisions of the South. She talked—especially when she was high, which seemed to be almost always now—about the War, the Pigs, the Movement, Che, Dylan, and MLK.

In December of 1966, she gave up all pretense of journalistic objectivity and joined an antiwar rally on the steps of Sproul Hall. A fight broke out, and there were arrests. Mary Jane was in jail and, like the others, had no wish to be bailed out.

It was Alexa who told Henry. He arrived at their room to find her sitting at the usual table, applying her usual primer of Pan-Cake makeup.

"What's it all got to do with us, anyway?" she asked lazily. "I've barely had a class in two weeks. This is not what my daddy had in mind when he took out a second mortgage."

"You don't care whether you have the right to protest the war?" Henry asked her, taking a step closer, appreciating, for the first time, the feline readiness of her eyes.

"No," she said. "I don't."

"You look really pretty today," he said, then paused. "And every day."

SHE MAY OR MAY NOT have been a virgin. Before they had sex, she said that she was giving Henry "her greatest gift," and he wasn't sure if that was Southern Belle for *best sex ever* or *first sex ever.* He didn't ask, which he knew was caddish of him, but he also knew the whole encounter was caddish. It didn't stop him. She was, in fact, both generous and clumsy in their night together.

In the morning, they went together to bail Mary Jane out, but she had already been sprung by an organized group. She appeared on the jail steps, giddy from her night of solidarity and purpose. The whole way back to the campus, she spoke about the thrill of the arrest, the strengthening numbers, and the potential for real change.

It was only after they had gotten back to the room and Alexa had excused herself to take a shower that Mary Jane turned on Henry.

"You asshole!" she said.

"What?"

"You know what. You asshole."

"What did I do?"

"You did *her.* Obviously."

"So what if I did?" Henry asked.

"So what? You showed up here and found me gone and this was the only thing you could think to do with your time?"

"I still don't see why that should matter to you."

She looked at him with exquisite rage, the product of her sleepless night, her nobility, and her hurt feelings.

"Maybe," she said, "you'll figure it out on the way back to Burbank."

HENRY ARRIVED BACK AT THE STUDIO to find that the reigning color was gray. Artists sketched at their desks, but at a noticeably slower pace, even when compared to the already careless approach they had taken all fall.

Henry called Fiona and asked her to meet him in the tunnel. Even she seemed not her usual self, however, cool as the tiled walls behind her—kissing him as usual but with her thoughts clearly elsewhere.

"Hey," he said. "Haven't you missed me?"

"Sure," she said.

"So what's going on?"

For a moment, almost hopeful, Henry wondered if he would be jealous if he found out that she had someone else.

But that wasn't what she had to tell him. It was Walt, she said. Only the top men had known about the boss's illness, but it turned out that he had had lung surgery just a few months before. Everyone thought he had recovered.

Now, she explained in a whisper—more sad than secretive—the word was that Walt had gone back to St. Joseph's Hospital, which was right across the street from the studio.

"We have to leave the lights on," Fiona told Henry.

"What do you mean?"

"At night. So Walt will think we're working, whenever he's awake."

THERE WAS SOMETHING FANTASTIC about the studio when Henry looked back at it from Buena Vista Street that night. The lights glowed like the lights in the *Snow White* cottage, the *Cinderella* castle, the London rooftops of *Mary Poppins*. Henry stood with his bike on the road between the place where a great man was dying and the place where his creations would be kept alive. In the morning, he was told that Walt Disney had died.

IT WAS LIKE THE DAY OF Kennedy's assassination, but worse: equally implausible but infinitely more personal.

Henry walked down Mickey Avenue, remembering his first day at the studio, the thrill of taking the drawing test, the taste of the pie that Cindy had served him. On every corner and in front of every building, people now sagged into each other's shoulders, speechless with grief, or too talkative. He knew that both Cindy and Fiona would be seeking him out, and he had no desire to see either of them. As he had on the day of JFK's death, he had the impulse to call Mary Jane, but he figured she would still be so angry about Alexa that he would have to do penance before he could tell her anything.

He walked all the way to the water tower, past any possibility for having to admit his pain.

He sat in the inappropriate sun and catalogued his losses. His father, of course, whoever he had been. Then Betty after his birth. Then Betty after the first year. Then Betty after New York. He had lost all the other practice mothers—both his own and the ones he had known in passing—and all their special languages and jokes and gifts. He had lost Charlie and Karen to the glee of their own giddy future. He had lost Martha, though that had been of his own choosing. He had lost Mary Jane after Lila, but then he had gotten her back, and now, because of Alexa, he had probably lost her again.

But this loss, Walt's loss, had a different feeling entirely: calamitous and cold. It was an irreplaceable loss over which Henry had no control.

By the end of January, he had broken things off with both Cindy and Fiona. He endured their various reactions of hurt, rage, disappointment, and blame with utterly feigned remorse. He wanted to have no one. If he had no one, he figured, he would have no one to lose.

PART FIVE

And, In the End

1

When She Talks

Just three months after Walt's death, Henry stood in the doorway of Martha's hospital room. It was already dark outside, but inside the room, it was bright daylight: the false daylight of fluorescent lights. Martha was sleeping. There was a smell.

It was not exactly feces or vomit, and not exactly chemical. It was closer to the smell of something you might find outdoors. A dark, brackish pond, maybe, or a dead animal on the side of the road. Henry froze for a moment, translating these scents into thoughts, and then he realized that the smell was of Martha's body rotting. She was rotting like a dead animal on the side of the road, and she was still alive. He could see, even from the doorway, that her knuckles were black. Her arms were sticks, with black veins on them.

Henry felt his stomach cramp, and he breathed lightly through his mouth. He took a step into the room and saw his reflection framed in the small window that showed the night sky. He looked exactly the way he was supposed to look: a tidy, responsible, young man of twenty—not one of those mixed-up hippies—coming to be at the bedside of his dying, beloved mother. Except that Martha Gaines was neither beloved nor his mother.

He hesitated, not knowing whether he should wake her or come back later.

A nurse entered, white and crisp against the black window. He turned.

"Are you the son?" she asked him.

He nodded.

"Is it just the two of you?"

He nodded again.

"I figured," the nurse said. "When she talks, you're all she talks about."

He tried to grin, and she smiled back sweetly.

"She'll be awake soon," the nurse said. "She never sleeps too long or stays awake too long. Why don't you sit and wait?"

Henry moved to the corner and slung his coat over the royal blue vinyl chair. The nurse tapped one of the milky plastic bags that was hanging from a metal pole. She lifted the mustard-colored pitcher from the rolling tray table and swirled it in one hand, then put it back down, satisfied by its fullness and the sound of its still-formed ice. Moving to the side of the bed, she lifted Martha's blanket, looking for Henry knew not what. He caught a glimpse of Martha's uncovered belly—shockingly flaccid and wrinkled, hanging heavily, like an elephant's skin. He looked away.

Martha stirred. The nurse smiled down at her and said, "Mrs. Gaines, you have a nice surprise here," then left.

Henry wanted to run after her and beg her to stay.

"SO," MARTHA SAID, her left arm unfolding shakily to reach for the hospital bed's controls.

"So, Emem," Henry said.

"Sit me up," she said, still fumbling for the button.

Henry took the six steps over to the side of her bed. He reached his own hand next to hers, easily finding the button with the headboard and the up arrow. As he pressed it, her hand found his, and he felt the impossibly stony coldness of her flesh.

"So you came," she said.

"Of course I came," he said.

"I wasn't sure you were going to."

"I told you I was going to," Henry said.

"I didn't know whether to believe you."

"You should have," Henry said.

"That's all right," Martha said, almost carelessly. "You don't always believe me, either."

Henry was startled. "I came as soon as I could," he said. "I had some work to finish at the studio."

Martha forced a conversational smile. "Tell me about California," she said.

"Well, it's warm," Henry began.

"I'd like that right about now," Martha said. She rubbed her hands together as if that could make them warm.

"Do you need another blanket?" Henry asked, looking toward the door. "I can go find the nurse and get you another blanket."

"No. She'll be back."

"Do you want some water? Your lips look dry."

Martha made an effort to lick them. Even her tongue was shaky.

"Do you, Emem? Want some water?"

She shook her head, looking worriedly across the room.

"What is it?" he asked.

"The picture," she said.

He followed her gaze to a bad landscape of a fisherman on a dock.

"Terrible," he said. "Tomorrow I'll bring you something to hang there instead."

She shook her head, stifling a cough.

"Not that," she said, and pointed again to the painting as the cough began to wrack her.

Henry looked again, then smiled. The picture was clearly crooked. He walked over to it and adjusted it slightly, trying to ignore the sounds that Martha was making. He continued to fiddle with it unnecessarily until she had managed to stop coughing.

"Better," she said, and they shared a practice house smile. Henry knew what to do now. He made a quick circuit around the room, gathering stray bits of paper, wrappers from gauze pads, empty juice cans, Styrofoam cups filled with stale water and bent blue plastic straws.

"I taught you well," Martha said.

Henry allowed himself the memory of the Christmas they'd spent alone together, the one when he'd been too sick to go downstairs, and Martha had given him the television set. They had watched Walt Disney for the first time that night, and she had laughed beside him, adjusting her scarf as always, fingering the gold pin at her neck.

"Is it just the two of you?" the nurse had asked him, and he had nodded yes. That was certainly what Martha had wanted, but she had wanted it too much and too late. There had always been other mothers, moving about in other rooms.

"I wish Betty had never come back," Henry said suddenly, impulsively.

Martha's eyes, which had been half closed, darted open fiercely, hungrily.

"Why do you say that?" she asked him.

"I don't know, Emem. If she'd never come back, maybe things would have been different."

"I never asked her to come back, you know. I never wanted her to come back," Martha said.

"You should have just taken me away somewhere," Henry said quietly. "Then I'd never have had to find out that you made all that up, about my real mother dying."

There was, finally, a silence. Henry realized that he had just had the most honest conversation with Martha of his life, and that she was almost dead. He waited for her to say she was sorry. She didn't. He said he was sorry.

"Sorry?" she asked. "For what?"

"I don't know. For being so angry, I guess," he said.

He waited for absolution. Martha didn't give it. She merely closed her eyes, and he watched a faint smile of victory register on her dry lips: Betty Gardner, rejected at last.

"I'm glad you came," Martha said finally. "My baby boy," she said, and squeezed his hand. "Oh, how I loved you."

What pierced and surrounded him, what he could not avoid—riding down in the empty elevator, walking through echoes in the empty halls—was the notion that he might not see her again. He had never felt it so strongly or cared so much. But it was the night, too, he told himself: the late-night feeling in the empty halls.

THE PRACTICE HOUSE was in the process of being transformed into a residence for visiting faculty and alumnae. The bedrooms—all but Martha's—were being redecorated, and the kitchen was being updated as well.

There was still no lock on the front door, so Henry merely let himself in. The house was dark and empty, which of course it had rarely been before. It smelled of plaster and paint. But Henry was too tired to focus or to care. He fell asleep on Martha's bed, and his last waking thought was the memory of her bringing him chicken soup on a tray.

ANOTHER NURSE CALLED IN the morning, and Henry braced himself for the news of Martha's death, but instead she told him that his mother was sitting up and asking to see him.

"Tell her I'm on my way," he said. He showered quickly and raced down the stairs, not stopping to answer the ringing phone.

She was dead by the time he arrived at her room. He did not want to see her dead, but the doctor and nurse seemed to think he would want to, and he gathered that simply declining the chance would seem somehow disloyal. He kept his jaw tight when he stepped into the room, and he made himself look at her. But while to the doctor and nurse he might have seemed to be absorbed in a properly devastated farewell, he was actually fascinated to see that the color of

Martha's lips was the exact shade of purple that had been chosen for the four vultures in *The Jungle Book*. And what was rising inside him, even as he looked on, was not grief or regret or even self-pity, but rather a raucous, wildly improper sense of freedom, unlike any he'd known.

2

Peace

If Henry had ever been in the Wilton chapel before, he certainly couldn't recall when. He felt he would have remembered the jeweled colors of the three stained-glass windows that rose into petal-shaped Gothic arches behind a simple wooden cross. The central window depicted Mary with Jesus in her arms.

The organ played. The candle flames shimmered. Henry was startled to find the whole front third of the chapel filling with mourners. It was not a large chapel, but there was nothing Henry had seen in the last few years of Martha's life to make him expect that there would be more than four or five people here. He wondered, sensing the rows filling behind him—people washing in like subsequent tidemarks on a shore—if Dr. Gardner had issued some sort of ex officio edict to make them come, or if it was standard at Wilton funerals for the whole faculty to turn out, perhaps amid intimations of their own mortality and the reassurance that they, too, would not die unheralded.

Dr. Gardner stood at the pulpit, smoothing a piece of paper and waiting for silence before he spoke. He squinted, and his mouth turned down; he seemed almost near tears, but then he flicked open his reading glasses with one hand and put them on.

"We are gathered here today to say goodbye to our friend Martha Gaines," he read. "For more than forty years, Wilton College has been at the forefront in the teaching of home economics, and the primary reason for that was Mrs. Gaines. When I was president of this institution, we were blessed to have had the leadership of a strong, intelligent, dedicated woman who spent virtually her entire career studying and teaching the science of child care to generations of young women, some of whom are in this chapel this morning."

Dr. Gardner looked up at the congregation, perhaps trying to locate these women, then back down at his eulogy.

"I'm well aware that Mrs. Gaines was known for being strict—not to say exacting—in her standards, and not only the practice house but the whole college was the better for it. She lacked tolerance for laziness, and she took disorder as a personal insult. I can recall hearing over the years that Mrs. Gaines was nearly absolute in her demands for hospital corners, proper feeding times, and even well-ironed pillowcases."

He looked up again and, satisfied by the expected light chuckles, returned again to his text.

"But anyone who knew Mrs. Gaines well," Dr. Gardner continued, "knew that her dedication to order was, more than anything, a profound affirmation of life. If you don't believe that life has deep value, it doesn't matter whether you keep it polished and dust-free. Mrs. Gaines taught us all to keep it polished and dust-free. She will be missed."

Dr. Gardner folded his piece of paper, removed his reading glasses, and looked up, as if surprised that what he had said had taken so little time and left so few people moved.

Henry had told Dr. Gardner that he would not speak. He hadn't thought he would have anything to say. But the coolness of his grandfather's remarks unexpectedly bothered him. Henry stood up and walked toward the pulpit, nodding at Dr. Gardner and proceeding to take his place. He looked out at the chapel and found people staring at him expectantly. He recognized the Wilton nurse and one of the groundskeepers. No one else.

"Good morning," he said. "My name is Henry Gaines." Then he stopped, immediately lost. He could not bring himself to say that he had been Martha's son, or that she had been his mother. "Martha Gaines raised me," he said instead.

His eyes moved restlessly over the high tide of visitors before him, scanning their faces, searching for the one that was missing: the one he hadn't expected to expect.

"I was the practice baby she kept," Henry said. "Every baby who came to the practice house came there because someone didn't want us. But Martha did. She wanted us all."

Unexpectedly, Henry was moved by what he had said, realizing it was true at the exact moment that he said it. He put his hands in his pockets. He looked down at his neatly tied shoes.

"It is a very, very strange thing to start life as an orphan," he said. "But Martha and the women in the practice house made us feel we were different in a good way. She made us feel more wanted than a lot of people's actual mothers probably ever make them feel."

That was, surprisingly, true as well. Henry looked at Dr. Gardner, Betty's indifference seething in the space between them.

"Martha gave us a start," Henry said, and once again—as he had in the hospital—he understood how unjust it was that her love hadn't been enough to conquer Betty's absence.

THE MINISTER READ THE SERMON. Henry didn't listen. There was much talk of good works on earth and peace in heaven. He did not focus on the details. He thought instead, without exactly meaning to, about all the sorting and cleaning that he would have to do in Martha's room before he could go back to Burbank. Then he stood and bowed his head for the Lord's Prayer, and he followed along with the hymn, which was named, appropriately enough, "Come, Labor On."

AFTER THE SERVICE, Henry stood with the minister and Dr. Gardner, shaking people's hands and thanking them for coming. One middle-aged couple, darkly dressed, came up with an aura of special mission.

"We're Sam and Laura Jacobs," the woman said. "We wanted to offer our condolences. Your mother was so marvelous."

Just to the left of them, a young woman about Henry's age stood wearing a suede jacket over a Beatles T-shirt emblazoned with the movie logo HELP! Henry guessed she was the Jacobses' daughter.

"Thank you," Henry said as the girl took another step away from them, then bent to comb out the fringes on her brown suede boots.

"How did you know Martha?" Henry asked.

"Well, we only met her a few times," Mrs. Jacobs said.

"We actually tracked her down a few years ago," Mr. Jacobs added. "We wanted to thank her in person for doing such a great job with our daughter."

Henry followed Mr. Jacobs's glance to the girl, who had abandoned the fringe on her boots and was now relooping a hair elastic around the bottom of one long brown braid.

"Was she one of Martha's students?" Henry asked, trying and failing to get the girl's attention, suddenly wondering whether she was hostile, or stupid, or merely stoned.

"One of her students?" Mrs. Jacobs said. "No. Oh, no. She was one of the practice babies. Like you."

There were people moving on the periphery of Henry's sight, a few more of whom he now recognized from the depths of his Wilton past. Vaguely, too, he was aware that Dr. Gardner was walking with the minister to the door of the chapel. But Henry was powerless to acknowledge the people, or to follow his grandfather's exit. He had never seen a practice baby outside the practice house, and he had certainly never met one who was older than an infant. He stared at the girl with the HELP! T-shirt. "Which one were you?" Henry asked her. "Hannah? Harriet? Horatio?"

The girl finally acknowledged Henry and smiled.

He pointed to her T-shirt. "Was it Help?" he asked, and she laughed.

"They called her Hazel," Mrs. Jacobs said.

Hazel. Hazy. The baby he'd famously kept safe in the two minutes that some ditzy practice mother had been locked out of the house.

"Hazel," Henry repeated. "Is that still your name?" he asked her.

"No. It's Peace," she said.

"Wow. Really?"

"Peace Jacobs."

"Cool," Henry said.

Her eyes were almost frightening: so pale green, so lucid, so suddenly fixed on his, so open. It was impossible not to look at her eyes— and not just look at them but look back at them, two dreamy doorways opening into—what?—in any case, a world. Her eyes seemed to promise excitement, humor, a strange sense of discernment, and one other thing Henry couldn't quite place, though it seemed somehow familiar. Immediately he wanted to know if this was the look she gave everyone. Perhaps it was simply her way.

"How would you like," he asked her, "to come see the practice house again?"

PEACE HAD TOLD HIM she might stop by that evening. But it was Mary Jane who arrived first. Her flight from San Francisco had been delayed, and she had missed the funeral. She had arrived at the practice house while Henry was still at the cemetery—the burial mercifully brief, just Dr. Gardner and Henry and a man from the funeral home who seemed unable to suppress his pleasure at the beautiful spring day.

"You missed all the fun," Henry told Mary Jane as he accepted a long, tight embrace from her.

If she was still angry about Alexa, she had decided not to show it.

"Did Betty come?" Mary Jane asked.

"No."

"Did she call?"

"No."

"Telegram?"

"No."

"Unbelievable."

"Believable."

"Do you have to deal with all this crap?" She gestured vaguely around Martha's bedroom, the repository of a life in which the limits of age, or perhaps of proportion, had meant an inability to discard anything. It was a mess, but an entirely organized mess, befitting the practice house standards.

"Of course I have to deal with it," Henry said.

"Starting when?" Mary Jane asked, picking up Martha's inlaid enamel hairbrush and immediately putting it back down.

"Starting now, I guess," Henry said.

THEY WALKED TOGETHER to the hardware store, renamed and re-painted since Arthur Hamilton's death. They bought tape, garbage bags, and cardboard boxes. Henry was startled by the stillness in the neighborhood. It was a regular Wednesday afternoon, but nothing seemed to be moving. The sky was Los Angeles blue, but that was the only similarity to home. There were virtually no people, no cars, no sounds.

"We'll do piles for things to give away, things to throw away, and things to leave for the college," Henry said.

"And what about things to keep?" Mary Jane asked.

Henry shrugged. "I guess," he said.

The clothes were easiest. Henry swept all Martha's undergarments and hosiery into one trash bag. The shirts, sweaters, and skirts were all immaculate as ever—spotless, perfectly folded, with sheets of tissue paper around and between them, as if they had just been purchased. Henry handed these to Mary Jane, and Mary Jane packed them in boxes. In Martha's desk drawers he found neatly stacked supplies: pads, pens, stamps, envelopes. The bottom drawer seemed jammed shut, and when Henry finally forced it open, he found at least a hundred of her Green Stamps booklets, filled and never used. It was the closest he came to crying.

"We need some music," Mary Jane said.

Henry turned on Martha's ancient radio, its signal strong and bizarrely modern, coming from the old wooden cabinet. Mary Jane sang along, off-key, with the Beatles' "Penny Lane" and the Turtles' "Happy Together."

I can't see me loving nobody but you for all my life . . .

"Are you going back to L.A. right away?" she asked him after they had decided the shoes were not worth keeping.

"I don't know," he said. "I'm not really sure I want to go back."

"I thought you were doing *The Jungle Book*," she said.

"I am."

"So?"

"It's not the same."

"Same as what?"

"The same as it was with Walt."

She stretched out now on the part of Martha's bed that was free from clothes. "What would you do instead?" she asked him.

She had a cigarette in her hand, and it bothered Henry suddenly that her shoes were touching Martha's pillows.

"I don't know," he said.

"Would you come back here?"

"No. Why would I come back here?"

"I don't know. Teach art. Chase students. Hang out with your grandfather."

"Are you high?" Henry asked her.

"Not enough," she said.

She put out her cigarette. From Martha's bedside table, she picked up a green porcelain box in the shape of a cabbage. "Christ, look at all this shit," she said, and somehow, surprisingly, Henry found that annoying, too.

HE WAS STARTLED, though he shouldn't have been, to find Martha's gold Omicron Nu pin. She had left it in a small cedar box, along with her Timex wristwatch and several pairs of simple gold earrings. Clearly she must have known that she wouldn't be coming back to this house—or going any place where time or affiliation or ornament would matter. Henry paused, uncertain, the box open on her dresser.

"What should I do with these?" he asked Mary Jane.

"Keep them, of course," she said.

"I think you should take the earrings."

"Don't be an idiot, Henry," Mary Jane said.

"I'm not being an idiot. I bet she'd want you to have them."

"She'd want me to be swallowed up whole by the earth, and that's what she always wanted," Mary Jane said.

"I see your point," he told her.

She laughed.

"But what about what I want?" he said. "What if I want you to have them?"

"Keep them, doofus," she said. "You might have a daughter some-day, you know."

They were words that conjured no image but were unaccountably soothing.

PEACE CAME AT AROUND EIGHT O'CLOCK, and despite the chaos of the room and the singular strangeness of the day, Henry found himself quietly delighted that he had been right to sense something in her eyes.

"Mary Jane Harmon," he said. "This is Peace Jacobs."

"Peace? Jacobs?" Mary Jane repeated. Her look was quizzical, press-ing, possessive, defiant: Henry could have drawn it from memory.

"Henry and I met at the funeral," Peace said, looking around and clearly trying to make sense of the room.

"You met at the *funeral*," Mary Jane repeated.

Peace shrugged.

"Peace was a practice baby," Henry explained.

"You're kidding," Mary Jane said.

"Her name was Hazel," Henry said.

"Hazel. You're not the one he *saved*, are you?" Mary Jane asked.

"Saved? What do you mean, saved?" Peace asked.

"Oh, I didn't actually save you," Henry said. "We were just locked in here together one time."

"Really? Just the two of us?"

"That's the story I always heard," Mary Jane said. "And heard. And heard."

"So what did he save me from?"

"I didn't save you," Henry said with a short but well-aimed glare at Mary Jane. "I just didn't do anything bad to you."

"Well, I'd take that deal most days," Peace said. She smiled directly at Henry, as if Mary Jane was not in the room.

Henry smiled back in much the same way.

Mary Jane looked at both of them. "Fine," she said, as if Henry had actually asked her to agree to something. In fact, the request had been entirely implicit: *Leave, so that I can forget everything by charming this total stranger.*

"Will you be here tomorrow?" Mary Jane asked, a question that had its own tacit meaning: a warning to Peace about the man she was eyeing with such unconcealed eagerness.

Annoyed, Henry gestured to the room at large.

"You think I have elves coming?" he asked her.

"I never know who you have coming," Mary Jane replied, and even through his annoyance, Henry had to admire her wit.

It was ten o'clock when Mary Jane left, and ten-thirty when Henry kissed Peace for the first time.

She tasted of the brownies she'd brought and proffered and—once Henry had eaten one—proudly explained that she'd laced with hashish.

"I baked them this afternoon," she said. "My mom was right there in the kitchen when I put the stuff in the batter, and she didn't have a clue."

Henry started to mind, and then he didn't, because Peace added, with unexpected and captivating pride: "And I baked them from scratch. I didn't even use a mix!"

———

PEACE JACOBS'S REAL NAME WAS SARAH, but she had changed it even before she'd decided that she wanted to be an actress. "Peace" went with the whole hippie aspect of her. She was just seventeen, and her appearance by her parents' side at Martha Gaines's funeral had been entirely anomalous. She had not been in touch with either of them for months beforehand, having dropped out of high school in search of herself. A trip home for funds had prompted a truce, and Martha's funeral had occasioned a show of good-girlism that no one with any insight could have taken seriously.

"I don't know why," she said to Henry, leaning back on Martha's pillows and lifting her arms up over her head. "But it feels like I don't like to stay in one spot very long."

Henry felt the giddy fog of the hash brownies overtaking him. He watched his hands move as he spoke, and found them newly fascinating.

"Me neither," he said.

"My parents say I'm crazy," Peace said. "Really, they always have. They say I should learn how to stay in one place. But what's the point of staying in one place? You can't learn anything. You can't meet anyone. You can't go anywhere."

Henry smiled, then started laughing.

"What?" Peace said.

He laughed harder, a being-high laugh.

"What?"

"That last one," he managed to say, "is pretty much the definition of it, don't you think?"

"Huh?"

" 'If you stay in one place, you can't go anywhere'?"

She was embarrassed for a split second, and then she started laughing, too. He liked that about her.

"Well, I love things that are new," she said, finally, when they had caught their breath.

"And people who are new," he said, and kissed her again.

———

HE STAYED SIX DAYS AT THE PRACTICE HOUSE, ostensibly to tidy up Martha's things, but really to explore Peace's considerable sexual talents and her unexpected mystery. Mary Jane, having sized up the situation perfectly, gave Henry a withering look and a halfhearted hug and left just two days after she had come.

"Why's she wearing that eye patch?" Peace asked after Mary Jane had left.

Henry hesitated. "She lost an eye when she was little," he said.

"Bummer. Couldn't they fix it?"

"They tried, but it turned out they'd waited too long."

"Bummer."

"Yah."

"How?"

"What?"

"How'd she lose her eye?"

"A long time ago," he said vaguely.

Talk at first seemed silly, and certainly superfluous. Peace had an acrobatic talent for sex; she could practically fold her body in half, while her face stayed fixed in profile, like a portrait on a coin. And she had other talents as well. She had an extraordinarily beautiful voice, part Mama Cass, part Patsy Cline. Singing illuminated her face, as did listening to music and even, apparently, to Henry.

One afternoon, when they were both so tired that they could not have packed another box, she told him to lie on his stomach, and, wearing only her panties and a hand-me-down vest, she straddled his backside and bent over him, the fringe of her long brown hair feathering his shoulder blades. She massaged him, starting with his head, working down through his neck, his muscular shoulders, his sides, the small of his lonely back. Her hands were incomprehensibly strong: kneading, holding, circling, fanning out and then twisting in, until there seemed no way to tell the difference between what he needed and what she knew. At every position, at every part of his body, her hands were answering the questions his body asked. How could she know this language? Where had she learned this exquisite art?

She stayed with him as the room around them grew emptier and colder, and whatever traces of Martha remained were the ones that had shaped them as infants.

HE COULD NOT REMEMBER having felt this kind of hunger. Within minutes of making love to Peace, he would want her again. Perpetually, he had the feeling he'd usually experienced only on the brink of a first kiss: the ravaging pang and rigid ache. With Peace, he was never entirely calmed if their bodies were not together. All thoughts of other women—the thoughts that had often propelled or sustained a sexual moment, or sweetened an afterglow—had exited his mental repertoire. He yearned to tell someone that he was in love. He had no one to tell. He told Peace.

"Really?" she said, as if she'd just been picked for a volleyball team. She smiled. The strap of her granny dress fell off her shoulder, over an irresistible shrug.

She wanted to come back to L.A. with him, she said.

"What would you do there?" he asked her.

"Live."

"And what would your parents say?" he asked.

"Maybe I wouldn't ask my parents," she said.

"You'd just run off?"

"*You* did," she said.

He didn't take her with him, but he was careful to take her address, her phone number, and the phone number of her best friend—just in case she ran away again. For once, he was not planning his own escape. He wanted to have Peace with him. Some instinct, however, told him that he would risk the thing's perfection if he attempted to have it too quickly.

He expected her to be angry, or at least to be visibly hurt. Rather, she lifted her chin an inch.

"That's cool," she said. "I'm cool with that."

———

HIS PLANE LANDED IN L.A. AT 6:00 P.M., and it was 8:00 by the time he opened the door of his apartment. The plant Cindy had given him months before was finally dead, its green leaves dusty and gray. Henry turned on the TV, then turned it off again. He unpacked his bag, all his clothes neatly folded from the laundry he'd done at the practice house. He put the shirts and shorts away, put his extra shoes on the closet floor. Then he spread out the things he had kept from Martha: a scarf, the necklace, the earrings, a box of his childhood drawings and schoolwork. He thought about Peace and imagined giving Martha's necklace or earrings to her. Then he placed Martha's scarf in the back of his sock drawer, put her gold pin on his key chain, put his drawings on his closet shelf. This was, for him, the real burial. He fell asleep and dreamed that he was standing at her graveside, but in the dream the day was gray and snowy, not the unmarred blue it had been. He woke to an unusual chill. He knew it wasn't Martha he was missing, nor any particular person or place. He just felt, as he had when Walt died, the weight of the list of what he had lost. And though he was only twenty, he felt certain that what he had lost would always remain more powerful to him than anything he could gain.

THE STUDIO SEEMED EVEN EMPTIER than it had right after Walt's death. In spirit if not in fact, D-Wing felt like Martha's bedroom at the practice house: a place defined uniquely by a vanished inhabitant. The crucial difference at Disney was the goal of preservation. The director of *The Jungle Book* talked explicitly about survival and, along with the top animators, seemed to see the film as a test case for the continued existence of Disney animation, even of Disney himself. The quest—it was nearly religious—was to do what Walt would have done.

Debating the nuances of Walt's wishes was hardly a new pastime. But now, with no chance of an actual verdict, the arguments were more fraught. Days dragged. Henry made the vultures flap. He made them jump. Shed feathers. Shrug. He made them yawn and speak and open their eyes in disbelief or excitement—all except for the eyes of the cockney-voiced vulture named Flaps, which were hidden by mop-top hair.

"I heard Walt wanted to get the real Beatles," Chris told Henry.

"For the vultures?" Henry asked lazily.

"Yeah."

They were stretched out at lunchtime on the lawn, knowing they should be back at their boards but equally unwilling to move.

"No way," Henry said.

"That's what I heard."

"Bullshit," Henry said—although he would later find it was true.

"But wouldn't that have been cool?" Chris asked.

Henry looked up at the sky. It was gray, unpleasantly so, and there was moisture in the air. He thought about Peace. He felt a stinging desire to see her. He wished now he had brought her back. He wondered what she was doing. He looked at his watch, as if that would tell him.

"Totally cool," Henry said.

"We should get back to work," Chris said.

"Yeah."

Each of them lit a cigarette.

"Imagine in-betweening the Beatles," Henry said.

"Ringo's nose would be exactly like the vultures' beaks," Chris said.

Henry laughed.

"Well, I've heard they need people," Chris said.

"What?"

"In London."

"What are you talking about?"

"Where have you been?" Chris said, and then he told Henry about a Beatles film that was being produced in London. An animated film, he said, that had to be finished in one year.

"Do they sing in it?"

"Yeah, I guess so."

"What's it about?" Henry asked.

"I don't know," Chris said. "Something about a submarine."

3

All You Need Is Love

Henry got the job by mail and by necessity: It turned out that *Yellow Submarine* had to be completed in only ten months' time, and animators were being hauled in from all over Europe as well as from the States. The key requirements seemed to be a willingness to work hard and a willingness to accept chaos. Even Joe Hinton, the hiring producer, made it clear to Henry from the start that no one in London had the vaguest idea what was going on.

Henry had money saved and was perfectly prepared to pay Peace's way, but her parents had apparently liked his clean-cut, fine-young-man look and had been moved by his words at the funeral. In any case, they decided that Peace going with Henry was preferable to Peace disappearing again. They paid for her ticket and sent her with cash.

"They called you that nice son of that nice woman," Peace told him when she returned his phone call in June to say that she could come.

She expressed no fear, no apprehension. The only doubt she acknowledged was about how long she would want to stay.

"I like to move around a lot," she told Henry.

"You said that before. You said it that first night in the practice house."

"So?"

"So it's fine," Henry said. "I move around too. Maybe we'll move around together."

He knew she was talking about a habit that was more than geographical. He was too. But he wanted, with absolute urgency, to be anchored, or at least tethered, and there was something in Peace—perhaps the surprise of their shared past, or how he imagined it might connect them—that gave him reason to think she was the one to whom he should be tied.

"Dear Miss Fancy," he wrote to Mary Jane on a homemade post-card with an outlaw drawing of Mickey Mouse wearing paisley shorts instead of the usual red ones.

> Well, chick, I'm leaving. These boots, as the song says, are made for walking.
> I got a job in London, and it's too good to pass up. I'm sorry I won't be around to see your graduation, but I figure there's an equal chance you'll burn the place down before then anyway.
> I'll let you know when I know where we'll be living.
> Meanwhile, raise your hand if you're happy for me.

And he drew a tiny picture of himself with a hand in the air. His only reference to Peace was the pronoun *we*.

Henry sublet his Tuxedo apartment to Chris in exchange for the promise that Chris would send some boxes to London once Henry had gotten settled. Two days later, he met Peace at Grand Central. She was carrying three suitcases and wearing a flowered hat, bright pink lipstick, and red velvet pants. She kissed and hugged him exuberantly. All the way to the airport, he found himself eagerly trying on the same pronoun he had used in his postcard to Mary Jane, the pronoun that this journey abroad would include: *We'll live; we'll find; we'll work; we'll spend; we'll go.*

THE STUDIO WAS IN SOHO SQUARE, where buildings were painted with huge Day-Glo flowers and shop doors were curtained by strings of beads. Several hundred people shared an enormous suite of mis-matched rooms, with the usual clutter of storyboards, character sketches, color palettes, and clay models. But, at least on the day

Henry arrived, there was nothing approaching a working script. All anyone seemed to know was that the story would somehow evolve from the Beatles' songs and that the Beatles themselves would have virtually nothing to do with the film. *Yellow Submarine* had not been their idea. They had been signed to a three-movie deal years before, and now, in the mania of their *Sgt. Pepper* popularity, animation seemed the only way to make a movie with them in it. Even their voices would not be their own but would be supplied by actors. On the mild June day when Henry arrived at the Soho studio, the closest things to actual Beatles were four life-size cutouts of their animated characters.

Joe Hinton showed Henry to an empty spot at one of three long tables that could accommodate ten or twelve artists each. With the tables and the low ceiling, the place felt a little bit like a lunchroom; the sensation was reinforced by the Ringo and John cutouts, poised like waiters behind the artists' chairs.

Henry gathered pens and pencils from a communal supply cart. He turned on his desk lamp. He brushed old eraser dust from the corners of his drawing board. All the while he kept glancing at, then away from, then back to, the cutout Beatles.

"Odd, isn't it?" the woman across from him said.

"Excuse me?"

"Odd, to have them here. Without the usual mob scene, I mean."

Henry laughed. "I'm Henry," he said.

Her name was Victoria Green. She was British, married, thirty-five, and had two children, she said.

She asked his age and where he was from. There was something frank and open about her.

"So you're the Disney boy," she said. "Got tired of Mickey Mousing around?"

Joe Hinton came back with a character sheet.

"I guess I should get to work," Henry said. He sat on the rolling chair and tucked his feet onto the tops of the wheels. He looked back up at Ringo and John.

Victoria exhaled her cigarette smoke, then waved it away with a wedding-ringed hand. She glanced over her shoulder and smirked. She said: "One piece of advice. Watch out for John. He'll talk your ear off."

HENRY HAD LEFT PEACE that morning with a map and a newspaper, and they had agreed to meet at six at the Piccadilly station. She was grinning when he emerged from the dark, deep tunnel into the bright summer evening. He had not intended her to make a decision without him, but her enthusiasm was captivating, and the flat she had chosen for them was, like her, both cheerful and surprisingly practical.

The flat was in Rose Street, a tiny lane closer to the theater district than to Soho Square, but just a block from the Tube, or a fifteen-minute walk to the studio. In the basement of an old row house, the place was funky in a way that Henry liked immediately. The walls were painted dark green on the bottom and light blue on top, the rudimentary backdrop of a landscape without foliage. It reminded Henry of his practice house closet walls, and he knew that he would paint it someday, but he had no idea with what.

The previous tenants had taken it upon themselves to label the main objects in the place, so that the words SHOWER and SINK had been painted onto the bathroom walls, and, in the main room, the words BED, DESK, and DRESSER floated helpfully under the ceiling. There was a tiny stove, no larger than the ones Henry had had at the Tuxedo, and a sink with a tattered skirt covering its legs. He felt he was finally home.

Then they started to unpack, and soon Peace took out her knitting—explosive pink and orange yarns in long, thick rows; she was using enormous knitting needles as thick as turkey basters.

"Where'd you learn to knit?" he asked her.

She shrugged. "I don't know," she said.

It was one of a dozen things she did unusually well, with surprising confidence, although it would not take Henry long to realize that her talent for picking things up was not matched by an equal talent for finishing them.

"Aren't you going to unpack the rest?" he asked her.

"Eventually."

"Eventually when?"

"Come here, Hen," she said. "Let's test the bed."

FOR ALL HIS PRECOCIOUS EXPERIENCE, Henry had never lived with a girlfriend before. Every aspect of it was exotic, from selecting a single toothpaste brand to negotiating the height of the shower curtain rod. On their first weekend in London, Henry and Peace went to King's Road and bought an Indian-print bedspread, sheets, towels, pillows, paper lanterns, a secondhand radio, and a secondhand color TV. They came home with their purchases and had sex before they'd unpacked them.

They had sex nearly every night. The undisputed soundtrack of their lives was John Lennon singing "All You Need Is Love." When it wasn't being replayed relentlessly on the radio, Peace was singing it in the shower or in the bedroom or on the street. Her voice was so sweet and strong, and sometimes, when she wanted to make love to Henry, she would simply sing "It's easy" in a pretty good Liverpool lilt.

Meanwhile, there were fifty or sixty shows being performed in the London theaters, and within days, Peace had staked out a spot at the stage door of the Victoria Palace and made half a dozen friends among the other hippies and hangers-on. By the second week, she had managed to talk one of those friends into introducing her to an agent named Martin Doyle. By the third week, Martin had become "the Great Martini," and had lined up a series of auditions for her.

In the mornings, after they had eaten breakfast, Henry would leave Peace sitting in the huge white wicker peacock chair that she had hauled home from a flea shop. She would invariably have a script in her hands and a blanched, open look in her eyes as she sat down, with utter earnestness, to try to memorize her lines.

The big prize of the season would be a part in *America Hurrah*, a huge hit in the States that was destined, everyone said, to make an even larger explosion in London. The play was a biting, avant-garde, daring indictment of modern society, and Henry was convinced that Peace didn't understand a word of it. He wasn't sure he did. But he would leave her in the morning hearing her practice lines like "I'm dead, thank you, I said, thank you, please, I said, I'm dead."

"Good luck," Henry told her on a Thursday morning in July, the day of the big audition and a month after they'd arrived.

"Martini says I don't need luck. I've got talent," Peace said.

Henry left the flat, stepping past the black-and-white mosaic doorstep, heading down Rose Street, loving her confidence, or at any rate the way she pretended to have it.

He passed the Lamb & Flag, the three-hundred-year-old pub where John Dryden got beaten up and Charles Dickens got drunk. He passed a cat in a doorway, and theater posters fixed to the sides of buildings like stamps. It was a warm summer, but never oppressive in the mornings or the evenings, when Henry walked to and from the Tube stop at Tottenham Court Road. He had even learned to say *Tottenham* so it had two syllables, not three.

AT THE STUDIO, Henry had been assigned to the team of animators who were drawing the Yellow Submarine amid the Sea of Monsters. Many of the monsters had already been drawn. There were the Kinky-Boot Beasts and Vacuum Monster, Snapping Turtle Turk and the fish with the human arms. But the Sea of Monsters was supposed to be a large sea, and in a non-hierarchical, non-Disney way, even some of the in-betweeners were being asked to contribute their own creations.

To the left and right of him along the long, cool table, Henry's colleagues madly sketched their own monsters at every possible opportunity. Frank had concocted American Monster, with the head of an eagle and the body of a flag. Dick was working on Many-Breasted Beast, which he alternately referred to as Many-Beasted Breast. Victoria was trying to counter with Muscle Man Monster.

In typical fashion, it had taken Henry only about a day to master the *Submarine* style—all flat, bold colors without shade or shadow; vibrant, bold ink strokes, and coloring-book fill-ins. But he felt no closer than he ever had to choosing a style, let alone a character, all his own. Faced with a blank page, Henry searched for inspiration. All that filled his mind was drawings he'd already drawn—of other artists' characters. "Doesn't have a point of view," the Beatles sang in the film about the Nowhere Man. "Knows not where he's going to."

One day early in July, when most of the staff headed out to the Dog and Duck for lunch, Henry stayed behind. Someone had put the standing fan on "oscillate" by mistake, and the air at regular intervals lifted the top cel on his drawing board. For a while, smoking a cigarette, Henry watched the cel rise and fall. Taking a sketch pad from the shelf behind him, he started to draw a fan monster. He made two fans for the eyes. Then he made the whole head a fan. Then he tried making the body the fan, with the blades looking large and dangerous. He imagined how Fan Monster might move: he might blow the submarine away; blow bubbles at the submarine; chop the submarine into pieces. He saw Peace's face and her smooth brown hair as she leaned back into her peacock chair. He thought about making a peacock monster. There could be a clock monster, he thought. Its clock hands could reach out with long, sharp claws, and its numbers could be launched as grenades. Henry wasn't sure he liked it enough to choose it above the others.

Choosing things, he knew, had been the challenge of his life. Choosing a woman, choosing a style. They weren't really that different.

He turned a page in the sketch pad, drew simple shapes—the old trick of Charlie's—then closed his eyes and tried to see what was in his own mind. In the darkness, he sensed light trying to get in. Insistently, the fan continued to make the room rise and fall. He imagined the street beyond the studio with all the black taxis and red buses rattling by. That didn't seem to be useful either.

He opened his eyes, completely dispirited, and began to draw too-familiar objects: the *Mary Poppins* penguins, the Mickey Mouse ears, the *Jungle Book* trees, the bulbous Blue Meanies.

At the sound of voices, Henry threw down his pencil.

"You're going to love me," Victoria told him, sweeping back into the room with Frank.

He looked up, smiling. "I already love you," he said.

"No, really. You're going to love me. I brought you fish and chips. I guessed you'd be starving."

"You're right," Henry said. "I do love you."

"I told you."

She handed him a brown paper bag that was spotted with grease.

"Just don't get oil on this table," she warned him.

Delighted to abandon his efforts, Henry took the bag into the sitting room, where he settled into one of several cast-off leather couches that sat amid mismatched coffee tables. The fish and chips, each in a little red-and-white paper boat, were too salty, but he didn't care.

Victoria followed him in.

"What's with you?" she asked him. "What's got your knickers in such a bunch?"

"How're you doing on your monsters?" he asked her.

"Oh. So that's it. Lacking inspiration, are we?"

He allowed himself the luxury of telling her the truth. "I'm drawing a blank," he said.

"What color?"

"No fooling. I can't come up with a thing."

"It'll come."

"Fish?" he asked her. "Chip?"

"No, thanks. You're the one who skipped lunch, remember? Why don't you show me what you've got?" She flashed him a flirty smile.

"Pardon me?" he asked, flirting back a little.

"Sketch pad, Harry," she said.

He pushed the remains of his lunch back into the bag, then balled it up and tossed it into a trash can.

———

HENRY GOT THE IDEA when he showed Victoria the sketch pad. There was his drawing of the Chief Blue Meanie, and there was his drawing of the Mickey Mouse ears. Later, he would confide in Victoria that he didn't consider it a pure idea. It was based on an accidental juxtaposition, he said, of two other people's pure ideas. She scoffed at his admission and said he was just fishing for compliments. Putting Mouseketeer hats on the Blue Meanies was a stroke of genius, she said.

She was not alone in her assessment. The sketch of the Chief Blue Meanie, wearing mouse ears, was quickly passed down the table, like a platter of cookies, and before the afternoon was out, it had met with the art director's enthusiastic approval.

IT AMAZED HENRY—but apparently didn't faze either the Great Martini or Peace—that she had gotten called back for the part of Girl at the Party in *America Hurrah*. This occasioned several more mornings of "I'm dead, thank you, I said, thank you, please, I said I'm dead," as well as several concerted if awkward efforts at staging. A week later— more amazing still—it was down to Peace and one other actress, and Peace called Henry at the studio to say that Martin had told her he'd heard the part would be hers.

Henry came home early to make her a special dinner. He turned on the radio and listened, inevitably, to the Beatles, the Stones, Pink Floyd, Jimi Hendrix. "Well," said the DJ, "this is the beat of the sixties, here for all you mods and rockers. It's a Thursday night in July in the year of our Lord nineteen sixty-seven, and here's a little something smashing for you from the Who."

Henry sharpened his kitchen knife, as Martha had taught him to do years before, and he sliced potatoes and minced onions, chopping in time to the music. He poured himself a glass of wine. He reveled in the fact that he could feel simultaneously attached and unconfined.

The dinner was ready at seven o'clock. Henry set the table with an array of the seemingly random objects that Peace had been bringing home from flea markets and who knew where else. There were mismatched plates, utensils, and glasses that somehow, once assembled, made a perfectly stylish whole, with the unmistakable flair of the perfectly stylish girl who had found them. Henry put fresh candles in the wine bottles Peace had made into holders, their sides already mottled with drippings of different-colored wax. By 7:30, Henry had fluffed the couch pillows, swept the carpet, and put the dishes in the dish drainer away. Just before 8:00, he heard Peace's key turn in the lock. She stepped in wearing a pink polka-dot raincoat and some kind of sailor cap.

"Hen!" she said, as if it was a surprise to find him in their flat. "Wow," she said. "You cooked?"

He tried to read her eyes, but they were hidden by the two curtains formed by her hair.

"Well?" he finally asked her. "Am I looking at the next Girl at the Party?"

"Nope," she said, and tossed her polka-dot coat, unsuccessfully, toward the front hall bench. She did an exaggerated stage curtsy. "Thank you," she said, as if to a vast theater audience. "Thank you so much."

"Oh, baby," Henry said. "I'm so sorry, baby."

He took her in his arms, smelling her herbal shampoo. Perhaps later they would bathe together, he thought, or shower, and he would wash her hair.

He loved so much to shampoo her, building her hair into soapy swirls, like white roses.

She broke quickly from his embrace.

"It's no big deal," she said.

"No big deal!"

She shrugged herself away.

"You were dying to get this part," he said.

Still standing up, she reached for one of the roast potatoes and ate it, then licked her fingers.

"You've been working on this part for weeks," Henry said.

She reached for another potato. "These are good," she said. "Hen. There'll be other parts."

Her focus shifted around the table. "So you cooked," she said again, and Henry lit the candles.

He glanced back to her, nervously.

"You may be taking this a little too hard," she told him.

He snapped his lighter shut, unnerved by encountering an indifference even greater than his own.

"Henry," she said. "For God's sake. There'll always be other parts."

4

So Much Harder Than It Looks

It was not the London of *Mary Poppins*. There were parks and rain and the occasional tea, but the similarities ended there. By autumn, the weather was raw, the sun set too early, and the one time Henry tried to impress Peace by drawing a chalk pavement picture of her in the park, a bobby came by—a fat, puffing man—and said: "Don't think you're going to be doing that here," as if the "that" was having public sex.

"My daughters loved *Mary Poppins*," Victoria admitted to him one late afternoon, when the sun—so rarely out—had somehow managed to flood their work table and force them to take a break. "What parts did you draw?" she asked him.

"Mostly the penguins," Henry said. "But I was just in-betweening then, too."

"*Just,*" Victoria repeated. "And you were, what, twelve at the time?"

Henry grinned.

"Anyway, my girls *loved* the penguins!" Victoria said. She put down her pencil and held up her Coke bottle. "Sip?" she asked him.

It was oddly intimate. He took the bottle and drank about a third of it.

"Oh, thanks a bloody bunch," Victoria said, grabbing it back.

"Tell me something," he said.

"Anything, pet."

"Is there a real street called Cherry Tree Lane?" he asked her.

She laughed. "Oh, Harry, you're hopeless," she said.

"Why?"

"Because you're still such a tourist."

"No I'm not."

"What you need," she said, "is a proper London education."

He guessed that she meant more than just seeing the sights.

HE CAME HOME FROM WORK that evening with a bunch of purple irises for Peace. But when he walked in, he found her standing in front of the bathroom door, her forehead pressed against the mirror as if she had just tipped over there.

"Peace?" he said. "Are you okay?"

"I'm groovy," she said.

"What are you doing?"

"I'm groovy," she said again.

"No," he said. "What are you doing?"

Her forehead was still against the mirror. "Waiting for my eyes to dry," she said.

He put the flowers in the old teapot they often used as a vase. He remembered, vividly and with dread, what it had been like to walk into Mary Jane's room the night she first dropped acid.

"Okay," he said. "How wasted are you?"

She giggled and turned to face him. The hair that had been behind her ears fell softly into two long Art Nouveau curves.

"No," she said. "I'm not high."

"But you're waiting for your *eyes* to dry?"

She giggled again and embraced him. As usual, her outfit was a brilliant blend of unmatched, unexpected parts. She was wearing her yellow miniskirt, a belt with mirrored buttons on it, and a new pair of tall white boots.

"I put on new eyelashes," she said, and she fluttered her lids for emphasis. She had rimmed her eyes, Egyptian-style, with dark eyeliner and had applied two pairs of false eyelashes—one on top of the other—as bushy and black as a new paintbrush.

"Can you see anything?" he asked her, laughing.

"How do they look?" she said.

"They look mod."

"Do I look like a dollybird?"

"Absolutely," he said.

She grinned. She lifted both her arms, not to embrace him this time but to celebrate herself.

"Guess where we're going," she said to Henry.

He took a step forward and kissed her. "Where'd you get the boots and the lashes?"

"Guess where we're going," she said again.

"Where?"

"We're going to the Scotch."

"The what?"

"The Scotch of St. James. The Great Martini gave me his card."

IT WAS ONE OF THE TWO OR THREE hottest discotheques in town. Henry had heard about it endlessly at the studio, because both Paul and George often showed up there, and various ink-and-paint girls were forever trying to get in. The Scotch was near Piccadilly Circus, down a narrow side street, right next door to the gallery where John had met Yoko. Peace led the way from the bar upstairs down a circular staircase to a long room dark with drama and jammed with people. Lights flashed, miraculously, in time to the music. Women in paisley miniskirts and men in velvet pants danced dangerously on the crowded floor. In the near corner, the band was dressed in what looked like Civil War uniforms, the drummer flailing away like a demonic Disney animatron. Along the walls were banquettes and small round tables, and at one of them, Henry could see two redheaded girls making out with each other.

He had learned from his days with Mary Jane at Berkeley that LSD was usually laced into sugar cubes or soaked into blotter paper. So when Peace, just moments after they'd gone downstairs, proudly produced two blue capsules, Henry wasn't sure what she was offering him.

"What is that?" he shouted at her, above the music.

"It's smashing!" she said.

"No! What is it?"

"What do you think it is?" she said.

THE MUSIC THRUMMED and beat against the walls. Every few minutes, Henry became convinced that he could see the sounds—pulsating outward in concentric shapes, like the rippled bands he drew for gongs or drums in animation. On the shelves and ledges that were cut into the cavelike walls, the rings of sound hit vases of flowers, stacks of books, bottles of whiskey, busts of poets and statesmen that were decked out in mod hats and sunglasses. In Henry's mind, the sounds splashed down and over all of these things, then pooled into puddles on the ground, where the hundreds of dancing feet splashed them and spattered them around.

So this was tripping, he thought.

He remembered the night he had followed Mary Jane around Berkeley, determined to take care of her and keep her safe. A wave of regret, like a shudder, or nausea, gripped him as he saw Peace looking back at him, beaming, tripping, not remotely Mary Jane. But then he was taken up by the music, and the two girls he'd seen kissing before were now with him on the dance floor, and it turned out that Peace knew one of them, and that led Henry to a different sense—of a vast, comforting embrace, the interconnectedness of them all, with the music and lights pulsing on and on, past the fear and regret and the nagging sense that something or someone was missing from his life.

AT TWO IN THE MORNING, Henry and Peace stood at their front door, Peace trying and failing to put her key in the lock. She would succeed in holding the doorknob, and even manage to locate the right key, but then she would collapse in a paroxysm of giggles.

"This is *so* much harder than it looks," she said.

"Peace," Henry said.

"No, don't tell me. I'll get it," she said, as if he had asked her a riddle.

She flipped a long strand of hair away from her mouth, then bent down again, the hair falling back over her face. He waited, trying to be patient, and then when her shoulder started to shake with laughter again, he said: "Peace. Let me. I'll do it."

"No!" she shouted, like a baby not wanting to give up a toy. And then she added, quite seriously, as if she was talking about a pair of crutches or having her arm in a sling: "I have to learn to do these things high."

When they stepped inside, Henry noticed that the purple irises he had brought home that night had already opened and drooped dramatically, stalks spraying out from the teapot like the lines of an explosion.

PEACE, AS IT TURNED OUT, did learn to do things high—and to a rather remarkable extent. Throughout the long, damp, but domestic fall, Henry got to the point where he thought he could tell exactly how much pot she had smoked, how recently she had been tripping.

Straight or stoned, she was without doubt the most effortlessly creative person he had ever known. She painted cabinets in different colors, cut out lips or eyes from magazines and collaged them onto doorframes, turned every surface she found in life into a plausible working canvas. She tie-dyed old sheets to make napkins, sewed a hilarious, belted miniskirt to replace the tattered, dowdy one around the kitchen sink, pasted wine labels onto the kitchen floor, and added new words to the walls around them—KITCHEN, CLOSET, SHOES, DOOR—in letters that dripped and floated and beat with psychedelic life. And with a style that Henry jealously recognized as entirely her own.

5

Mail Call

It was a Friday afternoon in late October, and Henry had been instructed by Jack Dixon, one of the animating supervisors, to leave the Blue Meanies and switch to the Apple Bonkers. The Apple Bonkers were tall, top-hatted gentlemen who used bright green apples to freeze the inhabitants of Pepperland. It bothered Henry that, based on the available storyboards, the apples didn't seem to need to be picked *from* anywhere and just appeared in the Bonkers' hands. The Disney man in Henry fought the lack of logic.

"They have to come from somewhere," he said.

"Why?" Jack asked.

"Because they do. Because you can't just get an apple from the air."

"Maybe you can in Pepperland," Jack said enigmatically, and walked off just as Victoria came back in from the front desk.

"Mail call, Disney Boy," she said.

"Mail?" he said. "I never get mail."

"Who's Mary Jane Harmon?" Victoria asked.

His face must have done something twisted or telling, because it seemed to startle her.

"She's just an old friend," Henry said.

Victoria held the envelope up to his desk lamp, grinning. There was a touch of Ethel's brassiness in her, Henry thought. Why did women always have to be either too hard or too soft?

"Wonder what it says," Victoria teased.

Despite Henry's wish to seem unmoved—despite his wish to *be* unmoved—he grabbed instinctively at the envelope.

"A stateside gal?" Victoria asked. "The gal you left behind?"

Then she saw the look on his face, and she softened immediately. "Oh. I'm sorry, Disney Boy," she said.

"She's just an old friend," Henry repeated.

He looked down at the envelope. The handwriting itself made him feel strange: tugged uncomfortably too far west. He didn't want to read the letter. He suspected that it would just make him feel low—and guilty for having left the States without having said a better goodbye. He put the envelope in his back pocket, picked up his pencil, and peered down at his drawing. He could sense Victoria looking at him, but he didn't look back at her.

He didn't open the envelope until nearly seven that evening, sipping a cup of cold coffee on one of the leather couches in the sitting room.

October 15, 1967

Dear Henry:

Ha! I found you! It took me four months, but leave it to old Eagle Eye and the bookkeeping department at Disney.

Well, I'm finally a college graduate, which of course is more than I can say for you, you stoner. Graduation was in June (of course) and everyone at Berkeley was very "Freedom now." I was just happy it was over.

Alexa kept asking me about you. "When's he coming back?" "I thought he really liked me." "Did he say anything to you about why he left?" So I said:

1. Beats me

2. You were wrong, and

3. Nope, nope, nope

Funny how she thought that—having been your best friend for 18 years and having flown across the country and back for your mother's funeral—I would have some coordinates for you more specific than London, England.

It doesn't matter. I figure you're heavily tattooed, with hair down to your waist, and are now living comfortably in an opium den with the latest three or four smitten kittens. You left America just in time for race riots to break out all over the place. It's so grim. I wonder if you think about it there.

For my part, I've settled in Greenwich Village with George (remember George? Of course you don't) and a number of projects, one of which has just come to fruition. To find out more, you'll have to write to me. That's right, write to me, doofus.

Love always,

MJ

Henry looked up. Victoria was standing in the doorway of the sitting room.

"I have had a profound insight," she said.

She walked to the other end of the sofa and straddled its arm, like a child playing horse.

"And what is that?" Henry asked her, wishing she'd go away.

"Do you realize that, other than a few screams, there are going to be absolutely no female voices in *Yellow Submarine*?"

"Huh," Henry said.

"Why do you think that is?" she asked him.

"I don't know," Henry said. "Maybe because there are only male characters in *Yellow Submarine*?"

"Aha! And why do you think *that* is?"

She blew a line of smoke rings into the air, her mouth a tough, inviting O, contracting as it pinched out its nearly opaque white circles.

Henry put Mary Jane's letter back into its envelope. "How do you do that?" he asked Victoria.

"Do what?" she asked, as if she hadn't meant her smoke rings to be provocative.

"Blow smoke rings," he said.

"Ancient secret."

"Teach me," Henry said.

"It's all about the tongue," Victoria said.

He did not want her, and it was not just because she was older and he knew her body would be less exciting than Peace's. He didn't want Victoria because she didn't paste magazine pictures onto doorframes, didn't make belts out of old neckties and purse handles out of old belts, didn't know how to give massages that were more like conversations than talk, didn't make him want to kiss her even after she'd asked him to. Henry did wonder—his wondering such things was after all a habit of being—if Victoria actually would cheat on her husband with him. It amazed and intrigued him that he had never yet slept with a married woman. But then he thought of Peace; she was the only one he really wanted or intended to want.

WHEN HENRY CAME HOME THAT NIGHT, Peace was wearing another new pair of boots, and she kept them—and only them—on when she led him to the bed to make love. Gymnastically, she got them close enough to his face so that he could smell their mixture of leather and marijuana—a head-shop, flea-market smell.

"Where'd you get *these* boots?" he asked her after he lit a cigarette and she lit a joint.

"Do you like them?" she said. She was lying beside him now, and she lifted her legs at a perfect ninety-degree angle, admiring the boots.

"You stole them, didn't you?" Henry asked.

She clicked the heels against each other.

"Did you?" Henry asked her.

"I think everything should be free," Peace said. "Don't you think everything should be free?"

She giggled and let her legs fall heavily back onto the bed.

"Where'd you steal them from?" he asked her.

She sang: "Stone free, do what I please. Stone free, to ride the breeze."

He knew he should scold her, but he was beguiled.

He asked her to pose for him.

"In just my boots?" she asked.

"Exactly," he said.

"Stone free," she sang. "I can't stay. Got to, got to, got to get away."

Henry sprang out of bed and found some charcoals and paper. He sat on a chair about two yards from the bed.

"Find a position you can hold," he told her. "Other than asleep."

She looked slightly wounded. "I *know* how to pose," she said.

"I'm sorry, baby. It's just, you know. It's not as easy as you'd think."

But she was a good model, reminding him of Annie. She was in fact excellent. She found a position, up on an elbow, and then another, curled around a pillow, and then a third, her back arched, her shoulders as perfect and polished as two stones.

"You're amazing," he told her, hungrily sketching.

She grinned.

"It's like you've been doing this all your life," he said.

She giggled.

"Well, not all my life," she said, but then she told him that, between auditions, she had been modeling for Geoffrey Whitehall.

Whitehall was famous—and not just in London—for his psyche-delic designs, which adorned everything from record albums to shop windows, posters, and clothing. His considerable success as a graphic designer had been converted to near icon status by the fact that he'd started a trend for painting on bodies. Women's bodies. Nude.

"How the hell did you meet Geoffrey Whitehall?" Henry asked.

"Martini introduced us," Peace said.

"Did you let him paint you?" Henry asked.

"I told you I posed for him."

"No. But I mean did you let him paint *on* you?"

"Not yet," Peace said. "But he says he wants to. Isn't that fab? He says my body's a perfect canvas."

"It is," Henry said. "But it's my canvas."

She looked at him. "Are you done drawing?" she asked.

He nodded, perturbed.

"Then let's go out," she said. "I heard that Jimi Hendrix might be at the UFO tonight."

"Who told you that?" he asked her, with a sudden desire to know everything she did during the day.

She shrugged. "I don't know. Someone," she said.

But he managed to talk her out of going. He gave her a massage, using the Tiger Balm she had brought home. He didn't ask her where she'd gotten it.

After he had made love to her again, she fell asleep, and he stood up to turn off the lights. Her skirt, sweater, and belt formed a checkerboard and patent-leather puddle at the foot of the bed, and beside it her new boots stood sulkily, drooping in opposite directions, as if they had had a fight.

6

Not Anybody's Baby

The Beatles walked into the Soho Square studio on a brisk November morning, and they were at once more vivid and less real than Henry could have imagined. They had, however, virtually no interest in being at the studio. They were under contract to come by twice during production, and this—six months into the project—was merely the first of their required visits. There were two still photographers and a film crew with them, following every gesture the Fab Four made as they encountered their two-dimensional cartoon selves. Predictably, they mugged with the cutouts, but to Henry they seemed to be downright bored. They were also a bit disheveled. Only Ringo's hair looked as if it had been recently washed. Paul had a five o'clock shadow, and though George was wearing bright red pants and a red silk ascot, he looked slightly gray—either hungover or just exhausted.

"What's it about, then?" John asked his cardboard double and flashed a peace sign to match the cutout's own.

Not until Jack led them into the editing room—where he ran several scenes for them on the Moviola—did their outlook seem to brighten. Suddenly, Paul was asking if it was too late for them to supply their own voices. John wanted to know if the Apple Bonkers' green apples were meant to look like the one on the Beatles' record label. Ringo picked up one of the models of the submarine itself and began to examine it from every angle.

Most of the artists ducked back down to their drawing boards. Even Victoria seemed to be hiding behind her floppy hat. But as he had long ago with Walt, Henry remained unfazed by fame, looking first Paul, then John, right in the eye.

"Hey, mate," John said and immediately walked up behind Henry's shoulder to look at his drawing board. "Mind if I have a go?"

As Ringo and George departed, and Paul embarked on a side discussion of distribution rights, John Lennon sat in Henry's chair, picked up a pencil, and began to sketch.

Lennon was wearing a black turtleneck and round wire-framed glasses, behind which Henry could see heavy-lidded eyes that seemed to mask any hint of inspiration. With Henry standing beside him, Lennon drew one simple flower, then another, then a third, the last one with a pair of petals that were flung out like ecstatic arms. The fourth flower Lennon drew had a face, and one of the petals was coquettishly hiding all but its eyes. Henry tried to appear neutral, but a small storm was starting in his heart. How was it possible for this man to come from nowhere and sit down without warning and simply create? No hesitation, no copying, no doubt, no mimicry. What John Lennon drew came from his pencil the way water might come from a faucet. There was no suggestion of any source more challenging or profound. In a way it reminded Henry of Peace: that same confidence and facility—the same instinct to fill surfaces with patterns, spaces with furniture, silences with sounds. It was the very instinct Henry lacked.

But perhaps it would be enough, he thought, to stay close to someone who did have that instinct, to have a little house somewhere: an eager, warm, brown-haired woman with a beautiful voice—and someday, perhaps, a beautiful child.

CHRISTMAS WAS ON A MONDAY and Boxing Day a Tuesday, and though Henry had had to work through the weekend, he had been given both holidays off. Defying the British custom—as well as her casual

Chanukah memories—he and Peace opened their presents on Christ-mas Day, beneath a tree they had trimmed the night before with pipe-cleaner peace signs, curlicues of used animation cels, painted tomato paste cans, and tissue-paper flowers. Peace gave Henry clothes and, implicitly, a lesson in mod. She had long since picked out his bell-bottom jeans and the wide leather belt that held them up. To his mild relief, she had not given him the pair of plaid bells she had pointed out on Carnaby Street the weekend before. Instead, she gave him a purple button-down shirt, a pair of secondhand boots, and an evil-eye bead on a black leather choker. Henry wore them all for the whole day, even though the boots were at least a size too small, and he could feel, practically before they reached the corner pub, the rawness on his heels. Peace gave him, also, the pink and orange scarf she had been knitting off and on since the day they had first arrived in London. It was easily ten feet long by now, but Peace had never gotten around to figuring out how to finish it. She had literally tied a piece of yarn through the final row, like a drawstring.

He gave her a guitar. He had bought it the week before at Macari's on Charing Cross. Victoria had been buying a flute for her older daughter, and Henry had gone along, with Peace in mind. She had been talking all fall about how much it would help her in her audi-tions if she could play an instrument. Henry knew the guitar was likely to be as much a fashion accessory as a career move. But he was delighted to see her face when he gave it to her, so fantastically happy.

Someone had already taught Peace three simple chords, and she practiced them relentlessly all afternoon and evening. Henry was ex-pecting her to try to sing something current, and it touched him inef-fably that what she seemed intent on playing first was "Twinkle, Twinkle, Little Star."

At five in the afternoon on Christmas Day, Peace's great stoned revelation was that the Alphabet Song shared the same music as "Twinkle, Twinkle." Another hour and another joint later, Henry started singing "Baa, Baa, Black Sheep" to her, and she collapsed in a heap of giggles.

"You're kidding!" she said. "That one, *too*?"

They had sex even while she was still marveling at this great discovery.

BOXING DAY MORNING, Henry lay under the Indian-print covers, looking up at the ceiling, where Peace had recently affixed a dozen or more flower-shaped vinyl stickers. On the floor there were, as usual, her cast-off clothes: today a purple sweater, some velvet gloves, and a black-and-white chevron-patterned miniskirt.

She was still asleep, her dark hair crosshatching her pale face.

"Morning, baby," he said to her.

She stretched, catlike, provocative. "Why do you always call me that?"

"Call you baby? Why? Does it bother you?" he asked.

"Yes."

"Really? Why?"

"Because I'm not your baby. I'm not anybody's baby."

Henry smiled what he thought was a shared-orphan smile.

"What?" she said.

"Well, you were someone's baby once," he said.

"I didn't mean that," she said, sounding truly annoyed. "God, Henry. Not everything's about that, you know."

The radio was playing "Big Girls Don't Cry," and for a moment Henry was back at Berkeley, sitting on Mary Jane's couch, listening to *The Beatles vs. The Four Seasons* and observing the patterns of bird droppings on her orange-tinted window.

HENRY HAD BEEN MEANING to write back to Mary Jane, but there had been something needy and vaguely punishing in the tone of her most recent letter, and the last thing Henry wanted was to feel beholden to her. In the afternoon, however, Peace decided to take a nap, so Henry finally sat down to the task.

Dear MJ:

Merry Christmas! Happy Boxing Day!

Of course I remember George. He was the guy who wrote you all that lowercase, e.e. cummings–wannabe poetry and looked like War-ren Beatty except without a jaw, right?

Here Henry inserted an impressively hideous illustration.

It was good to see your handwriting, even if you were scolding me. And you're wrong, I have not gotten tattooed. I keep wanting to tell you this—that I have finally done what you always told me to do, and that is make a choice. You've met her already. Peace Jacobs. Yes, the one I met at the funeral—the one who was the baby in the practice house. Honest and truly, MJ, I have not so much as kissed anyone else, and no it's not because I've suddenly grown a hump. And the weird thing is it must be the real thing because it's such a strange place and time to be picking one person. Everyone shags everyone here. Shag, you Yankee gal, means what you think it means.

Now, what are these projects you so calmly mention coming to fruition? Kidding aside, I hope you've landed the kind of newspaper job you always wanted and are raking muck all over the place. Any chance you'll be "crossing the pond" at some point? London is totally swinging. The movie has to be done by summer, so I've been working fiendishly. Here is one of the fiends:

Henry supplied a drawing of the Chief Blue Meanie. He mailed the let-ter on his way to work.

As the winter months unfolded and the staff struggled to complete the Sea of Holes sequence, Henry rarely did anything but work late and wake early. Peace didn't seem to mind his absence. After a winter of fruitless auditions and—as far as Henry could tell—fruitless acting classes, she had finally gotten a promising callback for the cast of the British production of *Hair*. She talked about the casting agent as if he was a mercurial deity. She called him Mr. Fate, and Henry never knew his real name. Throughout April, Peace's practicing for the *Hair* auditions made Henry almost nostalgic for the days of "I'm dead, thank you." Apparently there was a big opening number called "Aquarius" in which the whole cast was supposed to form a large circle and move in slow motion around some kind of altar.

For days, practicing the slow motion, Peace had not so much walked as drifted around the apartment. Every action had been excruciatingly prolonged: the peeling of a banana, the pulling back of a shower curtain, the toking on a joint.

"Why do they move like this?" Henry asked Peace.

They were walking to Geoffrey Whitehall's studio on a Saturday morning, Henry having won the battle to chaperone.

"Mr. Fate told me it's supposed to be like moving under water."

"So you're going to be dancing," Henry said to Peace.

"It's not exactly dancing," Peace said, and then she shrugged, but in an exaggerated, slow-motion, underwater way.

GEOFF WHITEHALL'S STUDIO was on James Street, four blocks over from Rose. It was not so much decorated as strewn with the evidence of Whitehall's supposed genius: posters, prints, record albums, book covers, portraits, advertisements, magazine stories, an entire cottage industry based on one artist's ability to invent a style and stay devoted to it. Henry hated him even before Whitehall extended his slightly damp hand.

According to Whitehall's instructions—and without the slightest hesitation—Peace lay on the floor wearing only her panties. The floor was painted with a Day-Glo rainbow and sky, and against it, her white body looked like a cloud. In one hand, Whitehall held a new sable paintbrush with a red handle and a white head. In the other he held a Cadbury's chocolates tin that was filled with black paint.

"Are you ready, luv?" he asked her.

She nodded, contented, as if she was lying on a soft baby blanket instead of a hard, painted basement floor. Whitehall's first move was to circle her left nipple with an inch-wide black outline.

Henry didn't know if he was more troubled by Peace's nude body or by Whitehall's unabashedly nonartistic delight in it. Whatever the case, it was clear to Henry fairly quickly that neither Peace nor Whitehall had the slightest interest in his presence, and it crossed his mind at least briefly that they might be waiting for him to leave.

7

Under the Table at the Scotch of St. James

Henry was lying under a table at the Scotch of St. James. He had sucked on a sugar cube an hour before, and the acid had just kicked in. Beside him was Martin Doyle, the Great Martini, and beside him— also under the table—was a record producer whose name Henry couldn't remember but whose face looked disturbingly—and, minute by minute, increasingly—like a clown's.

"You're Peace's shag, right?" Martini asked him.

Henry could see the words coming out of Martini's mouth, just as if they'd been drawn. He smiled.

"Right?" Martini repeated, and the word floated there. It was like the last scene in *Submarine,* when the words appear above John as he sings "All you need is love." Henry wanted to tell this to Martini, but he knew it was far too complex a thought. So he simply smiled again.

"She's a tart," Martini said.

"Apple tart," Henry said, not focusing.

"No, man. She's a tart. A real tart," Martini said, then crawled off to another table.

Henry looked up toward Peace's legs. She was wearing a pair of fishnet stockings, and in his state, Henry thought for a moment that he saw actual fish.

IT WAS NOT A GOOD TRIP, though it was more exotic than truly disturbing; what Henry saw—even as he tried to escape the experience—

was unpleasant but not unbearable. What he saw was an animalized world—actually not that different from the world he had learned to see and to draw at Disney. Martini, for example, was unmistakably a bear—somewhat along the lines of Baloo in *The Jungle Book,* but polar-bear pale. The small round tables on their center legs were storks, and the chairs were dogs and cats.

The fish in the fishnet stockings moved suddenly, slapping against each other. Henry grabbed hold of one of them, and Peace's hand appeared on her knee, then her face beside her knee, and then she fluttered down to sit beside him under the table. Peace turned out to be a bird—a dove or pigeon—her nose beakish, her hair feathery.

"Did you sleep with him?" Henry asked Peace. Her skinny knees, above the tops of her boots, looked as if they'd been drawn by two smile lines.

"With who?"

"With Mr. Fate."

"Of course," she said.

"To get the part?"

"Of course," she said. "That's what everyone does."

She was right, but Henry didn't care that she was right.

He tried to locate the feeling—as weirdly unfamiliar as a sudden illness or a stranger's rage. He knew he had felt it some time before: a blend of fear, amazement, and hollowness. But Peace's reaction to *his* reaction was easier to recognize. He saw it in the set of her lips, in the torque of her shoulders, the almost coquettish look in her eyes that said: *What did you expect of me? Don't tell me you couldn't have seen this coming.* This was the look he himself had given so many times before—starting all the way back with Daisy, way back on the night of the fire at Humphrey.

"It's the way it works," Peace said.

"Did you sleep with Whitehall too?" Henry asked her.

"What do you want me to say?"

"These guys are just using you," Henry said.

"And what's wrong with that? It's my body, you know. Nobody owns me."

Henry tried to answer Peace for a brief, awful, familiar moment, but he couldn't say a thing.

"YOU REALIZE, OF COURSE," Victoria told him, "that you are attempting to zig whilst the rest of the world is zagging."

They were sitting on one of the leather couches in the office on Monday afternoon, before a mess of lunch plates and cups that the previous diners had left behind.

"What do you mean?" Henry asked her.

"You're attempting the vine-covered cottage bit during the only time in history when not a single soul in the entire known world is being remotely monogamous."

Henry got to his feet and began to gather the paper plates and cups. Victoria lit a cigarette and watched him carelessly.

"Do you love her?" Victoria asked.

"Yes," Henry said. "I do."

"How do you know?" she asked him. He was aware that there was something more than sisterly in her inquiry, but for the moment he decided that he would ignore it and hear her advice anyway.

"I know because—I don't know. I don't get tired of her. I want to be with her."

"Really?"

"Really."

"Do you want to be with her now?"

Victoria asked the question as if it were clinical, not personal, but again it felt to Henry more like some form of flirtation.

"Now?" he asked. "This minute? No. This minute I want to kill her."

Victoria crossed her legs at the ankles, leaning back into the couch. "Kill her?" she said. "Really, Harry? I didn't think you could feel that."

"Feel what?" Henry asked.

"Are you sure you want to kill her? Or do you just want to trade her in?"

Henry looked at Victoria. "How did you know that?"

"Harry. You're hardly a mystery."

"I'm not?"

It felt good to flirt back. It felt as if he had just had something re-turned to him that he'd been missing. After all, he was much more ac-customed to this than to sincerity, jealousy, and rage.

Finally, he slid down the leather couch to sit beside her, and then he pivoted onto his right hip while she pivoted onto her left. They faced each other. She looked both wry and needy, but the wryness was more appealing to him than the neediness was unappealing. He kissed her, totally unsurprised by the enthusiasm with which she kissed him back. It was the rapid, not particularly interesting answer to a ques-tion that had been only marginally more interesting to ask.

He knew it would be their only kiss. It wasn't because he felt guilty about Peace, or even felt indifferent to her. It was, rather, his sense of Victoria, a sense of bottomless longing that was too much like Martha's, or maybe his own.

YELLOW SUBMARINE WAS DUE to premiere in July. Throughout the spring and early summer, days and nights—never religiously differen-tiated before—blended entirely. It was not unusual for an animator to come into the studio on a Monday morning and, buoyed by successive tides of naps, snacks, and carts of bangers and mash, not leave until Wednesday or Thursday night. There were always people sleeping on the couches now, and often there were ink-and-paint girls napping in the camera room. At Disney, the ranks of animators and painters had usually dwindled as units finished their work. But here, with an in-tractable deadline and increasing hysteria from the distributors, more people were being added all the time. As the deadline for delivery neared, the producers sent word out to the London art schools, and now in the evenings vans and buses pulled up to the Soho studio, dis-gorging students who formed a delighted night shift, donning white gloves to color in the Beatles and their fantastical world.

———

PEOPLE HAD SPENT WEEKS angling for tickets, and trying to get one for Peace would have done Henry no good, even if he'd been so inclined. With the rest of the animators, he had been relegated to a balcony seat at the huge London Pavilion.

"You'll sneak me in," Peace said on the morning of the opening.

"Not a chance. There are assigned seats, Peace," he said.

"Well, someone might not show," she said.

"Why don't you ask Mr. Fate to bring you? Or Martini? Or Whitehall?" Henry asked her bitterly.

"I did."

Their eyes flashed and met.

"Please, Henry?" she said.

"I can't."

"You could if you wanted to. You're just still mad at me."

She was standing in front of the mirror and using a long, fine comb to tease the top of her hair higher. Then she slipped on what he thought of as her Puss-in-Boots boots, swung her patent-leather bag over her left shoulder, and walked out the door. He wanted to say he was sorry, but she'd been right: He was still mad at her.

THE STREETS WERE MOBBED for blocks and blocks with Beatles fans wearing yellow shirts, yellow pants, yellow gloves, yellow sunglasses. Around the theater, bobbies in uniforms exactly like the constables' in *Mary Poppins* linked arms to hold back the fans, who were relentlessly singing the chorus of "Yellow Submarine" and hoping for a glimpse of the Beatles. Most of them never had a chance; the Four drove up in sequence and took turns posing with a huge Blue Meanie, as arm-waving and expressionless as any Disneyland figure.

Inside, Henry and Victoria sat in the balcony with a bunch of ink-and-paint girls. Victoria was a study in forced enthusiasm. Ever since their one kiss—with the exception of one silent, pouty follow-up day—she had been, in Henry's view, stoically peppy, married, and mod. She pointed out, in the packed audience below them, several of the Rolling Stones, as well as Eric Clapton and Ringo. Henry spotted Twiggy as well, and felt a pang: Peace worshipped Twiggy and would have loved to see her up close. But just as Henry was recalling the morning's conversation, he looked down from the balcony and saw Peace, with a yellow boa, flouncing down the aisle holding the arm of some man in a pink suede jacket. Something wrenched inside Henry, almost a physical tear, and he found himself changing positions in his seat, as if trying to get away from pain.

When the lights went down, for a moment before the film started, Henry could still hear the sounds of the crowd outside and imagine Peace navigating her way through it, yellow boa soaring. But then, quite unexpectedly, he was immersed in the world he had helped to make. "Once upon a time," the narrator's voice intoned, "or maybe twice . . ."

All along, they had joked that the story wouldn't matter as long as the music was loud. In reality, though, it was neither the story nor the music that pulled Henry along, or even the jokes and surprises and the rare mixture of styles. It was, in the end, the colors: the amazingly deep, incredibly vibrant, psychedelic colors. As often as Henry had seen them in the studio, he was astonished by what they did on the screen.

Even Victoria dropped her supercasual pose just long enough to seem similarly thrilled, nudging Henry in the ribs. "Bloody hell," she whispered when the long first scenes were over and the titles finally came up, along with the title song.

THREE MONTHS LATER, Henry sat in another opening-night audience, this time for the London premiere of *Hair*. It was all Peace had talked about when she had been home long enough and coherently enough to talk at all. The play was subtitled "The American Tribal Love-Rock Musical," and Peace never referred to the cast, only to "the Tribe." It wasn't until Henry was watching the show that he realized that Berger and Claude and Sheila were characters, not fellow actors.

Peace looked beautiful, a sash tied Indian-style around her fore-head. She danced and sang and swayed and, with the others, got briefly and unshockingly nude. Henry tried to connect her either to the woman he lived with or to the character she was playing. He could do neither. But despite everything—despite even his simmering anger at what he now knew were her constant infidelities—he was moved to another burst of hope by the words of one exuberant song:

And peace will guide the planets.
And love will steer the stars.

8

Lost Something, Sweetie?

It was their second autumn in London. Henry hoped that would make a difference. First times were for travelers and tourists, he thought. Second times were for people who had made a place home.

It was a chilly season, and rain, as it had the first year, came swift and gray, leaching the colors out of the city. Henry worked in color all day long. With the movie over, and no immediate substitute in sight, he had reluctantly landed a job through Geoff Whitehall, painting murals for a new discotheque called the Logical Alternative. The murals were entirely Whitehall's designs—already classic combinations of flowers, rainbows, stars, and mythic creatures. But the job was perfect for Henry, demanding patience, precision, and virtually no invention. He was one of a team of only three artists, and they worked in separate areas of the disco, close enough for the occasional tiff about the choice of radio station but far enough apart so that their brushes never met.

It was for Henry a particular joy not to have to job out the colors to the usual set of ink-and-paint girls. Not since the summer at Wilton, when he had painted first the practice house and then the building where Mary Jane worked, had Henry's hands, shoes, and hair been so often spattered with paint. Even now, even on a too-early October morning, with the empty club, the bad coffee, and the nagging sense that things with Peace were still not what he wanted them to be—even now Henry could remember the way the peach juice had trickled down his arm over the tangerine paint on the day he had first had sex.

November came, and as the brick walls of the club deepened with color, lunch was served up daily by whatever chef the owner was trying out. One of the artists flirted with Henry. So did one of the waitress trainees, and several of the auditioning dancers. Victoria called a few times, her pretexts growing more forced and her airiness less convincing. Henry perceived every one of these women as a viable option, and thus as at least a minor sacrifice. But he still wanted Peace.

Predictably, and perhaps alluringly, he saw less and less of her now. She was always asleep when he got up and left for work in the morning. Her show, it was true, didn't end until ten-thirty, and then there was the inevitable comedown—unachievable, apparently, without some sort of drug or drink. Most of Peace's contributions to the flat— even the ones that had involved theft more than industry—had halted now. Sometimes in the evenings, Henry would lie back on his side of the bed and try to plan what he would paint on these walls. The empty landscape stretched before him. It was still the inviting two-tone backdrop of green and blue it had been when they'd first moved in. It could have been Pennsylvania, or the woods behind Humphrey. It could have been California, or the British countryside.

Henry tried to decide what to put on the wall. There was pale blue sky and there was deep green grass. For a moment, he allowed himself to go back to Wilton, back to the closet where he had painted the field, the Ray, the car, and had first discovered the vibrant freedom of an existence without Martha. Nostalgia struck him, but without any precision.

Sometimes, even down their little side street, a car would pass, its lights would throw a shadow onto the wall, and Henry would try in vain to catch those shadows and find meaning in them.

NOVEMBER WAS FRIGID, and Peace took to pulling the covers away from Henry at night. Usually, she slept in total, almost scary stillness. Henry had watched her many times. He knew sometimes it was only drugs or drinking that made her sleep so deeply. But even when she napped or when she had had a night that was sober and straight, she was normally immobile in her sleep. These days, it seemed, it was more common for her to turn and startle.

He wondered if she was ill. He imagined nursing her. He would bring her soup on a tray, the way that Martha had brought it to him. As always, he was surprised when he had any memory of Martha, let alone a good one. But he could taste the chicken soup, feel the cold shiver of the darkness behind the window in the practice house.

Peace opened her mouth in her sleep and licked her lips, which looked dry. She scrunched herself into a tight ball. Henry put his arms around her and fell asleep, trying to keep her warm.

HE WOKE TO THE SOUND OF HER RETCHING, a forlorn and foreign sound that he mistook at first for a street noise. When he had located the sound, he sprang out of bed, as if there was something he was supposed to do. The bathroom door was closed, the collage on the doorframe looking puckered in the daylight, a two-dimensional time capsule of some things that Peace had liked.

He put on the kettle and took the tea down from the shelf. By the time Peace opened the bathroom door, he had remade the bed, fixed her the tea, and placed the cup on the stack of old magazines that served as her makeshift night table.

"Why aren't you dressed?" she asked him. "Shouldn't you be on your way to work?"

He said, "Are you okay?"

"I got sick," she said. She sounded and looked about five years old.

"I know, baby," he said, and for once she didn't object to the nickname.

"I'm sorry," she said, looking embarrassed.

"Come and get into bed," Henry told her.

She was wearing nothing but her panties and a sleeveless baby-doll nightgown.

"Come on, let me get you warm," he said.

"I'm fine," she said.

Her skin was the color of sourdough bread.

"Get into bed," he told her again.

She took a few uncertain steps toward it, and then she got in.

"Have some tea," he said. "It'll settle your stomach."

"I'm okay, Henry," she said.

She reached for the teacup, her fingers embracing it from the bottom, like the green base of a flower.

She slept. At ten o'clock, he called the disco and told them he wouldn't be coming in. Then he felt her forehead and left to find her some chicken soup.

SHE WASN'T IN BED WHEN HE RETURNED, and his first thought was that she was sick again. He waited for her, putting the soup on the stove and turning on the radio, so that the music could fill the silence. After five or ten minutes, though, he began to worry about her and walked up to the still-closed bathroom door.

"Peace?" he said.

There was silence.

"Peace?"

Silence again.

He knocked, waited, asked, called, pounded, and finally opened. The bathroom was empty, and the only sign of Peace was the toothbrush she'd left on the side of the sink, along with an empty box of false eyelashes and a dark mascara brush.

Henry worried, sensing she'd gone somewhere in an untamed state, unthinking and in pain. He put his coat on, wrapped the scarf she had made him twice around his neck, and went back outside.

She had not been to the drugstore two blocks down, nor to the market a block beyond that. Neither shopkeeper had seen her.

For an hour or so, Henry made his way through the neighborhood, passing the dry cleaners, the pubs, the head shop, the used-book store. At a side entrance of the small church six blocks away, he finally saw a familiar short red coat and white boots, breath clouds wisping out from the arched doorway into the gray-white day.

Henry's step quickened. Only at the last moment did he see the broom at the woman's feet, the broom handle in her gloved hands, the scraggly red hair, and the middle-aged face.

"Lost something, sweetie?" she asked him.

Henry, speechless, shook his head no.

Someone, he thought as he walked away.

HE WENT BACK HOME with one last hope that he would find Peace there. His worry grew into annoyance, then anger. When it was too big a feeling to confine to the apartment, he took it back outside. It would be rage by the time he reached the theater.

Snow was coming down, and Henry walked through the streets toward Piccadilly, remembering the tracks he had made in the snow the day he left Humphrey and ran away to find Betty. Betty, who had never even written to him after Martha's death and who, as far he knew, was still working for *Time* in Paris, just the English Channel and a lifetime away. He thought about what it had been like to have Betty as an unknown, a promise in his future. His future now seemed to lack so specific a hope.

The Shaftesbury was an old theater, with a castlelike turret on top. In the snow, it could have been a Disney backdrop except for the huge banner hanging across its famous corner entrance: HAIR: THE AMERICAN TRIBAL LOVE-ROCK MUSICAL. Henry had come to hate the poster and everything it stood for. What it stood for, to him, was Peace's absence.

Henry knocked at the stage door, and after a few minutes it was opened by a guy he recognized as one of the Tribe.

"I'm looking for Peace," Henry said.

"Who isn't?" the guy said.

"Jacobs," Henry added.

"Who isn't?" the guy said, smiling.

"Well, okay, is she here?" Henry asked.

"Try the rehearsal rooms. Look around. Hey, have you got any food? I've got to get something to eat," he said.

The ancient wooden walls of the backstage corridor were covered almost entirely with framed photographs and vintage posters. But the current actors—it was hard to know whether they were in costume or their regular clothes—left little doubt about the decade. Henry walked down the corridor smelling marijuana, coffee, stale flowers, perfume, and sweat. He could hear laughter, music, arguments, curses. He felt like a stick of wood being borne along a river.

Peace was sitting on the floor of a rehearsal room cross-legged, wearing an old leather aviator helmet. A guy was lying beside her with his head in her lap, and she was stroking his face intently, with both hands, as if she was curing him. She was saying something to him, or singing, and every few minutes she bent down at an impossible angle, gently kissing him. Only when an actress came over and swiped the hat from her head did Peace look up. Then she saw Henry.

Later, he would play and replay the moment and realize that her face had been remarkable not for the expression it held when she saw him but rather for what it lacked. There was no shock, no guilt, no regret, no anger. The look on Peace's face was perfectly open, perfectly welcoming. Henry might have been anyone. He might have come in to deliver food, or mop the floor, or anything.

"I want that back!" Peace shouted playfully to the girl who had taken the helmet.

"We'll see!" the girl called over her shoulder.

The guy on Peace's lap reached back up for her.

"Hi," she said to Henry.

"Hi."

"What are you doing here?" she asked.

"What are *you* doing here?"

She blinked. She shook her hair out and smoothed it down.

He realized in that moment that he was staring into a mirror. He had been blind to it—as incapable of sight as he had once been incapable of speech. Henry was looking at Peace and finally seeing the unaffected indifference, the strident autonomy, the inability to trust in one person; seeing, unavoidably, the absolute worst in himself.

THERE WAS A CLOAKROOM OFF THE CORRIDOR, and after a few minutes, Henry managed to steer Peace into it. In her bell-bottom jeans and flea-market cardigan, she looked like the schoolgirl she should still have been.

"What is it?" she said to Henry.

"Why aren't you home?" he asked her.

"Why would I be home?" she asked. "And why aren't you working?"

"For the same reason you should be home," he said. "Because I thought you were sick."

She crossed her arms in front of her chest. It was a petulant, protective gesture.

"Pregnant," she said.

It was oddly not shocking. Nevertheless, he repeated the word.

"Pregnant," he said.

"Yup."

She looked back over her shoulder in a way that made him completely certain he'd had nothing to do with the pregnancy and wanted nothing to do with it.

She took a step back, toward the coats that were hanging, arms intertwined.

He couldn't help seeing himself again, this time more than ten years before, on the day Betty had come to school, and Mary Jane had pulled him into the coatroom and he'd told her about Martha. He wondered, if he had told her his other big secrets, whether she would still love him the way she had loved him then.

That day, he had been the one stuffing his hands into his pockets, lessening the chance of physical contact. Now it was Peace, folding her arms, looking desperately down and away. Even as Henry's mind sped along to try to make sense of the new information, he understood for the first time how Mary Jane must have felt when he backed away from her that day. How that must have felt, he thought, as he took a step closer and saw Peace recoil.

"Do you—can we—" he began.

She shook her head emphatically.

"I got the name of a clinic from Cathy," she said. "It's legal here, you know."

"Don't you want to talk about it?"

She shrugged. "It was just a mistake," she said.

Someone came by to find her. "Half hour," he said.

"I've got to get into costume," Peace told him.

He nodded, staring at her. It was impossible to imagine that her schoolgirl self could be pregnant. Of course it had been, as she said, a mistake.

It was not until he was halfway home, trudging back through the canvas-white snow, that Henry thought about Betty and realized that she had been even younger than Peace was now when she'd chosen to let him be born.

9

The Most Moving Story Ever Told

There were two facing rows of blue bucket seats in the waiting room of the clinic, and a half dozen young women sat there—two with their mothers, four on their own. All of them seemed to be smoking, and all of them stared at Henry when he walked in with Peace. He was the only man.

A chubby receptionist with an unfortunate Twiggy haircut took Peace's name and told her to have a seat. Henry hung up their coats, and then he sat down beside Peace, the newest members of a wretched, transitory club.

On the table beside Henry there were worn copies of *Queen* and *Rave, Tatler* and *Woman, Time* and *Life*.

"Want to read something?" Henry asked Peace.

She shook her head. She was trying to look casual, but Henry could tell she was scared.

He reached for her hand, but she pulled it away, just forcefully enough to inspire both the mothers to look at Henry accusingly.

But he didn't feel guilty. If anything, he felt noble for having come with Peace and quite certain that from the start he had cared too much, not too little, about her.

She fiddled with the strap on her bag. He studied the floor— a threadbare carpet—and studied the heels of Peace's pink shoes. Who wore pink shoes to an abortion? A girl who wasn't old enough for anything real, he thought.

Half an hour passed. A nurse appeared in the doorway with a clipboard in her hands.

"Laura?" she asked of the room in general.

Laura put down her copy of *Woman*, stood up, offered a universal shrug, and followed the nurse out.

The group that remained readjusted. One of the mothers picked up the copy of *Woman* that Laura had dropped. On the cover was a smiling blond model, one story called "Looking Ahead to Christmas" and another called "My Babies" that was subtitled "The Most Moving Story Ever Told." For weeks people had been talking about Sheila Thorns, a Birmingham woman who had given birth to sextuplets.

"Six at once," the woman now reading the magazine said to no one in particular. "Can you imagine?"

"Six at once," her daughter repeated. "That would be so groovy."

No one pointed out how odd it was that the girl who thought six was groovy was clearly not as inspired by the prospect of one.

The mother kept up a stream of reactions. "Think of that," she said. "Poor sod." "I'd rather walk on coals."

Henry looked over to see whether Peace was interested, but clearly the sextuplet story had passed her by. She gave him one of her fake, forced grins: the invitation he suddenly found so false and so appalling. For more than a year now, he had watched her slide that inviting expression under the fences surrounding so many people she'd met. She'd done it with the groupies by the theater. The Great Martini. The cast of *Hair*. Even now, in the waiting room of a woman's clinic, he could see the invitation in her eyes, the promise of an intimacy she could feign with her body but clearly never feel with her heart.

By the time the nurse came for the next patient ("Suzanne?"), Henry hated Peace the way one can only hate a part of oneself. And by the time it was finally her turn—halfway into the bleak, lifeless afternoon—he was not all that unhappy when the nurse said he couldn't come in with her.

10

You Don't Look Anything Like Her

There was slightly more to pack for this move. Though Henry had spent far less time in London than in California, he had gathered more possessions with more pleasure here, and though he was already anxious to leave Peace, he found himself wanting to keep some of their things. On a raw day in February, Henry packed two entire cartons with the sorts of items he had never thought about bringing when he left a place. There was the teapot they'd used for flowers; a half dozen funky, mismatched bowls that he'd bought in an effort to match Peace's style; a set of Mickey Mouse sheets he had found on Portobello Road. He would have taken some furniture, too, if he hadn't had to cross the Atlantic. As it was, he pondered what to do with the two boxes. It took him a moment to remember that there was no one at the practice house who would know or care what to do with them. He thought about sending them to Chris at the Tuxedo, but that was, in any case, not where he wanted his things to end up. He wrote to Mary Jane instead:

Dear MJ:

I hope you won't mind, but I'm sending you a couple of boxes. These are not gifts for you, although I may well bring you some when I get there, which will be in a month or two. I am leaving London, leaving Peace, and coming back to New York. I have just one little side trip to make before I come, and then I'll want to see you.

———

HE HAD NOT EXPECTED a lot of emotion from Peace. In a sense, they had already said goodbye the night before the abortion, when she'd admitted that the baby could have been fathered by any of three or four men. That had been enough to draw the line forever between them, and Henry had been thinking of it that way—as if a frame that had previously included them both had now been redrawn to be two frames, with different colored backgrounds or even different landscapes. Peace would stay, perhaps forever, in the psychedelic landscape of 1968 London: an enormous Whitehall mural of go-go boots, comets, patent leather, Indian prints, *Hair* posters, and maroon lights bouncing off silver microphones.

Henry's background, by contrast, had already shifted to an imagined New York of Greenwich Village and painting and, above all, Mary Jane.

HE FLEW TO PARIS IN FEBRUARY. The whole way there, he thought about all the things that had been true of Mary Jane and true of no other woman. She was the only one who had known him as a child. The only one he'd hurt who had forgiven him. She was the only one he hadn't been able to conquer with a kiss. The only one he'd wanted but had never made love to. She was the only one he'd truly been able to trust and, perhaps because of that, the only one who had ever seen him clearly.

Henry sat thinking about her as the airplane drew a bright silver line through the buoyant pale blue clouds. All of the things that were *only had*s he remembered; all the ones that were *only hadn't*s he imagined himself doing.

First, though, there had to be Paris. There had to be a visit to Betty, or at least an attempt at a visit. Despite everything, Henry's morning in the clinic with Peace had made it impossible for him to imagine going back to the States without seeing the woman who'd given birth to him.

Later he would conclude that she would have ducked him completely if she hadn't happened to pick up the phone herself when he called her office.

"Gardner," she'd said in a bored, convincing newsroom style. Older. Scratchier. Deeper than he'd remembered.

"Hi, Betty," he'd said, and added, "Don't hang up. I'm calling from London."

"Who is—" she'd begun, and then there had been a pause. "Henry?" she'd asked, groggily, as if he had just tiptoed into her room in the middle of the night.

THE PARIS BUREAU of *Time* was in an unremarkable modern office building on the Avenue Matignon near the feathery fountains of the Champs-Elysées. Henry had left his suitcases in a locker at the airport, and so when he walked into the office, his hands were free to stuff into his pockets.

The receptionist at the front desk was speaking on the phone in French.

"*Oui?*" she said to Henry, seemingly put upon, when she finally hung up.

"I'm here to see Betty Gardner," Henry said.

She looked him up and down.

"I'm her son," he added in answer to what he thought was her unasked question.

"Yes, she told us you'd be coming," she said in a way that made Henry wonder what else Betty had told people. The thought that he existed in her life even when he didn't know it baffled and surprised him. He felt like a cartoon character, who could be drawn to do things he didn't want to do.

"Betty?" the receptionist said on the phone. "*Oui. Il est ici.*"

She hung up and turned back to Henry. "You don't look anything like her, you know."

BETTY DIDN'T LOOK exactly older than he remembered her looking, just more used. She seemed like a flattened, pinched version of herself, a clay sculpture in the making that was being overhandled. Her shoulders seemed narrower and her hips wider. Her face was flatter, and the smile she forced it to make could as easily have been a frown or a grimace; it was really just a minor change in the angle of her lips.

Henry hugged her, an awkward gesture filled with extra space.

"I'm so glad you called," she said, and to Henry, no one—not even Peace with a newly shoplifted pair of go-go boots—had ever sounded more false.

"Can we go out somewhere?" he asked her.

"Oh, I think we'd better," she said.

Even in the elevator going back downstairs, Henry knew there had been no point in his making the visit, and he also knew that he'd always be rather pleased with himself for making it.

OF COURSE, SHE KNEW PARIS. She knew French. She knew the brasserie to go to, the right way to order the sandwiches, and the right way to order the wine. But he was really the adult. He was the one with the choices before him and the absolution to bestow.

She could barely look at him until she had had her second glass of wine. She looked instead at the round, white marble tabletop, played with the long, narrow packets of sugar, said a too-eager hello to a pair of colleagues who passed on their way to another café.

"So you were in London," she finally said.

"Yes."

"Are they totally Beatles mad?"

"Yes."

"And the Rolling Stones?"

"Yes."

"And the sextuplets?"

"Yes," he said, frustrated.

"What?"

"Betty."

"What?" she said.

"*Mom.*"

It was only the second time he had ever used the word out loud. The first had been the night he had run away from Humphrey and gone to New York.

"Huh. 'Mom,' " she repeated, as if it was funny, and she took another sip of wine.

Henry lost, for a moment, any desire to forgive her; clearly she had forgiven herself, or at least forgotten how to blame herself.

"Mom," he said, as reprisal. "I've been living in London for almost two years."

He could as easily have told her that he'd been living in India, or Athens.

"That's great!" she said, clearly not comprehending that the point was how close he had been to her, how punishingly close he had been without her having known.

The waitress came by and asked something in French.

"*Oui,*" Betty said, a bit flustered.

"What was that?" Henry asked.

"She wanted to know if my sandwich was okay."

Henry looked at Betty's sandwich. She hadn't had a bite. "Why don't you have some?" he asked her.

"I will," she said, and took another sip of her wine. "How's yours?"

"Delicious," Henry said. "Do you come here a lot?" he asked her.

"A lot of lunches," Betty said.

"Do you like Paris?" he asked her.

"I love Paris."

"Where do you live?"

"In the Third," she said. "But you don't know Paris."

"No," Henry said. "I don't know Paris."

"That's okay," Betty said, perhaps a bit giddily. "I don't know London."

"I'm not going to be living in London anymore," Henry said. But she didn't ask him why not. She didn't ask him where he was going to live, or how, or with whom.

———

IT WAS, INCONGRUOUSLY, spring in Paris, a pale silver and green flowering. Back out on the street, Henry could feel the sun on the top of his head.

"Where do I get a taxi from here?" he asked.

"I'll take you to the stand," she said. "It's just a few blocks."

They walked toward the Arc de Triomphe, massive and unreal in the sun.

Betty checked her watch. "There's a lot of talk about de Gaulle stepping down," she told him.

"And you're doing a story?" he asked her.

"Yes."

The taxis were lined up, rounded and gleaming, like large boulders in the sun.

"Mom," Henry said. "I want you to know I wish you the best."

"Oh, I don't need that," she said, as if he'd offered her a handkerchief.

"I want you to know it," he said.

"Let's face it, Henry," she said. "I ditched you."

"Yeah, but you also kept me."

"What do you mean?"

"In the first place," he said.

"You need a cab," she told him.

She hugged him now, this time tightly, forcing herself to settle for a moment into the structure of his arms. He could feel her exhaustion, her tipsiness, her tininess. He could feel her shame, and her need to flee. He looked back once from the taxi, just in time to see her brush her hair from her forehead and tug on her ear.

11

Draw!

On the flight to New York, Henry sat beside a thirtyish French-woman who was wearing orange silk pants, a peace-sign necklace, and a surprisingly demure expression. He had her hooked by the time the pilot announced the altitude and the speed. Had her hooked despite the fact that she barely spoke English and his one reliable French word was *merci*. He used it strategically.

They clinked glasses over the horrible meal and laughed at their identical reactions to what passed for a chocolate parfait. Henry admired the way she tucked her feet almost shyly to one side. He liked the angles of her cheekbones, and the way she powdered her face as if she was wiping something away from its surface, not adding something to it. Henry let her ankle lean against his, and let her arm share the armrest. She smiled at him, and then fell asleep.

He felt like an athlete playing his last game as a professional, one who has made the choice, a bit nobly, to quit at the top of his game.

IT WAS RAINING IN THE AFTERNOON when Henry's plane touched down at Kennedy Airport. A gray sky framed gray buildings and sepia fields, black tarmac and dingy white airport trucks. Henry found his bags and stood in line waiting for a taxi, and though by now the rain had started to let up, he could feel the dampness in and around him, as if it was being painted on.

He had, of course, seen pictures of the World's Fair, the gleaming beginnings of Walt's greatest dreams, but Henry had several times declined the invitation that the studio offered employees. Now he asked his driver to slow down as the taxi passed the already lonely site. The tall towers loomed with their strange disk-shaped rooms, and the silver globe looked smaller and duller than Henry had hoped it would.

IT WAS FIVE O'CLOCK BY THE TIME he found a taxi, and just past six when he was handed the key to a small single room at the Roosevelt Hotel. Icy February air seemed to linger around him all night long. He woke every few hours, cold, confused, and jet-lagged, mentally juggling what he hoped for and what he regretted.

At six in the morning, he gave up on sleep. He showered, luxuriating in the force of the American plumbing and the fact that there seemed to be no end to the hot water supply.

Outside, on the frigid street, he walked for several blocks toward Times Square and found an open coffee shop. He sat at the counter on a green fake-leather stool, warming his hands on his coffee mug and trying not to stare at an old man two seats down who was eating soup and steak despite the early hour. Henry looked instead at the ambitious fortress someone had built of small cereal boxes, the kind that could be opened with a surgical cut.

A waitress stepped up to take Henry's order, tapping her pencil against her pad just the way Cindy used to do. The waitress had hair like Karen's, skin like Annie's, a voice like Betty's. She had nothing of Mary Jane's, though, and that was, Henry thought, exactly the way it was supposed to be.

SINCE SOPHOMORE YEAR AT HUMPHREY, with the unveiling of Stu Stewart's *Playboy*-inspired little black book, Henry had carried around a small address book of his own. By now, seven years and three locations later, most of the phone numbers were either defunct or irrelevant. There were, however, three people with New York numbers: a former student from Haaren, a fellow in-betweener from Disney, and a woman who had worked briefly on *Submarine*.

Henry tried the three numbers in alphabetical order. No one answered. He wasn't particularly surprised or disappointed. This was, after all, a Tuesday morning in a normal workweek, and there was no reason to think that anyone would be home.

He sat sleepily on a faded chintz chair next to the telephone. He turned on the TV. A soap opera. A game show. Another soap opera. He turned off the TV.

There was a fourth New York number, but it belonged to Mary Jane, and Henry knew he wasn't ready to dial it yet.

He sat, listening to the kiss, or hiss, of the bathroom's dripping faucet.

On the glass-covered desk was a stack of well-thumbed magazines: *Time, Life, The Saturday Evening Post.* On the cover of *Life,* a photograph of the moon seemed to float under the words "The Incredible Year." Henry flipped through the pages and found the table of contents. There were five chapters: Discovery, Shock, Dissent, War, and Comeback.

He felt he had been through all of them.

Then he turned another page, this time to the *Life* masthead, and saw Ethel Neuholzer's name.

HE CALLED HER AT THE MAGAZINE. She was still living in the old apartment and asked him to come by on Saturday.

"Kid!" she shouted expansively when she opened the door for him. She hugged him hard, a lengthy embrace that seemed unexpectedly meant for her as well as for him. "Come on in," she said.

She had redecorated the place, sixties style. The low couch had been re-covered in bright royal blue, with overstuffed striped and polka-dot pillows. The wooden coffee table had been replaced by a round glass one that was planted heavily in a round white fur rug. Even the orange chairs at the dining table were high-backed and futuristic. But the apartment's shabby moldings, painted-over phone wires, and worn parquet floors were unconcealed by the general makeover.

Ethel was heavier than when Henry had seen her last, and her skin drooped a bit. Like the apartment, she was decked out in mod, and, like the apartment, she didn't wear it all that convincingly.

"So you're a big guy now," she said to him.

"And you're a big shot," Henry said. "I saw it in the magazine."

Ethel laughed. "Yeah. They made me an editor. Imagine that. A woman editor."

"So what do you do?"

"It's really what I don't do. I don't get to use a fucking camera anymore."

Henry hesitated, then asked the next question looking down. "Are you still with—who was that guy you were with?"

"Who, Tripp?"

"Tripp, right. Are you still together?"

Ethel snorted. "Were we ever together?" She lit a cigarette and exhaled emphatically. "He left his wife," she said. "But then he left me."

"Sorry."

"What the hell," she said, adjusting a bra strap. "He was a shit."

SHE DIDN'T ASK HIM ABOUT BETTY, whose bedroom she had converted into an office. But Henry asked Ethel if she had heard about Martha.

"Yeah, kid," she said. "Good old Nurse Peabody wrote me about it. She told me Betty didn't come to the funeral."

"That's right."

"That must have been rough."

Henry thought back to the funeral, a moment he guiltily remembered for the pleasure of finding Peace rather than the pain of losing Martha.

He was silent.

"Let's get out of here," Ethel said. "Come on. I'll buy you lunch."

SHE TOOK HIM TO A RESTAURANT he'd only heard and read about: the "21" Club, just a few blocks from the apartment, on West Fifty-second

Street. It was quiet at lunchtime, and they were shown to a small table where Henry was surprised, and a little uncomfortable, to be seated on a banquette next to, not across from, Ethel.

"How are we supposed to talk to each other this way?" Henry asked.

Ethel shrugged. "I don't know. It's just how it's done."

Henry was conscious immediately of his casual clothes—the beige corduroy bell-bottoms and well-worn black turtleneck. It was an unaccustomed and unwelcome awareness of his own lack of means.

"They're going to kick me out of here, aren't they?" he asked Ethel, masking his discomfort with an attempt at nonchalance.

"Yes, Henry," she said. "That's why I brought you here."

A waiter came to take their order. Ethel ordered them two beers. Henry looked up at the ceiling, where hundreds of toys and signs and knickknacks were hung, like a three-dimensional collage. He saw an Esso oil sign. A teddy bear. A fire truck.

Ethel talked about the magazine, the growing worry that still photographs were being eclipsed by TV.

He ate a burger and French fries, reveling in their American flavor the same way he had his hotel shower. He told her about London, the Beatles, and Peace.

"Were you in love with her?" Ethel asked him.

"Absolutely," Henry said.

"And are you still?" she asked him.

He pictured Peace lying naked on the floor of Geoff Whitehall's studio.

"No," he said.

"Peace," Ethel said.

"Yes."

"That was really her name?"

"Yes."

"Serves you right. You should never date anyone whose name is a noun."

Henry laughed, wondering if the rule applied to Mary Jane.

Ethel offered to help him save money by moving back in with her. He was only briefly tempted. He did, however, accept her help with finding a job. She scoffed at his suggestion that he might teach drawing somewhere while pursuing his art career.

"And live on what?" she asked him. "This is New York, for God's sake."

SHE KNEW A LOT OF PEOPLE in the publishing world, and that—even more than her friendly, almost big-sisterly attitude—would be her real help to Henry.

"I got you an interview in the art department at Simon and Schuster," she barked at him one morning. "Go buy yourself a decent pair of pants and a decent jacket."

"Define *decent*," he said.

"*Decent,* as in *I'll lend you the money if you need me to, but get them, for Christ's sake.*"

In the next few weeks, Henry would wake in the morning, shower and shave, pick up a *New York Times* at the corner, and read it while eating breakfast at the coffee shop he had gone to on his first morning back in New York. He would sit at the counter, looking through the classified ads and trying to find a job that a background in animation and art could let him try for plausibly. In the afternoons, he would walk the streets of New York, which warmed slightly as February thawed. He went to museums, parks, movies. And every blond woman he saw made him think about Mary Jane.

Finally, in March, he was hired at Farrar, Straus by the woman who oversaw the book jackets.

For the next three months, Henry worked from nine-thirty every morning until seven or eight each night. His hope was that he would be able to design or illustrate some of the book jackets himself. For now, however, he was merely assigned to help out with the pasteup and to color-check the proofs.

In a life that was remarkably like the one Betty had told him she'd lived during her early days at the Barbizon, Henry came back each night to a dark, empty hotel room, only to sleep and to think about the reunion he wanted. For the first time, he understood what it had been like for her to live one life with the main hope of achieving a different one. He was absolutely determined that, unlike Betty, he would succeed.

IT WAS ON A SATURDAY IN EARLY MAY—and for no particular reason except that he couldn't wait any longer—that he decided it was time.

He reached Mary Jane at home. She yelped and told him to come straight over, and, riding the subway downtown, he closed his eyes and braced himself for the meeting they would have. He had assumed, from the tone of Mary Jane's voice, that George, or at least some boyfriend or other, was going to be present as well. She hadn't sounded like a woman who was waiting to be saved from a lonely life. It even crossed his mind, if briefly, that she might have gotten married.

He would take that on if he needed to. He would do whatever penance it took. Whatever punishment came his way would be fitting for all the choices he'd made: choosing Peace over Mary Jane, and Alexa over Mary Jane, and Lila over Mary Jane, and even, way back in their nursery school days, choosing not to make a choice.

He wanted to make a choice now. The rest—how they lived or where he worked or maybe even what he did—wouldn't matter, he thought. Mary Jane was what mattered, he thought: the most authentic part of his life.

She met him at her front door with a long, warm, unromantic embrace. He looked at her left ring finger and was relieved to find it unadorned.

She was living in a narrow carriage house in the heart of Greenwich Village, just a few blocks from Washington Square Park. Vivid green ivy slipped hopefully around her front door, which was painted bright yellow.

"Are you going to let me in?" he asked her. "Or don't you want me to meet him?"

"Him?" Mary Jane asked.

"Him," Henry said. "Is it George? Or is there someone new?"

They stood in the front hallway. The bright front door had led Henry to expect that there would be color inside her house, a Charlie-and-Karen paint box, perhaps. But the walls turned out to be tenement white, the furniture used and drab.

"There is someone new," Mary Jane said.

Henry nodded, neutral, trying to suppress the jealousy he knew he had no right to feel.

"But it's not a *he*," she added, and just at the moment of his greatest confusion—nothing being called to his mind in images, thoughts, or precedent—a little girl with white-yellow hair came running into the hallway and reached her arms up toward Mary Jane, who seemed to bend down, lift her up, and hug her all in one motion.

THE FLOWERS WERE PINK AND WHITE on the trees in Washington Square Park. Every petal looked like a dab of paint. Henry felt as if he and Mary Jane were walking through an animation cel from *Mary Poppins*. He knew their starting position: hands in their pockets, elbows occasionally brushing, eyes on the path they were walking. He knew what he wanted their end position to be: kissing under a shower of petals, promising everything. He would have loved to have an in-betweener move them through the intervening scenes.

They walked under the Washington arch, and Henry tried to ignore the memory of the arch in Paris, with Betty standing under its shadow, tipsy and ashamed.

"How old is she?" he asked Mary Jane.

"Nineteen months."

"So she was born—"

"In October."

"I was still working on *Submarine*."

"I know."

"You could have told me about her," he said.

"You disappeared, remember? And anyway. I wrote you that I had a project, didn't I?"

A bus drove by. A dog pulled on its leash. A teenage couple perched on the back of a bench laughed and shared a small brass pipe.

"Whose is she?" he asked Mary Jane.

"She's mine, doofus."

"You know what I mean. Who's her father?"

Mary Jane looked surprised. "It's George, of course. Who do you think?"

"And he flew the coop. Useless creep."

"He didn't *fly the coop,* Henry."

He grabbed Mary Jane's left hand and held it up, her pale, un-adorned fingers fanned out against the background of the flowering branches.

"Where's the wedding ring?" Henry asked.

She laughed. "You're so conventional, Henry."

"Please."

"Did it ever occur to you that *I* didn't want to marry *him*? Maybe I like him just coming and going."

"I wouldn't go," Henry said huskily, and Mary Jane burst out laughing, a little too forcefully, as if her laughter would be able to keep his evident purpose in check.

"I mean it," he told her.

She laughed again. "Are you out of your tiny mind?"

"You find this laughable?" Henry asked.

She looked at her wristwatch.

"Don't let me keep you," he said acidly.

"The babysitter's only staying till six."

"I'M GLAD YOU LEFT THAT PEACE GIRL, anyway," Mary Jane said as they walked back to her house.

"You only met her for two minutes," Henry said.

"True. But you've never met George, and you've already called him a worthless creep."

"Actually, I said a *useless* creep."

"Same difference."

"Where is he, anyway?" Henry asked.

She turned the key in the front door, ignoring his question completely. Within seconds she was assaulted by the toddler at her knees.

The little girl was wearing red Keds, blue jeans, and a red T-shirt. On another child, the outfit would have looked boyish, but the delicacy of her features and her winsome eyes made her utterly little-girlish.

"Haley, say hello," Mary Jane said.

Henry bent down and looked into both her eyes—her two undamaged, perfect blue eyes—and realized that this was what looking at Mary Jane must have been like, years before.

"Hi, Haley," he said.

He started to extend his hand in greeting, but Haley instead used one hand to spread two fingers on her other into a tiny, perfect peace sign. Henry followed suit, then pressed his two fingers onto hers.

"Hi," she said.

"Hi."

Mary Jane asked the babysitter to stay while she started dinner.

THE KITCHEN WAS A MESS. Toy pots and pans vied for counter space with the real items, as did toy plates, cups, and one well-smudged wooden toaster.

"She's beautiful," Henry said.

Mary Jane tried to hide her smile by opening the refrigerator door.

"She looks exactly like you," Henry said.

Mary Jane handed Henry four potatoes.

"See, I know that," Henry said, "because I knew you when you were just a little older than she is now."

"Potatoes," Mary Jane directed, handing Henry a potato peeler.

"I'm serious, you know," Henry said.

"I know."

"We grew up together. Think of everything."

"Just because we have a past doesn't mean we have a future."

"But it should," Henry said.

He embraced her. It was as tender a moment as any he'd had with Annie, as passionate as any he'd had with Peace. He had a hand on either side of Mary Jane's face, and he wanted her to feel completely encompassed, held and met and lifted up. He kissed her, watching till her one eye closed, and then he closed his own.

Then she took his right hand in hers and kissed the back of it, emphatically, three times.

"No," she said, and then repeated it when she saw the expression on his face.

Henry looked at her, shaking his head. Mary Jane sent him to the living room.

"Not now, Henry," she said, which he chose to interpret as meaning "maybe someday."

"Go be with the other kids," she told him, laughing.

"SIT?" HALEY ASKED HIM after the babysitter had left.

She was sitting at a low wooden play table.

"Okay," Henry said and took his place at a small matching wooden chair.

"Uppy?" she asked him.

"You want me to pick you up?"

He did, with one arm, and she slid onto his lap.

A wooden box with a sliding top sat on the table before them. Proudly, if with difficulty, Haley slid the top of the box back to reveal a riot of crisscrossed colors and the warm, waxy, earthy smell of crayons.

There was a stack of paper beside the box. Henry took one sheet for himself and another for her.

"What color do you want?" he asked her.

"Green."

He picked out a crayon for her. Spring Green.

She swung one leg freely against his, as if his leg was the leg of the chair.

For himself, he picked up Red. Just red. But as soon as he did, she took it from him, grinning. He laughed. "Okay," he said. He took a purple crayon next. She did the same thing again. Soon she held a huge bouquet of crayons, all the colors she could keep in her small hand.

"May I keep this one, miss?" Henry asked her, holding up the crayon called Burnt Sienna. She giggled and nodded.

From the kitchen, he could hear Mary Jane humming, but he couldn't make out the tune. Haley stayed on his lap, her entire face, her entire body, focused into one scrunched-up force of concentrated effort. She pressed her whole weight into the crayon, pushing it back and forth.

Henry stared down at the blank paper. Stared and stared as he tried to absorb the words Mary Jane had said to him, and the ones she hadn't said. Tears, as unaccustomed to him as need or regret, filled his eyes. One fell on the blank page. Henry outlined it with his crayon.

"What's it?" the baby asked him.

Henry laughed. "I can't tell you," he sang softly, "but I know it's mine."

She stared at him blankly.

"Draw!" she said, just sweetly enough not to sound too bossy.

"What should I draw?"

Henry looked at her. With his crayon still in his hand, he watched as she drew and drew: crazy colors, scribbled, dotted, zigzagged, criss-crossed, filling her page and then, without hesitation or doubt, spilling onto his own. She drew lines, over and over, her little fingers clutching first one crayon, then another, making a glorious field of every-colored grass. Henry picked up one of the crayons she'd put down and waited a long time, watching.

"Draw!" Haley said again, and finally Henry started to draw—one straight line, then a second one rising up out of the free, wild, colored grass, two perpendicular lines, the width of his hand apart. It was so simple. Henry drew the third line—parallel to the beautiful ground— and in an instant those lines completed a rectangle sitting in an open field, and with windows, a door, and perhaps a chimney, they could become a house.

This novel started with a real photograph:

I found it, quite by accident, on a Cornell University website about the history of home economics. On the opening page of the online exhibit, among other thumbnail images, was the captivating snapshot of a baby with a beguiling smile and roguish eyes. I clicked on the photograph and learned that "Bobby Domecon" (the last name short for Domestic Economics) had been a "practice baby," an infant supplied by a local orphanage to the university's "practice house," where college students learned homemaking, complete with a live baby whom they took turns mothering.

I know!

The first practice baby arrived at Cornell in 1919. She stayed for one year, as did dozens of subsequent infants. Cornell's practice baby program continued until 1969, but it wasn't the only one of its kind. During my research for this book, I learned that there were practice baby programs all over the country, so literally hundreds of infants started their lives being cared for by multiple mothers. For the most part, the approach seems to have been viewed as one that benefited the mothers as well as the babies, who were considered prime candidates for adoption when they were returned to their orphanages. There was, however at least one case that drew national attention when an Illinois child welfare superintendent questioned what the effects of this kind of upbringing might be. My wish for an answer is what inspired this novel.

‖ ACKNOWLEDGMENTS ‖

For their encouragement and many insights, I am grateful to Suzie Bolotin, Barb Burg, Cathy Cramer, Liz Darhansoff, Sharon DeLevie, Lee Eisenberg, Frankie Jones, Jon LaPook, Kate Lear, and Kate Medina.

I could not have finished this book without the extraordinary kindnesses of Donna Ash, Richard Cohen, Marcus Forman, and Saud Sadiq, and I owe them my deepest thanks.

Michael Solomon not only encouraged, but inspired, informed, and explained.

Betsy Carter offered wisdom, brutal honesty, and limitless reassurance, sometimes on a minute-by-minute basis.

I am lucky enough to live with not one but three gifted editors. The fact that two of them are my children only adds to my sense of good fortune. Stephen, Elizabeth, and Jonathan Adler are the irresistible forces in my life.

The factual background for this book came from many sources, including conversations or emails with Marty Fox, Sandra Leong, Floyd Norman, Priscilla Painton, Rinna Samuel, and Kerry Sulcowicz. In addition to thanking them, I'd like to acknowledge my reliance on the following sources:

Up Periscope Yellow, by Al Brodax; *Walt Disney's Nine Old Men & the Art of Animation,* by John Canemaker; *Stir It Up,* by Megan J. Elias; *The Girls Who Went Away,* by Ann Fessler; *Walt Disney,* by Neil Gabler; *Walt's*

People, vols. 1–4, ed. Didier Ghez; *Inside the Yellow Submarine,* by Dr. Robert R. Hieronimus; *Raising America,* by Ann Hulbert; *Good HAIR Days,* by Jonathan Johnson; *Becoming Attached,* by Robert Karen, Ph.D.; *The Good Housekeeping Housekeeping Book,* ed. Helen W. Kendall; *Mary Poppins, She Wrote,* by Valerie Lawson; *Dr. Spock: An American Life,* by Thomas Maier; *Hippie,* by Barry Miles; *You Don't Have to Say You Love Me,* by Simon Napier-Bell; *Household Equipment,* by Louise Jenison Peet, Ph.D., and Lenore Sater Thye; *Opening Skinner's Box,* by Lauren Slater; *Rethinking Home Economics,* ed. Sarah Stage and Virginia B. Vincenti; *The Illusion of Life,* by Frank Thomas and Ollie Johnston.

Back in 2001, students in a Human Development course at Cornell University collaborated with the Division of Rare and Manuscript Collections to create an exhibit and website about the university's rich tradition in the field of home economics. The result (still available online) provided a fascinating glimpse into a fading world that included practice apartments and practice babies and inspired this work of fiction. I will always be glad that Cornell made this wonderful material so accessible.

ABOUT THE AUTHOR

LISA GRUNWALD is the author of the novels *Whatever Makes You Happy*, *New Year's Eve*, *The Theory of Everything*, and *Summer*. Along with her husband, *BusinessWeek* editor in chief Stephen J. Adler, she edited the anthologies *Women's Letters* and *Letters of the Century*. Grunwald is a former contributing editor to *Life* and a former features editor of *Esquire*. She and her husband live in New York City with their son and daughter.

ABOUT THE TYPE

The text of this book was set in Legacy, a typeface family designed by Ronald Arnholm and issued in digital form by ITC in 1992. Both its serifed and unserifed versions are based on an original type created by the French punchcutter Nicholas Jenson in the late fifteenth century. While Legacy tends to differ from Jenson's original in its proportions, it maintains much of the latter's characteristic modulations in stroke.